MASQUERADE

MASQUERADE

ALL THAT GLITTERS
BOOK 3

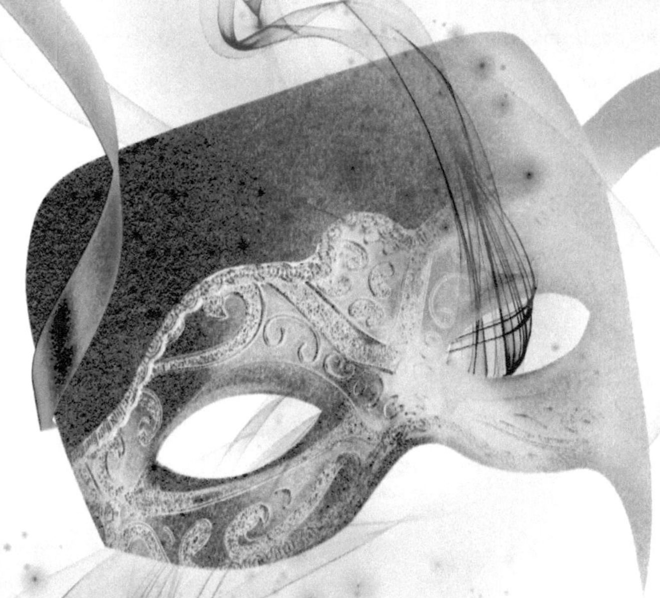

SHALAENA MEDFORD

Title Font: 403 Tarow Flare

Header Font: Ayres

Body Font: Palatino Linotype

First Edition: June 2024

eBook ISBN: 978-1-970291-02-5

Wide Paperback ISBN: 978-1-970291-05-6

KDP Exclusive Paperback ISBN: 979-8-878345-09-5

Content Warning

Piracy
Grief
Alcohol Consumption
Graphic Violence
Death
Mental Illness
Discussions of Slavery
Sexual Content
Off-Page Sexual Assault and Rape
Adolescent Death
Miscarriage
Abortion

Table of Contents

Hrănchu
Armalinia
Te
Great
Ocean
Jashedar

Andalise
Pishing
ich-Zardi
Kerriwen
Great
Ocean
Aibhànocht

Djorri Cove
Armalinia
Far'khtytii River
Pajisr
Screaming Cliffs

Qet-Qet
Kerriwen
Quodinlau Territory
Kal-Bar Territory
Pitique Territory

Andalise
Anarchaia
Lund
Tarn
Garda

Arqwin
Yörmuung Vyaard
Pishing
Carliolace
Yorvaald
Skaaldvik Vyaard
Ebrinar

Pronunciation Guide

Ahrek	ah-rEEk
Aibànocht	EYE-van-AWkh-t
Anarchaia	An-ark-ay-EE-ah
Andalise	an-dahl-eEE-ss
Anzi	AH-n-zEE
Argwyn	AR-g-wIHn
Armalinia	arm-ah-lEE-nEE-ah
Carliolace	kAHr-lEE-OH-lass
Chavìse-Kàmbhor	sha-vEE-shuh kam-vOH-r
Darian	dAr-EE-an
Dashaelan	dash-AY-lan
Daven	dAY-vehn
Ebrinar	ebb-rih-n-Ar
Edina	eh-dEE-nah
Elaric	eh-lAH-rih-k
Fiyora	fee-yOH-rah
Gerti-Aniisa	g-er-tEE ah-nEE-sAH
Igriid	ihg-rEEd

Jashedar	jAA-sheh-dAr
Kerriwen	kAIr-ih-wehn
kijæm	kih-jAm
Lưnyâk	lUH-nyUHk
Lyella	lie-EH-la
Madjra	mah-j-rAH
Myrmhin	mer-wIHn
Nebhàr	neh-vAHr
Pishing	pihsh-EEng
Quiicho	kEE-khOH
Ryk'r	rye-kER
Talegrove	tAYl-grOHv
Telbhaniich-Zardi	tell-vAHn-EEkh zah-r-dEE
Thersiàl Saigh	hur-shEE-AHl s-EYE
Thìse	hEE-shuh
Tsingsei	sing-sAY
Zeriida-Khiin	zeh-rEE-dah kh-EE-n
Zion Foggerty	z-EYE-ohn fog-er-tEE

It is not in the stars to hold our destiny,
but in ourselves.

~William Shakespeare

One

S UNLIGHT SPARKLED AND WINKED ACROSS THE RIPPLING OCEAN waters within Djorri Cove. Above it, the blue sky was clear as far as the eye could see. The wind carried with it the salt of the ocean. It swelled up onto the deck of the skyship and tangled through Song's dark brown hair, which hung loose over her black sleeveless shirt and sun-kissed shoulders. The deck aboard the Stars' Reprisal sat devoid of souls, save the one at the helm.

Song hadn't liked the idea of calling it the Stars' Bounty, but the name was sentimental to the few remaining members of the original crew. So they'd come to a compromise. They wouldn't be painting the zeppelin; they'd decided a golden zeppelin was far easier to recognize than grey canvas. A metalsmith had crafted a North Star of shining Armalinian brightsteel and affixed it to the vessel's prow. The white star stood out against the dark red wood, varnished and shining with its newness. Boots had yet to scuff the deck; cannons would later get the chance to stain the sides with their black powder. For now, though, she was perfect.

They'd secured the broken Stars' Bounty in a warehouse for later restoration. Song was still undecided on whether she would go back to the old ship once they'd returned it to its former glory, or if she might take both. It would be the first pirate fleet in history. Most pirate captains recoiled at the idea of multiple vessels attracting attention. It was easy to evade authorities as a single vessel flying or sailing alone. Song, however, couldn't resist the surge of excitement that fluttered in her belly at the idea of two or even three ships under her command. No one would dare fight back. People would lay treasures at her feet. Cannons from both sides would decimate anyone foolish enough to resist. It might happen one day…should she ever get back into the skies.

With a breath, Song smoothed her palm over the silky wood of the wheel, aching to feel the roughness of the old ship. She turned and lifted her bottle of whiskey from the map table. After a long swig, she pressed her wrist over her lips to hold it in as her throat threatened to cry it back out.

Weeks had passed. Or had it been months? Perhaps it had only been days. Song couldn't be too sure, as she spent her waking moments switching between hungover and drunk. Never sober. It didn't feel better this time. It didn't make her forget, or at least ease her sleep. She still woke with memories of a nightmare. The scream of an all-too-familiar voice echoed through her mind, even now—a scream she hadn't heard, yet her imagination forced it to replay over and over, ensuring her guilt and sorrow would never abate. Now it resounded within her head, fighting with the crackle of an angry, roaring fire.

"Thought I might find you here."

The cacophony of flames and despair came to an abrupt end as the voice yanked her back to the present. Sunshine stood at the top of one of the curved staircases, which wrapped like a horseshoe to cradle the double doors of the captain's cabin. Song raised her right arm to make a rude gesture at him. After she swallowed another drink, she looked at the appendage. It jolted her like a punch to the belly whenever she saw the bandages midway down her biceps. A fresh tear rolled from her eye as she dropped it down and took another drink.

"Don't worry, I know what you were tryin' to do," he said.

"Still better if I could do it."

"If there had been any other way…"

She could say, again, that he hadn't even tried to find another way. But they'd go around and around until she was screaming, he was shouting, and she'd end up wasting another bottle of whiskey by throwing it at him. Instead, she took another swig of her drink and stared out at the blue ocean.

"Have you eaten today?" Sunshine asked.

"Mmm…"

"Not even lyin' about it? Pleasant surprise. Come on, you can play with your new toy later."

Song closed her eyes and took in a deep breath of salty air. It made her stomach roil and her gnawing hunger scream louder. "I want cake."

"What?"

"For my birthday." She walked to him as he held out her coat to help her into it.

"Your birthday was over two weeks ago."

"Did I have cake for it?"

"No. Not like you could've kept it down, anyway."

She released an audible sigh as he buckled her coat. "Maybe I'll keep it down today. Depends on how much I drink."

"You're already tossed. If you stop now, you may just avoid throwin' up tonight." He lifted her hood and tucked her hair into it.

She studied him—looked over his soft expression and black eyes narrowed in the bright sun. He cared too much, and it annoyed her. But she was sure her sorrow would have swallowed her whole, had this man not taken it upon himself to care for her like an infant. He didn't do it in the same way Leslie had. After Dash died, Leslie treated her like a delicate person who knew damn well what she was doing. He'd been kind and understanding, but also forceful in his efforts to keep her from drinking herself into a grave.

Sunshine treated her like a kitten who didn't know how to exist in the world. He didn't tell her to stop drinking or demand she eat. Everything he did was a gentle suggestion.

As much as she loved him for it, she wanted him to be harsh. She wanted him to berate her for drinking herself into oblivion. It wasn't Sunshine she wanted doing it, though. She wanted Leslie there, telling her she was being an idiot. Telling her she's being a dramatic fool. But he wasn't there. And so she drank herself stupid every day and let Sunshine treat her like a helpless kitten.

"Well, if the food makes me ill, it doesn't matter how much I drank," she said.

"It's not the food." He took her by the elbow to guide her down the steps so she didn't twist her ankle or fall.

"It is sometimes."

"Oh? You remember those times?"

"No…"

"Then it's probably a lie."

Song chuckled and concentrated on not falling from the walkway. He forced her into the lift, since she was too unsteady to use the stairs. She closed her eyes to whimper through the steam-powered descent from the sky docks. They walked in silence through the sandy streets of Srkar to the tavern beside the inn. She'd learned to ignore the gazes which followed her wherever she went. She ignored the whispers and the people who crossed streets to get as far out of her path as they could. Anyone with half a sense would have seen how wobbly she walked and not given a damn. Then again, maybe they thought it made her that much worse.

Sunshine set her up at a small table with her back to a corner. He ordered her something, told her to stay put, and left. The barmaid placed a stein and a plate of food in front of her, then shuffled away without a word.

When they'd first arrived, the woman had been cheery. Word of the massacre in Carliolace followed, and she'd been terrified to even serve Song. But she became apathetic to the notorious, murderous pirate whom she served every day. Now she dropped the food onto the table to feed a hollow soul, then went about her business. She didn't say hello and didn't wait for a thank you. Somehow, it both angered and pleased Song. She wanted to be acknowledged, and yet she didn't wish to be reminded that she still existed.

Song stared over the paltry meal—enough food to call it

one, and yet not enough to fill a stomach. A disc of flatbread, a wedge of cheese, and a vine of grapes.

"Least it'll taste all right coming back up," Song muttered to herself. She lifted the whole vine of grapes to pry one off with her lips. After one bite, she spat the halves out onto the floor and tore into the flatbread instead.

When Sunshine returned, he set a little cardstock box down. "Your cake. Happy belated twentieth. Drink your water."

She made a face at the stein she hadn't touched.

"It'll ease your hangover."

"I know."

"So drink it."

She released a long breath. "Do I deserve the ease?"

"Song."

As though his warning tone was a slap to get her in line, she lifted the water and drank half. She reached for the box, but he pushed it away from her.

"Eat your grapes first."

"They're spoiled. I ate the bread and cheese."

Sunshine plucked a grape from the bunch and popped it into his mouth. He thought as he chewed the fruit. "They're fine. Eat."

"No. You have them. Give me my cake." She shoved the plate at him. When he didn't budge, she reached again. "I'm telling you, I'll throw them up in your lap if you make me choke those things down. Cake. Now."

After a silent standoff, he slid the box back in front of her and opened it. Sitting inside was a small, dark red cake with a whorl of frosting at the center. She grabbed it and took as big of a bite as she could. After a while of chewing, she shoved it into one cheek with her tongue.

"I like the color," she said. "Like blood."

"Seemed fittin'. Anythin' else you want for your birthday?"

She let out a long, contemplative breath. "Yes."

"Anythin' besides raisin' the dead?"

"No."

Not even thirty minutes later, as they passed the alley between the inn and the tavern, Song veered into it and bent over a metal bin to expel everything she'd eaten. She frowned at the red mess still connected to her upper lip by a thread of saliva. Her stomach betrayed her again, getting rid of more delicious cake. And now she regretted eating it. Sunshine returned as she finished. He wiped her lips with a handkerchief and handed her another stein of water to rinse her mouth and ease her stomach.

"It's a good thing I didn't make a birthday wish, because I'd get the opposite."

"It ain't an ill omen, Song, you're just drunk," Sunshine said.

He helped her to her room, where she sat on the bed. Her gaze panned the area, searching for something that wasn't there. She stayed still as he unbuckled her coat. When she didn't move, he patted her head and left the room, locking her inside so she couldn't sneak out alone again.

Song stared around. She was lost. Nothing made sense anymore. Everything surrounding her was alien. It started as a pout, then swelled to a sob as bleak thoughts rose to swallow her whole.

She sobbed into her one hand, cursing her loss of the other. She wept for Leslie and Dashaelan, Pinch, Doctor,

Bones, and all the names that ran around her head but had no faces, and faces with no names. Even Hardtack, whose fate on the Harpy's Claw remained unknown. She hadn't liked him at first, but he'd grown on her.

The few crew members she'd seen in the time they'd been in Armalinia had all tried to talk her out of drinking herself to death. Nothing any of them said had convinced her. Why should she stop? Why didn't she deserve this early grave? She didn't even deserve to reach her twentieth birthday. Not in her mind, at least.

Song reached under the mattress and withdrew the sorrowstone sword, along with its sheath. While she sobbed, she did her best to oil the blade, working her tears into the metal as they dripped onto it. But why did it matter? She didn't have an answer to that. Why keep polishing that damned sword every day? She couldn't use it. Its previous owner couldn't use it. Nevertheless, she polished it to the best of her ability with her single hand.

When she finished, she sheathed it and set it so the pommel rested on the pillow beside her. She kicked off her boots and fought with her trousers to unbutton and remove them. She cast everything to the floor in a heap, then slid into the bed beside the sword.

"I bet you're so mad at me," she said. "I bet you're screaming over my behavior." She swiped at the tears rolling from her eyes. "You want me to stop? Come and make me."

She held her breath, waiting for something. She didn't know what she expected, but when nothing happened, she closed her eyes and sobbed harder.

"That's what I thought, you coward."

Like every night since Carliolace, Song cried herself to sleep.

Two

Cold water splashed over Song. She lurched upright and took a shocked gasp of air. For a moment, she thought that was it—she was awake and nothing terrible would happen. Sunshine, however, as he'd done every day, had already set the bucket on her lap, so when her eyes watered and her head spun, it was there to catch her vomit. She gasped and spat, her throat raw and stomach aching from having nothing but bile to heave out this morning.

"One of these days I'm going to stab you for waking me like this," she said.

"So long as you make sure not to miss the bucket before you do."

Song made a face as reply and let him take the receptacle from her lap.

She couldn't see it—mostly because she didn't want to look in the mirror to see the stump hanging off her right shoulder—but she was gaunt. Dark circles had taken up permanent residence around her lightless blue eyes; what little fat she'd had on her body was almost spent trying to keep her from starving. Any moment it might start eating its way through her muscle. She didn't know any of this. She didn't know why sating her hunger resulted in vomiting, or why her hangovers were worse than she'd ever had. Song thought she deserved it. It didn't matter, though. None of it mattered.

Sunshine's gaze burrowed under her skin. She shot him a look, but he didn't stop.

"What?" she snapped.

"Just wonderin' if this is the day you stop."

"Is Leslie back?"

He let out a long sigh. "You know he's not comin' back."

"Then what do you bloody think?"

"Carry on much longer and you'll be joinin' him."

Song gave him a vicious sneer of a smile. "I fail to see how that's a threat."

He strode across the room and slapped her hard across the cheek. Before she could yell at him or retaliate, he left the room, slamming the door behind him. She didn't know what to think of this. She stared at her dirty fingernails, then did her best to try picking them clean with her thumbnail. Song tried not to cry, but her emotions didn't care. She lay back against the soggy pillow and curled onto her side, weeping.

Her body didn't want her to weep, though, as it demanded an outhouse and breakfast. So, chin wrinkled and eyes leaking messy tears, she shoved out of the bed and tugged on her trousers. She stared down at the buttons for a long time as the hopelessness rose once more.

"I don't need them buttoned," she assured herself.

She fought her way into her coat and stared down at the buckles.

"Damn everything," she pouted.

Song dragged her hood up and pushed her hair into her collar, then pulled the coat closed over her chest. She yanked the door open and stopped to stare at Sunshine. He leaned against the wall across from her, looking sour, a red irritation in his eyes.

"Will you help me?" she whimpered.

"Will you stop bein' a suicidal brat?"

She cried harder. "I'm sorry, I'm so sorry. I miss him so much that I can't breathe or think or…" She wiped her face with her palm. "Please help me to the outhouse, and I can grovel afterward."

"No need to grovel."

Sunshine buttoned her trousers. His eyebrows pressed together, and a thought appeared on his face, though he didn't say anything. He buckled her coat and led her around the side of the building to the outhouses in the alley. She finished her business with little grace and reemerged.

"Food, now," she said before he could ask. She again waited for him to button her trousers.

"There's got to be a way you can deal with your own clothes," he said. "Make your *kijæm* do it."

She sniffed, as though annoyed by the suggestion. "And take away all your fun? Never."

He gave her a long look, then turned for the tavern door. After they ordered, Song managing to at least get an ale out of the barmaid at that early hour, Song squirmed in her chair. Her head was a mess and her body ached. After she'd adjusted for the tenth time, grunting a little in her discomfort, Sunshine sent her an exasperated sigh over his eggs.

"Could you have chosen a noisier chair?" he asked.

She sneered at him. "You sat us here." She shifted again.

"What's wrong?"

"I can't get comfortable, that's all. My back hurts."

"Well, finish your eggs and we'll get you layin' back down, all right?"

She nodded and tried to rush through eating without making herself sick. Minutes passed as he ignored her shifting and squirming. Then a funny, familiar feeling crept between her thighs. She pursed her lips and widened her eyes.

"Key to my room. Now."

"What's wrong?"

"Don't worry about it. Room key. Hurry."

"What—"

"*Lady business!*" she hissed, so no one else heard.

He gave her the key, and she took off as fast as she could without running. She entered her room to dig into her trunk. It wasn't until she held up the hip belt and special cloth that she froze.

How am I going to bloody do this with one bloody arm?

Unable to put the belt around her hips, she gave up and stuffed the cloth between her legs in her underpants, which were already red with fresh blood. Song rinsed her hand in the basin and stared at the open buttons of her britches.

Just do it. Say the words.

But they refused to come. No matter how hard she tried, nothing popped into her mind—no commands and no words.

"Don't need you, anyway."

To her utter frustration, she began to cry again. Unable to button her trousers or remove her coat, she dropped onto the bed and tipped over. Her tears rolled over the bridge of her nose. She didn't even try to stop them this time, since it never worked, anyway. On one hand, she was tired of crying at the drop of a hat. On the other, she never wanted to stop crying. If she stopped, would it mean she no longer cared?

Sunshine found Song curled into a ball on her bed. She was crying again, her whole body shaking. He didn't say anything as he sat beside her and stroked her hair. Once he'd helped get her coat off, he stayed with her. He read to her from the translations Pinch had managed of the holy book of Aibhànocht. It had taken Sunshine a week to get over her theft of the tome's contents, but in the end he'd agreed that he would've done the same.

When her rocking, moaning, and sweating grew worrisome, he leaned forward in his chair to study her. "Are you all right?"

"Yes," she gasped. "Just…lady things."

"Should I get you a doctor?"

She wanted to say no. Wanted to be stronger. But the pain was growing worse. She nodded, and he left. When he returned, he had a woman with him. She spoke broken Common, but enough to communicate with Song. The woman gave her a sad smile and loaded up a metal syringe. Soon enough, the pain stopped and Song's world spun in lazy blurs.

The woman stayed with her for hours—maybe longer— and Song couldn't remember a single thing she said. She was kind enough to help Song use the chamber pot and get her back into bed with a wool rag and a square of leather under her hips. Song fell asleep a short while later.

SHE LOST COUNT OF THE DAYS AGAIN AS SHE SLEPT AND DRANK. This time Sunshine let her do so without a word, though he moderated the amount she consumed. When she was drunk, both the pain in her lower body and the pain in her heart subsided—though neither disappeared.

When Song could sit upright again, Sunshine sat her at the small table, hungover and grumpy, and forced her to practice writing with her left hand. This wasn't the first time he'd done this. The Pishing doctor she'd already forgotten the name of had been telling her things to do, like exercises to build strength, dexterity, and coordination in her left hand. He wanted her to have some semblance of normalcy, some return to activities she needed her dominant hand for.

Sunshine had consulted with a local doctor for a sort of prosthesis, something to fill out the sleeve and at least give the illusion of her being whole. That's why they had to bind her arm tight at the end. Song had met with a metalsmith named Anzi, who had set up shop in Srkar. She was world-renowned for her devices and inventions. She'd made fake arms for people before, and one for a Touched person—which is why Sunshine had gone to her. But being world famous had its downside for Song. Anzi's commission list was so long that she couldn't even start on the arm for six months. Song didn't have the energy to threaten her. In fact, at the time, she'd been drunk and had laughed as though the wait was another joke.

At the end of the week, when Sunshine had shuffled off for the night, Song dug out one of her hidden whiskey bottles. She sat on the floor in front of Leslie's chest. She'd been avoiding it longer than she had with Dashaelan's things. Every time she'd sat in front of the trunk, she'd pushed it back into the corner without opening the lid.

When her nose and ears were hot from drink, and her courage had risen, she opened the latch. Song held the lid in place for minutes, tears already pouring down her cheeks. She closed her eyes and opened the trunk. As the lid swung, the smell of him hit her across the face. She slammed it closed and bent to stretch her arm across it and sob.

She was onto her second bottle, her tears subsided but not gone, when an urgent knock rattled the door. Song pushed to her feet and stumbled over. She didn't have time to react as someone shoved into the room. She squinted at a tall, muscular man in a red shirt, his arms crossed and familiar face set in a mean expression. The door closed, and she focused on the mess of drab grey cloth. Tall black boots; long, grey, wide-legged pants; long-sleeved grey shirt; and a black shemagh wrapped over her head and in front of her nose and mouth. But Song would recognize those eyes anywhere.

"Smiling Eyes."

"What?" Lyella growled. The sultania tore the face covering down to reveal her ornate veil, then pulled the scarf from her head. She had tied her black hair into a ponytail and tucked it into the fabric.

"That's one more word than you knew the last time we met." Song leaned back against the door and took a huge swig of whiskey.

Lyella's eyes swept over her, brows pushed together in confusion. "I am…learn Common."

She furrowed her brow and held the liquid on her tongue to burn a little longer before swallowing. "Why?"

Lyella pointed at Song.

"For me? Why?"

Lyella slapped her across the face. Song widened her eyes. She'd actually slapped her! Lyella's eyes rounded as Song straightened to stand over her. Maybe she now knew what the name Song was attached to. The cruelty, the murder, the danger. Perhaps she feared this woman who didn't balk at the idea of harming a royal. Song snorted and broke down laughing.

"You slapped me!" She teetered forward and wrapped her arm around Lyella to giggle into her hair. "You're the only one I'll let get away with that."

Lyella shoved Song away, though. "You break promise."

She rolled her eyes and shook her head. "Only thing I broke was my arm. And my heart."

She grabbed the betrothal necklace hanging tangled with the keys for the Stars' Bounty and the Stars' Reprisal. "Armalinia sand. You mine."

"Oh, that. Yeah. See, I've been busy *losing an arm!*" she shouted the last bit, holding up the stump as though the sultania hadn't seen it.

Lyella flinched. After a long moment in silence, she eased

the whiskey from Song's grasp and set it on the table. "I buy you ship. I buy you arm."

She scoffed. "I bought my own bloody ship."

Lyella laughed and shook her head. Song made a face, realizing she had no proof that it had been her own quoine which made the purchase.

"I'm in line for a new arm already."

"I get arm."

"Can I tell you no?"

Lyella scrunched her nose. "Yes."

"Will you listen?"

"No." She giggled and sat on the bed, then dragged Song down beside her.

"How did you find me?"

"Srkar spies. Tell of Song to Sultan."

She blinked. "Oh. Daft of me to not think those exist."

"You mine."

"Can it wait? I'm really in no shape…"

Lyella studied her, brushing her greasy hair out of her face, her amber eyes lingering on the dark circles around Song's. After a moment, she gave a single nod. "Yes."

Song wanted to kiss the sultania, or do other things to please her, but her heart wasn't in it. So she leaned her head on the woman's shoulder and stared at Leslie's trunk again. She couldn't help thinking that she would trade every moment with this beautiful woman just to have him back.

"He was my best friend," she mumbled.

"Hmm?"

"Leslie."

"Oh! Jinjur! Where?"

Song shook her head. Tears rolled from her eyes onto Lyella's shoulder. The woman shifted and wrapped her arms around Song, holding her close. They lay back and Song closed her eyes and lost herself in her sorrow again, this time comforted by the soft hands of the sultania.

Song woke in the morning to that delicate arm draped over her. She stared at the woman lying against her side—at her thick, wavy black hair tangled across the pillow, her painted eyelids closed and her pouty mouth half open, leaving a spot of moisture on Song's shirt. Song's lips curved in the silliest of smiles as she stared. After a while, she giggled. Lyella opened her bleary eyes, which made Song laugh harder as they crossed and uncrossed, trying to focus on her.

"Why laugh?" Lyella asked, then yawned.

"Because you're so beautiful…but you're so ugly when you sleep."

The sultania gave her an unsteady smile, her Common not advanced enough for what Song had said.

"You'd think you'd look like a goddess, but no. You're kind of a mess. It's glorious."

Lyella blinked at her. "What?"

"Nothing, nothing. Just so happy you're not perfect." Song grinned, and the woman returned the expression, albeit confused.

The two conversed as best they could for the next hour. Lyella's Common was better than Song thought it could have been in a few months, though still not the best. When Sunshine walked in to wake Song, bucket in hand, he stopped with his lips pursed.

"That explains the bloke outside your door."

Lyella had scrambled when the door opened, and now lay back, lower face hidden behind the blanket. "Who you?"

"That's Sunshine. My new right hand…in more ways than one." Song waved away his confused expression. "Be a dear and bring us breakfast?"

He clenched his jaw, but left anyway. Sunshine stared at Lyella over breakfast as she leaned her head to send her veil forward so she could eat. He clearly didn't like the veiling custom, but said nothing of his objections.

After they ate, Lyella insisted they visit the metalsmith. Sunshine helped Song into her clothing as Lyella put on the desert attire she'd arrived in. Out on the street, Song received looks, but people seemed to ignore Lyella—which was the point of her disguise. Her guards also drew attention. Song remembered Ryk'r, but the other guard was new. He was petite, sporting the curves of a woman's body, though if he'd had breasts, he'd had them removed. A green tattoo stood out against the dark skin of his forehead, and Song frowned at the memory of Leslie educating her on the meaning of such markings.

The forge house where the metalsmith lived and worked comprised two buildings built side-by-side. She lived in one of the buildings, which was locked to the public. The other was a workshop with large glassless windows covered by metal bars, which she would cover with huge wooden shutters. The black shutters along the front were closed that day, but through the windows at the back, all could see the woman at the hot forge. The sharp clangs of her hammer striking metal echoed through the neighborhood.

Once inside the forge house, Ryk'r locked the door behind them as the other guard remained outside. Anzi finished working a piece of orange-hot steel, and shoved it into the burning coke. She removed her thick gloves and left them on the anvil. The metalsmith came to the front half of the workshop, which was set up as a welcoming little waiting area, with chairs, a table, and metalwork decorations on the walls.

"Sunshine, back again so soon?" Her accent was thick, though her Common fluid.

The metalsmith was a short woman, with muscular arms and broad shoulders, though her facial features were delicate and pretty. She kept her hair in a bun, wrapped tight with ribbons, and the front styled in waves. Song found it to be a beautiful contrast, to be so feminine, and yet built like a strongman.

"She insisted," he said, jerking a thumb at Lyella.

"Ah. And you brought Mister Song." She pressed her lips together at Song, then looked back at Sunshine. "I told you, I do not have an opening for six months."

Lyella asked her something in Armalinian. The two spoke back and forth before Lyella lowered her shemagh to reveal her veil. Anzi gasped and bowed low, her right fist over her sternum. The next thing Song knew, Lyella had ripped back Song's hood and yanked the necklace from inside her coat. Anzi's wide eyes settled on Song's face for a long time before she remembered her place and bowed to her as well.

"What's happening?" Song asked.

"On the request of the sultania, I will start your commission immediately," Anzi said to the dirt floor.

"If I'd known that's all it would take…" Sunshine muttered.

Anzi urged Song out of her coat and took measurements of what remained of her right arm. "Rumors say you are *balemari*. Is this true?"

Song gave her a blank stare.

"*Kijæm?*"

"Yes, it's true," Sunshine said before Song could muster the courage to say no.

"I will make you an arm that will look like a real arm and function like one. However, it is not as simple to use as a real arm, because you will have to give commands."

"Does it really work?" Sunshine asked as Song stared ahead, biting her tongue.

"Yes. My one other *balemari* client has never complained. Better an arm you talk to than no arm at all, yes?"

She stared down at Song, who stayed silent for a moment longer before she swallowed and nodded. The two Armalinian women spoke together as Anzi drew up a rough blueprint and took measurements of Song's left arm. Once satisfied, Lyella wrapped her shemagh back around her head and helped Song into her coat. The latter still chewed on her confession, hinges of her jaw pulsing as she clenched her teeth. In the end, though, she left without saying a word.

Three

L YELLA STAYED FOR ONE MORE NIGHT, THEN LEFT ON A SKYSHIP back to Pajisr. Before she'd gone, she smiled and set her palms on Song's cheeks. "Next time you come, you mine."

"I'll make damn sure there isn't a next time," Song said. "Sorry."

Lyella smiled, anyway. "*Ank'i yr* Castildi, Gould Tsingsei, *sultania drr* Andalise; Song Caleb, *sultan drr kharak.*"

Song released a wistful breath. "I like it when you speak nonsense to me."

Lyella captured her in a long, lustful kiss, then wrapped the shemagh around her head. "Ryk'r stay with you." She was out the door and down the stairs before Song could object.

Song met the man's gaze, then stared at his royal guard uniform. She pursed her lips. "You need less recognizable clothes."

His eyes remained steady on hers, but he otherwise didn't move. She shut the door, closing him out in the hallway.

Song watched Lyella's skyship pass over the city from her window, a frown tugging at her lips. She hadn't realized how much Lyella's presence had helped until she left. The sultania had been a blessed distraction, and now Song sat in the bed, staring at the wall, nursing a fresh bottle of whiskey.

The days returned to her new normal—drinking herself stupid every day, waking in the mornings being splashed with the bucket, though she no longer vomited into it. She thanked whatever gods did or didn't exist for that much, though her hangovers still left her nauseous. She lost track of time, again. Everything was a repetition. Wake, eat, hand exercises, drinking. Over and over. Sometimes she would go to Anzi for another measuring of her limbs.

Then one night, when she'd been staring at the trunk and yelling foul, drunken things at Sunshine, a knock sounded on the door. She bit her tongue as he cracked it to look out at the visitor.

Sunshine took a deep breath and let it out in slow relief. "I'm glad to see you, boy. Come in."

Song stood as a familiar brunette entered the room and Sunshine left. She pursed her lips at Ponce. "Oh, good, you're still alive. Quite nice, indeed." She followed the sentiment with a large swallow of whiskey.

"What happened?" Ponce asked, his brown eyes scanning over her.

"Oh, has no one told you?"

He clenched his teeth. "Toothy told me about Whispers. Said you lost an arm. Guess I just didn't expect it to be that much of your arm."

She stared at the bandage. "Mmm. Yes. I can't rightly put a hook on there, can I? What else did Toothy tell you?"

"Said you just drink all day. Don't give a damn about anything or anyone. Some of the men think you won't get back into the skies."

"I can't even fight anymore."

"I can teach you."

"What does it matter?"

Ponce shook his head. "It matters. The men want to—"

"Want to what?" she snapped. "Be led to their deaths by a stupid brat? I should never have been captain. Leslie should have. But now he's gone—and don't you dare tell me it's not my fault!" she said as he lifted his hands in a soothing motion.

"It *isn't* your fault, though."

"I should've just threatened Roman. But I was trying to be diplomatic for Leslie's sake. All I did was waste time and get him—"

She shut her mouth and blinked at the wall as Ponce wrapped his arms around her in a tight, comforting hug. After the shock wore off, she wrapped her arm around him and cried into his shoulder. They stayed like that for a long time, holding each other and crying. Song dropped onto the bed and he sat beside her.

Ponce took a swig of her whiskey. "What about your arm, though?"

She raised one shoulder in bitter apathy. "I said I would give my right arm to have Leslie not be dead. And so here I am, without an arm…but he's still dead. So…"

"Lost an arm for nothing. Boys say you're getting a new one, at least." He passed the bottle to her.

She pursed her lips after taking a drink. "I am. A metal one."

"Going to throw some wicked punches."

She shrugged. "Maybe. Maybe it'll just sit there. Useless."

"More reason to learn to fight with your other hand."

She made a face and passed the bottle back. "I'm rubbish at everything with my left hand."

"Well, now you've got me—"

"Ponce, I don't—"

"Look, I'm the most qualified to be your teacher. All you have to do is show up and shut up."

"I don't know what the point is. I really don't."

"How about I throw in something to sweeten the deal?"

She chuckled. "Something like what?"

"I promise not to fall in love with you." He grinned, though the smile didn't reach his eyes.

She laughed harder. "Oh, good. Because that's what was holding me back from accepting." She pursed her lips in exasperation. "You don't need to do this, Ponce."

"I want to do it."

"Why?"

He stared at his hands and released a long, weary breath. "Because I need some kind of purpose…to distract me."

Their eyes met, and she saw the truth written across his features. He seemed all right on the surface, but a deeper look revealed his desperate sorrow and dark depression. The man may well have barely been holding himself together. At least he was doing a better job at it than Song—though perhaps he was just better at hiding it.

"I suppose if it's just to help you…"

"It's settled. We'll start tomorrow when you're sober. For tonight, why don't you put on your coat and come with me?"

Song made a face at him. "I can't put it on by myself."

"Well, then, why don't I put your coat on you, and you

come with me?" He stood to retrieve said article and hold it out for her.

"Do I have a choice?"

"You do not. In you get." Ponce shook the coat, urging her into it.

Song released a long, drawn-out sigh, then stood and shoved her arm into the sleeve. She let him wrap her in the black leather, then buckle it across the front.

"Where are you taking me?" she asked after swallowing down more whiskey.

"On an adventure."

"Without Sunshine?"

"No, he can come."

"Ryk'r?"

Ponce blinked at her. "Who?"

"My royal bodyguard. Bastard sticks out like a sore thumb." She swung the door open so hard it punched a hole in the shoddy mud-brick wall. "Hello, Ryk'r!" She swallowed a long pull from the bottle and swaggered out, her ankles wobbling beneath her. "I've been meaning to ask you, but keep forgetting. What's *kharak* mean?"

The man in the hallway stared at her, but didn't move or make to answer.

She narrowed her eyes at him before Ponce flopped her hood over her head. "All right then, keep your secrets." She threw her arm around Ponce's shoulders as he closed her door. "We're going on an adventure. You're not invited unless you change your shirt."

The man didn't move. As the two started down the hallway, he fell into step not far behind. Song turned around, a rude belch ready. But as it came up, so did a little acid. She spat the bit of vomit into a corner, then chased the remainder down with her whiskey.

Ponce blinked at her. "Are you all right?"

"Perfectly perfect. Let's go."

He led her through the pirate city, down streets she didn't recognize. Every so often she would turn to make a rude expression at the guard on their heels, then trip on the loose-packed sand. Ponce would catch her and they'd resume as though nothing had happened. He took her to a tavern where music contended with loud voices. The volume of the patrons diminished as eyes turned to stare at her. She took a swig of her whiskey and glanced at the faces around the room.

"Oh, look! It's our friends," she said, pointing at a handful of her crew at a table. She swaggered over and dropped into a seat beside Knots. "Why is everyone staring at me?" she asked the man beside her.

"You haven't heard?" Knots asked as the previous racket resumed. His amber eyes locked onto her, his black brows furrowed. He'd gotten his mass of curly hair cropped close to his scalp since she'd last seen him. She didn't like it.

"I've been busy."

Ponce produced a folded parchment from his back pocket and dropped it onto the table in front of her. "I found that in Aibhànocht as I was leaving."

She fought the folded page, yanking it away when the man tried to help her unfold it. Once open, she stared down at the familiar sketch. "Oh, they bollocksed my nose again. That's almost the only feature they can even see, and they can't get it right." Song's eyes caught on the reward amount and she almost cried out in shock. "This can't be right."

"Wanted for piracy, numerous counts of murder, two massacres, mass arson, two counts regicide, and familicide, plus several less severe charges. It's quite the list," Ponce said. "Three hundred and seventy-seven *thousand* quoine seems about right."

She blinked at the page again. "I could buy a mansion in Garda for that. Not as big as my family's, but still quite large."

"Song," Knots said, his expression serious, "no one has ever had a price this high on their head."

"*Ever* ever?" she asked, incredulous.

"One hundred and fifty thousand was the previous record," Toothy said on the other side of Ponce. "Black Patch Bristol, one hundred years ago."

She held up the page so her guard who'd positioned himself against the wall could see it. "Ryk'r, look! I'm a large house!"

His dark brown eyes slid to the page, then resumed their resolute study of the room and the inhabitants who might pose a threat. He didn't make any expression, good or bad, like he hadn't even looked.

She scoffed. "You're still required to change your shirt."

The man didn't move, as though he hadn't heard.

Her brow furrowed on the page once more, reading each charge over and over. "What's this nonsense about familicide? And *two* counts of regicide?"

"Roman and Toren Duchamp," Sunshine said as he lowered into a seat on the other side of the round table.

"I didn't kill Toren! I would never kill a child, no matter how much that brat deserved it."

"Either way, he was the last of the Duchamp bloodline."

Song held her breath behind pursed lips, then let it all out in a whoosh. "How'd he die? Did the papers say?"

"Something about a toad. Probably one of those toxic ones Dash told me about." Sunshine accepted a drink from the barmaid as she set steins from a tray in front of each of them.

Song's lips tightened at the corners. The scene replayed in her mind as though it had just happened. Leslie, back glistering in the sun with his fresh blood. Toren winding back his arm to launch a toad at his torn flesh. It snapped into clear reality that the child had intended for the toad to kill Leslie.

"Oh… I suppose I did kill him. Inadvertently. The little wretch was trying to launch a toad at…" She cleared her throat, and no one questioned the name she wouldn't say. "I made it turn on him, instead. I had no idea it was toxic. Now that I do…I'd do it again."

"What do you suppose they do when a royal line ends?" Ponce asked.

Song shrugged. "Who cares? The entire country could burn down and I'd celebrate." She shoved the poster away and gulped down her ale. "Roll the next poster you see. I want one for my collection."

She stayed in the tavern with her men long into the night. They played cards, and it remained otherwise uneventful. She was grateful for that—for the other patrons leaving her alone. She didn't have to get into a fight with anyone when there was no way she could win anymore. When the night came to a close, and she fell into bed, staring at the ceiling, she almost welcomed the nightmares. At least in them, she still had both of her arms. And she could see Leslie again. At least in dreams, she was whole again.

Days passed. Song spent more time closer to sober than she liked. She begrudgingly worked with Ponce as he taught her how to do everything left-handed. He would sit behind her and guide her hand over the paper. The pages came out smeared, and ink stained the side of her palm. He promised it would get easier. She needed more practice to train herself not to rest her hand on the paper. Song didn't want to practice. She wanted her right hand back, so nothing had to change at all.

Some days she would go to the metal-worker's shop and sit through more measurements and estimates. Anzi would ask her preferences for things, and Song would shrug. She didn't want anything besides her own arm, and so she had no opinion on this fake thing that would be as useless as the empty sleeve at her side.

Most days, Ponce took it upon himself to help her more than he needed to. He forced her into a bath when she hadn't had one in so long due to Sunshine's fear of her passing out in the water. He made sure she had enough bubbles and scented whitening liquid to allow her a little privacy, and would wait in the corner, keeping an eye on her. He even washed her left arm, since she couldn't clean it herself. One such day, she sat on a cushion as he combed her hair.

"Why are you doing this?" she asked on a whisper, having forgotten the first time he'd told her his reason.

"What?"

"Taking care of me."

He released a long sigh and separated her hair into clumps at her scalp. "Because…" He began braiding her hair, as though he'd done the action many times before. "It's giving me purpose."

She sniffed and fought against her chin as it tried to wrinkle. "Maybe you're wasting time."

"You're not a waste of time. You just need to find what gives you purpose. So, shut up and let me use you for my benefit."

She laughed over the tears breaking free. "You're such a selfish cad… How do you know how to braid hair?"

He chuckled. "Toothy's sister taught me. She said I had to be useful somehow."

"Was this when she was trying to court you?"

"It was, yes," Ponce said with a laugh.

"Why are you doing it, though?"

"Because it's time we start training you to wield a sword again. I found a place to train, away from prying eyes. And no, you don't get a choice."

She took a deep breath in which she contemplated objecting and raising a fuss. Instead she said, "Thank you."

When they left her room, she stopped to stare at Ryk'r, who met her gaze without expression. He'd changed his shirt to a faded red linen, rather than the vibrant silk. He'd also traded his wide-legged pants for a pair of black leather trousers. The only thing remaining of his uniform was the wide cloth belt around his middle, hiding his kris.

After a long silence, she nodded once at him. "We're training with swords today. Won't that be delightful?"

He didn't reply, but fell into step a few paces behind them, as usual.

Sunshine met them at the training grounds—a courtyard behind a building Song didn't ask the purpose of. Ponce had paid the owner for complete privacy, so no one would see Captain Song struggling to keep the blade upright, let alone swing it in a straight line. Ponce stood behind her most of the time, chest pressed to her back and hand wrapped over hers. They repeated motions over and over, with Sunshine as the other blade.

When they stopped for a rest and something to eat, she sat alone in the corner, staring at her wrapped stump as she chewed a hunk of bread. She closed her eyes.

"If you're still there," she whispered, "strengthen my left arm. If I could just fight again…" She left it there, knowing the plea was futile.

Four

OVER THE WEEKS, THEY WOULD SPEND A FEW HOURS IN THE courtyard every day—even on days when the missing limb ached like she'd slept on it wrong. She had to push past the discomfort and pain, since there was nothing she could do about it. Ponce claimed she was improving fast, but to her it wasn't fast enough. Still, she couldn't deny that it came easier since that first session.

The day came when her prosthetic arm was ready. Ponce and Sunshine carted her down the street, neither having any idea why she was dragging her feet. Even Ryk'r blocked her path as she wriggled loose and tried to return to her room.

"If you shut up and get a move on, we'll take you to see the new bard visiting from Talegrove," Sunshine said.

"He's got a song about the slaughter of Carliolace," Ponce added.

"You know how much you like listening to those. We can go see how much he gets wrong."

Song released a long, tired breath. "They never get any of it right, except that I killed Roman."

They stared at her, pleading.

"Fine. Let's go."

They entered the forge house, and Song flopped into a chair. She stared at an intricate metal moth with filigree wings and a small winder at the back. It perched on a fake plant on the table, and had tempted Song to wind it up every time she'd seen it. She'd resisted this urge, though, not wanting to break the little invention.

When Anzi entered the room with a long wooden box, Song pointed at the moth. "What's that?"

Anzi smiled. "A failure, unfortunately."

"What's it do?"

She lifted the moth and twisted the knob. The wings flapped, but nothing else happened. "It is supposed to fly, but it will not."

"Not enough substance to the wings and too much to the body," Song said.

She nodded and replaced the crafted insect, then reached for Song's coat. "Do you mind?" She didn't wait for Song's affirmative as she undid the buckles and helped her from the coat. She slipped a tight-fitting cloth over her right upper arm. "This will help with comfort when you sweat. Nothing is worse than raising your arm up and all the sweat collected rolls down your sleeve."

"Speaking from experience?"

"Forging gloves get quite hot," she said, laughing.

Song's lips twisted into a sideways smile. "Fair enough."

The woman opened the case and moved aside for Song to behold her artistry resting on a purple silk cushion. Song swallowed as she stared at the fake arm. Without close inspection, she wouldn't know it was fake. She had forged it of Pishing sorrowstone. The joints were cogs made of brightsteel. Filigree patterns had been acid etched into the sorrowstone to glimmer silver in the light. The forearm had a realistic shape to it, and near-matched her left. Song bit the inside of her cheek. Again, her confession danced on her tongue, but refused to burst forth.

"Let me show you what I have done," Anzi blurted, having mistaken Song's hesitation for dislike. She lifted the arm and curled the fingers toward the palm, not quite like a punch, but close, and shoved the upper palm back so it bent at the wrist. A white blade about the length of a long middle finger shot from a slit at the heel of the palm. "A dagger for emergencies." Anzi's voice tightened with excitement. "And…" She pushed the hand down, so the blade retracted. She straightened the index finger and flicked a point at the tip, like a fingernail. It flipped open to reveal a tiny compartment. She used her fingernail to pull out a sharp cone of brightsteel, then closed the flap over it to lock it in place. It looked like a straightened claw jutting from the fingertip. "All four fingers and the thumb have these tips. They can come in handy for climbing, or…whatever Captain Song's imagination can come up with."

Ponce whistled low. "Almost want to cut my arm off to get one of those."

Song, Anzi, and Sunshine all lowered their eyelids at the man.

"How do I keep the sorrowstone oiled?" Song asked.

Anzi undid a clasp at the inside of the forearm and it split open to display the hollow inside filled with white rods, gears, and the blade in a sort of sheath. "Only the shell is sorrowstone, so oiling will be simple."

The metalsmith helped Song into the cuff. She had riveted a leather harness to the metal, which the woman put on her while explaining each step to the men. It buckled around her arm just below the pit, then had two more buckling straps that hung loose. Anzi crossed the room and returned with a short corset with leather straps and buckles attached in a confusing array.

Song stood to let the woman secure it around her and tighten the back. It didn't use the standard sort of eyelets down the front. It had a row of buckles, which the woman said she'd chosen as Song could remove it herself that way. With practice, she could put it on with one hand, too, though it would be difficult. Straps stretched over her front and back, securing to pads at her shoulders and forming a triangle over her body. Once she'd secured it in place, she connected the straps on the arm to ones dangling from the right shoulder pad. She tightened it until it wouldn't budge, but wasn't pushing hard against Song's biceps.

"At least this bloody corset is comfortable," Song grumbled.

"Yes, well, I tried other harness types, but none were as comfortable, nor as flexible as this. Move around and see how it feels."

Song hesitated, then twisted and tilted. The corset held her just tight enough to keep the harnesses in place, but not tight enough to bother her. The arm didn't fall loose, though the weight of it pulled on her shoulder. It wasn't an uncomfortable weight, barely heavier than her actual arm. But after months with nothing but air there, it felt like an anchor dragging her down. She didn't hate the weight, though. For once, she felt whole again. Except that it didn't move, and she couldn't make it.

"Try telling it what to do," Sunshine said.

She stared at it. Everyone waited, watching with bated breath.

After several minutes in agonized silence, Song whispered, "I can't."

"What do you mean, you can't?" Ponce asked.

She hung her head as tears sprang to her eyes. "I mean exactly that. I cannot conjure the words. They've all gone from my mind."

"Since when?"

"Since Carliolace," she whispered. "Just days after you took my arm." She sent an accusing gaze at Sunshine. "In my anger and sorrow I wished I had never been a Touched, because that's what took my arm from me. And somehow it heard me… It gave me a command in response. I said it, and it acquiesced. Before you ask, no. I have no idea what the phrase meant. I only know that now I'm not Touched."

"You corked your own font of *kijæm*," Sunshine muttered. "Whispers would've been happy…and I might've been before. But I can't help but see this as another tragedy."

She nodded. "Me, too."

Anzi blinked at Song, then at the arm. "I can…tighten the hinges so you can force it into positions. You will have to add checking the tightness to your routine while oiling, but at least it will hold things. Nothing heavy. But it would not hang limp."

Song sniffed and swiped a tear from under her eye. "That would work. Yes."

They remained quiet as the metalsmith tightened each hinge with a smaller tool, not unlike the one she'd used on the harness. The balls for the elbow, wrist, and joints connecting the fingers to the palm tightened with sideways screw pins.

"I'm sorry," Song whispered before the woman finished. "I know you worked hard on this, and… I should've said something."

She smiled. "No *balemari* has ever gotten rid of it entirely. I have a feeling it is still there, waiting for you to be ready to wield it again."

"You think so?"

"I do," Ponce said.

"As do I," Anzi said. She finished tightening the joints, then forced the elbow to bend and the hand to circle like holding a cup. It remained in position, even after she set a mug in the fingers. "There we go. Careful not to go too tight. You can have these." She slipped the tools into the little pocket within the case. "I have got spares, and can make another."

Without warning, Song lurched forward and dragged the woman into a hug. "Thank you," she muttered against her head. "You have no idea what this means to me."

"It was my pleasure, Song. I learned so much making that! I have got so many ideas for how to make one that could move for a regular person. Maybe power it with steam."

"That would be quite the cumbersome contraption," Sunshine said.

"Yes, but imagine if it works."

"If anyone can do it, it's you, Anzi." Song kissed the woman on the cheek, then let Ponce help her into her coat.

She moved the limb into a more neutral pose as Sunshine grabbed the box for it. "Right, then. I'll see you again, I'm sure. Maybe for another arm. Who knows?"

"If you break that—"

"I meant as a spare! Maybe an all brightsteel one for… formal occasions. I don't know!" Song said with a laugh as she strode outside; Anzi chuckled as the door closed. Once back on the street, she narrowed her eyes at the fading light of the sunset glinting from her new knuckles. "I need my gloves."

After a quick stop to drop off the box and retrieve her gloves, they set off again for the tavern where the new bard would be performing.

"Let's get a seat right up front," Ponce said.

"Are you tryin' to make the bard's heart stop?" Sunshine asked.

"One missed note and he'd wet himself."

"I won't kill a man for singing off key," Song said, scoffing. "I'll kill him for unflattering lies."

"You didn't kill the other bards," Sunshine said.

"I was too drunk. I'm sure the bottles flying at their heads were message enough."

When they reached the tavern, all the tables near the raised performing area were already occupied. Song sauntered to the front as a tense silence seeped through the room. She stopped at the centermost front table and stared down at the inhabitants—two men and two women. They stood and abandoned the table, taking their drinks and looking back over their shoulders.

She dropped into a seat with a satisfied smirk. No one was safe from her wrath, and they knew it. She'd killed a lord, and they believed she'd murdered a child. Any of them could be next. In reality, though, she couldn't be bothered to kill random people for minor infractions.

The babble resumed at its previous volume. Sunshine motioned for drinks as Song pointed at Ryk'r and then at the empty chair beside Ponce. Ryk'r didn't move or make any sign he'd seen her silent demand. Toothy dropped into the spare seat as the barmaid set drinks before each of them. She gave Song a nervous smile as the latter grinned up at her.

"Thank you, darling," Song said.

"Y-you're welcome, Captain."

Toothy chuckled as the woman left. "Someone with your reputation has no right being that charming, Song. The ladies won't know what to do. Scream and run, or spread their legs?"

"A shame the vast majority would go away disappointed," she said.

A door on the left side of the room opened. The man who entered and strode to the platform, waving at the cheering crowd, had a guitar at his side, the strap wrapped over a shoulder. His blond hair was short and styled. He was the most well-groomed of the bards she'd seen of late, telling her he was one who performed for high society and royalty, as well as earning a meal and a room at an inn through performance.

The bard froze, his eyes locked onto the hooded figure at the front and center of the audience. He released a single nervous chuckle. "Well, then… It's not often I get to perform for the subject of my lyrics. I hope you…enjoy this, Captain Song."

"If you lie, I'll cut out your tongue," she said. "No pressure."

He gave another nervous chuckle and took his seat on a high stool. "Good evening, ladies and gentlemen. You may have seen many bards before me, and you'll see many after. But I promise you will never see a show like mine." He signaled with a hand and barmaids turned down the lamps, so every light in the room dimmed, leaving them in near total darkness. "*Naw'eshkuhdortnih.*"

Song's eyes widened as swirls of blue-lit mist gathered around him. It twisted and tangled, forming shapes in the air over the stage.

"I am Elaric of the Winterlands. Join me as we watch this tragic tale unfold with our own eyes." He hissed a command under his breath and the blue light flowed into a sphere before him. It churned in a familiar, ever-moving mass as it waited. "I have performed this specific song many times — including for Senator Gould and his wife, who found it particularly comforting." He lifted his guitar and plucked out a gentle tune. "For this is not just a tale of tragedy and rage. This is not a tale of a pirate's wanton wrath or senseless murder. No…this is a tale of love and loss. This is the tale of Tsingsei Gould and the slave she loved…"

Song blinked in shock and sat up a little more in her seat. Until now, her presence in Pishing as Tsingsei had gone ignored in the papers and the other bard songs. She'd been forgotten due to everyone's outrage over what Captain Song had done.

Two figures formed in the mist—a man and a woman. She pursed her lips, knowing they were supposed to be Song and Leslie. However, the man was too rugged, and the woman was too short, and too busty.

That's all right. At least it aids my disguise.

Elaric began. His voice was soft and soothing, befitting a song of sorrow. As he sang the words, the *kijæm* played out the events he detailed, like a play performed by actors made of starlight. It even filled in gaps he'd omitted for lyric's sake.

"Our story begins with a kiss and a sigh
A lover's confession, a likewise reply
The princess of Andalise, silently brave
As she handed her heart to a runaway slave
They traveled the world, oh, adventures abound
Holding each other, a love so profound
She pledged him her soul, and he gave her his heart
Together forever, to never depart
But evil has ears, and it relishes pain
And it vowed that day to tear them in twain

Batten your windows and bar your door
For vengeance is coming to settle a score
A story of lovers now turns into hate
A sorrow so deep it will never abate

The high lord, he sent out the posters and price
Dead or alive, no, he didn't think twice
Once and for all of this slave, he'd be rid
The lovers they cowered, together they hid

They kept their heads down and begged for asylum
But fear gripped the people who refused to hide 'em
Until a savior came out of the sky
He took them aboard, and he didn't ask why
With outlaws and brigands, they now belonged
And so they found solace with Captain Song

Batten your windows and bar your door
For vengeance is coming to settle a score
You call it piracy; they say recourse
The high lord could take them, but only by force

I see that you wonder with innocent eyes
How a tale of such love fell to sorrow and lies
Her lover was found, and the bounty was paid
She took to the skies as she begged and she prayed
She offered her quoine, and she offered her father's
The high lord refusing every last proffer
He shackled the slave, hands reaching to the sky
Her lover took lashes, refusing to cry
She begged for mercy; she begged the whip halt
Her heart felt each strike of the vicious assault

Batten your windows and bar your door
For vengeance is coming to settle a score
Hold to your loved ones and stay out of sight
The streets will run red, oh, no one's safe tonight

The princess of Andalise, silently brave
Sneaked through the city to comfort her slave

She tended to his wounds, her heart an abyss
And then they exchanged what would be their last kiss
For in the morning, the high lord's mind changed
And one of the lovers was destined to hang
She ran to the gallows, and fate snapped the rope
The guards struck her down with a single sword stroke
She woke in the prison that night just to learn
Instead of the gallows, her lover was burned

Batten your windows and bar your door
For vengeance is coming to settle a score
Beg him for mercy, but know it's too late
What's done is done. You've sealed your fate.

She fled Carliolace, straight to Captain Song
"Be my reprisal, for I have been wronged."
The captain marched into the city that night
Revolver in one hand, a sword in the right
He swept through the streets, and he slaughtered the guards
Ignited the flames that would leave the town marred
Just like the slave that he'd burned at the pyre
The high lord's last moments were claimed by a fire
Our story began with a kiss and a sigh
And now it will end with a painful goodbye

Batten your windows and bar your door
For vengeance is coming to settle a score
Blood will spill freely, a city will burn
Take heed, all ye people, and learn

Batten your windows and bar your door
For vengeance is coming to settle a score
Call him a villain and call her a fool
But for your love, what wouldn't you do?"

The song ended and the entire room held its breath, fear a tangible presence pressing upon the patrons. Every eye glittering in the blue light of the *kijæm* was trained on Song. But she'd locked her gaze on the final image of her striding down an invisible street, sword drawn as the cloak of red *kijæm* billowed in her wake. Elaric whispered a command, and the image floated away. The room returned to darkness before barmaids dared turn up the lamp wicks. The bard's gaze fixed on Song, the smallest bit of fear in his eyes.

He'd known the right details, the ones not told in the papers, since she was the only one who knew the full story. Her mind reeled at the fact and chose now to remind her of all the little details he hadn't known. She could be irritated by the painting of them as lovers, but for some reason, it didn't bother her. What did bother her was how much he'd gotten correct. And now her mind tumbled through that memory for a while as the entire world waited for her to react to the song. She dragged herself back to the present and thought hard about how to react.

She stood and walked up to him, one slow step at a time. He didn't move, though he looked like he wanted nothing more than to run. Song stared at him for a silent minute. Then she reached into the pouch at her thigh and withdrew her small quoine purse, which had a modest amount in it. She held it out and, after a long hesitation, he opened his hand to receive the item. Once Song returned to her seat, Sunshine started clapping, and the rest of the tavern followed, giving the bard a standing ovation.

"Find out where he's staying," Song hissed when Sunshine sat. "I'd like to have a word with him."

Five

THE DOOR OPENED, AND ELARIC ENTERED. HE SET HIS GUITAR in the corner, then turned up the oil lamp on the table beside the door. The bard lurched backward, eyes wide as his gaze found the hooded figure sat on the single wooden chair in the middle of the room. Just behind, on the bed, sat Sunshine.

"Elaric, the Magic bard from the Winterlands," Song said. "Good show."

"Are you here to cut out my tongue?" he asked.

She laughed. "Why would I do that?"

"Because I lied?"

"Did you?"

He hesitated.

"Did you tell the story as your Gift told it to you? I assume that's how you knew the details so well."

"I changed the fact that you did it all one-handed," Elaric said.

She grinned. "Imagine if people knew that part. Then again, flashing steel and daring sword fights are far more thrilling than a happy trigger finger and extensive *kijæm* use."

"I didn't want people to fear Magics more than they already do."

"Fair enough." Song stood and took a few slow steps toward him. "I'm here to offer a trade."

He folded his arms, his thumbnail dragging along his lower lip. "Go on."

"I will fill in a rather significant gap in your tale, but you cannot add it to your song, and no one else can ever know what you do."

"And what do you get in return?"

"A bit of your *kijæm*." She removed her glove to show him the black and white metal hand. "I lost my arm after Carliolace. And then I lost my *kijæm*. I figure if you can infuse this with yours, then…maybe I might at least get my arm back."

He released a long, thoughtful sigh. "Is that your big secret? That you're no longer a Magic, and you're missing an arm?"

"No. There's one more major piece to the puzzle. For some reason, your own *kijæm* denied you the truth. Thankfully."

He licked his lips, his eyes sparkling with hunger for the secret. "All right. A trade. The whole story in exchange for hopefully a working arm." He held out his right hand, and she gripped it with her left to shake.

"Since I have to remove my coat to hand you the arm, you get the truth first. Tsingsei and the *free man*—he wasn't a slave anymore—were not lovers. And she didn't beg me for retribution. He was my first mate and…closer than a best friend." She lowered her hood. "I took the retribution myself."

Elaric's jaw went slack. "You're a woman?"

"I'm Tsingsei Gould. Your little light show got my appearance wrong. Which is nice. Helps with the whole Caleb Song thing."

"Let me see the arm," he said, dazed. "And tell me everything I got wrong."

"So long as you remember, this is a story you can never tell another soul. And if you do…I'm sure you're smart enough to know my response."

Sunshine stood and unbuckled her coat. He helped her remove the arm from the harness system, and set the prosthetic on the small table Elaric had dragged to the middle of the room.

"You're the only bard to not pin Toren Duchamp's unfortunate death on me, you know."

The man sat and stared over the arm, mesmerized by the craftsmanship. "Yes, well, I saw plain as day that you walked away from him, and he was still alive."

"How much of a toll do your light shows take?"

"Not much. I gather the information in little bits at a time. I learned early when to stop to avoid nose bleeds." His jaw tensed, and he looked up at her. "How do you use so much without the cost?"

"I pay that cost, same as you. After a fight with Captain Darian, I bled from my eyes and ears, too."

"You should be dead…"

Song nodded once, her lips pressed into a thin line. "Probably."

After she filled in the important details of all the events of Pishing, Elaric released a long breath, shaking his head. Rather than say something, as though he couldn't think of anything to say, he set his hands on the arm and muttered in that familiar language which Song no longer understood. The room illuminated as the blue mist flickered into existence. It spun around Song, seeming to lift flecks of light from her. It tangled around, blinking in and out, much like how it looked when she stole another's *kijæm*. The mass floated over to the arm and settled around it, seeping inside and affixing to the gears. The bard said a command and—with difficulty—the index finger cog joints lit up blue and the finger straightened, then went dark again.

"Well, it works," he said. "Little stiff, but—"

"I can loosen it," she said, snatching up the limb.

Sunshine helped buckle the straps connecting the arm to the harness system.

"How do you plan on using it if you can't control the *kijæm* anymore?" Elaric asked.

"I have no idea, but this is a start," she said. Once Sunshine had clasped her coat around her, she set her left hand on Elaric's shoulder. "Keep telling the same tale you have been. Tell them of a buxom Tsingsei Gould begging Captain Song's aid in retribution. You can decide whether to reveal that I did it all one-handed. Just don't let anyone know I am now one limb off from a full set."

"And if I do tell, I'll lose my tongue," Elaric said, now at ease with her, as though she was the least frightening thing in the room.

"Or your life. Depending on how cross you make me."

He laughed. "Has anyone ever told you you're quite charming? Even when making threats."

She grinned. "A time or two, yes."

"May I just ask one more thing?"

She hesitated, then nodded once.

"Was your first mate really not your lover?"

"No."

"Why not?" he asked as she strode for the door.

"Because he wasn't a woman." She winked back at him. "Enjoy the rest of your night, Elaric of the Winterlands."

"Do you know…?" He paused, staring at his hands.

"Yes?"

"Who shot the crossbow bolt?"

She turned back to him and stared into his eyes. Elaric muttered a phrase and *kijæm* lit the room. A gallows built itself up, with a man hanging in the noose. Then a little streak shot through and severed the rope so the man fell free.

"I don't know. I'm sorry."

He shrugged. "It's all right. I was just hoping to figure that out."

"Me, too."

It was late, and Song was tired and tipsy by the time she returned to her room. She stared at the arm, brow furrowed in concentration. Nothing happened. Not so much as a blue glittering on the metal, or a word in her mind. In the end, she scoffed and unbuckled the straps. She dropped the arm onto the table, then removed the harness and corset to drop in a heap beside the black metal. Song cradled the sorrowstone blade on her lap and oiled it, occasionally glancing at the arm on the table, which she would have to oil, too. It would be a lot more difficult to do with one hand, and she wondered the odds of Sunshine agreeing to do it for her. Then her eyes flitted to the trunk in the corner.

I have to go through it at some point. I can't keep a chest I never open and shove into a corner, can I? She sighed and slid the blade into its sheath. *Yes, I can.*

Song flopped into bed, hugging the sheathed sword to her. Tears rolled from her eyes, tickling across her temples and dripping into the upper curves of her ears. She hated the sensation, but didn't care enough to wipe them away. She'd wept for Dashaelan for so long—her heart still broke thinking of him. But it had gotten a little easier after a while. She didn't think she would ever stop mourning Leslie. Song had made bargain after bargain. She would give anything. And yet she knew it was useless. Her first offering had been her arm, and whatever higher power that may have existed had been more than happy to take it. But she'd offered it too late. Nothing could undo what had already been done.

Days passed, though each one felt the same as the last. She worked with Ponce to improve her finger dexterity on her left hand and practice writing. She even practiced the simple act of drawing and sheathing her sword over and over.

More of the crew joined in helping, trickling in one or a few at a time. Thumbs arrived in the courtyard one day with a bowl of his stew and a joke about teaching her to eat. Eating and drinking was as second nature to her as breathing, so she'd already mastered using her left hand for those before she'd even lost the right. But it wasn't about teaching her, anyway, and she knew that. Each man was, in their own way, rallying around her, heartening her into pushing herself and not giving in to the sorrow again.

She found it odd, though, that ever since her silent plea to strengthen her left arm, it had. Her coordination with it advanced far faster than it should have. Soon enough, she was mock fighting at the beginner speed she'd done years ago when Dashaelan had started training a brat.

Her right arm, however, remained a lifeless weight. She did exercises to strengthen her shoulder, hoping the strain from supporting the arm would lessen. It didn't, however, do anything to help the fact that it wouldn't move. No matter how much she willed it, the arm rested in whatever position she'd forced it into. The frustration built inside her day by day. Until the moment during a training session when it jostled and banged into her bruised side for what felt like the hundredth time, and she couldn't have done anything to stop it.

Song threw her saber to the ground and tore at the buckles keeping the arm attached to the harness. It fell into the sand with a heavy *thud*. She lifted it in her left hand and spun around to throw it with all her strength at the wall of the building, where no one had been standing. However, someone was there now. Someone in dark desert attire, a shemagh wrapped around her head and face.

Ryk'r lurched toward her, but was too far away. Lyella screamed and raised her hands over her face. Song's first instinct was to raise her arm up and avoid dealing the blow. As though reacting to the movement of her shoulder, the joints all lit up blue and the forearm of the prosthesis yanked upward, throwing it off course so it passed a hand's width from Lyella. It smashed into the wall and fell to the wooden porch.

Song rushed forward and grabbed the trembling woman in a frantic hug. "Are you all right? I'm so sorry, I didn't know you were there!"

Tears pooled at the corners of Lyella's eyes as her limbs continued to shake. She gasped, catching her breath. "Yes. Yes, I am good."

"Get her a chair," Song ordered over her shoulder, not caring who carried it out. She lowered the woman into the seat Knots set behind her. She crouched and stared into the smiling eyes as she gripped her hand. "If you want to hit me, I'd understand."

Lyella made a fist, her thumb tucked in, and punched at Song's shoulder. Thumbs laughed and knelt beside her, not asking permission before he fixed her hand's posture, curling her thumb under her knuckles and straightening her wrist. Lyella punched Song again once he'd finished. The sultania shook out her hand, then looked at her palm where her fingernails had dug little quarter-moon indents into the flesh.

Song chuckled. "Don't make punching people a habit. You'll ruin your manicure." She kissed the woman's injured palm. "What are you doing here, anyway?"

"Anzi says arm done. I came to see."

Knots stepped closer, the arm in his hands as he stared at the woman. "Is this the sultania you're betrothed to?"

"She is," Song said.

"What's your name?" he asked Lyella.

She met his gaze, but said nothing.

Song chuckled. "You're not allowed to know it. Or see her

face. It's a criminal act for you to even be seeing her without her *caddarik*. Right?"

"Right," she said. "I break rule to see *ghija*." She raised her arms, palms up as a hint for the man to set the prosthesis in her hands. Once she had it, she set it in her lap to look over the craftsmanship and investigate every little secret it held.

"Song…" Sunshine said behind her. "It moved."

She looked over her shoulder at him.

"It moved to avoid hitting the sultania. What did you do?"

She stared at the arm, her brow furrowed. "I…tried to move my arm as though it was still attached to me. I didn't really think about it, I just did it."

"Maybe that's what you need to do," Ponce said. "Stop thinking about moving the arm…and just move it."

She lifted her upper arm and thought about making a fist with the hand that wasn't there. But she couldn't disconnect the knowledge that she was trying to make something not connected to her move. Song closed her eyes and tried to imagine her arm still existing. It was easy, as quite often she felt it, and would disappoint herself all over again when she tried to grab something, but nothing had happened. Today had been one of those days where she felt that strange ghost appendage at her side, but like a sandstorm of pins and needles. She envisioned an arm made of *kijæm* instead, since it was easier to imagine than a whole sandstorm for an arm. She splayed out her fingers, then made a fist again.

The sound of metal snapping together urged her eyes open, and she stared down at the sorrowstone and brightsteel fist in Lyella's palm. She released a triumphant yelp, then tried to open her fist again. The hand didn't move. She closed her eyes and tried again, but nothing happened. After a moment of concentration, she growled in frustration, then made a rude gesture with her phantom hand. Metal shifted before her, and when she opened her eyes, the pinkie and ring fingers of the metal hand were straightened upward away from the fist to make the same rude gesture.

Song gritted her teeth and dropped to her rear. "Do you know how hard it is to not think about making an arm that isn't your arm move?"

"What do you mean?" Knots asked.

"If I think about making it move, it doesn't do anything. If I try to force it, nothing happens. Envisioning it is somewhat reliable. But it's only when I'm not thinking about the arm doing something that it actually does what I wanted." She glared at it and reached out to force the two fingers back down into the fist.

"It wants to be part of you," Thumbs said. "The *kijæm* wants you to treat it the same as any other part of your body."

Knots laughed. "You speak madness, man."

"No, he has a point. It actually makes sense," Toothy said.

"How?"

Maps leaned back against the wall and folded his arms. "She's said before, *kijæm* is like a separate entity. Maybe it's tired of being separate."

"Except that Song isn't Touched anymore," Sunshine said.

Everyone stared between the two as she sent her gaze down to the boards between her knees.

"I told it to go away, and it did. I can't even think the words, let alone speak them... And yet somehow..." She stared at the arm on Lyella's lap. "It's still there, I think.

Perhaps it's as much a part of me as the food I eat, even though I can't access it. It's like I locked it inside a chest and tossed the key into the ocean."

"We will help you figure it out," Thumbs said.

"Maybe you can unlock it again," Knots said.

She shook her head. "I don't know that I want to." No one said anything for a long time, and Song took a deep breath. "I have to wonder…if this is what the priestesses meant by 'melding'. It *melds* with the wielders. The more you use, the more it melds, and the less you're just you anymore." She hadn't meant to blurt it all out. But now the fears at the back of her mind, which had only been small whispers she'd thought manifested by drink, were out in the world for all to know. "What happens if you keep going? How much of you is left? How long before I'm nothing but *kijæm*? At what point does Song cease to exist because she's been replaced by some…*thing*? Will I even have my own face anymore?"

Ponce crouched beside her and wrapped his arm over her shoulders. "We'll help you figure that out, too. Without losing you. Keep that *kijæm* locked up forever, if you have to. We can figure it out another way, I'm sure."

She wrapped him in a quick hug behind his back. "Thank you. Now get off me before the others think I've gone soft." Song shoved Ponce over.

The men laughed.

"You?" Hairy said. "Gone soft? Impossible." His arm and leg had healed since the encounter with Captain Darian, but the man still walked with a limp. He would have that limp for the rest of his life, though it didn't seem to bother him.

"You're a right tough bastard," Toothy said.

"Put that arm on and let's get back to work," Ponce said.

After Lyella had helped return the prosthesis to the harness, Song retrieved her sword. "You're all really so insistent?"

"We belong in the sky, Song. Same as you," Maps said.

"We belong in the sky *with* you," Toothy said.

She met his gaze over the distance, and he smiled. She looked at the others, who nodded in agreement.

"How long do you think it'll take me to be ready?" she asked Sunshine.

He thought. "A month. Two at most."

"Most of the crew returned to their homes?"

"Aye. A lot of us have already come back here, though," Hairy said. "Word has been spreading fast. Even I couldn't resist the call to return to the skies with you."

"I haven't even said if I would."

"We returned out of hope," Maps said.

Song had heard here and there about what several crew members had been doing while she drowned herself in drink. A few had found jobs on the docks, unloading and loading cargo for other vessels. Thumbs had been cooking for the inn across the city. Most, of course, had gone home to visit family on something of a much-needed vacation. At least half the remaining crew would need to be replaced, as they'd grown weary of her behavior between losing the Krell men and getting eleven of them killed chasing Darian. On top of that, the Stars' Reprisal was larger than the Stars' Bounty, and so they would need to find more men, regardless.

She gnawed on the side of her tongue. "Maps, Hairy, Knots. Find out where the rest of our men are and bring back whoever wants to come. Toothy, spread the word that Song is looking to fill the crew of a new ship."

"Men who can fight?" he asked.

"Aye…and a cabin boy to help with my arm."

"When do we leave?" Knots asked as he paused in front of the door.

She stared around at their eager faces, then down at her metal hand. She thought about all the training she still had to do to be fit for fighting. Her lips cracked into a smile. "We take flight in one month."

Six

EVERY DAY, SONG TRAINED. EVERY DAY, SHE PRACTICED WRITING and fighting with her left hand. She worked with the metal arm, doing her best to train herself to think of it as her own arm, rather than some device which needed to be told what to do. No longer did Sunshine need to wake her in the mornings with a bucket of water. She didn't drink as much anymore, because she kept herself too busy to relax or escape with alcohol. Those who trained with her had trouble keeping up, but they tried in order to help push her to be ready in a month—going so far as to pit her against teams of two at a time.

Lyella stayed for a week this time. She took over helping Song bathe and dress, smiling the whole time as though she wouldn't want to be anywhere else, even if given the choice. If Song didn't know any better, she'd think that the woman was falling in love with her. Why else would a spoiled sultania who was waited on hand and foot take such care to do servants' work? Of course, there was the bathing custom of their culture. Lyella recognized her and respected her spirit. But dressing her? Doting on her? That wasn't part of it.

If the roles were reversed, Song wasn't so sure she would have done the same. It was something she imagined one would do for someone they loved. She liked her, sure. But love? No. That emotion had not attached itself to her heart in connection to Lyella. Maybe she needed more time with the woman, or maybe she was too damaged to love. She did at least care quite a bit for the sultania—enough to keep her close and spend nights pleasing each other.

At the end of the week, Song and her crew visited a tavern to have a sort of goodbye celebration for Lyella's last day there before she headed back to Pajisr. Song wouldn't get to see her again before they left—which was all right with her, but Lyella seemed sad. She clung to Song's side, as though making the most of the remaining hours.

The sultania sipped her wine through a hollow reed stalk as she hid behind the face covering of the shemagh. She stayed quiet, listening to the others.

"Are you sure you have to leave tomorrow, Bonnie?" Ponce asked.

The men had started calling her Bonnie Eyes, since they couldn't know her name or see her face. She'd accepted the nickname with a smile that crinkled the corner of her eyes.

"Sad, but yes. My baba will worry if not," Lyella said.

Song draped her arm over Lyella's shoulders. "What do you tell him you're doing? Are you honest about being in Srkar, or do you tell him something else?"

She released an embarrassed laugh. "I lie. I say go visit children in *yrshi*. No children, but Song."

She cocked her head. "What is *yrshi*?"

"It is, eh…where sun rise."

"Oh. West."

"W-west," Lyella echoed.

"What was it you said to me last time you were here? I understood everything, except *kharak*. Ryk'r won't tell me what it means. In fact, I'm starting to think he's a mute—not that I'm complaining. One less person to talk back to me."

Lyella giggled. "*Kharak* is, eh…" She pointed upward.

"The sky?"

"I think, yes?"

Song grinned and leaned her elbow on the back of her chair, then rested a cheek on her fist. "You called me king of the sky."

"I mean, you are," Ponce said on the other side of Lyella.

"Do you like that?" Song asked her. "That I'm, well… me. King of the skies. Pirate of pirates. Among many other things, of course."

"I like *you*," the sultania replied.

The way the two looked at each other spoke words which didn't need translation across languages, or even being said aloud. It was an instant understanding and agreement between them.

Song shoved to her feet. "Right, then. Gents, have a good night. *Ghija*, come sit on my face."

She dragged Lyella to her feet as Knots spat his mead back into the mug, then coughed out his laughter. Song didn't have a mind to ensure that she meant what she said. She'd discovered it to be easier than her trying to balance between Lyella's legs on one elbow.

At Song's room, the moment the latch clicked closed, Lyella ripped her shemagh and veil from her face and pounced on Song. She shoved her against the door and kissed her with a desperate fire. Her hands worked to free Song from the confines of her coat, then peel her own desert attire away. The woman was relentless and desperate, tearing at buckles and clothing in her rush. She left the prosthesis on, but detached the rest of the harness—Song worried the strap above her biceps wouldn't hold the weight, but couldn't dwell on it as the sultania dragged her by the untied cord on her trousers.

Lyella yanked Song's britches down, then shoved her onto the bed to finish stripping her, then herself. Their boots flew across the room in careless directions, followed by trousers and knickers. Song couldn't pause to think as Lyella climbed over her and kissed her. The soft skin of her hands searched Song's body, feeling every inch within reach. Song rolled over her, letting Lyella cradle her between her thighs. She set her left hand to the wet warmth between the sultania's legs and teased the spot just at the top with her thumb. She didn't want the woman to climax too fast, though, and so she abandoned it and slid two fingers into the welcoming heat.

When Lyella's moans made it impossible to kiss her, Song leaned up to stare down at the woman. She relished the noises and admired the expressions. Song set her lips to the furrow between the woman's brows. Lyella screamed out, her body twitching and hips rolling with Song's hand. Her fingernails dug into Song's back, scratching into her shoulder blades. Her other hand wrapped around the metal arm propped beside her head. Until that moment, Song hadn't realized the arm had been doing her bidding the whole time without faltering. She didn't dwell on this, though, as Lyella's nails clawed against her skin again.

When the sultania's cries diminished, Song slowed her movements so she could catch her breath. Lyella trailed her hand down until she found the desperate heat she'd ignited in Song, and she reciprocated. Song rocked with the motions. Her skin flushed hot as the woman knew where to press and how. She'd taken care in learning how best to satisfy Song—that much was clear. It didn't take Song as long as it had for Lyella to climax, as the sultania proved her expertise on the subject of Song's pleasure.

When her arms grew too weak to hold her up any longer, Song flopped down beside her to catch her breath. She stared up at the ceiling for a few minutes, listening to the woman breathing beside her.

"Right," Song said, "so how about that thing I told you to do?"

"What?" Lyella asked with a laugh.

"Sit on my face."

The woman didn't move.

"Now. I need one last taste before you go."

After another minute, where Lyella tested her knees weren't wobbling too much to support her, she knelt over Song's face. Song pulled her down by the hip until she could kiss the wet lips. She could go an entire lifetime with only a woman's flavor on her tongue. If she could bottle it, she would. But she couldn't, and so she had her fill of it; then had more, still.

By the time she allowed Lyella to move away, the woman struggled to do so. Her whole body shook as her knees trembled. She dropped sideways, causing the bed to shift. Lyella gasped and panted in the flickering lamplight, her mouth open, eyes closed, and wrist to her forehead. Song offered her a drink from a bottle of rum she'd hidden behind the bedside table, and the woman accepted, cringing down the contents, but grateful all the same.

"Too bad you can't stay," Song said. "Are you sure you can't run away on a skyship with me? I did it, and I wouldn't take it back if I could."

She shook her head. "I am next sultana."

"I know, I know. You have to guide your people, and all that nonsense. The burden of being so important." She gave the woman a devilish smirk. "I can dream, though."

She smiled as Song eased the bottle back to take a sip. "*Ank ly byrrnd,*" Lyella whispered, then captured Song in a kiss.

A gentle laugh escaped her lips as the sultania pulled away. "There you go, again, speaking nonsense that you and I both know you won't tell me the meaning of."

"Not sorry."

"Good. I don't want you to stop."

And so, for the next few minutes, Lyella whispered the phrase over and over as she kissed Song's face, knuckles, shoulder. She said other phrases as well. And Song listened and smiled, loving the way they rolled on the woman's tongue. After a while, as Song's eyelids grew heavy, Lyella's words came out softer, with longer pauses in between. Until finally, together, they drifted to sleep.

In the morning, Song accompanied Lyella and her guard to the skyship waiting at the docks. Lyella clung to Song's coat and cried for a long time before her guard forced her onto the ship. Song waved as they drifted away.

Sunshine shook his head beside her. "If I could get a woman to be that upset by leaving my side, I'd never let her go."

Song chuckled. "She's just sad because she knows that once I leave this time, I really won't come back. Won't let me get away with it twice. She wants her princess."

The skyship turned, arcing around the cove to head inland. Song waved to the figure who waved at her from the skyship. With a sigh, she headed for the first of her exercises for the day.

She, Ponce, and Sunshine arrived at the courtyard. The owner of the shop connected to it was a kind woman, always excited to see them. Song suspected it was their quoine she welcomed with enthusiasm, rather than the patrons themselves.

Crew members trickled in as the hours wore on, and as usual they rotated in to spar with her. She'd settled her prosthesis near the small of her back, fist clenched as it stayed out of her way. The sun was high in the sky, beating down on her bare shoulders. Sweat dripped from Ponce's forehead, but her skin was misty from the desert heat. She half wondered if she would never sweat from exertion again.

"Look out!" Toothy shouted.

She jolted as the metal arm jerked around, dragged her shoulder up, and caught something with a loud *CLANG!* Song stared up at the rock held in the fist right beside her head. She looked past it at the two older teenagers, whose laughter stopped the instant her eyes landed on them. They disappeared behind the wooden fence. Toothy and Ponce used a chair to climb over and give chase.

Song blinked at the hand again, at the rock she hadn't even seen coming. She used her left hand to pry it from the fingers gripping it. Sunshine helped rearrange her arm as she glared at the stone. For a long time, she contemplated using it to hit the boy who'd thrown it. On second thought, he'd just taught her something about her new limb. Then again, if she didn't teach the little scab a lesson, he'd do it to someone else, someone who might kill him for it—though that option was also quite tempting to her.

When Ponce and Toothy returned, they only had one teen gripped in their fists. She scowled and strode forward. As she reached him, her mind not made up on what to do, she dropped the stone and withdrew her revolver to press the mouth of the barrel to his forehead.

"You think it's funny to throw stones at someone?" Song hissed.

"N-no *jrra*. I am sorry, *jrra*," he said.

"What is *jrra*?"

"Ma'am."

Her eyes narrowed. "Makes me sound old." Song pulled back the hammer, and the boy flinched. "What's your name?"

"Madjra."

"Do you have a mother?"

"No."

"Sister?"

He shook his head.

"Father never taught you to respect women?"

"I'm an orphan."

Song took a deep breath and held it. "So you're saying no one would miss you?"

Madjra's eyes widened and crossed to stare at the barrel still pressed to his forehead. "Please don't kill me!"

"I'll make you a deal. Be my cabin boy—a competent one—and I'll let you live."

"Cabin boy? Like on a ship?"

"Yes."

He swallowed, his eyes crossing to look at the revolver again. "A-all right. I'll be your cabin boy."

Song holstered her weapon. "It's about lunchtime. You'll join us."

Sunshine helped her into her coat, his eyes glancing to the teen. Once clasped inside, her hood raised, Madjra's eyes widened.

"You're Captain Song!" he hissed.

"I am. Tell a single soul, and I take your tongue."

At the tavern near her inn, they all sat at neighboring tables. Song forced Madjra into the chair beside her. After they ordered, she sat in silence, studying him, which made him shift in discomfort.

"You've got good aim," she said after a while. "I was a moving target and you would've hit me."

"Got good at hitting lizards from a distance. They move fast," Madjra said.

"Your accent isn't as heavy as most. Lots of time around pirates?"

He nodded. "Grew up here. Lot of orphans in Srkar are half pirate, anyway. Some aren't even orphans, just unwanted."

"Brothel whores?" Song asked.

"Aye."

"That's rather cruel."

Toothy chuckled. "Keep your child or your job. Happens around the world. Mostly in poorer areas where they can't afford to prevent a child, or can't…eliminate it."

"The children have a better chance at surviving in an orphanage," Ponce said. "Rather than with a parent who can't provide for them."

Song pressed her lips into a tight line as she thought. "From what I know of orphanages, it's not much of a better life. A lot of children end up on the streets in Garda."

"Only one country has solved the problem of unwanted children," Sunshine muttered. "Not a single street urchin there. Lots of children's homes run by religious matrons. It's seen as an honor to have them in good workin' order. The children are well taken care of. They never want for anything."

Song furrowed her brow. "You know, aside from your priestesses, Aibhànocht might be the best—"

"I weren't talkin' of Aibhànocht. You'll be shocked to know it's Pishing."

She scowled. "I see. Take good care of their future slaves."

"Pretty much. A starvin' person ain't good for anybody. Someone livin' on the street is a stain—and useless to boot. Voluntary slaves are commonplace, just so they have a place to sleep, and meals to eat."

"Except for the slavery part, that actually sounds like a great system," Song said. "I imagine Dash told you all this."

He nodded and took a drink from the stein the barmaid set before him. "It was the only positive thing he ever said about that damned country."

She clenched her jaw and stared at her drink, then shook her head. "Right, no need to dwell on that." She returned her sights to Madjra. "What about your friend?"

"What about them?"

She stared at him, an eyebrow raised at his use of 'them' for a single individual. She decided it must have been something to do with the culture's spiritual acknowledgement. Perhaps Madjra's friend was something akin to the people with tattoos on their foreheads to denote an opposite gender from the body they possessed.

"Well, I imagine you'd like to stick together, or some nonsense," she said.

"I don't follow," he said, his tone careful.

"I'm currently recruiting a crew. Is your friend a worthless urchin, or would they—it is *they*, right? I don't want to offend the Great Spirit, or…whatever."

"Yes, they."

She nodded, taking it as a confirmation of her theory. "Would they like the chance to see the world, eat actual meals, and make quoine to boot?" She took a long pull from her drink as he contemplated.

"I can ask them."

"How old are you two?" Toothy asked.

"I'm sixteen, they're fifteen," Madjra said. He cringed at the ale after taking a drink; she suspected he lived on water most of the time—which was a risk to one's health in this area, in particular.

"You'll be required to sign a contract."

"I can't write."

"An X works," Sunshine said. "So long as you're the one that does it."

Song let out a long breath. "Right, so…" She scratched her eyebrow with her thumbnail. "Your duties will include doing anything and everything I ask. You will help dress me, help with my arm, and my coat. You'll have to oil it every day. Thoroughly. Can you do that?"

He nodded. "I think so."

She studied him as the barmaid set their plates in front of them. Madjra's widened eyes scanned over the food like he'd never seen so much just for him at once. He didn't touch it, though. He looked at her as though asking permission.

"After you eat, find your friend. If they have a mind to come along, then I expect you both to show up in three week's time. If they don't join, it's no bother. But *you*…if I don't see you on the docks at dawn, I will hunt you down and kill you. Do you understand?" Song met his gaze as his lips pressed into a pale line.

"Aye, Captain. I do."

"You may eat. It's yours."

He dove into the meal, moaning sounds of enjoyment at each bite. He only ate half, though, and pocketed the remainder as the rest of the crew finished. Song dismissed him and pointed across the room to the first face she'd seen after waking up in the Carliolace prison: Jerome — otherwise known as Bootleg J.

The man's skin was tan, making it almost the same color as his hair. She suspected he had some Kerri in him, and perhaps some Jinjur, going by the hint of red that showed up when the light hit his hair just right. He'd let his beard grow out a little, and it, too, was a dark mahogany shade. The man had shown up the day before, after hearing she was building her crew back up. He'd been smuggling in the area, but none of her crew had even seen him, though he'd seen them and had even followed a few. The man was a master at stealth, sleight of hand, and subterfuge. He was also one of Leslie's childhood friends, and as much as she wanted to ask more about Leslie's past, she didn't dare risk falling back into a bottle because of it. So she decided to avoid the subject altogether.

Jerome stood at her side, a wicked, almost knowing gleam in his eye. "Captain?"

"Tail Madjra until we depart. Make sure he doesn't skip town. If he does, bring him and his friend to me," she said, her voice low.

"Aye." Jerome left out the same door the teen had.

"What will you do if they try to leave?" Ponce asked.

"Kill them both, instead of just the one."

"Little unfair," Toothy said.

She pursed her lips at him. "He gave me his word. Anyone who can't keep their promises doesn't deserve a second chance. Besides, they saw me without my coat. Flee with that knowledge, and I can only assume you mean to spread it or sell it. Can't have that, now can I?"

Ponce seemed uncomfortable, but kept his lips tight. Toothy gave an absent nod, as though coming to terms with her reasoning. Sunshine remained impassive, seeming apathetic to it.

In the back of her mind, the little voice belonging to Leslie murmured, 'You're being unreasonable, Song. Mercy is the better option. Trust that some people can keep their promises.'

She clenched her jaw and stood. *Maybe if Leslie were here to say it himself, I would listen. But he's not. So shut up.*

Seven

THE NIGHT BEFORE THEIR DEPARTURE, SONG FOUND HERSELF staring at the chest in the corner. She'd worked hard to mend her body. She could fight well enough left-handed, had a fake arm that had reached the point of working half the time—now that she'd gotten better at treating it as her own limb.

It continued to do strange things, as though it had a mind of its own. They were either useful things—like catching the rock or a sword she'd failed to block with her own blade—or silly little pranks. It had to be the *kijæm* looking out for her, or playing with her, depending on the situation. No way was taking her drink and hiding it in the fist under the table anything but a prank. After the third time, she didn't search for it, but ducked below to chastise the limb.

It also seemed to enjoy making strange gestures at people. It had an odd one it particularly liked, which meant nothing to any of them, so she would ignore it until the middle finger curled back into the fist. Song liked the actions, though. It felt like having a best mate at her side, making sure she remembered to laugh whenever she'd rather cry and get lost in a bottle.

As hard as she'd worked to fix her physical shortcomings, her mind still felt broken. It had taken her so long to be at least a little functional after losing Dashaelan. Now, every time she was alone, her thoughts dwelled on Leslie, and tears forced free from her eyes no matter how hard she fought them. Any moment she had time to relax her body, her sorrow returned to drown her. And now, with Lyella gone, she couldn't even turn to someone else as a distraction.

She slid from the bed and crossed the room in what felt like an eternity crawling on her knees. Tonight was the night. She was going to open the chest and not slam it closed. Song set her palm to the lid, closed her eyes, and held her breath. Tears rolled down her cheeks as she pushed it upward. When she took a breath, she had hoped the scent of him wouldn't still linger in the air, but it did. His belongings had trapped his smell, and the closed lid had preserved it, keeping it so fresh that at any moment she expected him to be right beside her. It wasn't a terrible smell, as this contained the cleaned clothes still folded and waiting for his return. It was, however, a comforting one that squeezed at her heart like a hug and a painful vice all at once.

Song opened her eyes and stared inside. The row of books placed spine up and secured to the corner by a belt might've been strange in another man's trunk, but in this one, nothing could've belonged more than them. His quoine pouch sat tucked to one side. He didn't seem to own many things, she realized. The rest of his clothing would have taken up the empty space within. She reached in to pluck up a little silver box. The delicate lid popped open like a locket. Inside was a small bundle of honey-colored hair braided together and tied with ribbon. She didn't dare touch it, and so she closed the box and returned it to where it had been.

Beside the box with hair was a silver-colored metal cube fastened together at the corners with patterned bronze plates. On one side was a bronze crank. The box sat in her palm for a long time before her right arm crept into view and—so delicately she thought it, too, feared breaking this device— turned the crank until it refused to wind any farther. She set her left index finger to a little button that slid along a track to release the mechanisms inside.

A sweet tune plucked out. She closed her eyes and listened. When it ended, it played again and again as she sobbed. It slowed to a crawl, and the arm wound the crank again. When she could bear it no longer, she pulled the box away from the hand, slid the button to stop the sound, then placed it back into the trunk, and closed the lid. She'd never heard the tune before; it was mournful and yet sweet. The only description she could think of was that it was a farewell lullaby.

She picked herself up off the floor and removed the limb and harness from herself. Still weeping, she oiled the sorrowstone arm. She started with the outside, then popped open the forearm to work the oil in there. She finished by swiping some inside the cuff that cradled her biceps.

By the time she started in on Leslie's sword, her tears had stopped, but her chest still knocked with an occasional hiccup, and her chin wrinkled every so often. Once finished, she sheathed the sword and packed everything away. Song slid into the bed, hoping the excitement fluttering in her belly at the prospect of getting back into the skies wouldn't keep her up. The weariness from crying overpowered the jittery feeling, and she was soon fast asleep.

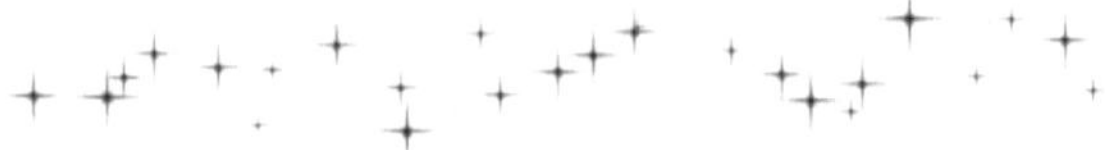

IN THE MORNING, SONG ENJOYED ONE LAST BATH. PONCE ARRIVED once her hair had dried, and he twisted it into a braid. She stared at the sorrowstone blade for a long time. After a while, he left to get Sunshine to help carry her and Leslie's trunks out. Neither noticed her saber wasn't clasped to her belt on the table anymore.

When Song made her way to the docks, people stared at the figure striding through the city, rather than stumbling. Eyes drifted to the red leather scabbard at her hip. She couldn't explain why it had called to her all morning to wield it instead of her usual sword. Perhaps it was the feeling of having Leslie close by, with his sword at her side. It felt right, and she wished she'd done it sooner.

Her crew had gathered on the dock beside the new ship, as though waiting for her to board first. Standing a head above them was Bruce, whom she'd feared wouldn't return to the crew without Leslie. She hadn't seen him once since docking in Srkar, and she was curious to know where he'd been. She also wondered if he blamed her as much as she still blamed herself. The other crew members' eyes flashed to the sword, then to her, and each nodded or smiled in approval.

"He would be honored to know you wield that," Thumbs said.

Toothy stood beside her and turned to the crowd of men. "Returning crew, get your personal items on board, claim your hammock, and start loading supplies. New members will listen to the rules of the ship, and if you agree to them, you'll sign our contract. After that, find a hammock for yourself, then report to Sunshine to help load supplies." He pointed at Sunshine, who moved away from the group so they could see him better.

"Captain Song," Sunshine said, "after you."

She took a deep breath, then crossed the ramp onto the deck. She smiled and spun to face them. "Gentlemen, welcome to the Stars' Reprisal."

They cheered and filed aboard. Song strode to the double doors and unlocked them, then entered. She stopped to stare at the new gleaming black upright piano fixed against an otherwise bare wall.

"Sunshine!" she called.

"It was me," Ponce said at her shoulder, causing her to jolt. "You don't have to play it—"

"As if I could."

"—but I would like to. Every once in a while. Figured safest place was your cabin, and you wouldn't mind."

She raised one corner of her mouth. "I wish you had asked, but I'll allow it. Anyone who harms it will lose a finger."

Toothy cleared his throat, and she spun to see the first of the prospective crew members. Ponce retrieved the signature page as Song searched the writing desk against the wall for where Sunshine had hidden the pens and inkwell in its drawers. Halfway through the line of new crewmen, Jerome entered with two teens—Madjra and his friend.

"Oh good, you made it," she said. "Come and sign before we run out of room."

"This is Yraz," Madjra motioned to his friend.

"Did your friend tell you why you're here?" she asked.

They nodded, but avoided looking at her. They crossed an X beside their name and stepped to the side, gripping the handle of their small, deflated sack of paltry belongings.

Ponce threw his arm over the teen's shoulder. "Come with me, Skittish, we'll get you and the cabin boy set up."

As he steered Skittish out, Song noticed Ryk'r standing in the line, a glare on his face.

She waved him forward. "Didn't realize you had an interest in piracy."

He said nothing and didn't move.

"She ordered you to go with me, didn't she?" After a minute, she stood and entered his personal space. "I'm going to need you to give me some kind of hint that you understand what I'm saying, and that you can and will follow orders."

After another minute staring each other down, he gave a single curt nod, and bent to sign the page in the swirling script of Armalinia. Beside it, he wrote out his name in the Common letters. He straightened, nodded once, then took up a motionless sentry position beside the piano near the door.

When the final space on the page filled, signaling the last spot available on the crew, Song gazed over the long line and the hoard of men still waiting outside.

She leaned to Toothy. "Why are there so many more than I told you to find?"

He shrugged. "Lots of men looking for adventure? Maybe they're eager to fly with *the* Captain Song?"

"Do they know what happened to our last ship?"

He shrugged.

"All right, then. Get the leftovers out of here, and let's prepare to shove off." Song ascended to the helm, where Maps had already set up a world map and made himself comfortable on the stool beside the table.

"Where to?" he asked.

She'd had a month to ponder that question. Try as she may, she couldn't think of anywhere specific. And so now, staring at the map, she let her still-smoldering sorrow and desire for revenge on a man she'd already killed decide. She pulled a pin from the cork on the corner and jammed it into the ocean off the Pishing coast.

"There."

"What're we doing there?" Maps asked.

"We'll circle around the continent, stopping merchant vessels, specifically. We'll make this crew rich off Pishing goods."

He eyed her, a hint of worry in his eyes. "Anywhere else?"

"No. Chart the course to border Pishing. Focus their trade routes with Andalise, Kerriwen, and Telbhaniich-Zardi."

"For how long?" He stared at her with an insistent look on his face.

She thought about this, then gave him a sideways smile. "Until we've refilled our empty coffers, and the Bounty is ready to fly again. Does that satisfy you?"

"So we'll be going back to the Bounty?"

Her smile widened. "No. I think we'll fly both. What would we call that? The Stars' Armada?"

"I don't think two is an armada. Maybe a fleet?"

"Hmm…Stars' Fleet… No, that's terrible. I'll have to work

on it later. Anyway, chart us a course to riches and glory, my good man."

"Aye, Captain."

The men had finished loading the supplies. Dock workers pulled the ramp away from the ship. Toothy swung the railing gate closed, then dropped the balusters into notches in the deck. Aside from the pin hinge at the railing, no one could have guessed that was where the gate opened, it fit together so seamlessly.

There was one last thing to do before they left. Song stood at the bow, ignoring the audience on the deck and docks. Everyone waited, motionless. She wrapped the rope around her right hand, and the fingers clamped around the end. Sunshine held the most expensive bottle of champagne money could buy tied to the other end. He'd told her it could be any old bottle, but she disagreed. An expensive one had to be luckier. An offering to the stars that guided their way. Give them an expensive offering, and they were sure to repay her crew. It was something Dashaelan had written in one of his many journals, and she figured it made as much sense as any superstition, so what was the harm?

"To the maiden voyage of the Stars' Reprisal. May she guide us safely and bring her crew good fortune!" Song tossed the champagne over the railing.

The world around them held its breath, all eyes on the bottle. Song's stomach knotted as, for a split second, she wasn't sure what to do if it didn't break. But glass shattered against the bow and everyone cheered.

She hauled the broken bottle up. "Ponce, hang this in my cabin. Sunshine, take us out."

Ponce took the rope from her and gripped the bottleneck to avoid impaling anyone. Song followed Sunshine to the quarterdeck. He steered them away from the docks as she stood at his side. This new ship didn't creak as the wind pulled at the ropes and chains connected to the zeppelin like the Stars' Bounty had. She missed the creaking, but at the same time, her eyes shone with pride. This was *her* ship. No one had ever captained it before.

Once they'd flown far enough that no other ships shared their airspace, and Srkar was a memory, Song called all the new crewmen onto the main deck. About one-third were Armalinia natives; most of the rest were Andalise, Jashedar, or Pishing natives; two seemed to be from Telbhaniich-Zardi. Her eyes settled on a Kerri, with fierce facial scars and tattoos. The one on his forehead was that of two spears which crossed at the bridge of his nose; above it was a feline skull. His head was shaved on the sides, and his long hair had been rolled into dreadlocks and bundled together with leather cords.

"I don't remember the Kerri from the contract signing," she said to Sunshine.

"Were you paying attention the entire time?"

She pursed her lips. "No. Maps, retrieve Thumbs, please." After the navigator descended, she addressed the waiting men. "We'll start in just a moment."

Thumbs made his way to her. "You needed me?"

"Is that Kerri man's tattoo an enemy of yours, or can you two exist harmoniously on this ship? Where is he from and what do his tattoos mean?"

He stared at the man, then chuckled. "He is from Qet-Qet. It is a city in a small area in the north of the country. They are no one's enemy. It is a place of trade for other countries, and for all tribes. A Qet-Qet man is more likely to travel than someone from the inner land, like me."

She nodded. "Right, well, if anything happens, let me know and I'll get rid of him."

He nodded. "I will be sure to. May I return to galley inventory?"

"You may."

Once he'd gone, Song stood at the midpoint of the right staircase, leaning her left hip against the railing. "All right, gentlemen. I've gathered you here because you're new, and I'd rather get this out of the way once. I want to first remind you that you all signed a contract to keep your crew-mates' secrets, including mine, or you will lose your tongue. One of those secrets is my identity. I have killed men who've seen my face. Consider your tongue a mercy." She lowered her hood and the eyes on her widened. "As you can see, I would rather the world not know who is under this hood. If anyone has a problem flying under the leadership of a woman, speak now. You will be kept in the brig until we make port somewhere—whenever that is."

No one said anything, aside from Skittish whispering to Madjra.

"Perfect. Madjra!"

The boy stumbled forward, eyes wide.

"In my cabin, so we can go over your duties." She stopped on the bottom step as she remembered something. "Oh, and, anyone thinking about making bets or overtures, or passes at me…don't. You can ask my original crew members how well that went over when *they* did it."

A laugh burst forth from the back of the group. A few men moved to the side to give her clear sight to Ponce, arms folded and mischief gleaming in his eye.

She gave him a wry smile. "You, in my cabin as well."

Ponce strode past her, and she followed him inside, closing the doors behind them. She unhooked the binds that kept the grey curtains in an hourglass shape over the windows of the double doors.

"All right, Madjra, one of your primary duties is maintaining my arm. I can take it off on my own, but I can't put it on. It's also a pain in my arse to oil with one hand." As she spoke, she unbuckled her coat and slid it from her shoulders. "Same with my coat."

"Why do you only use one hand to remove your coat when I know your other one works?" Madjra asked.

"Because it didn't work before. And it's still unreliable."

She talked him through the process of oiling the arm, answering all his questions. His eyes darted to her upper arm several times, but she ignored it. She assumed he would get over the initial shock of seeing the amputated limb.

After a while, Madjra admitted, "I thought you just had metal wrapped around your actual arm."

She chuckled. "That would be simpler."

She had Ponce help her back into her harness and coat as a demonstration to the boy, then removed it all again to talk Madjra through it. He didn't tighten it enough, as though afraid to hurt her. Ponce pulled the harness tighter.

"That's all right. You'll figure it out. Preferably by tomorrow, as I'm not a patient person," she said.

He swallowed away a nervous knot and stared at the arm again. "Aye, Captain."

"Now, go find something else to do until I need you."

"Help in the galley," Ponce suggested. "But don't steal any food or Thumbs is sure to cut your hand off."

"He what?" Madjra asked, eyes wide.

"It's true. Kerri warriors are fierce and don't even hesitate to take body parts."

Song caught on to what Ponce was doing and nodded. "Oh, yes. Don't you know about Kerri warriors? Tempers worse than mine. Thumbs was one of the best."

"But he's a cook!" Madjra sputtered.

"Aye," Ponce said. "Because if we let him fight, the bloodlust would take over, and he'll kill us all before we could blink."

"Now, go help in the galley, and don't do anything to make him angry," Song said.

Madjra left, and the two stared at each other, then broke into snorting giggles stifled by their palms.

"How long before Thumbs realizes that kid is terrified of him for no reason?" Ponce asked.

"How long before Madjra realizes Thumbs is harmless?" she replied.

"Ten quoine says within the month."

She smirked. "Ten quoine says within the *week*."

He took her left hand in his, and they shook on it. "Excuse me while I go convince Skittish that Bruce eats children."

A laugh burst from her lips as he let himself out of her cabin.

Eight

THE STARS' REPRISAL ENCOUNTERED ONE VESSEL ON ITS WAY to Pishing—a merchant ship flying a Telbhaniich-Zardi flag as it headed to Armalinia. After a moment of contemplation, Song had given the order to maintain course. She wanted to give the crew more time to learn how to work together, since most of them didn't know one another.

Many of the new recruits knew how to fight with a sword, so Ponce trained the ones who couldn't on the cannons. Though, since Song was continuing her left-handed lessons, others came on deck to learn and practice. Many would stand to watch, forgetting their duties as they stared at this woman with one fake arm as she battled a man who didn't hold back. One wrong move and she could lose her other hand. But she and Sunshine didn't hurt each other. After so long sparring together, they could read each other's movements to avoid landing an actual blow.

One day, she descended into the bowels of the ship. She lifted the trapdoor at the bottom and crouched to look down at Toothy in the crow's nest. "Oi!"

He stared up at her. "What?"

"Come up to the main deck and let me hit you." She closed the trapdoor and walked away to find a man nicknamed

Birdie—after how much he enjoyed sitting in trees and even crow's nests. She sent him below to replace Toothy, then stopped in the kitchen area. "Thumbs, how is everything going with the younger crewmen?"

He gave her a long, even stare. "I know what you did."

"What did I do?"

Thumbs chuckled. "I do not know the specifics, but the kids act as though I will attack them for anything."

Song smirked. "How odd. I can't imagine why."

"They also asked if Bruce eats children."

She held back her laugh. "What strange imaginations they have. What did you tell them?"

"That he considers sixteen to be children, too."

They laughed, and she looked over her shoulder at the huge man minding his own business in the crew's quarters. She excused herself and strode to him. Song crouched in front of Bruce and set her hand on his arm to get his attention.

He smiled. "Hello, Song."

"Hello, Bruce. I missed you these past months."

He frowned. "I was sad."

She nodded. "I'm still sad. But I'm happy to have you here with me."

"Still home. Even without Leslie."

Her chin wrinkled, but she resisted crying. "Different ship, though."

"Still home."

"I agree."

"I thought you were going to hit me," Toothy said from the doorway.

"I am." She stood. "You're good in a tussle. Closest I'll come to…"

"Maybe I don't want you beating me up?"

"Don't be a baby."

"Spar with Thumbs!"

Song released a single *ha!* as Thumb's vicious laughter echoed from the galley. "If I wanted to be knocked out in one hit, I would."

On the main deck, she and Toothy sparred as best they could. He didn't fight the same as Leslie had. In fact, he almost wasn't a challenge. She had half a mind to give up, but didn't. She was rusty, and even this untrained man would help her sharpen the skills she'd worked so hard to build over the years.

The sparring served a second purpose. She had to learn how to make her arm punch when she wanted it to. She had to make sure to pull the punch as well, since the device could hit Toothy hard enough to break whatever bone it struck. After a while, when the man was sweating and she'd become frustrated, the arm hit him hard in the shoulder. Toothy threw his hands in the air and backed away to grip the spot.

"Sorry!" she said.

"I was ignoring you hitting too hard with that bloody hand, but that last one… It'll be purple by dinnertime." He looked into the collar of his shirt as though checking if it had already begun to discolor.

"Why didn't you say I was hitting too hard?" she shouted.

"Because we're sparring!"

"Toothy, I have to learn to hit like a normal person!"

"Congratulations, you're not a normal person, Song! You're a woman with a sledgehammer for a fist."

"I have to learn to fight fair!"

"Why?" he asked. He set his hands on her shoulders and looked into her eyes. "Why should you be the one to fight fair? Darian didn't. Duchamp didn't. Your father, and politicians, and royals everywhere don't fight fair. Now you physically have an advantage over anyone who would use any means to stop you. So I ask again, Song. Why do *you* have to fight fair?"

She toed a plank and shrugged, her chin wrinkling at the mere thought. "Because Les—… He would've wanted me to."

He released a long sigh, his jaw tensing and releasing as he held back what he wanted to say. "Then I guess you should fight fair. But don't allow yourself to *lose* over fairness. That's how we lost…"

"Leslie. Pinch. Bones, Bishop…and all the others."

Toothy nodded once. "Aye. That and the Bounty."

"So…you *do* blame me—"

"No! I blame fairness. I blame Darian for being too much of a coward to fight you like a real man. You are not to blame, Song. Lesser men are."

"Couldn't have said it better myself," Sunshine said behind them, then took a long drink of his tea.

She released a deep breath and nodded. "All right. Toothy, you may go. Same time tomorrow?"

"Abso*lutely* not," he said as he disappeared below deck.

WHEN THE STARS' REPRISAL REACHED THE COAST OF PISHING, they adjusted course to circle like a shark in the water. One day passed before they encountered a passenger skyship. Song shouted the order and they gave chase. She opened the little spout beside the helm, which would relay her voice throughout the ship.

"Hold!" she shouted to the cannoneers.

The passenger vessel had three cannons on one side. If the Stars' Reprisal stayed near the back, they could avoid them altogether. She pointed it out to Sunshine, who adjusted to not run alongside the other skyship. On her order, men shot grappling hooks and spears from the ballistae on the starboard-side bow. They hooked into the port side stern of the other vessel. Men collected at each rope to pull the two ships together, fighting against the other propeller still spinning in mad desperation. Bells shot a spear and managed to plant it into the wood between the blades, bringing it to an abrupt halt.

Her men swung across and made easy work of the few crewmen and guards who fought back. Song stood at the bow. She held out her arm to stop a man.

"What's your name?" she asked.

"That's Toothpick," Knots said when the man hesitated.

Her gaze settled on the toothpick in his teeth. "Apt. Help Knots get this plank across."

They settled the plank from the Stars' Reprisal's railing to the passenger ship's. She stepped up a crate and strode across, a knot in her stomach, which she found to be irritating at best. She'd never been afraid of heights, and it had only gotten more negligible to her when she could save herself.

Now, without access to her *kijæm*, the idea of falling seemed a bit more frightening—but not enough to keep her feet on the ground, or on deck.

Like many passenger vessels, this one was three decks deep. The first would be reserved for the passengers' rooms and a dining area; second for crew, cannons, and the galley; the lowest deck would be for cargo and luggage. The top deck had a few chairs for the passengers to lounge in, but otherwise remained clear for the crew to work uninhibited. She'd been on her family's similar skyship in her youth, but only to go to major cities in other districts. Her family had taken carriages to the house in the country, rather than the skyship.

Song descended to the second deck, where the passengers had gathered against one wall, holding one another—parents shielding children, and men shielding women. She walked down the row, smirking as women flinched and buried their heads, as though not looking would make them invisible to her. She stopped at a beautiful woman in a green dress, her hair a dirty brown with hints of red. The woman jolted in shock and tried to make herself smaller when she realized Song hadn't moved on. The man shielding her straightened as though trying to conceal her from view.

"You in the green dress, step forward," Song said.

"No," the woman squeaked.

The man in front of her didn't move.

"Get out of her way," Song said.

"She's my wife," he growled in the more regal Pishing accent similar to how Leslie's had been when he wasn't forcing the fake Andalisian aristocrat's accent.

"Oh, bravo. Congratulations, truly. She's quite beautiful. Now," she unholstered her sidearm and pointed it between his eyes, "*move.*"

He did so at the woman's begging, but continued to grip her hand.

"Come, come." She beckoned the woman forward with the barrel of the revolver. "What's your name?"

The woman stood before her, tears streaming to her chin, eyes pointed to the floor, an arm reaching back to keep a grip on her husband's hand. "Fiyora."

Song tilted her head. "Interesting. I knew a Fiyora once, when I was little. Is that a common name?"

She nodded, sniffing. "It's a flower. I-it represents love."

Song smiled and slipped her revolver into the holster. "I like that. Well, love, I'm going to ask you to come with me. Do what you're told, and not a single gorgeous red hair will be harmed on your beautiful head. Can you do that?"

She took a few strengthening breaths. "Yes—"

"Fiyora!" her husband hissed.

The woman held out a calming hand. "I can do that, so long as no one else is hurt, either."

"So long as everyone cooperates, no one will be harmed," she assured. "I swear on my honor." Her right arm hooked out for the woman to take, and she did.

Song motioned to her crew, and they came forward to take personal possessions from the people against the wall. She guided the woman to the short hallway with doors on either side—cabins for the wealthy passengers who would never be caught sleeping in something as undignified as a hammock.

At the first door, she opened it and urged Fiyora inside. The woman stood beside the bed, clenching her fists, her head ducked as Song closed the door to prevent her running. Then she circled the woman—who flinched as she passed—and shook the pillow out of its silk case. She shoved the cloth toward the woman, who stared at it, then at Song in confusion.

"You're going to put everything of value in this room into that pillowcase for me," Song said.

"…That's it?"

"For this room, yes. Then we'll do the next, and the next. Why?"

Fiyora opened a drawer on a vanity table, her back to it as she faced Song. "That's all you're going to do to me?"

She chuckled. "Surprising, I know. But I promise I won't touch you. You're just going to accompany me."

The woman paused in uncertainty before turning around and emptying the jewelry from the drawer. Song checked the dresser, but found nothing of interest. They crossed the hall, and Fiyora started emptying that vanity of jewelry.

"Why me?" she asked.

"I like your hair color."

A crease formed between her eyebrows as she looked at Song. "What do you mean?"

Song closed the last drawer of the dresser and dropped the two golden cufflinks she'd found into the pillowcase. "I like the red. Reminds me of some people I knew."

In the next room, Fiyora didn't hesitate as she grew more comfortable around Song. She started emptying drawers, glancing back at the hooded figure every so often.

"The slave?" she asked.

Song froze. "Oh. You've heard the song, then?"

"The song is forbidden in Pishing, but we heard it in Andalise. So…did the slave have red hair?"

"He did." She led her to the next cabin.

"Did Tsingsei really love him?"

"She did."

She hesitated. "And did you?" She squeezed the mouth of the pillowcase as no response came. "Or did you avenge him because you love Tsingsei?"

"Miss Gould is a brat who can't do anything right, so I had to clean up her mess. And by the way, he wasn't a slave. He was a free man, and had been for years before Roman's bloody posters went up."

"So, it *was* him you loved."

Song slammed a drawer closed. "Are you finished interrogating me?"

Fiyora laughed, now seeming at complete ease with Song. "You didn't have to answer the questions."

Song grunted in response. In the next room, she leaned against the wall to watch the woman. "Do other ladies treat you like you don't belong because you're part Jinjur?"

She paused, having touched nothing as she stared over the items on the vanity. "They do."

"What's the story there, if I might ask? How did a Jinjur become a noble?"

"My great-great-grandmother was raped by a slave. At least, that's the public story."

Song released a long, weary breath. "Let me guess, she lied to save herself from a crueler punishment?"

"She didn't love her husband. She also had trouble conceiving by him. One night with a Jinjur, and oops!" She released a little laugh. "She would've been disowned, or at least shamed. Her son would've been sold as a slave if she'd not lied. And I would not exist—at least not as I am and in this life." Her fingers settled on a little jewelry box as a loving smile twitched at the corner of her lips.

"And the slave?"

"Escaped. Supposedly." After a deep breath she lowered the silver box into the pillowcase, rather than throwing it without a care, as she'd done before. "What about you? Do you have any dark family secrets?"

Song smirked. "I am my family's dark secret, and they don't even know it. The benefits of wearing a hood."

"You should consider adding a mask. A lady my height can see a little more of your face up close. You're quite handsome, you know."

"Are you flattering me in the hopes I won't make you shove your belongings into that sack with everything else?"

Fiyora frowned at the broach she'd been fiddling with.

"You were so quick to steal from every other room. Serves those women right for calling you a Jinjur like it's filthy. As though it muddies your blood and lessens your worth." Song set her hand over the one fidgeting with the broach. "You're worth more to me than they are. You have more right to call Pishing home than they do."

She blushed. "Has anyone ever accused you of being charming?"

"A time or twenty." Song stooped and reached into the pillowcase to fish out the jewelry box. She set it on the vanity and held out her elbow to lead Fiyora from the room. "Consider that your reward for being bullied by bratty aristocrats your whole life."

In the last room, she scooped expensive items into the sack without a care or a pause. "You know much about bratty aristocrats?"

Song snorted. "More than you'd ever dare imagine."

"Miss Gould, or others?"

"Her and others, yes."

Once finished, Song extended her elbow for Fiyora to take, and gripped the pillowcase in her other fist. She walked the woman to her husband and bowed, kissing the top of her hand.

"Thank you for accompanying me, m'lady." She set the woman's hand in her husband's. "Take good care of her, sir. She's quite the rare beauty."

"What did you do to her?" he demanded, then enveloped Fiyora in his arms. "Are you all right?"

"I didn't do anything," Song said.

Birdie approached and reached for the woman's necklace as she shrank away from him. Song's right arm clamped onto his shoulder and ripped him backward, sending him to the floor.

"If I wanted her robbed, I would have robbed her," Song hissed.

He blinked up at her, a bit dazed, but nodded in understanding. "Aye, Captain. Sorry."

Song waited until her men had gone above before she joined them on the main deck. As she ascended, she thought over what the woman had said about the mask. It couldn't hurt. She could have benefited from wearing one in the past to avoid being recognized. Perhaps she could fly to Tarn to have Stitch make her some new clothing, including a mask. Besides, she would need dresses and jackets with long sleeves to cover her arm if she ever needed to be a lady again.

She let out a long breath and strode across the plank. The last of her men followed and the Stars' Reprisal disconnected from the craft. They left it there and flew away to continue their patrol around the country.

Song stared at the man doing everything in his power to ignore what loot was still on deck, waiting to be carried below. She made her way over to Ponce and stood beside him. His hands fidgeted with a paper—the manifest for the vessel they'd just pillaged. He stared out at nothing, a furrow on his brow and a frown on his face.

"You don't have to do the manifest," she said.

Ponce sniffed, as though trying to hide how badly he wanted to cry.

"Sparring with Toothy…felt like a betrayal."

They stood in a mournful silence, neither crying, but both wanting to.

"So, I won't make you go down there alone. I'll find someone else. Until then…care for a stiff drink?"

He stared at the paper in his hands, then nodded. "Thought you'd never ask."

Nine

SONG DECIDED TO HEAD FOR TARN SOONER RATHER THAN later. She wasn't on any specific timeline and had nowhere else to be. The world was hers for the taking later, just the same as it was that day. On the way there, they stopped another passenger vessel, and again she took the prettiest woman through the rooms to loot for her. It wasn't entirely that she couldn't do it herself—her arm still liked to act out or act up now and again, just to irritate her—she wanted to stare at a beautiful face for a while. At the end of the encounter, this woman had also been charmed, though still terrified. Not that Song didn't like the fear. On the contrary, she enjoyed watching these people cower and obey without her so much as lifting a finger.

The next day, Toothy called Song out on deck. She followed his voice out of annoyed curiosity. He stood at the bow, holding a spare plank upright in his hands. Other crew members had gathered, clearly in on whatever scheme he'd come up with.

"What are you doing with that?" she asked, her distrustful gaze sweeping around the group.

"You're going to hit it," Toothy said.

"I what?"

"Hear me out. You punch too hard to not injure one of us. So, practice hitting this. Thumbs?"

The man stepped forward, knowing already what was being asked of him. He positioned himself in front of the board and hit it as hard as he could. Toothy's arms jolted and bent at the elbows, but he recovered fast.

"All right, that's how hard you should hit in order to be slightly above normal person standards," Toothy said.

"But how will I know how hard I'm hitting?" she asked.

"You won't. I will. I'll feel it in my arms."

"Why's the cook the one you're basing it off? He doesn't fight," one of the new crew members said.

"You think you can do better?" Ponce asked with a wicked grin. "Go ahead, then."

"I was more meaning Bruce. The man is enormous!"

Bruce glanced up from the sketchbook held up to his face as he sat against the railing. "No."

"Bruce doesn't fight," Song said.

"Why's he on this ship, then?"

Her eyes flashed a warning. "Bruce is family. You, however, are not. Remember that next time you question me."

"I see for Song," Bruce said.

"And what do you see?" the crewman asked.

He settled his eyes on the man, scanning him up and down. His lips twisted into a smile. "A coward."

He sputtered in embarrassment, but failed to come up with a retort.

"Can I try hitting the plank?" the other Kerri man asked behind Song.

She turned. "I haven't managed to catch your name."

He smiled, and while it should have been reassuring, it appeared more sinister, due to the crossed spears at his brow. "An uninspired soul once called me Dread because of my hair. Unfortunately, it stuck."

She snorted. "Truly uninspired. Should we call you something else?"

"I am used to it by now." His accent was thick like Thumbs, though had an odd quality to it that made it a touch more similar to a Pishing accent.

"Well then, let's see how hard Dread can hit," Toothy said.

Over the next several minutes, the crew all tried to hit as hard as Thumbs had. He grinned with pride as none came close enough to call it a draw. Then, the one crew member Song hadn't expected to even move stepped in: Ryk'r. He said nothing, just wound his arm back and hit the board as hard as he could. Toothy clenched his jaw as the shock traveled through his arms.

"I think we have a match!" he said after a minute. "And now I beg that someone else holds this. I can't feel my hands."

Ryk'r took the board and stood where Toothy had. The latter shook out his arms and flexed his fingers. The former pointed at Thumbs and motioned at the board so they could reestablish the baseline. After that, Song worked at hitting, guessing how much power to put into each punch as the man made hand signals. She'd thrown one hundred punches, give or take, but she'd gotten the exact right force to put into it. It felt like she was holding back so much, but she had to trust that people with actual feeling in the area being struck would know better than her.

"One last punch," Knots said. "Hit it as hard as you can!"

"Five quoine says she breaks the board in half," Ponce said. His gaze caught hers and he shrugged. "Sorry, couldn't help it."

Song laughed. "I'll allow it this time."

"I'll take that bet," Bells said. "Splintered, but not broken."

Soon, Ponce was taking bets from each man, writing names on a paper. Song took the time to rotate her right shoulder to recover from the jarring impacts.

"All right," Ponce said, "One hit as hard as you can."

Song took a few steps back and whispered, "As hard as we can."

Her right arm lit up in a blue glow, not only around the joints, but within the silver patterns of the black metal, and along the back. She stepped forward and pulled her arm back. The light brightened as something shoved forward from behind. Her arm streaked through the air, leaving a glowing trail like a shooting star. The fist made contact with the plank and smashed through as though it were paper. The force ripped the two halves of wood from Ryk'r's grasp before it knocked him to his back.

The deck grew quiet as Song gripped her shoulder—the arm was built for the abuse, but she realized her actual joint was not. Ryk'r stared up at the zeppelin overhead. After a long time in which no one was sure how he'd react, he opened his mouth to laugh. He had a deep, smooth voice when she'd expected something like a growl. Others joined in the laughter, and some cheered.

Song helped the man to his feet, grinning at him. "So you *can* smile. Good to know. Who bet knocking Ryk'r on his arse?"

Ponce glanced over his sheet, his brow furrowed. After a minute, his eyebrows rose. "Bruce was the only one!"

The big man laughed and gave Song a knowing smile. She returned it, well aware of how sure he might be of what the arm was capable of. He could very well know more than she did. As the men dispersed, Song approached him.

"Hello, Song."

"Hello, Bruce."

"Need something?"

She chewed on her bottom lip and took a deep breath. "I know there's *kijæm* in my arm, but…do I still glitter?"

Bruce smiled at her and gave a single small nod. "You do. This ship does. It waits."

"For what?"

"For you."

She wanted to ask what he meant, to point out that she was right there, and had been the whole time. But her mind halted her tongue, reminding her she wasn't there, not for that Gift. Part of her wished she could get rid of it. The other part was terrified of being truly alone.

Heavy breathing woke Song in the middle of the night. An occasional slapping sound accompanied it. Having bunked with men in the past, she knew what she was hearing—though in the past she hadn't realized what it was, and had been too innocent to acknowledge it. She used to pretend to still be sleeping. Now, however, she was in her own cabin, in her own hammock, and no one should have been in there at this hour.

She turned her head to spy her cabin boy sat in a chair, sweat on his brow. In his lap, running up and down his exposed length, was her metal arm, fingers shaped to encircle him as he controlled it with a hand around the wrist. Swallowing back bile, she curled the fingers, causing him to jump. But he wasn't fast enough to remove it from his genitals as the palm jerked back and the brightsteel blade shot out, straight into his erection. He screamed, but otherwise didn't move to avoid jostling the blade.

Song kicked her feet up and sideways to roll out of her hammock—a motion she'd discovered to be far easier than trying to be dignified—a sneer on her lips. "You vile little whelp."

She gripped the forearm of the prosthesis, twisted, and ripped it from his grasp. The blade sliced through his organ in a spray of blood, which splattered across her.

"How many times have you done that?" she bellowed.

"J-just twice!" Madjra gasped, grabbing his groin.

"You disgusting pissant!" She dropped the arm to the floor and gripped his collar to drag him upward. "Outside. Now."

He stumbled, hunched over and whimpering. She opened the door and shoved him out onto the deck, where a few of the night crew leaned against a railing. He tripped and fell, still gripping himself, though he dared not move from where he'd fallen.

"Get up!"

Trousers around his ankles, Madjra shoved to his feet, shaking, sobbing, and blubbering apologies she refused to hear. Song put her hand to his throat and guided him to walk backward. His Adam's apple bobbed against her palm as his lips continued to form pleading words. His thighs caught on the railing and his eyes widened.

But Song didn't stop.

She pushed, and he scrambled to grab onto her, hands slicking his blood along her arm and slipping across her skin. She stopped long enough to give him a false sense of security, then shoved him over the railing. He screamed as he fell into the blackness below. The sudden cessation of his voice without a splash told her they were over land.

She turned, a furious fire in her eyes as she gazed around the deck. "You!" she pointed at the man Bruce had called a coward that afternoon. "Coward—"

"My name—"

"*Do I look like I bloody care?* Wake Ponce and Skittish. Jerome, fetch me a bucket of water, soap, and a clean rag."

Neither moved, eyeing her with unmasked fear.

"Now, or you'll join Madjra below!"

As she neared the quarterdeck to return to her room, Sunshine said, "Are you all right, Song?"

She stopped and stared up at him through the wheel spokes. "I am. Thank you."

"What'd he do?"

"Used my prosthesis for his own…amusement."

He sneered. "If you hadn't've tossed him over, I would've."

"I know."

Song lit the lamps around her room, trying not to step in the scarlet pool. By the time Ponce and Skittish arrived, the room had been lit enough for them to see the blood spattered and smeared across her and the cabin.

Ponce raced to her. "Are you all right?"

"It's not my blood."

"What…" He stared down at the metal arm, blade out and lying in the worst of it. "What happened?"

She turned her glare on Skittish. "Madjra was *entertaining* himself with my prosthetic hand while I was sleeping."

The look on their face told her they knew.

"So congratulations, Skittish. You've been promoted to cabin…person."

Their face paled, but they said nothing.

"Your first duty is to scrub every crevice on my sorrow-stone arm. And then you get to scrub it again and again until every last bit of Madjra ceases to exist upon it."

Skittish shook as they looked over the shocking amount of blood, then out on deck where it led. "Wh-where is Madjra?"

"I let him off the ship early."

Tears misted in their eyes. "You didn't even give him a warning?"

Song strode to them, her jaw locked tight and a scowl furrowing her brow. "*This* was my warning to him. Being my cabin boy was the warning he got for throwing a rock at my head. Now, pick up that arm and *get scrubbing!*"

The two crewmen stood in the doorway, Jerome with a bucket and cloth, the other with a bucket and mop.

"Enter. And thank you for grabbing the mop."

"Aye, Captain. Assumed it was a good idea," Coward said.

Ponce dragged a clean chair across the room and set the second bucket beside it. She sat and let him clean off her arm. It angered her that in this moment she couldn't do it herself; she had to rely on someone else. At least it was Ponce, though. Of all the men in her life, he and Sunshine made her the least uneasy when it came to caring for her the way Johanna, her handmaid back in Garda, had done. She frowned at the floor between her bare feet. For some reason, she missed Johanna more now than she had since the first month away from home.

"Are you actually all right, though?" Ponce whispered.

Song clenched her teeth and shook her head. "I know the arm isn't part of me, but it feels like he physically violated me."

"It is part of you, and he did." Ponce held her gaze a moment longer.

She nodded. "Then I'm not all right. But I will be."

"Course you will, you're Captain Song. Toughest bastard I know."

She chuckled, then shook her head. "I liked Madjra. Did I overreact?"

"Could you ever look at him again without wanting to throw him over the railing if you hadn't done it?"

"No."

"Then you didn't overreact. I'd even go so far as to say rule five applies in this situation. He signed the same contract as the rest of us, and chose to rape your prosthetic hand, knowing the cost. Good riddance."

He set up her room divider so she could remove her bloody shirt and knickers. She at least could wash the rest of her body herself. He helped her into new clothing, then joined the others in cleaning up the splatter across every surface. Jerome stood hunched on a chair, cleaning a bit from the beam that ran across the ceiling to provide support for the quarterdeck above. It was low enough to catch some splatter, but too high for the man to reach while standing on the floor. Skittish sat at the table, tears streaming from their eyes as they used a boar bristle toothbrush on the knuckle cogs.

"Get them a clean bucket of water," she said.

Jerome dropped his rag into his bucket and trudged out with it.

Song sat opposite the teen. They did everything in their power to not look up and risk meeting her gaze.

"He was your best friend."

They nodded.

"Why did he throw the rock at me that day?"

Skittish sniffed and sucked on their teeth. "I dared him to."

"Hmm." She leaned back in the chair. "Your guilt right now must be incredible."

"Did…did he suffer?"

"Greatly."

They looked into her eyes as though checking how serious she was.

"My prosthetic's hand was still gripping his *little sailor* when the knife came out. He would've bled to death or had to be completely emasculated because of the damage. That is, if I hadn't been so furious I tossed him overboard."

"Was he still alive when…"

"He screamed all the way down, if that's what you're wondering." She studied their expression as they studied hers.

"Do you even care that you just killed him like he was nothing?" Skittish asked, their voice a near whisper.

Jerome returned with the bucket of water. Song stood and yanked the arm from Skittish's grasp, then swished the hand and forearm through the water to rinse it. Afterward, she slammed it back down in front of them.

"He *was* nothing. And so are you. Remember that if you ever have the same stupid idea to use any part of me for your own pleasure. You want to be something? Be someone? Then be better than Madjra. Be honorable. Do that and you will learn to fight, earn a good wage, and most of all, you'll survive." She sauntered to her hammock and dropped inside, ready to finish her night's rest. "You came from the streets, Skittish. You can go back to starving, or you can make a name for yourself on my crew. The choice is yours."

Song didn't wait to see if they would make a choice right then and there. She made herself comfortable and draped her forearm over her eyes, letting the swaying fabric rock her back to sleep.

Ten

By the time the Stars' Reprisal docked in Tarn, Song had trained her new cabin person in their duties. She wasn't sure they'd stick around once let loose in the city, so as they reached the ramp, she grabbed them by the upper arm.

"Let me know ahead of time if you plan on disappearing, so I can replace you before we leave."

They swallowed. "Aye, Captain."

"Song," Bruce said behind her as she let Skittish go.

She stared up at him and frowned at his demeanor. Tarn had been where Dashaelan had picked up Bruce, Leslie, and William. In the back of her mind, she'd known this, but it hadn't clicked in until she saw Bruce's sorrowful expression.

"You don't have to leave the ship," she said.

"Leslie had keys," he said. "Can I have them?"

She nodded. "Yes. Of course. Let's go find them."

She stood back as Bruce moved Leslie's things around to find a little ring with two keys on it. He pocketed them, set everything back where it had been, and closed the trunk.

"His seedy back room," Song remembered aloud.

"And flat."

"What are you going to do with them?"

He thought, staring at the floor. "Give them to someone good."

She smiled. "Let me know if you need help with any of that, all right?"

Bruce gave her a single nod, then left her cabin. She stared at the trunk in the corner for a minute longer, then strode from the room, locking the doors behind her.

Stitch's shop was still open near the docks. Song entered and stood to the side as the woman finished with another customer. The man jolted when he turned and spotted the hooded figure, minding her own business, feeling fabric samples. On the wall was one of the new wanted posters for her with the enormous reward and paragraph of charges.

"Oh! There you are, darling!" Stitch shouted, causing the man to flinch. "Been so long, I started to think you'd forgotten little old me."

Song hadn't realized she'd missed the way the woman spoke until she heard her again—Stitch's stuttered, skipped t's, and the frantic tone in her voice, as though there weren't enough hours in the day to finish her work.

"No one could ever forget you, Stitch," Song said. "Finest clothes for over-nighters." She hugged Stitch as the woman shuffled past to grab a spool of twine. "Something to remember me by?" She tapped the poster with her fingertips.

Stitch laughed. "Who wouldn't want to boast that they'd made the coat of such a famous figure?"

"Literally anyone who didn't seek to be interrogated, you silly woman."

She tittered and returned to the counter. "What're you here for, love?"

"A few custom items. Finish taking care of this gentleman. I can wait."

The man hadn't moved as his eyes bounced between the two. Stitch rang up his items and wrapped them in a burlap cloth bundle tied with twine. As he passed Song to exit the shop, she gripped his arm.

"If you do anything stupid that would get Stitch's shop closed, I will slaughter everyone you love while you watch. Do we have an understanding?"

He cleared his throat and nodded, then exited the store.

"Are you threatening my other customers?" Stitch huffed.

"Look, I just don't want some snitch running to the police precinct over me again. They could shut you down. And then where would I get my clothes?" Song gave her a charming smile and leaned on the counter.

"Someone's grown confident in the years since I last saw her."

"I've no idea what you're talking about."

She pressed her lips together and lowered her eyelids at Song. "What are you wanting this time, love?"

"Another coat, some special dresses, and shirts. Oh, and a mask to cover the upper half of my face."

"I hope you plan on staying longer than three days for that many items."

"I can. I have some new dresses I haven't even had the chance to wear, which you could make matching jackets for?" She grinned, pleading.

"What's the need for the special items, dear?"

Song ushered her behind the room divider and removed her coat to show the woman her metal arm. "I need to cover this up when I'm playing dress up as a lady. Also, if there's a way you could make gloves that don't come off, that would be lovely. The one I have slips down the fingers all the time and it's a pain."

Stitch measured Song's bust and the length from her neck to just below her sternum. "Half jackets are in fashion right now. They'll take much less time to put together. Just wear this contraption under the dress." She measured from the middle fingertip of the metal arm all the way to her neck. "If we add a button to this shoulder pad, I could make a long glove that fastens to it."

"I would like black leather and some dressy ones. And spares, of course. I'll try not to ruin them, but—" She held the hand away from the woman and made the blade shoot out from the palm. "Accidents might happen."

"Why don't we start with one pair of black leather, one pair of white satin, one dress jacket in cream—it'll match anything—three shirts—"

"Sleeveless, please. It's easier to get on with one arm."

"Three sleeveless shirts, and one more of your signature coat—which I already have on-hand."

Song stared at her in mild shock.

"What? It was a delight to sew. I wanted to make another with more durable stitching. Thought you'd be back much sooner." She worried her fingers over the seams Song had had to re-stitch over the years, and the roughly mended tears in the leather from blades slicing it open.

"All right, how long will all this take?"

Stitch sucked in a breath. "I've got a lot of orders, but

you can pay to expedite. May need you to stick around for a week."

She dragged her coat back over her shoulders. "All right, fair enough. Add items for me to pick up later this year?"

"I can do that, yes."

Song paid the down payment and left to find herself an inn.

Bruce found her during the week. He took her down an alleyway to a small room behind a tavern. He smiled as he looked over the dusty poker table and the chairs housing cobwebs. In the corner was a curtain and a cot.

"I lived here," Bruce said.

"In Leslie's seedy card room?"

"Before I knew him. Yes."

She made a face. "Awful. But who am I to judge?"

Bruce chuckled. They exited to find a man waiting. He stared at Song, then at Bruce.

"This ought to cover it," the man said.

He handed a sack of quoine to Bruce, and the latter set one of the two keys in his palm. They nodded to each other, and the man disappeared inside the little room he now owned.

Bruce led Song through the streets. Four blocks away, he entered a dingy apartment complex. On the second floor, he unlocked a door and led her into a single room, save for the separate washroom. In one corner next to the washroom was a pathetic excuse for a kitchen, and at the other end were two beds separated by a bookshelf filled with books which had collected a layer of dust.

"This is definitely Leslie's flat," she said, her throat threatening to close. "Overly-humble, with lots of books. And, aside from the dust, it's clean and organized. I'm surprised it hasn't been rented out."

"He owned it. Cards are good quoine."

She stared over everything, stopping on her reflection frowning back at her in a mirror. "It always amazed me how vain such an otherwise humble man was. Did you notice?"

Bruce chuckled. "Yes."

"Why did you bring me here?"

"Do you want anything?"

She spun in a slow circle, frowning. "Everything he cared about most in the world, he kept with him. These are just… things. Get rid of them."

Bruce fiddled with the key still on the ring, his gaze trapped on it as he took deep, steady breaths. "I thought…"

"What?"

"I thought he could be here."

"Somehow escaped and hiding in Tarn?"

He nodded.

Song closed the distance between them and wrapped her arms around him in a gentle hug. "For the longest time, I thought I heard his footsteps headed toward me in the darkness. But I was in a bed in Srkar, not my hammock on the Bounty."

After a while, Bruce crossed the room and pulled on what appeared to be four books, but when they remained together, she realized it was a small box. Inside was a huge sack of quoine.

"What's that?"

"He saved."

She frowned. "For what?"

"Peace and quiet." Bruce chuckled. "Away from cities."

"A country house?" Her lips couldn't decide if they wanted to smile or frown. "He would've loved that."

He held out the sack to her, and she stepped back.

"No," Song said, "That's hi—… You can have it. You can have all of it." Her throat ached and threatened to close. "I don't want anything. Just him." She fought back tears burning her eyes. "Excuse me." With that, she left, rushing back through the streets as she fought off sobs, damning herself for still crying at the drop of a hat.

If tears were payment to the Guardian of Souls, I could afford to bring them all back.

Not that she believed in the Jinjur god. But it was handy to have a different god for everything, so she always had someone to be furious at. Song locked herself in her room at the inn and took several deep breaths as she leaned against the door. The tears broke free, but she refused to sob. She picked up her forbidden Jinjran tome and sat cross-legged on the bed. She flipped it open to where she'd left a ribbon in the pages and tried to read. The words blurred behind her tears. She cursed, wiped her eyes, and stared at it again.

She'd found the tome good for keeping her emotions in check and distracting her. It was dull as any educational book, and helped her mind numb over before she dozed off. Today, however, it didn't seem to work. Today, her tears refused to be denied. She slid the ribbon into the pages and closed the book. It must have been inevitable that she could only fight it back so much before it broke through. The worst part of all, though, was that she could never just cry for one man for a minute. Once she started thinking of one, another face would follow. And soon she would be bawling for everyone she'd lost.

That's what happened now, and she resented it, yet mourned them all the same. She cried in the midday sun shining through the window onto the bed. It warmed her, and yet she wanted to be cold. She wanted it to be dark and wanted to freeze her tears from her face. Of course, the world would never bend to her wants. And so she curled up on the lumpy mattress and fell asleep, cheek against the wet spot her tears had left on the pillow.

Their stay in Tarn was, thankfully, uneventful. She sold a few plundered items to a jeweler, and made sure the ship would have supplies for a longer time in the air. To her surprise, Skittish remained. They shared a room with Knots, since they couldn't afford their own, yet. The two stayed at the same inn as Song, and the teen made an effort to be seen by her at the end of every day. Sometimes, though, the look on their face would break her heart. She didn't regret throwing Madjra overboard for what he did, but she did feel a sting over taking a lifelong friend from someone. That kind of pain had to be close to what she felt, she assumed. She'd never had a lifelong friend to lose, but she'd had Dashaelan and Leslie.

Bruce's new fortune could have taken him anywhere. He could have bought a small house in the poorer district of a city. But he stayed by Song, watching her. She could no longer speak to him in the *kijæm* language, but that didn't matter. She could still understand him after a moment to work out his meaning. The day before their scheduled departure, Sunshine found her to report Bruce donating a large fund to the ship's coffers. Song frowned, but couldn't do anything about it. If he wanted to spend Leslie's money on his new home and his crew family, then she had to let him. Her heart couldn't take the look he would give her if she refused. At least it would aid in the eventual restoration of the Stars' Bounty.

After dusk, a messenger arrived to take her back to Stitches. The dress jacket had a high neck and was a dark creamy color with black lace and accents. The coat she'd had much more time to work on was more elaborate than the first, with fancy stitching and detailed linen lining the interior. Stitch borrowed her harness to sew a button on the right shoulder pad. Once clasped back around her, Song pulled the white glove on first. It slid on with ease. Then she pulled on the black leather glove and slipped the button through the slit at the top. She moved her arm around to make sure it didn't impede her range.

"Perfect, as expected. You've earned your reputation," Song said.

Stitch giggled. "As have you, dearie."

She scoffed. "No. Some of those are lies."

"Which ones?"

"I didn't murder a child."

Stitch helped her into the new coat and waited. "And?"

"And his death was an unfortunate accident that might slightly be related to something I did. But I did *not* murder him. On purpose."

The woman lowered her eyelids as she folded the clothing into a neat pile. "That's still only one thing, and manslaughter is just slightly better than murder." She lifted the mask for Song to look at.

"I just don't like being lied about. I'll own up to anything, but don't you dare make false accusations."

The mask was black with a thick, somewhat stiff fabric for the face. Fancy embroidery in black gave it a subtle sort of beauty that was only noticeable up close; a large swath of fabric was attached to it. Stitch set the mask over Song's face. The fabric covered her head and tied at the back. It fit comfortably, the nose slightly larger than needed—which she was thankful for, rather than it being too small. It covered enough of her face that in the mirror she could have thought a man with her eyes stared back at her.

"I was right to come to you."

Stitch carried the stack of clothing to the counter. Song lifted her hood and pulled her left glove on as she followed her out.

"Come back in a few months and I'll have an entire collection for you, right?"

Song smiled. "Perfect. So, should I start behaving myself so you don't feel ashamed of making clothes for me?"

Stitch released a single laugh. "Do what you want, dearie. I'm not your mother, now am I?"

Song chuckled as she paid. She gave the woman a hug, then carried the burlap-wrapped bundle back to her inn room.

Eleven

THE MUSIC BOX SAT ATOP THE PIANO IN SONG'S CABIN. THE notes plucked out at a painful crawl. She sent her tearful gaze to it, then wound it back up and set it down to let it play again. Song could feel the eyes staring in at her from on deck. She hadn't stopped playing the tune for most of the day as they flew back toward Pishing.

After a while studying the wanted posters of Dashaelan, Leslie, and herself nailed to the wall over the instrument, she lifted the piano cover and marveled at the ivory keys which Ponce had yet to play. With her left hand, she tapped away, harmonizing deep notes as an ominous juxtaposition against the sweet plucking of the music box. By that evening, she'd mastered that part, her right hand understanding the task.

She wound the box up again and listened without playing. Ponce sat beside her on the stool. He set his hands on the keys and tried to find the notes she'd been using before. Without a word, she set her hands over his and guided him into playing.

"It's like thunder," he said after a while.

She furrowed her brow. "I suppose it is."

He wound the box up when it slowed. They stared at it in the fading light.

"Where did you get this?" he asked.

She didn't feel like crying, and so instead of saying Leslie's name, she pointed across the room at his trunk.

Ponce frowned. "Oh. He never took it out or played it."

The two grew quiet as the tune started over. When it circled back around, the sweet sound of a violin drifted in from the open doors. Sunshine stood in the doorway, concentrating on his instrument as he dragged out long notes in melody with the music box. Ponce pressed the low notes as he had before, glancing at Sunshine every so often. When they stopped, Sunshine nodded once and Ponce smiled.

"It's like a storm," Toothy said, now standing on the other side of the doorway. "Like Ponce said. There's the wind," he motioned at Sunshine, "the thunder," he motioned at Ponce. "The music box is the rain."

Song shook her head. "It's not fast enough. A storm would have quick, furious raindrops."

"Maybe you can be the rain," Sunshine said.

She stared at the piano and released a long sigh. "Maybe another time. It's getting late, and I could use a bite to eat."

She closed the key cover and stood. They headed below together, letting the music box continue the tune until it slowed to a stop.

IN THE MORNING, SONG COLLECTED SEVERAL CREW MEMBERS TO go over a flight plan. They all agreed it would be better than aimless meandering. Maps had spread out a large parchment with the world drawn across it over her table. Some men in the cabin were new sign-ons that were putting in the work to make a home of the ship. She wanted to include them and show that she valued their presence—even through the threats of throwing them overboard. They crowded into the room, looking over each other's shoulders, but stayed quiet as senior members discussed.

"We should take one or two more ships—depending on their cargo—and then head to Telbhaniich-Zardi to offload," Sunshine said.

"With so many fjords in Pishing, it's hard to guess where most ships would be coming from," Maps said.

Song leaned on the table to get a better view of a wide gouge on the northern side of the continent, just left of a triangular mountain mass. A loud *thump* echoed through the room, manifesting as a physical impact that vibrated through the table, up the metal arm, and into her shoulder. She pressed her lips into a thin line as no one said anything. The others looked around for the source of the noise. Her eyes drifted to her right hand—fingers curled and forearm at a ninety-degree angle from the tabletop. She pulled the slightest bit with her right shoulder, but the arm didn't budge.

"What about there?" she asked, breaking the silence. She pointed at the fjord with her left hand. "Yörmuung Vyaard."

"That could work," Maps said.

Song nodded. "Right. Get back to your posts."

He rolled up the map and shuffled through the gathered men to chart the course. The others took the hint and filed out as well.

"Sunshine, please stay a moment," she said.

He closed the doors when the last man left. "Yes?"

"I need your help."

"With?"

She clenched her jaw, not wanting to admit it. "I'm stuck."

"Stuck?"

She gave him a meaningful look.

"I can't read minds." But there was a playful glint in his eye.

"All right, all right, fine. I nailed myself to the table, and I need you to yank it out."

He stayed back where she wouldn't be able to hit him and chuckled.

"Get over here and help me!"

Sunshine wrapped his hands around the metal one. "Good thing you weren't wearin' one of your fancy new gloves, eh?"

"On the bright side, this has never happened to me before."

"That's what all the men say."

She narrowed her eyes at him. "I don't understand the joke."

He grunted at the arm. "Take it off. I'm afraid I'll hurt you if I pull too hard."

She scoffed and removed her coat to unbuckle the straps holding the arm on.

As she did this, Sunshine explained, "You see, sometimes men have trouble *performin'* intimately."

"Oh!" She pulled her coat off the arm and made a face. "Damn you. I knew that. I just try not to think about it."

Sunshine chuckled as he ripped the arm from the wood of the table and helped her put it back on. She sent the little blade back into the palm, making a mental note to not lean on tables with her fists tight anymore.

As someone called for lunch, they exited together. She listened and learned about each of the men. Even Skittish was warming up to everyone, though their eyes would still settle on her, and a frown would pull at their lips. She met their gaze in a silent, steady challenge. Song didn't know if the teen had sinister plans or innocent ideas swirling through their grieving mind, but she would make sure they never acted on any of those thoughts. Either way, she knew it was only a matter of time before either they left or she would have to get rid of them. Until then, she gave them no more than that warning glance every so often as they both focused on the other crewmen's talk.

THE STARS' REPRISAL ENCOUNTERED A PASSENGER VESSEL FLYING west across Andalise. They adjusted course to intercept. The other skyship practically bowed down to surrender to them—no cannons fired, and no swords drawn.

Knots stopped her as they prepared to board. "Toothpick's been saying some rather questionable things of late." His eyes remained trained on the subject of his words.

"Such as?" she asked, staring at the man in question.

"He complains you break rule five every time we board a passenger ship."

She let out a single humorless *ha!* "I never touch the women."

"We said as much, but he insists we just don't know what goes on behind closed doors."

She intercepted Toothpick, dragging him to the bow by the elbow. "Word is you question if I follow my own rules."

He didn't say anything, but rather responded with a loud gulp.

"I follow them. Same as you. Same as every man aboard my ship. Are we clear?"

He nodded. "Aye, Captain."

"Get back to it, then."

Toothpick rushed away, as though being detained by her would cause his death.

Song released a long, irritated sigh as she returned to Knots. "Keep an eye on him."

"Aye, Captain."

When Song swung over, the other ship's crew was already kneeling, hands on the back of their heads and eyes cast to the deck.

"How did you know you didn't stand a chance?" she asked, grinning.

"The star on your ship," a man said.

"And here I thought changing ships would hinder my reputation." She nodded to her men. "Tie them up. You five, with me." She gestured at a group, and they followed her below.

The first deck was set up for lavish comfort. She smiled as she leaned in the doorway and the aristocratic women shrieked at the sight of her. A man stood, his chest full with a confident breath. She unholstered her firearm and held it up to his forehead.

"Sit down or die."

"Daddy!" one woman screamed.

The man straightened, swallowed, then lowered back into his seat. Her crew entered and tied up the few men in the cabin, searching their pockets as they went. Song sauntered through the women. She stopped to stare at one, a jewel-encrusted necklace cradled between her humble breasts. Song was more interested in the necklace than where it rested — though she appreciated the placement all the same.

"What's your name?" she asked, removing her left glove to feel the woman's golden hair. It was soft in her fingers, and she could almost smell the floral perfume on her.

"Leave her alone!" a woman down the bench from this one shouted as she stood.

Song straightened and looked at this older version of the first. "And who are you, to make such demands of me?"

"Please, it's her birthday," the strangely familiar woman said. "She's only fifteen."

"I didn't ask her age. I asked her name." Song pushed the girl's chin up with a finger. "And I still haven't gotten it."

"Hester," the teen sputtered, trembling so hard the golden chain shimmered like ocean waves dancing in the sunlight.

"See? That wasn't so hard, was it? You are very pretty, Hester."

"Please leave her alone!" the woman shouted, tears rolling down her cheeks as she trembled. "Take me instead."

"Isabelle, no!" a woman who must have been their mother cried out.

A slow grin spread across Song's lips as it hit her. It had been years, and they'd been undoubtedly kind, but now she recognized the first girl she'd ever kissed. A woman, now. And a beautiful one at that. Song took a few slow steps toward her as she dragged her glove back over her hand. Isabelle's confidence wavered as her eyes scanned over the other passengers.

"Not in front of my family," she sputtered, holding back a sob. "Please."

It occurred to Song what she was offering. She didn't even try to hold back the wicked grin her lips twisted into at the irony.

"Lead the way," Song said.

She cast her devilish smirk to her men. Ponce and Toothy paused, then fell into raucous laughter. She signaled for the latter to loot the other passenger quarters; he strode after to head into the first one.

Isabelle led her to one of the cramped bedrooms at the back. Tears slicked her cheeks as she turned to look at the hood.

"Sacrificing your own virtue to save your baby sister? How…noble of you," Song said.

"Just get it over with."

When Song didn't move, Isabelle untied the high collar of her dress and undid the buttons down the bodice. She stripped her top half down to her undergarments, then untied the silk slip beneath her corset and yanked it down to expose her breasts, sobbing the whole time. Song didn't move. Her attention did, however, catch on the necklace which hadn't been visible before—a locket large enough for a picture. Compared to the necklace Hester had been wearing, this was a cheap piece. Perhaps a gift from someone far less wealthy than her family.

Song strode closer until Isabelle boosted herself up to sit on the little vanity, knocking makeup powders to the floor. She spread her legs, squeezed her eyes closed, and turned her head away. Song leaned close, inspecting her face and listening to the trembling breath moving in and out of her nose.

"I once stole a kiss from a girl like you," Song whispered. "First girl I ever kissed."

Isabelle peeked one eye open, then flinched it closed again at Song's proximity. "Did you assault her, too?"

"Too? I haven't even touched you." And she hadn't. Even now, standing between the woman's spread legs, she hadn't so much as felt a hair on her golden head.

Isabelle opened her eyes to study Song's lips as she took deep, calming breaths. "Why haven't you?"

"Is that what you want?"

The woman didn't respond.

"Do you fantasize about a pirate taking you by force? Is that why you jumped up so quickly to defend a girl I wasn't even going to touch?"

"But you—"

"I what? Followed you in here? Let you open your bodice and spread your legs? I didn't ask you to do any of that. No, Isabelle, there is only one thing I want from you." Song leaned closer and reached her hand up to rip the locket from around her neck.

"No! *No! Please!*" Isabelle lurched forward as Song stepped back.

"Oh, putting on a show and everything? Or does this little trinket really mean that much to you?"

"I'll do anything, please. Please." Isabelle sobbed.

Curiosity made Song open the locket. "Clearly."

Someone had fixed a picture of a man inside. Not a painting, but an actual photograph. Those were rare things which Song had never had the patience to sit still for. He was young and not of aristocratic beauty. Song had to wonder if all these years later, this was that poor boy Isabelle had claimed to love, and maybe still did.

"Friend of yours?"

"Please," Isabelle whispered, fresh tears rolling down her cheeks. "I'll do anything. Just don't take that."

"Oh, but now I have to."

"Why?"

"Because you care enough about whoever this is to let a pirate have his way with you. Which, by the way…thanks, but no thanks. No one on this ship is getting raped. No matter how wet your knickers are over the thought."

Isabelle wrapped her arms over her bare chest and gave Song a disgusted look. Satisfied with the woman's horror, she strode from the room. Isabelle raced after, gripping her bodice closed.

"Please give it back!"

Song held the locket up, then dropped it into the pouch at her hip. "No."

Isabelle collapsed to the floor to bawl. "Please…"

Song ignored her and strode to the front. She paused and gazed over the aristocrats cowering around the room. No pendant glittered around Hester's neck any longer.

"Where is her necklace?" she pointed at the teen.

"It's here. Wanted it for yourself?" Knots said as he dug it out of the sack of items.

Song took the necklace. She strode over and secured it back around the girl's neck, pulling her hair from inside it. "Lovely." She pinched the girl's trembling chin in her thumb and forefinger to make her look up at her. "Happy birthday, Hester." She took the girl's hand and kissed the top.

Though she was terrified, a blush graced the teen's cheekbones. "Thank you," she whispered.

"What about me?" Isabelle begged from the floor.

Song released a long breath and reached into her purse. She tossed two quoine to the floor in front of the pleading woman.

"What's this?" Isabelle demanded.

Song grinned. "I always pay whores."

Twelve

AFTER ENCOUNTERING AND PILLAGING A MERCHANT VESSEL, Song decided to head for Telbhaniich-Zardi earlier than planned. The Stars' Reprisal docked at the north-western end of Chavìse-Kàmbhor, opposite from where they'd gone before. They arrived in the morning and had to find a free area on the second level of the docks. They would only stay a few days to sell items, since they'd just resupplied a few short weeks before, and planned to return often with how much she hoped they could get from traders.

Song stared at the lift packed with men. She swallowed, her fists clenched tight. *It's just a lift. Stop being such a coward!* But her feet refused to move. She turned away and started walking, hoping to find a staircase. There had to be one somewhere, she figured. Steam could be finicky or break down. There had to be an alternative to—

Tak-tak-tak-tak—

Footsteps raced toward her. Arms wrapped around Song from behind and dragged her sideways. Her metal arm reached out and tangled the fingers through the grating of the skywalk. It held on tight as they tumbled over the side. Panic jolted through her as her amputated arm shifted, threatening to slide out of the prosthetic limb's cup. The harness had been designed to keep the arm from falling off her biceps, not to keep her from falling out of the prosthesis.

She turned her wide eyes on the person clinging to her. Skittish glared at her, jaw clenched and eyes lit with vengeful fire.

"You're doing this *now?* You've had *weeks* to get your revenge," she said.

"On a ship full of men loyal to you? They would've stopped me before I could do anything."

"If I fall you fall, too."

"You think I don't know that?" they shouted.

The weight of two people proved to be too much for the harness, as it slipped down her biceps.

"Is revenge really worth your life?" she asked.

"Wouldn't you die to avenge the one person who meant the world to you?"

She chuckled. "No. I wouldn't die for anyone. I would make my enemies pay, and I'd stay alive doing it. One of the first lessons Captain Dash ever taught me…was only a fool seeks revenge."

"I'm a hero for removing a cruel captain from the world!"

She laughed outright. "You're not a hero. No one will even remember your name. I've already forgotten it. You're a fool."

"I'm not a fool!"

"You're right. You *were* a fool." Song unsheathed the eilfaas tusk dagger at her waist and stabbed it into their side.

They cried out, but held tight. She stabbed them again and again until their arms lost their strength and they slipped free.

They fell, a hand on their side as their feet spun to point upward. Their head smacked into the skywalk on the next level down, and their body went limp. They tumbled end over end in an uncontrolled free-fall all the way to the cobblestone street below.

She sneered and brought her arm up to deposit the bloody dagger and grab the grating. Ryk'r stood above her, staring over her shoulder. He knelt and took her left hand to drag her back onto the skywalk. She adjusted her right arm in the cuff, then picked up her dagger to wipe the blood away and sheath it. They stared down at the corpse, now surrounded, as bystanders and policemen converged on the scene. Faces turned upward, and some people pointed at the two on the walkway.

"Well, it looks like you and I get to answer some questions."

Ryk'r released a long, weary breath, which she felt on a spiritual level.

"All I wanted to do was sell our spoils and buy a woman's company. But no, now I have to explain why that mess in the street is *not* my fault."

Luck was on their side, however, as they reached the bottom of the stairs. An officer held open the gate and walked with them to the scene. Song stared at the splatter that used to be her second cabin boy. She didn't even recognize them from the impact on the skywalk and the street. Blood surrounded them, streaking out from their body like a grim halo.

"Would you believe me if I told you it was self defense?" she asked.

"Aye," the officer said.

Her gaze snapped to him. "Aye?"

"Two witnesses saw him push you, five more saw him hanging off you."

She released a long, grateful sigh. "Oh, good."

The officer opened a notebook. "Any idea why he pushed you?"

She raised one shoulder and gave him a one-sided smile. "Haven't the foggiest. Maybe they envied me."

"And why would he be envious?"

"I'm Captain Song. Who wouldn't be envious?"

He gave her an unimpressed glance. "Do you know his name, at least?"

She cast her gaze to the corpse. "No. Just some pathetic fool."

SONG MET UP WITH A FEW OF HER MEN, WHO STOOD NEAR THE lift, staring down the street at the gathering.

"What happened over there?" Toothy asked.

"Skittish tried to push me and fell to their death. Has anyone found an inn yet?"

Ponce blinked at her as they all grew silent.

"What?" she said.

"They tried to push you?" Sunshine asked.

"They did. We were dangling right up there. If I didn't have a fake arm with a mind of its own, I would've died, too. It was exciting. Now, an inn?"

"There's one across the street with three rooms," Toothy said.

"One is mine. Bugger off." With that, she crossed the street as fast as she could, ignoring Ryk'r on her heels.

She paid for her room, and one for Ryk'r, obtained the key for hers, and rushed to it. Once on the other side of the door, Song sank down, her knees and hands shaking now that she wasn't holding it back.

She'd never been afraid of heights in her life. As a youngster, she would walk out onto the roof of her family's mansion without a care in the world. When she'd been Touched, she felt invulnerable to the heights. It didn't matter if she fell or jumped, because she could catch herself.

Now, though, she was helpless. The worst part was that she was helpless through her own doing, and would continue to be because of her stubbornness. But was it stubbornness? Or was she more afraid of it killing her than anything else?

Up until that year, she'd had a Krell to look after her and make sure she didn't kill herself—to be there if she used too much and lost consciousness. They were often the first faces she saw, and she hadn't ever questioned if she would never wake up from an incident to any other face. She never wanted to, either. Even surrounded by her crew, it stuck in her mind that none of them were a Krell. And somehow she felt less sure of her own safety using *kijæm* because of it.

When she'd calmed herself down, she realized just how much she wanted someone to hold her to them and comfort her. But she didn't want her men to know how afraid she was—how weak she was without her *kijæm*. So, she left her room, taking her satchel of clean clothes, and set off in search of the bathing room, so she could find herself a brothel after. She wondered if it was normal to pay someone just to cuddle.

"Oh, hello, Captain." Knots stood in the hallway, holding his own knapsack.

"Is there a line for the bathing rooms?" she asked.

He smirked. "I wouldn't know. There are a few places around the city which are better for…lonely travelers."

"Go on?"

"Brothels where you can pay for a naked woman to wash and pleasure you all at the same time."

Song stepped aside for him. "Please, lead the way."

By the time they arrived, Toothy, Bells, Thumbs, and Ponce had joined. The brothel was lavish and gave off a more demure atmosphere than one would expect. Song suspected this was an expensive place where wealthy individuals visited for a good time, rather than a place with more affordable prostitutes. The matron of the establishment approached, unconcerned with a collection of smelly pirates in her foyer.

"Good morning, sors," she said. "All together or separate?"

"Very separate," Song said from behind the others.

She glanced into the parlor at the women, who stared at the group with interest and expressions of invitation. Four men clothed in suits stood in the room. Her gaze lingered for a moment before ignoring them and settling on three women wearing expensive silks and sitting on red velvet couches. One in particular caught her eye. Her skin was rich brown, but her hair was an auburn so deep it rivaled mahogany. She settled her hazel eyes on Song.

"Do you have," Song interrupted what the others had been saying around her, "any women who enjoy…other women?"

"They're whores, dear. They enjoy what you pay them to," the matron said.

Song tore her eyes away from the woman who'd captivated her, so she could purse her lips at the matron. "That is not what I asked. I don't want to pay a woman to enjoy something. I want her to enjoy it."

The woman smiled, even though Song had snapped at her. "Tell me who you'd like, and I'll tell you her personal proclivities."

"The woman in the yellow dress."

"Zeriida-Khiin. Excellent choice. She enjoys women as much as men. Quite expensive, though."

"I can afford her."

"Which other woman did you want?"

Song stared at her. "Other?"

"You wanted one who also likes women, so I assumed you'd be paying for two."

She pressed her lips together. "We'll see how I like Zeriida first."

The others selected women they wanted, and then came Ponce's turn. He stared in at the selection. After a long time in which he seemed to question if he truly wanted to do this, he cleared his throat.

"Him. On the left." Ponce pointed in at a man with yellow-blond hair and green eyes, his skin pale, though not porcelain like those of Aibhànocht. "If he's…of the persuasion."

"He is." She addressed all of them, then. "You'll pay for an hour, minimum. Don't get cocky and pay for more, as there are no refunds or discounts for your own lack of performance. If you spend longer with them, you'll make up the difference afterward. I presume you're all here for the premium treatment, which is an extra twenty quoine applied only to the first hour."

They each handed over their quoine—Song paying the highest. If she hadn't had a glove on, her palm would be slick with nervous sweat.

"One hundred quoine for that woman to give you a bath," Toothy muttered. "Don't go over an hour with that one. Hope she's worth it."

Song didn't care, though. She would pay anything just to lie her head on that woman's bosom and close her eyes. She chose to ignore the fact that the unique features of the woman reminded her of Leslie and Lyella altogether in one gorgeous package. Zeriida-Khiin had a mixed pedigree, like everyone on this island, except her features were more precise, as though she'd been born of a Kerri, an Armalinian, and a Jinjur, and somehow the most recognizable features of those people shone through. When she approached—her eyes scanning over Song, as everyone must have known who she was by now, even if this country wouldn't hold it against her—Song noted a spattering of black freckles across her dark cheeks and nose.

"This way," Zeriida-Khiin said. Her accent was thicker than Knots', but lighter than many merchants had.

Song glanced behind as each of her men met with their chosen entertainment. She followed the woman through the hallway and into a room midway down. In the middle of the room, set into the floor, was a round porcelain tub large enough for three people. Soaps and oils surrounded it. On the other side, away from the door, was a bed, and beside it a table of devices Song couldn't make out from there. Zeriida-Khiin locked the door and stared at Song, as the latter stared back like a clueless git.

"Would you like me to undress you?" she asked.

Song raised her arms to her chest, stopping the woman. "Sorry. I, uh…"

"First time?"

"No! No. First time *paying*, yes." She shifted away from the woman's hands again. "One moment. I, uh… Does your price include secrecy? Nothing goes beyond the two of us?"

Zeriida-Khiin giggled and moved Song's hands away from her torso. "Are you saying you don't want to be the subject of whorehouse gossip?" She pulled Song's satchel from her shoulder and set it on a chaise.

"Preferably."

She released a secretive chuckle. Her smile dropped as Song again curled her arms across her chest to keep her from unbuckling her coat. "Would you like me to talk you through how this works first?"

"Sure."

Zeriida-Khiin took a breath and smiled. "All right. I usually help clients out of their clothes—there's something comforting and even erotic about someone else undressing you, don't you think? After that, I bathe and pamper you. Intercourse can take place before, during, or after the bath. Or all three, if you've the stamina. Or not at all, if that's what you want. All clients who participate in intercourse must wear a prophylactic. We have some on hand. If you're of an unusual size, then you should have your own."

"Sorry, erm… What's a prophylactic?"

Without dropping her smile, she crossed to the table beside the bed and returned with a small bowl, which she pulled a long tube of sheep's gut from. "You can take this with you afterward, as no one will want it once used by another man."

Song backed against the wall, cringing. "And that goes where?"

"Andalisian, what did I expect?" she muttered, more to herself.

"Maybe we put down that…thing, and go back to the part where I pay you extra to ensure you don't tell a single soul what I look like naked, right?"

Her eyes widened a little, then she glanced at the pro-phylactic still dangling in the air. "Oh. Oh, I'm sorry." She put the bowl back where she'd gotten it. "It's nothing to be ashamed of. Men in the past have paid extra for me to keep it a secret. It's more common than you think, really. And it doesn't matter how well you do or do not fill out your trousers, I can work with anything."

Song cringed. "Bloody hell, that's not what I meant."

"Well, maybe stop being so coy and speak frankly!"

Song growled and tossed her hood back. She ripped her mask off and pulled her braid forward. "I'm not a man, and there is nothing in my trousers for you to 'work with'."

Zeriida-Khiin's eyes rounded and she stared at Song in a stunned silence. "And you're the real Caleb Song?"

"It's an alias, but yes."

"My silence is fifty quoine. Not another person will ever know."

"Seems excessive, but if you'll keep it quiet…" Song dug the quoine from her purse and handed it to the woman.

Zeriida-Khiin set the money on the table and returned to undress Song.

"Missing limbs don't bother you, do they?" Song asked.

"I'm paid to enjoy whatever you—"

"That's not what I asked. I don't care what you're paid for."

Zeriida-Khiin smiled and released a breath as she worked Song's coat off. "No. It doesn't bother me. One of our ladies is absolutely terrified of amputations. Ran away screaming when a client…" She stared at the metal arm. "Your entire arm is fake?"

Song lifted it, and the woman jolted in fright. "I can leave it on or take it off. Whichever you're comfortable with."

"Sorry, I just… Oh, that's right, you're Touched, aren't you? Is that how it moves?" The woman took the metal hand and began investigating it. She bent close to examine the hinges on the fingertips and the slit in the palm, then flipped open the latch that held the forearm closed to hide the gears and rods.

Song couldn't help but smile. "Is all this included in my hour, or does my time start after you're through examining my arm?"

"My apologies. How unprofessional of me." She snapped the forearm closed and started unbuckling the harness.

"Can I be honest?"

Zeriida-Khiin nodded.

"I think I like unprofessional. Feels less suffocating. Would you mind if we pretend we're strangers and no one is getting paid for it?"

"I can do that."

"Just one more question," Song whispered as she reached for the strings holding the woman's bodice closed.

"Yes?"

"Am I allowed to kiss you?"

"You're allowed to do whatever you want, except hurt me. Since you're adamant I enjoy it, I'll let you know if there is anything I am uncomfortable with if it comes up. Take anything too far and I have an alarm, which will call the guards into this room."

Song nodded. "Understood." She jerked on the string and locked her lips with Zeriida-Khiin's, sliding her tongue into the woman's mouth.

Her lips were soft, and she tasted of strawberries and chocolate. Her bodice opened and Song slid her palm over one of the soft breasts, cradling it. They stripped each other bare, save the arm and straps to keep it on. Before Zeriida-Khiin could get her to the tub, she pushed the woman to the chaise and knelt in front of her. She kissed the lips between her legs.

"I thought I was the one that's supposed to pleasure you," Zeriida-Khiin said.

"Tasting a woman brings me pleasure. And making a woman scream brings me pleasure." She ran her tongue along the sensitive area. "Don't you dare fake it."

"I'll try not to."

Song draped the woman's legs over her shoulders. She took her time, savoring her. She tasted different from Lyella, and yet she still enjoyed the flavor. Zeriida-Khiin also didn't have the same pleasure spots and thresholds as the Armalinian woman. Song had to work to find the right places to touch and how much attention to give them. When Zeriida-Khiin finally climaxed, it was with a loud scream and a wet release as her fingers tangled in Song's hair.

"So," Song said, a self-satisfied smirk on her lips, "about that bath."

Thirteen

BY THE TIME THE STARS' REPRISAL RETURNED TO THE SKIES, Song had acquired a new cabin boy. The young lad was all of thirteen, and eager for the adventure. His shortname was Qiicho, but the men called him Keyhole after a misunderstanding on the pronunciation. The boy loved it, though, and quickly worked his way into the hearts of the crew. While his duties were to Song, he helped wherever he could. He learned fast and wanted to know everything he could in order to be a better pirate.

Song sat on the steps with him after a sword lesson. She looked over his black hair, dark skin, and vibrant blue eyes. "Does your mother know you're on a pirate ship?"

He laughed. "No, sor. She thinks I'm working for a merchant."

"A good lie to tell a mother," she said.

"I love my mum. I just don't want her worrying about me."

"We'll take good care of you so you can return to her and lie about your exploits. Don't worry, she'll see how much quoine you've made and won't care how you got it."

"I sure hope so." He speared a chunk of meat onto his fork.

Song made a face at the jar in his hands. "How can you eat that?"

"What? Eel?"

"Yes. And pickled."

He laughed and held up a fresh piece.

Song leaned away. "No, thank you."

"I grew up on the stuff. Mum sent some with me so I'd feel more at home."

She smiled and leaned back on the railing. "I'm positively jealous of the mother you have. Honestly, mine is…a nosy, bossy terror."

"You don't miss her at all?" Qiicho asked.

"Not anymore."

"Your papa?"

"I was daddy's little girl once. And then everything else became more important than me. Suddenly it was this new law, or that proposed bill, or some government or pirate-hunting thing I never cared to learn about. I'm sure after the shock of me running away wore off, they stopped missing me. I like it better out here, anyway. No one can tell me what to do."

"And if they try, you'll knock their head off with a wicked right hook."

She laughed and patted his shoulder. "All right, Keyhole, I believe Maps wanted you next. You know, he hasn't even taught me how to navigate?"

"Because then I'll be out of a job!" Maps shouted from the helm.

"I would never!" she said with a scoff. "Besides, I'd have to work at it for years to get even half as good as you."

"I know you're just trying to assure me, but I'm fairly certain you're right."

Qiicho closed his jar and trotted up the steps for his lesson. Song met Ryk'r's eye as he leaned against the mainmast. She stood and approached him.

"Are you any good in hand to hand combat? No weapons?"

He gave her a single nod.

"Spar with me. And yes, it's an order."

Ryk'r turned out to be a suitable sparring partner. She pushed past the tightness in her chest, reminding herself that she needed to stay on top of her practice. It had been months since everything happened, and she'd remained drunk and sedentary for too long.

Sparring with the man became a daily habit. He said nothing through the whole thing. Rather than a man of few words, he was a man of none, and Song couldn't decide if that bothered her or if it made her more comfortable. She had to wonder if he chose not to speak, or if he was incapable of it. Her cabin boy joined some of the sparring sessions. Ryk'r treated him kindly and would teach him positioning, stance, and maneuvers. The man said more with his actions than anyone could with words.

When they encountered merchant or passenger ships, he stayed below, watching over Qiicho at his cannon. The boy had suggested hiding in the cargo hold, but the splatter on the wall which had been Doctor flashed through her mind.

Qiicho reminded her of herself. Though, he had a great deal more world experience at four years younger than she was when Dashaelan had taken her under his wing. He was intelligent and learned so fast that she could see him being a captain of his own ship one day.

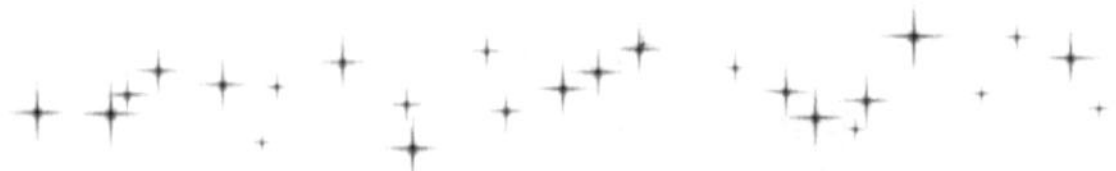

Song's nightmares were getting worse. The first ones had been Dashaelan. After the Harpy's Claw, her nightmares grew to include the broken bodies of her crew. Then Leslie joined them.

Hands shook her and Song snapped awake. She unsheathed the kris hiding beneath her pillow. Sunshine caught her wrist before the dagger could pierce his neck. He pursed his lips down at her.

"You were screamin'," he said.

"Oh, good, because in my nightmare no sound came."

"Well, it was terrifyin'. Thought somethin' happened."

Song sat up and rubbed her sweat-slicked face. "Is it always like that?"

"No. Usually just moans, which I ignore. I'd hate for them to be the good kind one day, and catch you in some indecency."

She made a face at him, and he chuckled.

"What's different tonight?"

"I didn't have any liquor before bed. Usually I have a glass. Thought I'd try something new by not being a drunkard."

He released a long breath. "One glass don't make you a drunkard, Song. Gettin' so sloppy drunk you can't stand on your own does. If the drink helps, may as well keep doin' it."

"All right. I'll try not to let it escalate to sloppy." She lay back and breathed out at the ceiling. "You may go. Oh, and don't wake me like that again. Let me scream all night, if you have to. I'd hate for you to fail at catching my blade. Nice reflexes for an old man, though." She giggled as he gave her an unimpressed look.

Sunshine poured two fingers of whiskey into a glass and waited as she swallowed it down like medicine. He set the glass back inside the cabinet where it wouldn't fall.

"Go back to sleep, Song." He patted her head and left.

She closed her eyes and let the hammock rock her back to sleep.

As time wore on, they continued to harass Pishing vessels. When their cargo holds filled, they returned to Telbhaniich-Zardi to sell everything. Song stopped in every time to visit Zeriida-Khiin, having grown a strange fondness for the woman. Besides, it was easier to stick to the one woman who already knew her secret.

To get back in the air sooner, Song rented a large flat from a landlord who didn't ask questions. They used it to store cargo, and hired a man to fence a little. She would return later to see how he'd done and if she could trust him. If he made off with her quoine or loot, she vowed to track him down and kill his family. He found it excessive, since trade was something honored to the country's people. Nothing was more despicable to them than a thief, and so he gave his word. All the same, she wanted proof that she could trust him.

They returned to the skies and waited, vessels seeming sparse that week. Perhaps they were catching on, or perhaps it was a bad time for trade. Either way, she grew bored after two weeks of inaction. Then the whistle came from below—

two pips for a pirate ship. Several spyglasses set to eyes to scan over the horizon.

She found the vessel, and her breath caught in her throat. She recognized that ship—the deep belly with a massive four-pronged grappling hook settled at the keel. Her skin grew cold and clammy as her neck flashed hot and palm sweat. Her gaze flicked across the deck, where her men stood, awaiting her order.

Qiicho lowered the spyglass. "Captain?"

Song cleared her throat. "Get to the cannons! Prepare for evasive actions! Everyone get below deck, *now!*"

Maps stood at her shoulder. "Song—"

"You, too, Maps."

"What are you thinking?"

"I'm thinking I refuse to lose another man to that damned ship. Now get below and brace yourself."

He nodded once, an eyebrow raised. "Aye, Captain." He took Qiicho by the elbow and led him below.

The Harpy's Claw turned to intercept. Song steered off course to run alongside the other ship at a distance which the claw and ballistae couldn't reach. As they neared, the *thu-thunk, thu-thunk* of gears boomed through the sky between them.

Song's breath hitched, and she struggled to take in little gasps of air at a time. Tears burned at her eyes and her throat ached with fire. She became dizzy, but forced herself to stay at the helm. Song resisted, with every ounce of her being, the urge to turn the wheel and flee.

She opened the spout beside her and shouted, "Portside cannons at the ready! Aim for the wheel at her belly!"

The other crew stared in puzzlement at the empty deck of the ship skirting their reach.

"Down the line as you get in range," she ordered. When the first of her cannons lined up with the belly, she shouted, "Fire at will!"

A cannonball exploded from the ship beneath her with a thunderous *boom*. It slammed into the wood beside the claw wheel as the next cannon fired. They continued down the line, most of their aims true.

"Bells, on deck!"

The man appeared moments later and made his way to her as she turned the wheel to spin the ship around.

"Get to a ballista. Sever the rope from a harpoon and stop their propeller. Then get back below."

"Aye, Captain." He rushed to the prow to carry out her order.

"Cannons, reload and stand ready," she shouted into the spout.

Bells fired his ballista as they neared the Harpy's Claw. The harpoon soared through the air and embedded in the stern between the propeller blades. He gave a triumphant laugh, then scurried below.

"Fire at will!" she shouted.

The first of the cannons exploded forth against the Harpy's Claw's starboard side. They continued down the line. Darian stood on deck, bracing against the mainmast of his ship. Their eyes met across the distance, and she sneered, heart thundering in her chest as a violent rage caused her hand to tremble and her phantom arm to ache.

As she turned the ship around for another attack against the other skyship's port side, a man leaned over the railing of the Harpy's Claw, waving a white cloth. Darian strode across and punched him, then stole the cloth. The two braced themselves as the cannons tore into the hull again. When the Stars' Reprisal passed for the cannons to fire on the other ship's starboard side, she gave the gaping hole in the hull a satisfied sneer.

Song came about again, circling the other craft like a shark in the water. She repeated the order to fire at will, ignoring the men shouting from the other ship for her to stop. Many tried to surrender, but Darian refused, dragging each to the deck, even shooting one in the leg to make an example of him.

You rely too much on your hook, she thought, staring at the man in the green coat. *Too heavy for you to have cannons of your own.*

A moan grumbled from the other ship. The cog tilted sideways as the supports on one side failed; it creaked, caught against the keel. A cannonball shot from below her and landed with shocking accuracy against the final piece holding the whole thing up.

Wood creaked. Metal screamed. With one last crack, the cog wheel fell away from the hull of the ship and crashed into the ocean below. Bodies followed—some flailing, and some already mangled by cannon fire. Men scrambled about, as the sudden loss of weight caused them to rise higher into the air. She watched for another minute before turning her back on the scene and setting her sights on the horizon.

Maybe they'll float all the way to the stars.

Her men trickled onto the main deck, looking behind with spyglasses to witness the skyship's ascent. Maps dropped onto his stool and sighed down at the table, but said nothing. Toothy and Ponce strode to her, Sunshine arriving a moment later with Qiicho on his heels.

"What was all that about?" Toothy asked.

"That was me not fighting fair."

Sunshine stared at her in thought. "And what about your friend?"

A humorless laugh burst from her lips. "He's already dead. I've been chasing a ghost this whole time."

"How do you know?"

"Because if he was alive, and if he was truly my friend, I wouldn't have to chase him around the world, would I?" she shouted. "We were in Srkar for *six months* and he didn't come to find me. So either he's dead, or he is not my friend."

"And Hardtack?" Ponce asked.

"He probably died along with all the other men Darian killed that day."

"Song—"

"*I will not sacrifice more of my crew for ghosts!*" she bellowed. "Not one more man dies for Altain or Hardtack. Do you hear me? I'm done chasing a corpse. And now that the Harpy's Claw is out of the equation, next time we encounter Darian, we board, and we kill all of them."

"What if they surrender?" Sunshine asked.

"We…*kill* them." She settled her glare on him. "No quarter for a single man who flies with Darian. And then we blow whatever ship he's flying out of the sky and watch it burn until it sinks to the bottom of the ocean."

They stared at her in uncertain silence.

"Aye, Captain," Sunshine muttered, then turned away to go below deck.

Qiicho fidgeted as the others left. He stayed beside her for five minutes in excruciating silence. "What if your friend was still on that ship, sor?"

"He wasn't," she said through gritted teeth.

"But…you don't—"

"You're right, I don't know. But the last time I engaged with the Harpy's Claw, I lost eleven men and one more after. Are the lives of this crew worth one boy I knew, what, three? Four years ago? For a month at most? I've known you longer, now. I would never sacrifice you for him."

He shrugged up one shoulder. "To be fair, I wouldn't leave you hanging for that long, either. I'd have found a way back, or gone home."

They stayed in silence for a minute.

"Maybe he's gone home."

Song released a long sigh. "Maybe. Either way, it's time I stop chasing him. Darian is nothing to me now. The feud is over."

"Feels like a celebration is in order."

She laughed. "No, one is definitely not."

"But a celebration would give me a reason to eat my last jar of eels."

She glanced sideways at him. "You were saving it for a special occasion, like a fine wine?"

"Aye. And I was hoping you'd finally try some."

She made a face.

"Last jar for a long time, Song. You won't get another chance."

"I don't even want *this* chance!"

He tugged on her metal arm. "Come on, sor. I thought Captain Song wasn't afraid of anything."

She sucked in a deep breath, then let it out. "Fine. One bite. Maps, take over."

Qiicho rushed below and returned with the promised jar. He sat on the step beside her and opened the lid. The acidic stench of fish and spiced wine hit her. She didn't hate it, since she loved fish, but she wasn't sure what to think of fish being pickled. He speared one of the bite-sized chunks onto a fork and handed the utensil to her, then used a second fork to get his own piece.

"Cheers!" Qiicho clicked his fork against hers and popped his eel into his mouth.

Song stared at him, then giggled. "Cheers." She shoved it into her mouth and paused, taking small, almost tentative nibbles.

The texture was more soft than regular fish, but it wasn't terrible. It had a mild taste—she'd certainly had fish that were more fishy-flavored. The pickling liquid was a salty red wine with shallots, carrots, and a bit of spice she didn't know the name of. All in all, it wasn't half bad. She jammed her fork into another chunk of eel and stuck it in her mouth.

"Well?" he asked.

"It's not terrible, actually."

"You like it," he said, his voice a low growl as he chuckled.

Song quirked the corner of her lips up on one side. "Yeah, I think I like it."

"It's my mum's recipe. Best I've ever had."

She stole another piece of eel. "Might need you to get me a jar next time we dock in Chavìse-Kàmbhor."

"Aye, Captain."

They continued to talk as they shared the jar of pickled eel. Song's tight stomach unwound itself and ease rested on her shoulders over the encounter with the Harpy's Claw. The longer she sat with this boy, the better she felt about choosing the crew she had now over the ghost she'd once known.

Goodbye, Altain. Sorry I couldn't save you.

Fourteen

SONG HAD BEEN EXPERIMENTING WITH THE PIANO SINCE PLAYING alongside the music box. She'd trained her right hand to hit the correct notes without her being able to feel the keys under the fingertips. It was a painstaking practice in dexterity and patience. More than once she'd stomped away, furious as the hand continued to hit two notes at once or not know which key to press. It was the first real communication failure between herself and the arm since Srkar, and it left her feeling helpless all over again. Over time, though, it got easier, and she missed less and less.

Qiicho loved the music box tune and would wind it up for her as she tapped away. Often as he sat beside her on the bench, she would catch him pressing invisible keys in as close to synchronization with her as he could. The day after she'd broken the Harpy's Claw, he sat with her, practicing on his invisible piano. He couldn't move his fingers as fast as she could. She assured him that over time, with lots of practice, he'd one day be able to play like her. She wasn't a concert pianist by a long shot, but she'd been playing from a young age.

Ponce shooed Qiicho out of the seat as Sunshine's tuning plucks drifted in from the doorway.

"Let's give what you just did a shot," Ponce said, cracking his knuckles.

Qiicho wound up the music box and held it behind them. It played through the tune once, then Sunshine joined with long, sweet notes in melody with the music box, like winds tugging a sail. Ponce joined in at the low end of the piano, pressing the notes hard so they crashed like booms of thunder.

After a while, Song joined. She played at the right side of the piano, one hand striking chords and the right picking out quick notes one after the other in a cascade like a downpour. Once finished, they sat in the atmosphere afterward, the music box plucking away as they gathered their thoughts.

"It's like the storm I feel in my heart has come to life," she said after a while.

"I feel the same way," Ponce said.

"It is a beautiful sort of pain," Thumbs said at the doorway.

"You can feel the love and the sorrow in it," Knots said.

Song frowned at the crew gathered around the doors, staring in at them.

"Play it again?" Jerome asked.

She took in a deep breath. "All right. One more time. Then it's to the deck with you for sword lessons, Keyhole."

"Aye," the boy said, as he wound the music box again.

When they finished performing the song, the audience outside the cabin door clapped, then dispersed to return to their duties. Ponce obtained paper, pen and ink, and a flat edge. He sat at the table to draw lines across pages in the unmistakable design for sheet music.

Song joined Qiicho on deck. He unsheathed the little rapier he'd had since joining them. She had to go easy on the weapon, unsure if it could hold up against sorrowstone. Typically, the boy would work with her for an hour, pushing himself further if he grew tired. Today, however, his limbs seemed sluggish. After a while, he sheathed his sword and sat on the steps, his eyelids drooping as he leaned his head on a baluster.

"Come on, we're not finished," she said.

"I don't feel good, sor," he said.

"What's wrong?"

"A bit dizzy. Tired." His words slurred out of his mouth. "Stomach hurts."

Song let out a long breath and sheathed her sword. "All right, we can rest. I'll get you some water."

She turned for the stairs, but stopped as he coughed and gagged, followed by a wet splash. She gritted her teeth at the mess of vomit across the deck. Down the stairs, she shouted for a swabby and the new doctor—the man formerly from the western coast of Pishing, where they called them medics. Some had called him Medic until they learned why he'd been in the Carliolace prison. He'd been charged with murdering his elderly and terminal patients, but he insisted it was out of mercy for their suffering, which they'd begged him to end. Now his nickname was Mercy.

Song grabbed an empty bucket from the crew's quarters and rushed up on deck—others followed close behind her. Qiicho threw up again right as she shoved the bucket under his chin.

"Let's get you into my cabin," she said. Song held the bucket with one hand and wrapped her other arm around him to help him walk. "Ponce, clear out."

Ponce collected his work, eyes wide with concern on Qiicho, and left the room. Qiicho stretched out on the cushioned bay bench, his head on several pillows she piled up for him. Mercy came in to check his temperature and look him over. He ran his fingers through his dark hair as he examined the boy. He made a thoughtful noise, and stood to urge Song out of the room.

"Seems to be a stomach bug. We should keep him hydrated and quarantined," Mercy said.

She was getting used to his accent by now, which was thicker than Leslie's and Dashaelan's, and replaced all the f's he said with v sounds.

"If he's quarantined, how do we keep him hydrated?"

"Wear a cloth over your mouth and nose when you enter the room."

She pressed her lips tight, shifting out of Jerome's way as he and Toothpick mopped the deck. "I should stay in there with him. He's stuck to my side all the time. There's no way I wasn't already exposed."

He nodded in agreement.

When Song entered the cabin again, she had water for him. Qiicho took little sips. He didn't lift his head or open his eyes wider. She cared for him as best she could as he lost his ability to speak. Helplessness weighed on her shoulders, but she resisted crying. She had to be strong, no matter how scared she was. Hope churned within her that this was, indeed, just a stomach bug, albeit a severe one she'd never heard of.

As the day wore on, Song felt weaker. She couldn't place the feeling, but it was unlike anything she'd ever experienced. Her stomach hurt and vertigo caused nausea to bubble inside her. After a while, her vision blurred. Her eyelids drooped, eyes refusing to focus or move to look anywhere but at her feet in front of her. Minutes passed. Her mouth sagged open, and there was nothing she could do about it. At least she had some control of her body still, as she lurched sideways to vomit into the bucket Qiicho had used. She couldn't rinse her mouth, though, and so suffered with the smell and taste of acid tainted porridge.

She sagged against the bench. As time progressed, her shoulders weakened, and it became a struggle to hold up the weight of her real arm, let alone the metal one at her side. By the time someone came to check on them hours later, Sunshine entered to find her on her side, weak and expressionless—alive and aware, but unable to move or respond. Alarm rose on the ship. Mercy banned all but himself and Sunshine from entering her cabin. They set her up on a stack of pillows at enough of an angle to keep her mouth from falling open. With the sudden trouble she had swallowing, she was somewhat glad for the strange dryness of her mouth.

"Follow my finger," Mercy said.

He moved it from her right to left, up and down, but she couldn't follow it. Her eyes refused to move or focus, remaining locked in place, staring straight ahead. He and Sunshine left to speak in private. Not long after, her body started to tingle and ache like a sleeping limb—only it was under the skin, in her muscles, and across her bones. Her entire body buzzed like the sandstorm arm she envisioned whenever the missing limb acted up.

Mercy and Sunshine returned and stopped in their tracks. They strode forward as one and dropped beside her to look at her glowing red eyes, their skin tinted by the dim light.

"Bugger me," Sunshine said, "she still has *kijæm* after all."

"But what is it doing?"

They watched her with interest as nothing seemed to happen—at least that they could see.

A sensation like warm fluid filled her mouth. It felt alive, squirming across her tongue, weaving between her teeth, and sliding across the roof of her mouth. It filled and filled, until a pressure built on her tongue, forcing her lower jaw down. Her lips parted, and a slithering red mist spilled out to illuminate the room around them. It continued for meters upon meters, emptying from inside her. It collected into a ball that hovered in the corner near the ceiling, away from everyone. The last of it joined the sphere, and the light shifted to a shade of orange like steel in a forge. Heat caressed Song's face even at that distance as the light brightened to yellow, then white. A sizzle accompanied a puff of smoke, and the light dimmed once more, then faded to blue. The ball dispersed, and the light faded out of existence.

She couldn't put descriptive words to it in her mind, but somehow she felt better. Her condition hadn't changed, and she still lay helpless on the floor, but she didn't feel quite as awful as she had.

"Song? Are you all right?" Sunshine asked.

In response, she managed to at least lift one finger of the metal arm.

"We're heading to Telbhaniich-Zardi," Mercy said. "Hopefully Keyhole can hold on that long."

"Don't worry, everything else is under control," Sunshine said. He pet her head and left the room.

Night fell. Mercy had been flipping through a book for some time, scanning the pages. Qiicho's breathing had been growing weaker as the day dragged on. It reached the point where she had to strain to hear it over the beating propeller. The moment came, though, where she couldn't hear anything but the propeller.

A blizzard of icy panic consumed her. She couldn't move, couldn't speak, and the best her vocal chords could manage was a faint *eeh* that whispered through her nose, too quiet to be heard. On the table just within her lower periphery, where Mercy sat, was her arm. Her body was weak, but that shouldn't matter with that arm. Song made motions with the phantom limb at her side, hoping the arm across the room would mirror the movements. It didn't take long for the man to stand and cross to her.

"What's the matter?" he asked as he checked her eyes and the pulse at her neck.

She couldn't respond with words, but tears formed and rolled out across her cheeks. It took Mercy a minute to give up trying to understand. He turned and checked on Qiicho. A long, heavy breath escaped his lips.

"He's gone," he said, as though now he knew what she'd been trying to tell him.

Her heart clenched at the confirmation. Mercy left, then returned with Bruce and Ryk'r. The latter moved Song, and Bruce moved the pillows. They helped wrap Qiicho in a blanket. Ryk'r carried the small body from the room as Bruce sat beside Song, head tilted as though listening to something.

"They took it out of you," he said after a long while. "You will heal."

She knew he meant the glitters had done it. She wanted to ask why, but couldn't. Why had they saved her when she'd rejected them? And why hadn't they helped Qiicho?

After a minute of silence, he said, "They need you."

Song's breath hitched for a second. How had he known what she'd thought? And there had been a long delay, as though he'd waited for both the question and the answer.

He grasped her left hand, lifting it from where it rested on her abdomen. He stroked it in a gentle, comforting manner. "They waited so long. You made a promise. They followed you. And they saved you. They chose you. Now you choose them."

Song had to choose to let them in. They wanted something from her. She didn't care to know, and she didn't care to help, either. Why should she help them when they'd let such a young boy die? He didn't deserve it, and she was furious.

She'd never hated the Gift so much since she'd gotten it. If she could remove it from her body now, she would. She'd forced it into some sort of hibernation. It no longer played an active role in which she controlled it. Instead, it remained within, strengthening her, giving her a working arm, and saving her life from whatever had just killed the cabin boy she'd hoped would stay at her side forever.

Bruce left and returned with his drawing book. He sat beside her in silence as the pencil scraped across the paper. Every so often he would look over at the tears glistening on her cheeks, wipe them with a handkerchief, and resume drawing.

THE NEXT DAY, SONG WOKE WITH THE ABILITY TO BLINK AND breathe a little easier. Her eyesight was still blurry, but at least she could move her eyes—with great difficulty. None of the rest of the crew showed any symptoms of becoming ill, and so they ended her quarantine.

Ponce came in to clean her lower half, which was humiliating. She assumed it was something others had done for her before then, but at least she'd had the blessing of being unconscious and near death. Now she wanted to cease existing, because this time it hadn't been involuntary; she just couldn't hold it any longer.

On the bright side, though, Ponce didn't seem to mind. He talked her through it, and she could at least move her legs to assist with the removal of her soiled trousers. Her arm was still weak at the shoulder, but they'd propped her hand on her stomach. She did the best she could, motioning with her hand. It devolved into Ponce asking yes or no questions— 'Are you comfortable?' 'Is it all right for me to remove your underpants?'—and she would move her hand up and down like a nod, or left and right like shaking her head.

He confessed that all these years he and Doctor had been the ones to clean her up when she'd been unconscious for days. None of the other men felt it appropriate to touch her, but since someone *had* to, Dashaelan had selected him the first time, at Toothy's suggestion. That much was, at least, comforting to her, even though she hadn't known him as well at the time. Once he'd finished, he settled a square of leather and wool under her—usually reserved for lining her hammock during her lady's blood—covered her with a blanket, and left the room carrying the bucket with her soiled clothes.

Thumbs fed her broth by hand. It wasn't quite filling, but the salty, thin bouillon was the only thing she could reliably swallow.

Knots sat with her a while as well, reading to her from the Jinjran history tome, since it was closest. He stumbled over the Jinjur words with a giggle each time—Song did her best to make a giggle in reply to make him feel better—and his Zardiian accent made some words hard to understand. She was happy for the company, either way.

Bruce came in later, as the sun was setting. He sat beside her again, smiling as he held his art pad. She waved with her left hand.

"Hello. I made you a story."

She nodded her fist and slid her eyes to his blurry figure. Bruce flipped through until he found the page he wanted. He held it up for her to see. She motioned with her hand to move it closer, so he did. It hovered in the air a hand's-length from her nose, but she could see it now, albeit a bit fuzzy.

The picture was less detailed than his usual works, giving away how fast he'd worked on it. Regardless, she recognized herself in her gown from the Midsummer Ball, her tan coat buckled over it. She stood on a skyship deck, a man's hand gripping her shoulder.

If she could furrow her brow, she would have. Instead, she looked up at Bruce.

He turned the page. On the next was a picture of her falling over, her temple colliding with the railing. The next had her lying on the deck, eyes wide, mouth agape, looking quite dead, or close to it.

Did… Did I die? Or just almost? How accurate is this?

The next image showed Song covered in little dots she realized must have been the *kijæm* when it wasn't lit up. It traveled across the deck, up her body, and into her ear. The next drawing had her blinking.

It saved me. I died—or very nearly died—and the kijæm *saved my life. That's when it granted me its power. Does that make me a puppet? Or did it leave my identity intact?*

The next image showed two skyships from a distance, a glittering mist billowing against one like a gust of wind. It knocked against the other as a figure in a gown fell from it. A collection of the same swirling patterns pressed against her back to catch her.

Bruce closed the book and stared at the cover. "That's all they showed. They show pictures. I don't know what some mean. So I draw. These were for you." He gave her a soft smile. "To know."

To understand how I became Touched; how the kijæm *saved me. But I still have so many questions.*

Her questions could wait, though. To be fair, she had no choice but to tuck them away for later.

Fifteen

B Y THE END OF THE WEEK, SONG WAS UP AND WALKING SHORT distances. She still suffered the occasional droopy eyelid, but otherwise seemed to be healing up just fine. She made it out onto deck one day, not bothering with her metal arm. Her muscles were still weak, and she didn't want it weighing her down.

At the bow sat a little coffin constructed with spare red wood planks that should have been for repairs. She frowned at it and shuffled over, ignoring Knots as he helped steady her, though she didn't push him away. Dread had a wooden mallet in one hand, which he pounded on the end of a knife with to carve into the wooden top. Ryk'r stood over him, scrutinizing his work. When she neared, the guard pried her from Knots's grasp, as though it was his duty. He pointed down for her to look at what Dread had put on the lid of the coffin—a North Star. Below it was *Qiicho*, and underneath that was '*Keyhole*'.

Her face pinched, and tears pooled in her eyes. "He was going to be one of us forever, damn it."

"He had so much life to live," Dread said.

"What did we have? What killed him?" She looked at the men standing around the bow, but they shook their heads.

"Someone fetch Mercy for me. Ryk'r, help me to the step. I want to sit in the fresh air."

He guided her across as Knots disappeared below, and Dread resumed carving out the North Star. She leaned against the railing and closed her eyes, enjoying the breeze as though she'd never breathed such glorious air. Somehow she felt more alive, and more thankful to be that way. She'd had near-death experiences before, and yet this one felt far worse. In the past, it had been her *kijæm* almost killing her. Something easy to avoid, if she could resist the urge to use it all the time. But whatever this had been had left her feeling powerless and vulnerable. It was something that could take anyone—and it had.

I could have died…

She thought about Bruce's words. She had to choose her *kijæm*. It would stick around, waiting forever if it had to, but she had to choose to be Touched. Until then, it wouldn't let her speak the words for her to command it. She was something between a Touched and whatever Bruce was—she didn't even know how he could communicate with the *kijæm*, or see it when it wasn't sparkling. She knew now it showed him pictures, and she wondered if that's how he knew the sort of person someone was before they'd said a word. He'd known she was not a boy the first time he'd laid eyes on her, because it showed him the reality under the hood.

Now the question of how she could latch onto those like him or Myrmhin and puppet them remained her truest mystery. It would have to wait, however, as Mercy strode over and dropped onto the step beside her.

"You're recovering far faster than you should be," he said.

"I suspect it's this Gift of mine."

"Aye. I figured that, too."

"Did Knots tell you why I wanted to speak with you?"

"Aye." Mercy stared at his hands between his knees. "What did you and Keyhole do together that no one else was a part of?"

"There's always someone else around, except when he helped me into my harness in the mornings. We never did anything without—" Her brow furrowed. "I...shared his last jar of eels from his mother."

Mercy released a long sigh, nodding as though he'd been expecting this response. "Found it in one of Doctor's texts. It's not something we understand much. But improperly pickled fish is right up there at the top of the dangerous list."

"What was it?"

"It's called botulism. By all rights, you should be dead, too."

Song swallowed away a knot. "How do I tell a mother she killed her own child?"

"I don't know. You'll think of something, I'm sure." His gaze drifted out over the railing to the dark mass of land on the horizon. "Perhaps just tell her how he died, rather than who is to blame." Mercy patted her knee and stood to join the others at the bow.

Song set her head in her hand and closed her eyes on the world, wanting nothing more than to block it all out, and maybe rewrite reality.

By the time they docked in Chavìse-Kàmbhor, she'd been able to rest a little and prepare for what she had to do. Ryk'r helped her into her arm and coat. She accompanied the men carrying the coffin in the lift, her fingers digging into her royal guard's arm, as he was unfortunate enough to be the one helping steady her. She held her breath almost all the way down, save for a few small, jolting gasps whenever the cage jostled the littlest bit. He didn't say anything or make a scene. He stared straight ahead and let his arm take the abuse.

At the bottom of the lift, the crowd parted for the group. The street fell into a respectful silence. Men removed their hats and everyone cast their eyes to the ground for a minute before continuing on their way once the casket passed. The stillness of the city at the sight of them was almost beautiful in the most haunting way.

"Does anyone remember his last name? Or at least where he lived?" Song asked.

"I know the way," Knots said behind her.

"Lead on."

They followed the man through the streets, the four other men with the coffin on their shoulders and Song off to the side. No one got in their way, and if they were in the path, they moved.

There was something comforting in the way people acknowledged it without a need for words. No matter what country they were in, this reception for the dead would have been consistent. Something which united everyone—brought peace between pirates and lawmen, merchants, and civilians—was death. The long sleep; the final goodbye; the lost tomorrow. The metaphor didn't matter; death was death, and everyone understood it.

At the correct house, Knots stepped aside for Song to knock. She'd never had to return remains to a family. After Pishing, other crew members had handled it, since she was too far gone to even think about performing her duties, let alone doing it. With a deep breath, she knocked on the door. The woman who answered was much shorter than Song. Her blue eyes lit with an unquestionable kindness, her lips in a sweet smile as though it was second nature for her mouth to be settled that way.

"Can I h—" Her eyes found the small coffin. "No…" she whispered.

"Are you the mother of Qiicho?" Song asked.

"Not my boy!" She fell forward as though wanting to attack Song or go to the coffin, but her knees collapsed beneath her. "You killed my son!"

"No, we—"

"Damned pirates, you took my boy."

Song bit the inside of her cheek as she gripped the woman, letting her wail into her coat and beat on her with a fist. His mother blamed her over and over on distraught babbling. She pounded on her and cursed her name. Song said nothing and didn't stop her. She took the beating and the accusations. She accepted the blame as three more children stared out in confusion, tears forming in their eyes, though the youngest didn't seem to understand.

"For what it's worth," Song said, "we loved him like family. He *was* family."

"He was *my* boy."

"I know. And I had intended to bring him back to you alive. We can take his body wherever you need us to. It's the least we can do."

She glared up at Song. "You've done enough. Leave him with me."

Song moved to the side so the men could carry the coffin into the house. She set a hand on his name carved into the wood as it passed, but didn't go inside with them. Before leaving, Sunshine set a full purse on the casket—Qiicho's earned wages and then some.

As Qiicho's mother closed the door, Song reached out and slapped her palm against the wood to stop it. She clenched her jaw, staring in at the other three children that ate the same food. They seemed fine, so maybe it had just been the one jar. But it still didn't sit right with her to not at least warn the woman of the danger—without outright accusing her.

"You've got three beautiful children left," Song said to the glaring woman. "You may want to throw out any remaining pickled eels from the batch you sent with Qiicho. And be more careful making them in the future."

She removed her hand, and the woman stared at her in a tearful, bewildered silence.

"The world will be darker without him." She turned and left with her men.

SONG DIDN'T WANT TO GET ANOTHER CABIN BOY SO SOON. SHE didn't want to replace Qiicho before they'd even laid him to rest. She had to hire someone, though, and so she sent out a few men to look for street urchins or other young boys who needed the work.

The next day, Song stood in the cemetery among the field of headstones several rows away from Qiicho's funeral. Her crew gathered behind her, as the boy's family put him to rest. His mother noticed them. She didn't say anything, though. The funeral was small, and Song didn't understand a single word the pastor said, but she knew the basics of any funeral rites, and that was enough.

After Qiicho was in the ground, a mound of dirt over him and a temporary grave marker hammered into place, Song left. Her crew had dispersed a few at a time, but she had stayed until the grave diggers picked up their shovels and trudged away.

She didn't know where she wanted to go, and so found herself wandering near the brothel. With a deep breath, she entered. She didn't have to say anything. Zeriida-Khiin stood and scampered to her, a smile on her face. Song handed her quoine to the matron, but not the extra for the premier treatment. This time, the woman led her upstairs to her own bedroom.

Once behind a closed door, Song urged the woman onto the soft bed and lay beside her, resting her head on Zeriida-Khiin's stomach. She stared around the room at the armoire, the little tea table, a nightstand, and the paintings on the wall. Her room was lavish—worthy of a place in an aristocrat's mansion. Proof of the woman's high value.

Sitting quite out of place on the tea table were small gears and mechanisms, which when put together might form a music box, or a little clock, or maybe something Song couldn't even conceptualize in her mind. Beside it sat a collection of brass tinker tools with mahogany handles. She wondered if the woman hadn't cared to put them away, or if maybe clients weren't supposed to come in here and see the mess.

"Everything all right?" she asked, her voice vibrating in her ribcage.

"I'm surrounded by so much death all the time. And I keep losing the ones I become quite fond of." She let out a long breath as the woman didn't speak. "So no, everything is not all right. And I would like to lie here a bit, using you as a pillow, if that's fine with you."

Zeriida-Khiin ran her fingers through Song's hair, her nails gently scratching along her scalp. Song closed her eyes and enjoyed the comforting motion. She hadn't realized how much she needed that sort of attention until right then, and she released a sigh of contentment.

"You're paying high quoine for a cuddle," the woman said after a long time in the silence disturbed by other voices in other rooms.

"It's my quoine to spend how I choose."

Zeriida-Khiin giggled. "Fair enough."

"Oh, I also brought you this." Song reached into her left hip pouch and withdrew a yellow gem-encrusted brooch made of gold and shaped like a butterfly. "Took it off some Pishing noble. She was an ass, to be honest. Brayed like one, anyway. I thought it would look beautiful with that red dress you had on the last time I stopped in."

"Oh, I love it!" She accepted the gift and stared at it, her thumb running over the rough texture of the stones. "Thank you, Song."

"Do you ever wear the hairpin I brought you?"

"I do. It matches my green dress so well."

This made Song smile. There was something nice about having a beautiful woman to bring gifts to. One who didn't mind where she'd obtained them, either. Perhaps Lyella could have been the woman she could spoil with stolen items—except Lyella wanted to marry her. And Song didn't want that. Marriage meant staying put. Maybe one day she would want to stay in one place, but for the foreseeable future, she wanted to keep moving, keep pirating, and keep taking out her endless rage on Pishing.

When her hour ended, she hauled herself out of the bed and left the brothel to find herself an inn. She spent the night thankfully, but also regrettably, alone.

Sixteen

THE ROW OF ADOLESCENTS WAS UNIMPRESSIVE, THOUGH THAT was understandable. Young boys rarely wished to join a pirate crew. They would much rather work on a merchant vessel, or something with a better reputation, as well as a better chance of staying alive. She had to wonder, though, if news was spreading about her previous cabin boys. She'd already gone through so many in under a year, which was unheard of, even for pirate standards.

Midway down the row, one stood out to her. He ducked his head as though trying to hide. He'd a flatcap on that seemed fuller than it should be. Something made Song stare a bit longer. Then she realized that at the nape of his neck was what seemed so off. Rather than short hairs or longer ones down his neck, they looped upward into the cap, and the fine hairs stuck out at odd angles as they escaped — too short to fit into the cap, but too long to stay out of the way. The popped collar didn't hide them near enough to be convincing.

Song strode over and lifted the cap, causing the teen to flinch. Dirty-blonde hair in spiraling curls tumbled out onto the girl's shoulders to frame her round, brown face.

"How old are you?" Song asked.

"Fourteen, sor."

"Why do you want to be a cabin boy bad enough to disguise yourself?"

"Because you were a cabin boy, once. Right, sor?"

"Aye...?"

"I want to be someone important. Someone people fear. I want to learn to fight so I can come back here one day and show my bullies how it feels."

"Brave. But why should I take a girl as my cabin *boy?*"

"Because girls are just as good as boys, sor."

Song bit the inside of her cheek to keep from smiling. "And why should I take *you* above all the older boys? Why shouldn't I take one of the stronger ones, or one who already knows how to fight?" she asked, though she'd already made up her mind.

The girl's brown eyes drifted downward to search for her answer on Song's boots. "Because I have no family and no friends. I have nothing. I deserve this honor over every boy here. This is the reward for a hard life, is getting what I want. I've earned it."

Song smirked at her ambition. "We'll see just how much you deserve. Be ready to leave in two days. Arrive at the port at dawn, and the job is yours."

The girl beamed. "Thank you, sor! I won't let you down!"

"What's your name?"

"Gerti-Aniisa! Shortname is Gerti."

"I like that. Right, you're all excused." Song motioned down the line. "And if anyone lays a hand on Gerti hoping to take her place, I'll make sure you regret it before you beg to die as a mercy."

Two days later, Song exited her inn room to find the young girl sitting out in the hallway, a small bag containing at most one spare outfit and nothing else. Song met with her fencer, who had proven to not only be trustworthy but also excellent at his job. She approved an increased cut from the sales for his pay, and took what quoine he'd made this time around, along with the sales list, so she could go over everything later.

As she settled the heavy sack into her satchel and looked at the profit from the goods he'd sold, she smirked to herself. Even with his percentage taken out, it was an obscene amount of quoine for a pirate ship to have made without lifting a finger. Such was the benefit of having all the fun stealing without having to do any of the fencing. Less time selling meant more time in the skies. They almost had enough to start the repairs on the Stars' Bounty.

Gerti stared at the satchel as they walked. "That's a lot of quoine, sor."

"Indeed, it is. Do your duties and a cut of that is yours."

Once in the skies and away from the city air traffic, Song took Gerti into her cabin and lowered her hood. The girl stared wide-eyed at her.

"You're a girl?" Gerti exclaimed.

"I am. And I'd already decided I wanted you the moment I saw something of myself in you."

"What's that?"

"The foolish courage to walk into a pirate tavern disguised as a boy in order to become a cabin boy for a notorious skyship captain. Stick with me, and you might fly your own ship one day." Song smiled at her, then took off her coat to go through the girl's duties.

Gerti didn't enjoy learning to fight, as they found out the next day. She didn't want the bruises that came with getting knocked around or falling over. She squeaked and curled into a ball, still standing on one leg when anyone came at her with a sword; dropping her own, rather than lifting it to block the blade.

Song learned something in that one afternoon that she'd never known about herself before—she did *not* have the patience to train someone so terrified of everything. She wanted nothing more than to yell at this girl and send her below for a week for acting so brave that Song knew she'd had to hire her, only for the brat to be more useless than she'd been when Dashaelan had had the displeasure of whipping her into some kind of shape. Outside of fighting, though, she did the rest of her duties well.

Four days out, they encountered their first passenger vessel at the northern end of Pishing. It put up a brief fight, but in the end, the crew surrendered, rather than losing any lives. Everything went to the cadence of the practiced dance they did. It was like a well-oiled machine at this point. Her crew handled the other crew. A handful of her men accompanied her to the passenger deck while others found the cargo hold. Song charmed the passengers, then picked out the prettiest lady to make her do the stealing.

The woman who caught her eye this time was shielding another woman, rather than hiding behind a man. Song liked that boldness. The woman's hair was black, and her eyes a bright blue. The woman behind her had the same. Sisters, if Song had to guess.

"You." Song pointed at the woman cowering behind the first. "Come with me."

She flinched and emitted a high squeak of a whine.

"Take me instead," the brave one said.

Song chewed on the inside of her bottom lip. "What's your name?"

"Gemestha."

"Named for the Holy Sun goddess. You know, once upon a time, only one of Gemesthie's *gotu* could hold such a name. It wasn't something one was given at birth."

The woman grappled for words, confused by the impromptu history lesson. "I didn't know. Impressive that you do."

Song smiled. "All right Gemestha, you come with me."

The woman breathed out as though relieved, yet still terrified. She hesitated, giving her sister's hand one last squeeze before coming forward and following Song to the first of the rooms. Once the door closed, Gemestha turned around and reached behind her to attempt undoing the buttons down the back of her red and black dress. Song didn't move as she watched her fight with herself, trying to get her hands to reach far enough. After a while, she huffed and gave up.

"Please don't ruin my dress. It's my favorite," Gemestha said.

"You're quite calm, except for the flutter at your neck. Are you not scared?"

"Not really, no." She took a step closer. "You're the real Captain Song?"

"I am. Why? Have you met others?"

"Not met them, no. But I've heard of them."

"I bet they're all idiots who don't know the first thing about being Song."

"What would that first thing be?"

She stepped closer to touch Gemestha's hair. She tried to think what the first thing would be besides her not being a man, but instead focused on the woman's unflinching gaze—in fact, she almost leaned toward Song, as though hoping for a kiss. "You're not the first woman to offer herself willingly to me. How many of them do you suppose said I forced them?"

"They had virtue to keep intact," she said.

"And you don't?"

Her head shook the slightest bit.

Song released a long breath. "My poor dear. I will tell you what I told all the others. I won't be touching you. None of my crew will touch you or anyone else here." She stood closer to the woman, holding her chin in her fingertips. "We're pirates, love. Not monsters."

"I won't tell anyone you forced—"

"No. I will not betray my code, even for a…willing participant."

She gave Song a sad smile. "Perhaps if I—"

The door opened and Bells leaned in. "Captain, we've got a problem."

"What?" Song followed him down the hall to where the

muffled sound of a woman crying came through the thin cabin door.

"Toothpick took a girl in there. Door is locked."

A hot anger flashed through her. She pulled her metal arm back. Bells leapt to the side as she rammed her fist into the handle as hard as she could. It jolted in her shoulder, but the door frame splintered around it. One more strike and the door popped open to reveal Toothpick holding the woman's mouth as she cried. He didn't have time to raise his trousers as Song rammed her left fist into his cheek.

"Take him above deck and hold him there," Song bellowed as she shoved him out of the room.

Toothy and Bells grabbed the man, allowing him to at least drag his britches up before they carted him off.

"You're a hypocrite, Song!" Toothpick shouted. "You tell us to keep our hands to ourselves, and yet you take women in secret!"

"I told you, I never—"

"Liar!"

"Shut up, dead man," Bells said as he smacked the side of Toothpick's head.

Song closed the door and held out her hands toward the woman, who'd shoved herself into the corner to sob into her palms. She pressed herself farther back when Song took a step toward her. To her dismay, it was the terrified woman whom Gemestha had been shielding.

"I won't hurt you. I promise. What's your name?"

"Myooru," she managed in a whisper. "Please don't… Please…"

"You're safe. I promise."

"No woman is safe with Song!" she shouted. "You and your crew are honorless bastards!"

"My men signed a contract, same as me. And that contract promises death to anyone who breaks it."

"Liar."

"Why would I lie?"

Myooru glared at her.

"Do you want to know what I did to the man who gave me this?" She pulled her collar down and her hood back so the woman could see the scar on her neck from William's knife. "I told him I would break his hands for touching me. And I did. Then I killed him. Anyone disgusting enough to force themselves on another person doesn't deserve to breathe a minute longer. Take my hand and I will grant you some vengeance. It won't undo what's happened, but it might help you feel better knowing one less monster is in this world."

Myooru stared at Song's hand for several minutes, fighting to catch her breath. She set her trembling fingers in Song's palm and let her haul her up to her feet. Song supported the woman as she walked on shaking knees.

"Myooru, no!" Gemestha gasped as they exited the room.

"Ladies and gentlemen!" Song shouted in the main passenger room. "I invite you all above deck to witness what happens to those who break the rules of Captain Song's crew."

Several followed out of morbid curiosity as Song ascended, her arm wrapped around to support Myooru in more ways than one. Her men who had been on the main deck had all abandoned whatever duty they'd been at and stood circling Toothpick. Blood dribbled from his nose, telling of at least a few doling out some punishment before their captain arrived. Song ordered him held prone beside the railing. She stood Myooru before him, then unholstered her revolver.

"Do you know how to shoot a gun?" she asked.

"No," Myooru whispered back.

Song set the revolver in the woman's hands and made sure she positioned them just right. "Keep your hands steady, palm on the base. Now use your thumb to pull back on the hammer." She wrapped her hands around Myooru's. "Aim…" She guided the revolver to point at his chest. "And when you're ready, take a breath and squeeze the trigger."

A minute passed in excruciating silence, all eyes on the woman.

Myooru whimpered. "I can't."

"It's all right," Song said. "He earned it."

"I can't do it. I can't shoot someone like an animal."

"He *is* an animal," Gemestha said. After a few seconds, she strode across the deck and eased the firearm from her sister's hands. She took aim. A gunshot cracked through the silence, tearing across the deck like thunder.

Toothpick howled in agony, trying to double over to grab his groin, but unable to as Hairy and Dread held him in place. Blood seeped down the insides of his legs, staining his trousers as it went.

Song grinned. "Nice shot!"

Bang! Bang! Bang! Bang! Bang! Click! Click! Click!

She set her hand on Gemestha's, stopping her continued attempts to shoot the man. She eased the gun from her shaking fists, taking in how beautiful her fury was. Gemestha shoved past Song and dragged her sister into a tight embrace. Song sauntered toward the man, scrutinizing the trail of bullet holes leading up his body. If Gemestha had had two more shots, the last would've hit his head.

"Rule number five, lads," she shouted and spun on her heel.

"No raping," her men shouted back.

"The punishment for breaking rule number five?"

"Death!"

She turned to stare at Toothpick as he gasped, blood and spittle dribbling from his lips. "Death. There is no room for monsters on my crew. And there is no room for monsters in my skies."

She raised her foot and kicked his stomach as Hairy and Dread released him. Toothpick tumbled over the side and down to the hard ground far below them. Song returned to the sobbing woman wrapped in her sister's arms.

"There, there," Song cooed, stroking her black hair. "Let's get you into a bed." She met Sunshine's gaze. "You're in charge. Finish up fast."

The rest of the passengers followed in silence, returning to their seats without protest as Song walked with Myooru and Gemestha. The two women entered a room and lay together on the bed, Myooru sobbing into the pillow. Gemestha met Song's gaze, and it surprised her to not find blame, even though Song blamed herself. If she'd left Gemestha there to block her sister, or had taken Myooru instead, then perhaps this wouldn't have happened.

As the Stars' Reprisal detached from the passenger skyship, Song let out an exhausted sigh. For all her attempts at keeping her crew honorable, one had sullied their record. Which didn't matter, anyway, since it seemed lies had spread from the women Song had refused to touch. She clenched her jaw, hoping the story of Toothpick's punishment spread farther and louder than the lies about her and the rest of her crew.

In her cabin, she found Gerti practicing writing. It was one of the few lessons which didn't produce whining from the girl.

"Gerti, did you know Toothpick?" Song asked as she slid into a chair.

"A little. Why?"

"Did he ever touch you or force you into doing something?"

She wiggled the pen in her hand. "No, sor. I don't think I really ever talked to him."

Song released a relieved sigh. She hoped she could protect her—which would be a lot easier if the girl put in more effort toward learning to fight and defend herself. Unfortunately, it had been William making Song feel helpless that had made her work hard with Leslie. If she could wake the girl up somehow, without scarring her for life, that would be ideal.

Song never got that chance, though. Days later, another pirate ship ran alongside them, determined to intercept. Men from the other crew swung onto the Stars' Reprisal. She had ordered Gerti to stay inside her cabin, as she had with the passenger vessel.

Instead of following orders, the girl came tearing out with the small sword she used for practicing. The man she engaged with disarmed her without trying. He wrapped his arm around her and grabbed a rope to swing across to his own ship. Gerti fought against him, then turned her head and bit into his neck.

Halfway between the two skyships, he released his grip. The weight of the girl ripped out a chunk of his flesh. She clawed all the way down his bare arm as she screamed and tried to hold on, leaving torn skin in her wake. In mere minutes she'd gone from being safe in Song's cabin to falling down through the air toward the ocean so far below them, the girl may as well have hit solid ground.

Seventeen

They returned to Telbhaniich-Zardi to repair holes from cannon fire and nurse injuries from the encounter with the pirate crew. Song gave the order to find yet another cabin boy, this time deciding a girl was too big a risk.

While the loss of Gerti upset her, she wasn't as torn up as with Qiicho. After all, she'd known her for a week. Being honest, Song would have paid Gerti and sent her on her way once they'd returned to Chavìse-Kàmbhor. The girl had acted brave, and yet she'd been so averse to learning how to fight. She hadn't wanted to learn, she wanted to already be good at it.

At the end of the two weeks docked for repairs, Song visited Zeriida-Khiin for the second time during their stay. The woman was excited to see her again so soon. Song suspected she enjoyed having a client who preferred to do all the work to pleasure her, rather than the other way around. Being fair, though, Song enjoyed the little gadgets the woman had. Zeriida-Khiin called them her toys, and would use them on Song. It was an odd word to use for something designed for pleasure, rather than play—then again, sometimes it did feel like playing.

Song had asked about these gadgets and the tools she'd seen before. Zeriida-Khiin confirmed her interest in tinkering, but she hadn't invented the little devices. She repaired them if they broke, but her real interest was in little constructs of creatures. She hoped one day to get them to move on their own. It was merely a hobby, but one she loved.

Song indulged herself this time, spending longer with the woman than the prepaid hour. Song wanted her beautiful sultania to lie beside her through the night, though. She could spend the night here, but eighty quoine for every hour she stayed was a steep price just to sleep next to a beautiful, naked woman.

They were resting after a second round of fun when a little bell jingled in the upper corner of the room, where the walls and ceiling met. She had no time to question it as Zeriida-Khiin slid from the bed and gathered Song's clothing, then stuffed it into the hidden bottom drawer of the armoire. She unbuckled Song's metal arm, slipped it off and set it on top, closed the drawer, and returned to the bed. Her eyes widened before she tore Song's necklaces off, and shoved them into the nightstand drawer.

"Act natural," she hissed. "Don't say a word."

"What? What's happen—"

Zeriida-Khiin held a shushing finger to her lips. The door opened and two guards in shining breastplates entered, glaring down at them. Another man in a constable's uniform lingered in the doorway. He delivered an apologetic smile to the women.

"Get up," a guard demanded.

"Is it just you two?" the other asked.

The Zardiian constable sighed at the two men.

Song gripped the blanket over herself. The other man held up a paper as though comparing Song's face and what she suspected was a sketch of her. It occurred to her that these men had Pishing accents and wore guard uniforms—blue underclothes and stag horns on the breastplates.

Her eyebrow raised the slightest bit as she recognized the crest from the night she'd killed Roman Duchamp. Now she was desperate to know which house they belonged to, that they had the authority to come to the most neutral country to search for her and not get turned away.

"Who are you looking for?" Zeriida-Khiin asked. She stood at ease and confident, pinning up her hair, though she remained nude and unbothered by the men.

"Caleb Song," the first man said.

"Oh. He left. Went right out the window not long ago."

He grabbed Song's left arm and dragged her from the bed, then ripped the blanket away, exposing her nudity for their scrutiny. He cringed at the stump where her right arm should have been. "Who are you?"

"Hands off," the Zardian constable growled; the guard released her arm and shot the constable a scowl. "That's your only warning."

"Answer the question," the other guard said to Song.

"Dedre is new," Zeriida-Khiin said. "Poor thing is mute." She brushed her fingertips over Song's forehead to move her hair. "Performs well, though. Worth the high price if you've the quoine…?"

"And the arm?"

"Some people find that sort of thing exciting, and even erotic. We don't shame desires. At least, we're paid not to." As though trying to entice the guards, she ran her fingertips along Song's body. "Do you have any...interesting desires?"

Song's skin tingled and heat swelled inside her as the woman continued to touch her, as though selling her to these men. She should have been worried—should have covered herself. But they were looking right at her, and right at a poster with the lower half of her face.

They'd caught Captain Song.

And yet, they looked right through her. To them, she was nothing more than an ugly, mangled, high-quoine prostitute. The thrill of it raced through her as she bit back triumphant laughter and the urge to pin Zeriida-Khiin to the bed and see how far she could get before the men figured out that she was the client, not the worker.

To push things the littlest bit, as the man with the poster walked through the room to check under the bed and in the armoire cabinet, Song turned and dragged her left hand up the woman's inner thigh. After a minor hesitation, she nestled her thumb somewhere warm and wet as Zeriida-Khiin gasped in surprise. The guards watched for another minute before the first cleared his throat.

"When Song returns, you're to notify the local police immediately."

"Oh, did they grant you the *au*-thority?" Zeriida-Khiin asked, trying to remain composed.

Song kept her gaze on the men. One's eyes caught on what she was doing with her hand as the other's swept over Zeriida-Khiin's whole body. The first had to adjust his trousers. Song kept going as the thrill shivered up her spine.

In the doorway, the constable checked his pocket watch, as though immune to the naked women. "Unfortunately," he muttered at his watch.

"An understanding was come to, yes," a guard said. "So, if you see him—"

"What makes you think he'll return?" Zeriida-Khiin asked, her voice breathy.

"Everyone knows you're his favorite *whore*," he spat.

With that, they left.

The constable released a long breath and shot a glare at the guards. He nodded an apology to the women. "Sorry to disturb your work, sors. Have a good evening." He pulled the door closed and their footsteps retreated down the hall.

The woman deflated and Song removed her hand from between Zeriida-Khiin's legs.

"You didn't have to protect me," Song said.

She bit at the inside of her bottom lip. "It's what you pay so much for. We protect our clients, here."

Song sighed and took her by the hand. "I'm not an idiot. I know I pay for your company. But you mean more to me than that."

"Don't."

"I don't mean it like that. It's hard for me to trust people. I'd like to think you lied to them not just because I pay for you to."

"You don't need to treat me like I'm not a prostitute. I know what I am, Song. I don't hate my job, and I'm not ashamed," Zeriida-Khiin said.

"Was it your first choice, though?"

"Of course not."

"You wanted to be a tinkerer, didn't you?"

"Yes. But don't you dare offer me a way out of this."

"Why do you think I would?" she asked.

"Clients have gotten possessive of me in the past and tried to 'rescue' me. My life isn't some tragedy. I worked hard to get where I am now, and I get to tinker in my time off. I don't need to be rescued."

Song smiled as she bit at her bottom lip. She lifted her hand to set on the woman's cheek. "Funny, looked like you're the one who saved me, just now. Quoine or not, you had no obligation to."

"You're…my favorite client."

"Why?"

"You were the first one to ask if I *enjoy* something, without having to be paid for it."

She shrugged. "It's no fun if the other person isn't having an authentically good time as well."

Zeriida-Khiin smiled. "I don't love you, though."

"And I don't love you. I just want a lady waiting for my return, whom I can gift nice, stolen trinkets, and we can please each other for hours. I don't want a woman keeping me somewhere I don't want to be, or demanding I stop being the way I am. Are you that woman, or should I start sampling the rest of the menu?"

She giggled. "I do like gifts."

Song returned her hand between the other woman's thighs and backed her up against the wall. "Then we have an agreement. I won't love you, and you won't love me. We're just here to entertain one another."

"Sounds like a fair deal to me."

Song kissed her. They tasted each other's tongues as the heat between them grew. They moved back to the bed as Song worked to create the noises from Zeriida-Khiin that made the woman worth all the quoine Song was willing to pay.

The matron entered the room, cutting their activity short. She jolted and stared down at the two.

"Who is this? Where is Captain Song?" she hissed as she closed the door.

"I'm right here," Song said. She grinned at the woman's shock. "The guards just left."

Zeriida-Khiin sat up. "They're waiting in the lobby, aren't they?"

"Of course they are," the matron said. She looked at Song. "You can have your second hour free as an apology for the interruption. Zeriida-Khiin will take you out the back way, but the streets will not be safe for you."

As she thought, Song sucked the wetness off her finger as though it were marmalade. "Do you have a courier?"

"I can have one of the men run a message."

As though she'd already asked, Zeriida-Khiin found a slip of paper and a pen. The matron wrote out the note Song dictated, then left to allow her time to finish her free hour.

By the time Song finished and was letting the woman wash her with water from the basin, someone knocked on the door. Zeriida-Khiin opened it to let in one of the male prostitutes, who had a satchel in one fist.

"Your man is waiting in the lobby for you," he said.

"Tell him *Dedre* will be right down," Song said.

He nodded and left.

"Can you make me look expensive?" she asked Zeriida-Khiin. She opened the bag and dumped out her sky blue dress, white gloves, and tan overcoat.

"Of course I can."

Song sat still as the woman did her hair and makeup—after borrowing a more suitable shade of face powder from another woman down the hall. She returned Song's necklaces to her and helped her into the harness over her underclothes. She helped secure the white glove up the metal arm and onto the button on the shoulder, then buttoned up the back of the dress once Song had gotten it on. This was one of Song's favorites, with the high collar and the lack of bustle. She pulled on her dress shoes as Zeriida-Khiin shoved her pirate garb into the satchel.

"I'll have Kyron take this to the inn where he got your man."

"All right. Hopefully no one blows my disguise," Song said.

She caught a look at herself in the mirror and had to stop. If she hadn't known it was her in the reflection, she'd have thought the woman was pretty in a strange way. The kind of woman that didn't take her breath away, but she couldn't look away from because of how perfectly her odd features fit together.

Zeriida-Khiin smiled. "With the right makeup, anyone is beautiful. You especially." She set her fingertip under Song's chin to turn her head and look at her handiwork. "Next time you stop in, let's dress you up like a woman so I can have some fun with *this* face."

"If it excites you, I'll do it," Song said.

Out in the hallway, Kyron waited to escort her downstairs. She set her right arm at an angle so it looked fake and immoveable, fingers together and wrist straight. The matron jolted when she saw her, but kept her lips tight.

"Your lady, sor," Kyron said, presenting her to Sunshine.

"I thought she was a prostitute?" one guard said, though he was staring at her with a bit more interest than earlier.

She hated how much a pretty painted face changed how they treated her—just like her mother and anyone else who saw her before they had made her up back in Garda.

"Our women and men can be rented as company for a dinner," the matron said. "It costs a great deal of quoine and must be booked in advance, to ensure their safety, of course. Are you interested in wining and dining one of my ladies? Or lads… We don't judge here."

"We're here on business," the one who wouldn't stop looking at Song said.

She couldn't help but notice it specifically was not a no.

"Maybe another time," he said. He looked at Sunshine. "That one worth it?"

Sunshine stared at Song, who smiled at him. "Oh, yes. Excellent conversationalist."

The guard laughed and Sunshine took that as his cue to lead Song right out the front door, past the very men looking for her. Once in the street, she let a small laugh growl out of her nose.

"What's so funny?" he asked.

"Zeriida-Khiin told them I was a mute."

He released a soft half-chuckle.

"And a high-quoine prostitute because of my amputation. I'm worth so much, no matter where I go. It's flattering, really."

"Calling you high-quoine also means men like that can't afford you. She was doing you a favor."

"All right, let's get out of the city as fast as possible. Hopefully they're not watching the ship, too. I'll have to wear dresses until we leave, just to be safe." She locked her eyes on another pair of guards in the same uniform, nailing a poster of her to a message board. "Someone in Pishing is trying hard to get their hands on me. I wonder what they promised the leaders of Telbhaniich-Zardi in order to get permission to hunt a pirate on the island. Even my father never managed that." She paused and waited for the men to walk away before striding to the board. Song stared at the poster, her tongue caught in shock.

Wanted: Alive
400,000q Reward

She rushed after the guards and convinced them to give her one of their posters, then returned to Sunshine. "For my collection."

"It's been a year and a half since you killed Duchamp. Why up their efforts now? And why change their minds and take you alive?"

"Once I figure out which lord bears that crest, I'll have to pay him a visit and find out."

Eighteen

THE CREW ESCAPED CHAVÌSE-KÀMBHOR WITH LITTLE DIFFI-culty—except when it came to Song. Guards watched the dock where the Stars' Reprisal had anchored. She couldn't walk onto the ship as a woman, nor could she wear her hood. And so she climbed into a crate to be transported up with the last of the cargo.

Thumbs pried the lid off and smiled in at her. "What is this, a stowaway?"

She laughed and took his hand to get out. "Have we left yet?"

"Not yet."

"Get me out of this dress. I want to say goodbye to the guards as we leave port."

He laughed and helped her out, then took her things into her cabin as she dressed and washed the makeup from her face. She tied her mask over her braid, lifted her hood, and waited. Once they were pulling away, she strode up and waved over her head so the guards saw her.

"Good luck finding Captain Song!" she shouted at them.

The four she could see scrambled to get to a lift or stairs as one ran for a skyship.

"Really, I hope you find him. Right, slippery bastard, that one!"

She and Thumbs laughed, satisfied with the chaos.

"There's no way they leave port fast enough to catch us," Maps said.

"And good luck figuring out where we'll go next," she said.

"Where are we going?"

"Let's return to Tarn for those clothes Stitch promised me. See if we can't find a cabin boy there."

"That'll be hard," Toothy said. "Word is spreading that your cabin boys are cursed."

She scoffed. "They're not. It's just bad luck."

"Doesn't matter. You know how superstitious people can be. Four kids in one year? May as well be cursed."

She grunted, but otherwise said nothing.

They didn't stay in Tarn for long, only stopping in for the clothing and a cabin boy, if they could find one. The one thing that made Song pause the whole trip was when Stitch told her of a man coming into the shop and demanding Song's coat. Of course, she'd refused to make one for him and sent him on his way, but it was the first time it had ever happened. She described him as an aristocrat or royalty, handsome, with an accent she'd heard before but had never asked where it was from. 'Hard R's' she'd said, which didn't narrow it down, as every country's were harder than Andalise's.

Song herself found a new cabin boy. He was an orphan, too old to stay at the children's home anymore, and was begging on the street as she'd left Stitch's shop. At seventeen he was the oldest she'd come across, but it was the age she'd been, and so she thought nothing of it. His name was Oliver, and like so many Andalisian orphans who'd never known parents, his surname was based on the orphanage—Tarnome, for the Tarn Home. The crew, however, called him Alleyrat as a nod to where she'd found him.

He was quiet in a careful manner. Alert, she thought. He was kind in a way that made her protective of him, as though she could shield all the bad parts of the world from him. His behavior differed from the previous teens she'd hired, who at least had some sort of ambition. Not Oliver. He just wanted a place to call home—three meals and a reprieve from cold winters—no matter what that entailed. She hoped it would at least keep him alive. Still, if she could have her way, she'd want Qiicho back.

Song tried not to treat him as though she wished he were someone else, though. She didn't want to change him or make him feel unwanted. She just needed to get over her own reservations about anyone new after having found such a perfect cabin boy in Qiicho. Song knew she shouldn't hold others to that standard, and would hate if someone did it to her. Instead, she gave him his fair shake. She helped train him to fight with a sword and better complete his duties.

They first stopped in Srkar to pay the storage fees for the Stars' Bounty. They'd acquired enough for a down payment on the first of the repairs. If Ponce's math was correct—which she didn't doubt—they would have enough quoine to finish the repairs by summer. Song couldn't resist the excitement tangling through her. She would have to choose someone to captain the other vessel and hire a whole new crew. But damn if it wasn't the most thrilling prospect, despite all the work it would require.

Oliver was the one who spotted a ship she could never forget if she tried. They'd just returned to Pishing airspace when he called her down from the helm to look at the strange new vessel.

It was huge compared to the Stars' Reprisal, long and likely held twice the crew. It had a black zeppelin held on by spiked metal collars attached to chains and two mainmasts, a black body, and black canvas wings jutting out from the sides. At the front of the zeppelin was a sharp barb attached to a protective plate—likely to keep the canvas safe when piercing through other zeppelins. It was the sort of vessel which could do dangerous maneuvers and sharp turns. And at break-neck speeds she could only imagine, if the two propellers—one on the zeppelin, one on the stern of the ship—and steam stack at the back were anything to go by. She scanned over the ship with her scope, discovering the name painted in silver at the bow.

Darkness

"Bloody apt," she said.

"I've never seen anything like it," Sunshine said beside her.

"It is a warship," Dread said, looking through a scope at it. "Likely made of the strongest wood, so your cannonballs bounce right off. Built for ramming into other ships."

"You've seen one of these before?" Song asked.

He shook his head. "No. Only heard about the *idea* of them through rumors. This was two or so years ago. Everyone in Qet-Qet called the man crazy…"

"Well," she said with a sigh, "Maps, steer us away from that bloody Darkness. Lads, if you see it, say something. We're not going anywhere near it. Understood?"

Ayes rippled across the deck as she handed the scope back to Oliver and descended to the bottom to open the trapdoor.

"Birdie, look off the starboard bow," she shouted to the man in the crow's nest. "See that black nightmare? You see that again, whistle one long, one short, and one more long. Got it?"

He looked through his spyglass at it and grimaced. "Aye, Song."

THE NIGHTMARE WAS THE SAME AS EVERY TIME BEFORE—THE dead all coming to swarm her. Those she had loved the most crowding at the front. Now every young face of her previous cabin boys joined the legion of phantoms haunting her dreams. Qiicho especially disturbed her. She often found herself caught between a skeleton screaming on a burning pyre, and Qiicho standing behind her to block her escape, his eyelids droopy and face expressionless. He stared at her with unblinking eyes, and she was helpless to do anything. The faces surrounded her, demanding why and cursing her name. She tried to flee, tried to scream—anything. But she couldn't move. Trapped in crystal and forced to look upon her own failings.

Song, it's only a nightmare.

Song, wake up.

Song—

She jerked upright. The kris swung through the air as she shouted at the figure over her. Oliver's eyes widened. His blood seeped out across her hand, the jugular pulsing it out around the serpent blade in his neck. He collapsed to the floor as she rolled out of her hammock and knelt over him.

"Sunshine!" she shouted. "Help!" She looked into Oliver's eyes and frowned. "It's going to be all right." Even as the words left her lips, she knew it was too late. She'd warned every cabin person not to wake her, and yet the doting boy had done so, anyway.

Sunshine ran in through the open door and stopped in his tracks, having arrived just in time for Oliver's final gagged breath to rattle through his bloodied lips. He stood over her in silence, then knelt down to close the boy's eyes.

"Tell me I'm not cursed," she whispered, tears rolling down her cheeks.

"You're not cursed, Song. I'll get a swabby."

Several minutes later, Ponce entered with Coward. They wrapped Oliver in spare canvas and took his body out to the deck, then started cleaning up. Song rinsed her hand in the bucket of water, frowning at her distorted reflection. Ponce knelt to help wash the blood from her arm.

"You're no longer a swabby," she said.

"What?" Ponce stared at her.

"I'm promoting you to—"

"*Please* don't say cabin boy."

She pursed her lips. "Captain's Assistant."

He released a long breath, then nodded. "That'll work, I suppose."

"What did Alleyrat do wrong?" Coward asked.

"Nothing," she said on a mournful breath.

"But..." He gestured out toward the deck.

"He woke me from a nightmare," she said. "It's my fault

for keeping a dagger under my pillow, I suppose."

"It's smart to do it, though," Ponce said.

"Consider it your only warning to not wake me from a nightmare."

Coward chuckled. "Just poke her like this." He angled the mop handle to jab her shoulder with the tip. "Can't stab someone halfway across the room."

She batted the handle away, not in the mood for jokes. "That's fair." She gave Ponce a sad smile, which she hoped was reassuring. "Don't worry, I won't kill you."

"Maybe not intentionally," Ponce muttered.

They continued circling Pishing after a burial at sea for Oliver. The funeral was short, as nobody had much to say about him. Song wondered over how tragic it was for him to die so young with no one close enough to mourn him the way he deserved. No one beyond her crew would know he'd died. She had to wonder if anyone would have even cared. Afterward, Bruce gave her two drawings, one of Oliver, and one of Qiicho. She hung them on her wall beside the piano.

The arrangement with Ponce seemed to work over the next week. He didn't need training or instructing, as he'd already helped her in the past.

The only vessel they happened across was another pirate ship as they rounded the northern arch of the country. Song wasn't going to give the order to intercept, but some of her men had been acting antsy for a fight, or something to do besides play cards or other time-passing games. And so she blew her whistle, and the men came to life, scurrying to their posts.

They ran alongside the ship, boarding before the other crew could board them. As injuries mounted on both sides, she pulled the more dishonorable move and shot across the distance, killing the other vessel's captain. It left a bitter taste in her mouth as the action reminded her of the day she'd lost Dashaelan. No one on the other crew cried out or mourned. No retaliation came for her. In fact, they dropped their weapons and surrendered before their captain's corpse had time to grow cold.

Song left the others to tie the crew up as she descended with Toothy to check for anyone hiding below. A handful stopped at the cannon deck, led by Bells, to collect those men. Song continued to the lowest level of the small ship. It served as both cargo and crew's quarters, with hammocks strewn wherever space allowed. In the cargo hold, though, was the most interesting thing the ship had to offer. One of the crew stood outside a brig cell, pointing a revolver in at a figure curled into a tight ball.

"Problem pets?" Song asked.

He turned the weapon toward her, but didn't fire.

"The rest of your crew has surrendered. You'd be wise to do the same."

He glanced at the figure, then uncocked his revolver and held it up as he raised both hands into the air.

Song strode over to take the weapon as Toothy followed to grab the man. He jerked his chin at a single key on a hook across the room from the cage. She retrieved it, and as she slid the key into the lock, the man grew bold and started a fistfight with Toothy.

"Do you need assistance?" she asked.

"No, I think I—" The man punched Toothy hard in the mouth, the latter spat out one of his precious few remaining teeth. "You bloody tosser!"

Song left them to wrestle on the floor as she entered the cell. The figure smelled something foul. It was a woman. Her dainty hands gripped over her grime-coated rat's nest hair to cover the back of her neck. Song cringed at the state of her. The woman's arms were practically skin and bones, blackened with filth and dried blood. The plain white nightdress she'd been stuffed inside fared no better.

"Hello, darling," she cooed.

The woman curled tighter into the corner. "Just kill me," she begged on a desperate whisper. "Please."

"I'll do no such thing," Song said. "I'll take you away from here, if you'll let me." She set her palm on the other's shoulder and the woman's entire body flinched. "I won't hurt you. I promise."

The woman turned to look at her, her brow furrowing as her eyes scanned over the coat.

"Do you have a name, darling?"

"Song?" she gasped in disbelief. "Are you really here?"

"Yes," Song brushed her hair back, trying to shine more light on her features.

She shoved herself against Song, gripping her tight as she whimpered weak tears into her chest. "I was looking for you."

"Why were you looking for me? Who are you?"

"Amelia. Do you not remember?"

Song's mouth fell open. She remembered that name, now. The pretty farm girl she'd met so many years ago.

"I remember you, Amelia. How could I forget? Why are you here?"

"They said they knew where you were. Said they'd take me to you."

Song resisted calling her a stupid girl for trusting a pirate's word. Song had once been a stupid girl, too, and had gotten lucky with Dashaelan being so honorable. But Amelia hadn't been so lucky. She'd been tricked and abused for her naïveté.

Song stood, an anger burning inside her. "Toothy, I need you to—"

"Just a second," he grunted. He was on his back, gripping the other man's wrists to keep him from landing any blows.

Song strode over and kicked the man in the face, knocking him onto his back beside Toothy. He screamed for mercy as she unholstered her sidearm, pulled back the hammer, and fired on him. His shouting stopped and blood seeped from behind his head. She turned her attention to Toothy as she holstered her revolver.

"I need you to take Amelia to my quarters and have Mercy look at her."

Toothy pulled himself from the floor and rushed into the cage, where he scooped Amelia into his arms. She wailed for him not to hurt her. He ignored her weak limbs pushing against him and strode from the room.

Once alone, Song tracked down the powder barrels she knew the ship must have had. She rolled each from room to room and placed them in strategic locations along the ship, connecting them with a single fine trail of black powder. Once satisfied, she found a spool of spare cannon wick and connected it to the barrel beside the cannon room door. In the galley, she found a flint stone.

"All hands return to the Reprisal," Song shouted as she emerged from below, trailing the wick behind her.

Ponce stared down at a man he held at knifepoint. "Should we untie—"

"I said *clear out!*" she shouted.

They unhooked the grappling hooks and swung across or used the plank. She waited until her crew was safely on the Stars' Reprisal before she lit the wick with the sparking flint. Without a moment's hesitation, she swung across to her own ship and shouted for the crew to cut the ropes to any remaining grappling hooks. She ran to the helm and freed the propeller, urging the skyship to hasten their retreat. They'd just cleared a safe distance from the other ship when the explosion erupted beneath the bound men, engulfing them in flames.

Sunshine followed her into her cabin where Mercy examined Amelia, laid out on the bay bench. "Is this why you blew up the ship? Who is she?"

"Her name is Amelia. And this—" she unholstered her revolver, "belonged to her brother."

"Old friend. I see."

"How is she?"

"I gave her something to sleep," Mercy said.

"But how is she?"

"Weak. Malnourished. If she doesn't get to a real medical facility, and fast, I don't think she'll live much longer."

"Sunshine, have Maps plot a course for the nearest city that isn't in Pishing," she said.

"Closest city with a good hospital is Garda," Sunshine said.

"Plot the course."

"Song, are you sure—"

"I said plot the bloody course!"

"Hasty actions bring ill-favored results."

Song released a long sigh at him. "I know. But it's our only option right now." As he left the room, she shouted, "And have Ponce bring a bucket and rag."

"What's he saying?" Mercy asked.

"It was one of Dash's favorites," she said. "Our former captain. Had a whole list of one-liners as his code. No one was safe from hearing them at random without provocation."

She crossed to sit beside the woman, Song's nose wrinkling at her putrid state. In the years since meeting her, Amelia had matured, but her features had also been pulled tight, her face cast in a sickly shadow from malnourishment and nameless illness and abuses.

"How do you know this woman?"

"She saved my life once. Long ago, when I was still a Gould."

Ponce entered, and the two worked in silence to clean the woman. Her hair was a mess, and would take hours to wash and untangle—which Song didn't have the patience for, but Ponce did. She left him to it and wandered out to sit on the steps. No one said anything for a long while.

"What's the plan?" Sunshine asked eventually.

"I can't go into Garda as Song," she said. "The entire city would notice."

"And if you go in as Tsingsei, the entire city will notice, anyway."

Maps let out a long breath. "A no-win situation."

"Going in as Song risks people knowing who is under the hood when you're apprehended," Sunshine said.

"Going in as Tsingsei would prevent that, but I'd be forced to go back home." She sighed up at the zeppelin. "After I leave, Toothy is in charge. Take the ship to Talegrove so she's not impounded, and you lot taken in. I'll have to wait it out. Sooner or later, my parents will let their guard down and I'll be able to slip away again." She spotted Jerome and Coward at the bow. "Oi, you two! Grab a bit of canvas and rope and cover the figurehead and name."

The two disappeared below.

"I'll need two men to carry Amelia on a stretcher. Obviously, Ponce will have to go with me."

"I'd like to go, too," Sunshine said. "Sounds like a nice vacation."

She chuckled. "All right. We'll have to call each other by our real names. Tsingsei, Henry, and…"

"Thersiàl."

She quirked her mouth up at one side. "So you *are* the man Dash wrote about in his journals all the time." She released a long breath and stood. "Right, then. I'm going to go get packed. I suggest you do the same."

"Aye, Captain."

In her cabin, she informed Ponce of the plan. To her relief, he didn't argue or try to get out of it. He finished untangling Amelia's hair, and left to prepare. Song packed everything she owned into two chests—one for her pirate clothing and one for her lady's attire.

She pulled on her new powder blue, high-collar, long-sleeved dress with lace accents and dark blue embroidery that Stitch had worked hardest on. She styled her hair into a lady-like updo, and painted her face as best she knew how. Song frowned at the ugly woman in the mirror hiding behind a poor attempt at makeup, wishing for Zeriida-Khiin's magical hands. It would have to do, though, as she didn't have the desire to try again.

Now that she was ready, she sat in a chair to stare at the wall and wait to finally go home again, four years later.

Nineteen

G ARDA…

She stood at the railing, wrapped in a fancy coat that wasn't as warm as her hooded one, and stared out at the city she'd grown up in. It hadn't changed—or if it had, she didn't notice. To the southeast around the docks were warehouses and industrial buildings. Beyond that was cheap housing, inns, and seedy taverns, the red-light district to the right of them. Straight ahead was the commerce, business, and governmental part of the city and the massive train station. The left side of the city, as it stretched deeper inland, became nicer houses for the rich.

The crew stood at her side, staring in awe.

"Which one is yours?" Jerome asked.

Song stared at the men, who stared at her in anticipation. "That one."

They turned their sights to follow her pointing finger, and many gasped or muttered.

On a wide, flat hill, all the way to the left, so it was near enough to the ocean for a spectacular view, but far enough to avoid the filth of the docks and poverty, sat the Gould Estate. Even from here, she could make out the red and yellow bricks, the stables, servant quarters, sprawling gardens and hedge maze, the fountain at the center of the round gravel path leading from the gate to the front door.

It didn't belong in the middle of a city. It belonged outside the limits as a country estate. Perhaps once upon a time it had been outside the city. Now, though, other large houses surrounded it—which were dwarfed in comparison. Most of them sat close together, and some had humble yards that, along with the house, could fit into the small area of her family's hedge maze. The Gould Estate was an audacious feat of wealth and vanity.

For the first time in her life she recognized her own deep-seated desire to be an audacious and vain pirate—showy, attention-seeking, over-shadowing others in her desire to be seen as better, and not even a little self-aware about it…until now. It was a short-lived self-reflection that she did not put a pin into for later study. In fact, she consciously ignored it and decided she enjoyed being vain and flashy. She liked the pirate she'd become.

Nerves coiled within Song's abdomen as they slid into the harbor. She was smart enough to know there was no possible way she could avoid being noticed or recognized. Other places around the world she could take that chance, but here was another story. These people knew her. They'd known her for her entire life. A faint hope that she could avoid discovery whispered in her ear, but it was such a small hope that her anticipation smothered it into silence.

Ponce rushed ahead to hail a carriage as the rest of the men set about making ready to leave once the five had debarked. Song sighed as the frosty winter air bit at her cheeks and caused her breath to plume out as vapor in front of her face.

"At least it's not Aibhànocht," she said.

"That's the spirit," Sunshine said on a chuckle.

A few of her crew helped move her trunks off the ship, then one by one, every man hugged her goodbye. Tears stung at her eyes and she grumbled, not wanting to cry off her already dreadful makeup.

"You act like you'll never see me again!" she said.

"In case we do not," Thumbs said, gripping her so hard she couldn't breathe.

"We could just stay here," Bells said. "Find us somewhere out of the way."

"And if someone discovers this is the Reprisal?" she asked.

He made a face, but had no retort.

"Give Shadow my regards," she said as the last man hugged her tight. "Toothy is in command while I'm gone. If you all decide you'd rather keep running amok, at least don't blow holes in my ship, all right?"

Dread laughed and leaned his elbow on Thumbs's shoulder. "It would not be the same without you."

A chorus of 'aye' sounded across the deck.

"Ready?" Ponce asked from the dock.

"No." But she crossed the ramp, anyway, Ryk'r right behind her.

She stopped on the dock and started to object to him following, but realized he would never accept an order to stay behind, as Lyella's orders superseded her own. She closed her mouth and nodded at him. He nodded back.

They descended in the lift—Song clinging to Ryk'r the entire way down—and loaded into the carriage. First the two dropped Song and Ryk'r off at the hospital with Amelia, who was just waking up from whatever Mercy had given her. Sunshine and Ponce left with Song's belongings to get an inn room to stay in until she was inevitably found out.

The hospital staff asked Song and Ryk'r to wait in the lobby while they examined Amelia. She occupied her time studying the huge tome on Jinjran. She was reading a section on their special holidays based around their many gods, and wondered if any of them had been adopted into the culture of the colonizers. Had Leslie or Dashaelan participated in any of these sorts of festivities? Or were these traditions long dead to all but those who possessed copies of this book?

The doctor came to speak with her after a while. Amelia would need to stay with them for weeks, but he claimed they could treat her for her poor nutritional health and, once strong enough, they could cure the venereal disease the pirates had given her. Song clenched her jaw, especially glad now that she'd blown up the entire ship.

They allowed her back to visit Amelia. Ryk'r followed and stood at the doorway to give them privacy while keeping guard. Now awake and having had water and broth, Amelia looked like less of a ghost, though her cheeks were sunken and dark circles rimmed her eyes. Song took her right hand between her own.

"Where did you take me?" Amelia asked.

"Garda."

The woman frowned. "Oh. Oh, I'm sorry, I—"

"It was my choice. You didn't force me into it."

Amelia nodded, but stared at her lap. "I got the shock of my life the first time I saw your missing poster, you know."

Song chuckled. "I would think so. It was pure luck that you didn't know who I was."

"Have you talked to your parents yet?"

"Not yet." Song bit at her bottom lip. "Why did you chase me down, Amelia?"

She shrugged, her face caught in a sort of disbelief at herself. Instead of giving her an answer, though, she yawned and said, "I'm so tired."

"Rest, Amelia. I'll come see you again, I promise."

Amelia closed her eyes and drifted out of consciousness. Song left the room to find the doctor and a nurse waiting in the hallway.

"Miss Gould?" the nurse asked tentatively.

"Yes," Song said.

"There are reporters and police outside waiting for you. Word has spread that your parents are on their way," the doctor said. "I refused to let the crowd into the hospital."

She released a small sigh. "That's at least something."

It didn't take long for her parents to arrive. Her mother swept in through the doors and grabbed Song in a tight hug before she could even stand. As far as Song could tell, she was the same mother she'd left behind. The same perfectly made up face, and unwavering hairstyle.

After Mrs. Gould moved aside, her father enveloped her in the kind of hug she'd only ever dreamed about receiving from him—the kind which Dashaelan had been generous with. While her mother hadn't changed, her father had developed a few streaks of faint greying in his short, black hair.

"Where have you been?" Annie Gould demanded.

"On an adventure," Song said.

"I've missed you so much, my darling girl," Elroy said, still refusing to release her.

It brought tears to her eyes, but she tried her best to ignore the urge to cry. She couldn't help but think that if only she'd known this was how to get the affection she'd craved from him as a child, then maybe it would have been a lot harder to run away with Altain.

"Adventures *where?*" her mother demanded.

"I'm quite tired, and my friend is very ill," she said. "Can I tell you later, in more palatable segments?" It was more so she could come up with lies, but they were not going to know that.

"Of course, of course," her father said.

"I don't want to have to come to the hospital every day to see Amelia. Can we set up one of the spare bedrooms as a hospital room for my friend and hire someone to stay with us to care for her?"

Her mother released an indignant scoff. "You go away for *four* years, without a word, and show up out of the blue, asking—"

"Of course you can," her father said. "Just so long as it means you're home with us again."

"Will *you* be home enough to notice?" she asked.

A look of guilt crossed his face. "I'll do my best. Things have gotten…complicated."

"How so?"

"Nothing for you to worry about."

Her mother pushed into her face and used a handkerchief to fix her makeup as best she could. "There are reporters outside, and you look simply dreadful."

Song leaned away from her. "I did my best, mother. Are you really so obsessed with appearances that you care more about that than the fact that I'm here?"

"That's not— I don't—" Tears came to her mother's eyes. "How can you say such a thing? Of *course* I missed you!"

The tears of an aristocrat could be genuine, or they could be manipulation. She'd learned that long ago, and so now could never trust if her mother was putting on a performance, or telling the truth. Song turned away, refusing to look at the crying woman. If she wanted to prove she'd missed her, then she would have to do it without tears.

"Why don't we get you home? I'm sure you're tired after so much excitement," Elroy said.

She released a long breath. "Not really, but it's better than staying in this hospital. Mother, have you got one of those fans in your bag?"

She produced the hand fan, her small handbag organized as ever, and not filled with needless clutter. Mrs. Gould returned to dabbing at the tears threatening to ruin her makeup.

"Thank you." Song flicked the fan open and held it over her face. "There, now no one has to see how dreadful I look."

Her mother paused and eyed Ryk'r as he fell into step behind them. "Who is this?"

"*Akh'tilak* Ryk'r of Armalinia. My bodyguard."

"Why do you have a bodyguard?"

Song smiled. "I can explain later."

They walked together out the front door. A cacophony of voices asking questions hit her as she hid behind the fan. Ryk'r walked ahead, intimidating people to move aside as her father followed after him. Her mother wrapped a hand over Song's elbow and set her other hand between her shoulder blades to urge her along, as though she wouldn't move on her own. In reality, she wanted to run as fast and as far as she could.

Odd clicking sounds surrounded her, and she peeked out at large devices set up with covers over the people behind them. She recognized them as accordion cameras, though the clicking was new to her.

"What are those cameras?" she hissed to her mother.

"Oh, someone found a way to make cameras take faster pictures. They can even capture a moving subject. Isn't that exciting?" Mrs. Gould hissed back.

Song made a face. "Not really, no."

Her mother gave a dismissive sigh, but said nothing. Once shut inside the family carriage, Ryk'r beside her and the curtains drawn, Song lowered the fan. She deflated against the seat and stared at the item in her lap.

"Tsingsei," her mother said, leaning forward as though she had a secret to tell. "Your arm is…rather cold. Are you all right?"

She met her worried gaze and nodded. "I'm fine, mother. It must be a trick of the coat."

She *hmm*ed in agreement, though her face betrayed her continued concern.

"There's a song about you," Elroy said as the carriage broke free from the crowd. "How much of it is true?"

She tried not to give a wry smile at the mention of the ballad, but failed. She met his gaze. "Most of it. Why do you ask?"

"Do you know Captain Song?"

"I do. In fact, Song's ship just left port after I debarked."

Elroy shifted in his seat and moved a curtain aside to stare up at the sky. "I expect you to give me a full account of him. I want to know if Caleb Song is his real name, what sort of man he is, and what he looks like."

Her smile turned mischievous, though she hoped it wasn't obvious. "In order… Caleb Song is not his real name; he's not any sort of man; and he kind of looks like you."

He blinked at her and dropped the curtain back into place. "Not any sort of man? What does that mean?"

"Song is not like any man you've ever met. Very…unique." She chose her words with care that time, hoping her quick wit hadn't gotten her into trouble.

He glanced back out the window and deflated upon seeing nothing. "All right. You can go into more detail later, when you've had time to wind down from the excitement."

"All right."

She couldn't help but notice how he hadn't asked if she'd actually loved a slave and had gotten her heart broken because of it. He only cared about Captain Song, not his daughter's heartache. She clenched her teeth and stared at the curtain over the window.

Some things never change.

Twenty

AT THE GOULD MANSION, FACES SHE DIDN'T RECOGNIZE GATH-ered to greet her. She forced a smile and said 'hello', and 'I've missed you' to everyone. She stared each person in the face and lied. They cooed as though it meant the world to them. She'd been back in Garda for two hours, and already she hated every second. She despised having to put on this façade. It was all performance and no heart. And the worst part was, none of them seemed to notice. They were content with her lies.

The one face she was eager to see, though, was Johanna. The woman appeared in front of her, face a wet mess. Song gripped her tight, crying. Those were the first tears she shed over being home. Out of everyone, she'd missed her handmaid the most. She'd feared her parents would have let the woman go after Song's disappearance, but here she was, sobbing in her grasp.

After the excitement died down and people had gotten in their 'welcome homes', Song asked for a bath to be drawn in her own personal bathing room. Her porcelain tub was what she'd missed most—the long clawfoot with a raised back so she could submerge herself. And it was never a question of who had used it before her and when had it last been scrubbed out. It was hers. No one had ever used it but her, and a maid scrubbed it after every bath.

Song stopped in the doorway to her room and stared at the walls of dolls; Ryk'r did the same, staring with an expression somewhere between wonder and discomfort. Someone had kept them clean and dusted over the years. She had the urge to break out every one of their eyes so they'd stop staring ahead with blank, unsettling expressions. But they were an expensive and rare collection. Better to sell them, she thought. The quoine would be more useful spent elsewhere—perhaps on a house of her own somewhere in Telbhaniich-Zardi, once the hunt for her died down.

She opened her armoire to pick out a dress. Song frowned at her winter selection, all with sleeves built for arms without muscle and especially without a prosthesis. Gowns she'd once loved now reminded her of the stupid skinny brat she'd been.

"They're a little young for you now, aren't they?" Johanna said in the doorway. She stared at Ryk'r and rushed past him as though he might stop her.

"They're four years out of style, as well," Song said, though she didn't actually care. She glanced at her bodyguard. "He's not going to hurt or stop you."

"All right." She laughed nervously and came forward to search through the armoire. "Style doesn't matter when you're staying home, now, does it? Do you not have new dresses?"

"My friends have my belongings. They rented an inn room for the time being." Song pulled out a simple summer dress with no sleeves, which matched the coat she had on enough that it would suffice. "This will do."

"We'll have to get you fitted into the new corset—"

"No. I'm not interested in new corset fashions—or any new fashions. I'm not interested in being a lady or a partygoer or any of that. And no one is going to force me into it this time." She paused and narrowed her eyes at the woman. "Are ladies still tightlacing here?"

"Oh, goodness, no. That didn't even last the year."

She smirked. "It was only a matter of time before the rest of them realized they enjoyed breathing."

Johanna chuckled and took the dress. "All right, let's get you to your bath."

Once Song had locked herself inside her bathing room, Ryk'r standing guard just outside the door, she stared at the steaming tub. It hadn't occurred to her until that very moment that she'd always had someone there to help bathe her, or dress her when she'd finished, or at the very least, attached her arm for her. She almost tossed her hands up and drained the tub. Instead, she squared her jaw and nodded once in determination, then stripped.

She lowered into the hot water with a sigh, leaning back and closing her eyes as it heated her muscles. She'd missed the perfumes and salts she'd grown up with, which Johanna had used to scent the water. It was comforting, even as she tried not to let it be. After she'd soaked long enough, she washed her hair again and again, then scrubbed every inch of her she could reach until she was raw.

Next came the hard part. She climbed out of the disgustingly grey water, careful to keep her one hand from slipping on the rim of the tub. She stood on the fluffy bath mat and dried herself off, having to fling the towel over her shoulder and rub against the wall to dry her left arm.

"Now, onto the *really* hard part," she said. "Should've waited for Ponce, you idiot." For a moment, she considered calling Ryk'r in to help her. For the sake of avoiding questions, gossip, and scandal, she didn't. Everyone in the house would have lost their minds if she brought a man in the bathing room with her.

After a long struggle, she gave up trying to pull on the harness first. Song gripped the metal arm between her thighs to keep it steady as she shoved her biceps into the cuff. After a bit of fighting with it, she managed to tighten and buckle the strap in her armpit.

Now two-handed, she could don the corset and clasp all the buckles to the harness. The dress was a bit on the annoying side, with a back that laced up. Of all the dresses she could have grabbed, this was the worst to put on by herself—though, at least it wasn't buttons. She managed it, though. It wasn't the prettiest job, but it would do. Finally, she slid her white glove over her prosthesis and buttoned her coat over the entire ensemble. She stared at the woman wearing a girl's dress in the long mirror, then made a face at her and left the room.

"Would you like me to make you up?" Johanna asked as Song opened the bathing room door and entered her bedroom.

She almost said no, but nodded. "Please."

It would be harder for anyone to recognize her lower face behind the makeup. Then again, maybe like at the brothel, her father would look right at his daughter and not see the pirate sketch. Because who would look at a woman and recognize what they thought to be a man? Still, though, it was a risk she didn't want to take.

"Where is Ryk'r?" she asked when she didn't see his red shirt and imposing figure.

"I set him up in a guest washroom, since you were taking so long."

"He doesn't speak, so I'll say thank you for him." She sat at her vanity table and stared at herself in the mirror.

"Why are you wearing your coat? Are you going somewhere?" Johanna asked as she combed Song's damp hair.

"No, I'm just chilly," she lied.

Song spent the afternoon re-familiarizing herself with the house, Ryk'r a few feet behind, ignoring everything in order to keep his eyes on her. He had taken the bathing opportunity to shave and dress in the vibrant red silk shirt and black wide-legged pants of his guard uniform. Even though his outfit was not something one saw in Garda, he seemed to fit in better that way.

She stopped inside the music room and stared at the piano. After a while, she wandered in and sat at the bench to play. Soon her fingers fell into playing the song from Leslie's music box.

"That's beautiful," her mother said from the doorway.

Song stopped and released the pedal, so the haunting echo came to an abrupt end.

"What is it called?"

She'd never thought of calling it anything, and so blurted the first thing that came to her. "Song's Storm."

"Did Captain Song write that piece?" Johanna asked as she stepped in beside Mrs. Gould.

"Yes," Song said.

"He's a talented musician."

"Did you need something, Johanna?" her mother asked.

"There are two gentlemen callers for you, Tsingsei."

She shoved to her feet and rushed from the room with Ryk'r on her heels. The women followed them to the parlor, where she gave Ponce and Sunshine each a hug. The two had washed and shaved, then dressed in their best clothing, though it was still quite humble and battered compared to anything within that house.

Ponce chuckled. "It's only been a few hours."

"Yes, and I already want to leave," she murmured.

"Who are your friends, dear?" Mrs. Gould asked.

Song stepped aside to present them. "Thersiàl Saigh of Aibhànocht, and you actually know Henry Xavier Barton the Third, of Anarchaia."

Her mother strode forward with a smile. "Henry! Whatever happened to you? Your parents said you'd gone away, but wouldn't say where to." She gave him a kiss on each cheek.

"I wouldn't think they'd announce having disowned me," he said. "But that's the reality of it. Been trying to make my own way ever since."

"And it brought you right back to Tsingsei, hmm?"

Song and Ponce made matching faces of discomfort.

"I think she'd agree that we end at friends," Ponce said.

Sunshine kissed the top of her hand when Annie turned to him. "A pleasure to meet you, Mrs. Gould."

"Johanna," she called over her shoulder, "inform the kitchen that we'll need two more place settings."

Song smiled. "Oh, good, I didn't even have to ask."

Ponce seemed to have no trouble at all falling back into high-society expectations. Sunshine, though, had no idea there were different kinds of forks, and he was expected to use each one for specific things. Ponce laughed and helped him, though the man grumbled about it.

Elroy arrived a little late, stopping to introduce himself to the men. "To what do we owe the pleasure?"

"They are two of my travel companions," Song said.

"On Song's skyship?" He eyed the two, and they stared at her.

"Yes."

"Why didn't you leave with Captain Song?" Elroy asked.

Ponce blinked, realizing the story she'd spun. "We were always closer with Tsingsei."

"Bodyguards, like Ryk'r," Sunshine said.

In the corner, Ryk'r nodded, but remained silent.

"You can sit and eat, you know," Song said to him. "Please."

"What is the story with him, by the way?" Mrs. Gould asked.

Song thought as she finished chewing and swallowed. "Oh, that's quite a long story. Can it wait for another day?" She looked at him again. "Ryk'r, please. You must be famished."

After a moment, he took the empty seat beside her. Someone from the kitchen scrambled to bring him a dish, which he looked at with curiosity. Song tapped the correct fork, and he took it, then cut into the meat more delicately than she thought he knew how. He chewed the piece as everyone watched in curiosity. He smiled, and those at the dinner table may well have ceased to exist as he gave his full attention to his plate.

"Does he not talk?" Annie asked.

"No," Song said. "Not a word since I met him." She cut into her own meal and paused. "Father, do we still have spare rooms which my friends might inhabit for a while? It would be a shame to make them waste quoine on an inn when we've so many unused rooms in this house."

Elroy released a long, unsure sigh as he stared her in the eyes. "These men are technically pirates, are they not?"

"What?" she asked, feigning shock. "These three? No! Ryk'r is an Armalinian royal guard, the most upstanding of citizens you can find. Wouldn't you agree?"

"And the other two?"

"Thersiàl is an attendant for the Aibhànocht church—rather, he was until he chose to keep me company. And Henry, of course, is Henry Xavier Barton the Third! He comes from a good pedigree. The idea that he might be a pirate is as preposterous as insinuating that I, myself, am a pirate."

The three men and her father blinked at her. The former because she'd lied so well without so much as a stutter—though it was an argument she'd practiced in her head—and her father because he had no retort for her protestations.

Elroy released a long, patient sigh. "Any sign of indiscretions or pirating habits will see you thrown in jail and tried as pirates. Do I make myself clear?"

"Crystal," Ponce said.

"Absolutely," Sunshine agreed.

Ryk'r grunted and shoved a forkful of seasoned green beans into his mouth.

After dinner, Ponce and Sunshine left to retrieve their belongings from the inn. Servants helped bring everything in, and Song waited impatiently as her trunks arrived in her room. Her chest tightened as Leslie's remained unaccounted for.

When it arrived, she shut herself within her room and set about ripping all her old clothes from the armoire and hanging up the new ones—taking one to pull on, so she could toss the old one into the pile. She left her pirate garb and weapons locked in that trunk, shoving it beside the armoire and spreading a folded quilt over it so it appeared more innocuous.

After that, she had Johanna take the old dresses to be donated—even as her mother complained with needless, excessive verve about donating such expensive garments. But Song insisted and won the argument.

She checked on the room being set up for Amelia's arrival—it was almost bare, save for an armoire and a large, comfortable bed. A vanity sat against one wall, and Song made a mental note to fill it with makeups and perfumes for her when she could choose her own. On that thought, she realized she'd need to purchase new ones; Johanna had used a bit of hers, as Song's were long since spoiled.

After the excitement of that day, Song's world came to a sudden halt. Boredom was her new housemate as she wandered from room to room, shadowed by her guard. Her entire body was restless as her heart longed to look out over the blue ocean and think about the adventure and the plunder on the horizon.

She thought about the plans they'd made before the Stars' Bounty had been destroyed. She wished again that she had ignored the Harpy's Claw. Leslie would be alive. Pinch would be alive. Ten other souls would not have been lost. The Stars' Bounty would be intact. They'd be off somewhere in the middle of the Great Ocean, searching for something which may not exist. But it didn't matter if it existed or not, they would search for it all the same.

Song's Island.

Even now, it had a ring to it. She wished more than anything to be out hunting it down, rather than wandering from room to room as though memorizing how many steps it took to get from one staircase to each door in the second-floor hallway.

It occurred to her that's what she'd been doing. She'd been counting every step between rooms. Song had been memorizing the layout as she had with both ships—learning her way around so she could find herself in the darkest of nights. She could take the pirate out of the sky, but she would never take the pirate habits out of herself.

Twenty-One

THE HOSPITAL ALLOWED AMELIA TO LEAVE THE NEXT DAY, after they'd hired an in-home nurse. The doctor would have to visit daily to administer the treatments, and he gave her strict instructions to avoid intimate activities. It was an unfortunately easy task, as Amelia had no interest. Song had to wonder if that would change, or if her desire had been scarred forever. For her, the idea was horrifying, for she so enjoyed her time with Zeriida-Khiin or Lyella.

Amelia sat in the bed, fidgeting with the luxurious comforter, as though unsure what to do after Song's revelation of her metal arm and the circumstances which caused it. She stared at Song in silence, and Song stared back, caught in an equally mute disposition. Song had long ago stopped thinking about the girl she'd once met. She hadn't thought about what she would say to her since before she'd forgotten her face. They were complete strangers now.

"You seem well," Amelia said. "All things considered."

"What I seem is a lie," she said, then clenched her jaw. "Sorry. I'm...fine, I suppose. You seem..." But she couldn't finish that sentence, because Amelia seemed positively wretched.

"I feel it, too," Amelia said, a smile on her lips that was both wry and sad.

They sat in an awkward silence for several minutes. Song started and abandoned a question several times.

"Just say it," Amelia said.

"What were you doing on a pirate ship?"

She jolted, as though not having expected that to be Song's question. "Oh, I was....looking for you."

"Why?" Song practically snapped. She bit her lips together to avoid telling the woman how stupid she thought that reason was.

"I didn't want to marry Rory." She opened her mouth to say more, but stopped and she stared at her hands in her lap.

"What, Amelia?"

"I…wasn't being married off. It didn't feel like that, at least. I was being traded like livestock. And I wouldn't have been a wife, I would have been a servant. When I met with him, he treated me like a pest. He told me he preferred women to be silent, and he expected me to obey and honor that preference. I wanted to marry someone I loved, not to be turned into nothing more than a coat rack who does chores."

"I'm sorry. No one deserves that. But did you have to hop on the first skyship you saw? Do you have any idea how dangerous that is?"

"Well, I do now!" Amelia all but shouted. "And no, I didn't hop on the first one I saw! I waited and worked in a tavern for so long, hoping you would turn up. Instead, those ruffians found me and said they knew you. They promised to take me to you!"

"They lied."

"Obviously!"

The awkward silence returned, now tinged with a tension that gnawed at Song. Maybe she should have tried to comfort the woman, make her more comfortable despite how she herself felt. But Song couldn't bring herself to lie for this woman the way she might have lied to appease Leslie or Lyella, or even Zeriida-Khiin. Another lifetime ago, Song thought she could have loved Amelia. Now she hadn't the heart to put in the effort. Somewhere in the back of her mind, she blamed it on a fear of being hurt again. She'd lost Leslie; she'd pushed the sultania away; Zeriida-Khiin was just a prostitute.

"Pirates are terrible people, most of the time," Song said. "Even I wouldn't trust the vast majority of them."

"I wanted to be brave, like you."

"Amelia, I wasn't brave. I was stupid and reckless, same as you. I got lucky with Dash and his crew. They have honor, when many do not even know the meaning of the word."

"I wish you had come back for me."

Song clenched her jaw. "How was I supposed to bloody know you wanted me to? I don't read minds. And if I remember right, *you* weren't even sure!"

"Don't shout at me!" Amelia said, tears glistening in the corners of her eyes.

"You're being naïve!"

"And you're being cruel!"

Song let out a breath. "I suppose you're right. I'm sorry." And there it was—the lie to appease Amelia. It didn't bring her any peace of mind, though, just annoyed her for having said sorry when she didn't mean it.

"I had hoped our reunion would be joyous," Amelia said. "Instead, we're fighting. It's not fair."

"Life often isn't fair. But perhaps we can set all that aside and it can still be the reunion you've dreamed of."

"Have you dreamed of it, too?"

Song swallowed and shook her head. "Maybe once. But a lot has happened since then. I haven't really had time to stop and dream about anything. When I do dream, it's nightmares. Easier to drink enough every night, so neither happens at all."

Amelia chewed on her lower lip and nodded, though her expression betrayed her attempt to hide how upset the revelation made her. "Did you ever find your friend?"

"No. He probably died that day. I wasted years chasing a ghost. Lost good men over it. I was a damned fool for ever thinking he was still alive, and I would get him back."

"What would you have done if he was alive, and you had found him?"

Song stared at her, dumbfounded. Long ago, she'd had the idea of finishing their adventure. But now? She didn't even know where to fit him into her new life. She no longer had a place for him. Altain, the boy who had consumed her thoughts for so long, the sole reason she was a pirate captain…no longer belonged in her life. She had no more use for street rats with fantastical ideas for grand adventures. No, a boy with a fake map and no plan had no place anywhere near her or her crew.

"Song?" Amelia pulled her from her thoughts.

"Oh, um…I think I would have brought him back home, dropped him off, and returned to the skies. It's where I belong."

"Do you plan on leaving now?"

She shook her head. "Unfortunately, I can't. My parents would likely chase me down if I so much as walked down the street unaccompanied."

"Would you stay for me?"

Song smiled and spat out a second lie. "Of course. I'm here for you, Amelia. I'll make sure you recover. And perhaps we can use this time to get to know one another like we'd wanted to before."

She knew that starting a relationship with two lies wasn't the best beginning, but maybe with time, those lies would become true. All that mattered now was Amelia's comfort. So what if Song gave her that peace of mind through dishonesty?

AFTER AMELIA'S VISIT WITH THE DOCTOR THE NEXT DAY, SONG entered the room to find her staring ahead in a state of shock. Song sat in the chair beside the bed and said nothing, waiting for her to show signs of life. Johanna stayed quiet as she stood against the wall. They steeped in an uncomfortable silence for a minute before Amelia's face scrunched and she began to bawl.

"What's wrong?" Song asked, taking her hand.

"There has to be a way to get rid of it!" she said.

"Is it your illness?"

"No!"

"Then what?"

"I'm pregnant!"

Song leaned back in shock as Amelia slapped her hands over her face. She sobbed as Song said nothing. She'd never known how pregnancy happened, but something in her gut told her it was the fault of the abuse the pirates had put her through.

"Like…with a child?" Song blurted, just to break the tense quiet. After a long silence in which no one else acknowledged her stupid comment, she muttered, "Well…obviously."

"I can't have this baby," Amelia said. "I can't live one more second with this thing inside me. Does that make me a monster?"

"It makes you normal," Johanna said. "It would take an incredible amount of strength to live with a reminder of your abusers. I admire women who could separate the child from the terrible circumstances of its conception. I wasn't able to."

Song stared at her handmaid, unsure now how to treat her. Did she regard her as a victim? Or continue as she always had?

"What did you do?" Amelia asked.

"I obtained some Pink Pills, and they took care of the problem."

"Where can I get them?"

"They're not exactly legal, so it's hard to get your hands on them…unless you know the right people to ask."

Amelia sniffled. "Oh."

Johanna set a comforting hand over hers. "I happen to know the right people. I'll get them for you, dear. Don't you worry about a thing."

"You're a blessing," Amelia said on a sob as she smiled. "A godsend. Thank you so much."

Johanna's smile came stiff and forced. "Get your thanks out of the way now, because you'll be cursing my name once the pills take effect." With that, she left the room.

Song sat, listening to Amelia's now happy crying. She didn't know what to even say, or if there was anything she could say. Her one near attack by a man had ended in her being rescued and then killing him. She had no identical shared experience, and so felt it was not her place to try sympathizing with Amelia's plight. Should she have said something? Or would she be told that her own experience didn't count, and there was no way she could understand, or be considered a kindred?

Mrs. Gould entered some time later, having been apprised of the situation by Johanna. She held Amelia's other hand and wiped her tears. She admitted she'd never been through anything like that, but that ladies should always stick together in tough times, and so there she was. It was a side of her mother Song hadn't seen before, and she rather liked it. It gave her hope that maybe her mother wasn't quite as cold as she'd grown up thinking.

Johanna returned some time later with the promised pills. The doctor entered with her. He talked Amelia through it, agreeing it was the best course of action. It was her choice, and he made absolutely sure she knew that she had the right to make it. His stance, of course, could cost him his license. And so right there he wrote on her paperwork that the treatments for her venereal disease had caused her to lose the pregnancy. Through eye contact alone, the five people in that room agreed to never tell another soul.

When he left the room, Annie gave a mischievous smile. "If he'd objected I would have thrown him out the window and given you the pills, anyway. The audacity of needing a man's approval to do anything as a woman. *Tsk!*" She huffed and left the room, muttering to herself as she often did when planning something and needing verbal reminders of her to-do list.

Song and Johanna stayed in the room with Amelia, waiting for the pills to take effect. They played a card game—one without bets or excitement, as was more suitable for ladies. Sunshine stopped in every half hour to make sure none of them needed anything. After a few hours, the medication started working. It began with a pinched face and sighs of discomfort. After a while, it progressed to moans of pain as she lay down and squirmed.

Amelia squeezed Song's hand so hard it ached. Song eased her fingers free and set the metal ones in her palm to squeeze instead. Johanna spread a wet cloth over Amelia's sweating brow.

"It hurts so much," she whimpered.

"Do you wish you hadn't accepted that medication?" Song asked.

Amelia shook her head. "I couldn't live with the reminder…"

"What does it feel like?"

She clenched her teeth together and released a soft moan. "My lower back hurts all the way to my knees. And I'm uncomfortable no matter what position I'm in. It's like the pain of my lady's blood, but so much worse."

Song gave her a wry, one-sided smile. "I've had a bleed like that. It was awful. Worst pain I've ever been in."

"Worse than your arm?"

She sucked in a breath and thought. "Close second, I suppose."

Her gaze drifted to where Johanna stood against the wall, staring at her, brows furrowed in thought over her brown eyes. When her handmaid didn't look away or relax her expression, Song shot her a glare.

"What?" Song demanded.

"If I didn't know any better, I'd say you experienced the pain of losing a child… But you've never lain with a man, right?" Johanna said.

She faltered, then forced her mouth to say, "Right."

Her night with Leslie replayed in her mind. It haunted her as she tried to ignore the nagging thoughts surrounding it. Her sight drifted to where Sunshine stood in the doorway beside the red sleeve of Ryk'r's uniform. His eyes flicked down to stare at the floor rather than meet her gaze for long. The way his guilt made him twitch wound her stomach tight and wrung her heart until it choked her. She lurched to her feet and pried her hand away from Amelia's grasp.

"I'm going to see about something for the pain," Song blurted. She strode from the room before anyone could object.

She blinked back the moisture pressing at the sides of her eyes. Her lungs forced her breath to remain steady. She opened the door to the parlor where the doctor sat having tea with her mother.

"Can you do something for Amelia's pain," she said on a faint whisper. "Please." The last word sputtered out on a soft gasp. Before either could respond, she turned and shuffled away as fast as she could, her heels clacking on the smooth tiles of the floor.

An hour passed before anyone found her again. She sat in a rarely traveled hallway on the third floor, surrounded by carafes pilfered from her father's office. Ponce stood over her as she wiped her cheek and took a huge gulp of brandy.

"Miss Gould," he said in greeting.

She didn't acknowledge him.

"What brings you to this dark hallway with so much liquor?"

A sob choked itself from her lips, causing brandy to dribble down her chin.

"I see." He sighed and leaned back against the wall opposite her, then slid down to sit on the floor as well. After a while he said, "Is your bum cold? I can feel the chill of this floor through my trousers. It's not pleasant."

She turned her glistening eyes on him, then pushed a carafe across the smooth floor with her toes. "This helps."

Ponce lifted the jeweled stopper and sniffed the contents before taking a drink. "Haven't had anything this expensive in a decade. Or more." He hummed with approval and took another long drink. "So, why are we getting sloshed?"

The words sputtered on Song's lips, incomprehensible to even herself. She tipped over to lie on her side, using her skirt as a cushion against the cold floor. After a while where he stared at her and she continued to murmur, she gripped the other side of her skirt and dragged it over her head, folding herself inside.

"I see," he said. The liquor splashed as he gulped back another long drink.

"I think I was with child," she said, her words forming now that she'd hidden herself from the world.

"Leslie's?" he said, his voice a whisper.

"Of course," she whined.

"How do you feel about it?"

"Awful. And relieved. And awful because I'm relieved."

Ponce lifted the edge of her skirt, and lay facing her. He closed himself within the dark purple confines of the cloth. He didn't say anything. Ponce looked at her with an expression that assured he was there to listen, and nothing more.

"I'm relieved because I really don't know what I would've done. I can't be a mother. I'd be awful at it. I don't even *like* children. They're…sticky and drippy and helpless. And I'm not patient enough for all that." She accepted the handkerchief he offered to blot her eyes and wipe her nose. "But it would've been Leslie's. And it would've been Dashaelan's grandchild. Of course I would've happily carried such a child. But I also…don't want to have children. But it was a Krell. But it would've taken me out of the skies… But it was a piece of Leslie that will never exist again."

Ponce reached out and set his hand over hers and gave her a soft smile. "I understand."

After a long time in sorrowful silence, she took a deep breath. "I didn't know that's how babies happen."

"What? Sleeping with a man?"

She nodded. "I thought it just happens."

"Like…spontaneously?" He chuckled.

Song nodded. "I thought that once I married, it would just…happen."

Ponce laughed.

"Stop it."

He laughed harder.

"Ponce, stop laughing."

He wrapped a hand over his mouth and tried to hold it back.

"You're being rude!" But her lips twisted into a smile and she held off a laugh pushing up her throat to escape with a sob, should she let it. "Stop making fun of me! How was I supposed to know?" By the end of her complaint, she was giggling, too.

"Did you really think it was just spontaneous?"

"After marriage, yes." She hid her face as her lips grinned, but her eyes continued to cry.

"Oh, don't feel bad." He pried her hands away from her face. "If it makes you feel any better, Toothy had to teach me all that when I left home. And he laughed at me, too." Ponce shoved her skirt off them and grabbed their drinks, then helped her sit up straight. "To Dash and Whispers. The only men to ever make Song second guess having children."

She delivered a sad smile as she raised the carafe and took a drink.

"Almost a shame."

"Why?" she asked.

"Handsome as you are and Leslie was? Your kids would've been positively gorgeous."

Song's cheeks heated over the flush of intoxication. "Shut your stupid mouth."

"It's true, though. Gorgeous little redheads who dance like leaves on the wind and swear like a drunken pirate."

A laugh exploded from Song's lips as she covered her face. "Stop it, Ponce!"

"A little girl who wears beautiful dresses to hide pistols strapped to her thigh."

"A dagger in her boot."

Ponce nodded as he laughed. "Or a boy who is the most gentle of all men but could knock you flat in one punch. Hopefully, he would have volume to his voice, at least."

Song took a long drink and stared down the hallway at the sunset-painted sky on the other side of the window. "I really am glad I lost it, though. Whatever it was."

He nodded in understanding. "With how ill you were… probably saved your life."

Song's face contorted into an ugly sob.

"It's all right, get it out," he said, and took a drink of his brandy.

"He knew," she said, as her drunken mind put pieces together, which she'd gone out of her way to ignore.

"Elaborate?"

"Leslie… The night before they tried to hang him, he asked for one last kiss, no matter what happened. And at the gallows, he didn't seem surprised. He wasn't going to fight. Leslie knew. And he said goodbye to me. But I didn't know."

He took a drink as she fell to pieces again. Ponce waited, not saying a word or stopping her breakdown.

"I didn't get to say goodbye," she choked out. "I didn't get to tell him I will never be the same without him. Even now, after so long, I sometimes forget that he's dead. In the morning, I'll find myself eager to start the day with a training session. But then I really wake up and remember that he's gone. He's not on holiday—not somewhere else for a while. He's permanently gone. I will never, ever see his face again or hear his voice. I lost my other half, and I don't know if I'll ever be all right again."

"It's been almost two years."

"And I'm tired of mourning! But I don't think I'll ever stop. Have you really stopped mourning Nebhàr?"

His gaze shot to the container in his hand as a frown ripped his lips downward, causing his chin to wrinkle. "No. Not sloppy over it, though. My tears won't turn back time any more than they'll bring him back. All I can do is keep moving forward and chasing the end of the pain."

"Aren't you afraid that if you stop mourning, you'll forget him? I'm terrified to move on. How would he feel if he knew that—"

"It doesn't matter, Song. They can't feel. They won't come back and see us still living. So all we can do is move past it. I'll sit and mourn every dead Krell with you, but I think our men would want to see us happy, not spilling enough tears to fill an ocean. Whispers so loved to make you smile. Stop crying for him and start smiling again."

She sniffed and forced a small smile. "I suppose you're right."

"To the Krell line. May they rest in peace."

They lifted their carafes and took long drinks.

Song lifted hers again and wiped at her eyes with the other hand. "To Nebhàr. May he also rest in peace."

Ponce took a deep breath, as though bracing himself, then raised his drink. "To Nebh-Nebhàr." His brave front cracked the smallest bit.

Song suspected he was lying about how far he'd come with his mourning. She took her drink and studied the man, wondering if maybe he still broke down in private, but would never admit it to anyone. Lying or not, she would let him have that possible secret.

After several minutes, she sucked in a deep breath and held it, her eyes closed. "I'm already sick of being home."

"It's been three days."

"That's three days too many. I don't think I can pull off a second disappearance. The entire world stops to stare when I pass. Even when I'm alone. I can feel it. I'm a caged bird."

"Let's give it a bit. A month, maybe. Then see about sneaking you off in the night. Until then, I will happily drink stolen hundred-quoine brandy in abandoned hallways with you as we blubber over men taken from us too soon."

She chuckled and leaned forward to clack her carafe against his. "Thank you. It's an honor to cry with you."

Twenty-Two

Much to Song's chagrin, her parents announced a grand ball as her reintroduction to society. She could complain all she wanted, but her mother wouldn't hear any objections. She'd also wanted it to double as a birthday party, and that meant gifts, so Song sighed and accepted. At least she'd get something out of it besides sore feet and an overwhelming desire to run away all over again. They'd scheduled it a month out, so guests could travel from farther regions. It wasn't until that moment that she realized she'd missed her birthday, and hadn't even noticed. Somehow, being twenty-one felt the same as being any other age. The number was meaningless, and she couldn't even be bothered to care.

While caring for Amelia over the next two weeks was time consuming, Song wanted more to her day than taking turns with her mother to sit with her and keep her company. But perhaps this was the opportunity to get to know her like she hadn't been able to so many years ago. It felt like an entire lifetime ago. And the girl Amelia had known and could have liked didn't exist anymore. But Song would give it a real try—at least then she could say she had.

Boredom carried Song from the manor. She'd grown restless after so long in a dress playing lady. So, that night, she locked herself in her room and waited as Ryk'r's footsteps retreated. She pulled on her pirate garb and slipped out her window to walk through the city with her revolver and eilfass dagger as protection.

Down by the docks, she entered a tavern seedy enough to not question someone keeping their hood up. She found a seat in a dark corner, put her back to the wall, and motioned for the barmaid to approach when she had a free moment. Once served with her glass of chilled whiskey, she leaned back to observe the ruffians she now preferred over aristocrats.

An individual with a long black coat with his hood raised caught her attention. After what that woman on one of the passenger vessels had said about copycats, she had to wonder if this man was one of them. She watched their card game for a while. The man in the hood seemed to be winning. When a chair opened at the table, she couldn't resist, and so sat down.

"What's the buy-in?" she asked, motioning for a refill on her drink.

"Fifty," the dealer said as he shuffled the deck.

She set her quoine in his hand and accepted the colored chips. "Hope you fellas are ready to fill your pockets with my quoine."

"What's your name, boy?" he asked, chuckling.

"Caleb," she said.

"Not *Song?*" a man asked on a laugh, eyeing the other hooded person at the table.

"Song don't own wearin' a hood," another player said.

Song stared at her cards, deciding to say nothing.

"No, but I don't like when others do it to impersonate me," the man in the hood said.

She snorted a long scoff through her nose. "And who are you that anyone would pretend to be you?"

"The *real* Song."

She released one quick *ha*, and shook her head.

"Don't believe me?"

"Not at all."

"Why not?"

She took a drink and let it rest on her tongue. Song smirked and tossed a few chips to the center of the table. After a few rounds of listening to this man, she leaned back. She decided to have a bit of fun and perhaps expose him as the fool he was.

"Well…*Song*… We got off on the wrong foot, didn't we? Allow me to buy you your favorite drink." She motioned the barmaid over. "Dear, could you bring my friend here a chilled whiskey?"

His head tilted to watch the woman leave to get the drink. "That's not my favorite drink."

Song smirked. "That's what Song always orders. Apparently, it's got sentimental value, right?"

"What game are you playing, boy?"

"Five-card draw, same as you." She set two chips into the pile. "Are you good at bluffing?"

"Are you?"

"Not really. Quite the fault of mine."

The barmaid set a drink in front of the man, and he eyed it.

Song handed the woman more quoine than the drink was worth, her fingertips lingering in the other's palm for a moment, and gave her a gentle smile. "Thank you."

The woman blushed and nodded, then returned to her work.

After folding that hand, Song leaned back in her chair. "So… Why don't you regale us with a story from your adventures, dear captain? Perhaps you could tell us about the men who trained you. They must be skilled, indeed."

He won the pot and scoffed at her. "You have an obsession, boy?"

"Just not a fan of liars. But, if you can prove you're Song…"

"Captain Krell trained me. He was a tough teacher. Didn't like me much, but that didn't matter."

"Where is dear old Captain Krell, hmm?"

"Retired."

Song's lips quirked to one side with an expression of regret. "If only."

She kept the man talking, telling lie after lie. If not for her training to be a proper, emotionless lady in public, she might've shot him right there. Instead, she listened, growing more furious by the second. When she finally won a hand, she'd had her fill of the man's tall tales.

"I'd like to buy out," she said, then leaned back to wait as the dealer counted up the chips and sent his assistant to a back room to fetch her paltry winnings—which amounted to an overall loss when the buy-in was figured in.

"Gonna leave without telling us some of your own adventures, lad?" the imposter said.

She took a deep, patient breath. "You wouldn't believe me if I tried." She stood and leaned close to whisper to him. "No one called him Captain Krell. It was always Dash. Until the day he died. And I was his favorite. He was like a father to me."

He scoffed. "Liar."

"Try me." She left, stopping to kiss the barmaid's knuckles and thank her for the drinks.

Once she stepped outside, she leaned against the wall to wait. A few minutes passed before the copycat came outside.

"Knew you couldn't resist," she said.

"Can you prove you're the real Song?" He shook his head when she said nothing. "That's what I thought. Piss off, lad."

"I don't have to prove who I am. But…if you insist." She turned and headed down the alley, knowing he would follow. "Men are such simple creatures, aren't you?"

"What?"

"You'll follow anyone into a dark, lonely alley so long as you think you'll get something out of it. So trusting. Typically, when you follow a lady into an alley, you expect to take advantage of her…"

"You're not making any sense."

She spun to look at him. "Aren't I? Isn't it clear to you now?"

"Is what clear?"

"That you followed a lady into an alley…but you're not going to get lucky." Her lips turned up in a slow grin. "But I am."

He stepped back, and she withdrew her revolver.

"Don't you dare think of escaping, you coward. You go into the tavern, sully my name with lies, and expect to walk away unscathed?" She tutted. "My dear, that's just not how Song works."

He pushed her hand away and threw a punch, but she back stepped. She kicked him in the knee before he could run away, then knocked him to the ground. She sat on his stomach as she withdrew her dagger and gripped his jaw.

"Careful, now, you don't want my hand to slip."

"I won't claim your name again!"

"I don't believe you."

"Mercy!"

She let out a long breath. "When are people going to realize I don't deal in mercy?"

Fighting against him, she pried open his mouth and sliced out his tongue. He moaned and held his mouth as she gripped his tongue, took his dagger, and stood.

"I would say if you do it again, I'll kill you. But something tells me you won't be claiming my name again." She laughed, kicked mud at him, then returned to the mouth of the alley.

Song strode into the tavern and in a swift motion pinned the tongue to the middle of the card table with the man's dagger. Without a word, she left.

After wiping the blood from her gloves and dagger, she walked home, feeling light. Something stirred in her chest—a fluttering excitement over the night's events. After so long in boredom, away from that sort of life, it thrilled her beyond belief to have gone to a tavern and even exacted some light torture on someone who deserved it.

People stared, but didn't make it too obvious. She could be anyone, especially since her ship had left port already. At the Gould manor, she waited near the gate until no eyes were on her, then she slipped inside and ran from bush to tree until she reached the shadows of the house. Song jumped onto a low balcony and crouched to remain in the shadows of the railing, then let herself in through the balcony door to Amelia's room.

Amelia lay sleeping on the bed, a needlepoint hoop still in one hand. It was a hobby she liked to spend her time on, and was getting quite good at. Mrs. Gould herself had taken to teaching her special stitch patterns as she sat with Amelia to share gossip about people Amelia didn't even know, but listened and reacted all the same. Seeing her there, so beautiful in her sleep, Song had the overwhelming urge to kiss her. She crossed the room and took away the hoop to set on the nightstand, then leaned over the woman.

It would be wrong to kiss her while she's sleeping.

She set her fingertips to the woman's cheek and stroked softly. Amelia's eyes fluttered open and Song smiled at her. But her eyes widened as she shoved backward and opened her mouth to scream. Song slid her hand over Amelia's mouth to muffle the noise, then ripped her hood down and yanked her mask off.

"It's just me! Just me, Amelia!"

Tears came to her eyes as she cried with relief. "You scared the life out of me, Song."

"I'm sorry. I just…you looked so lovely and I wanted to kiss you, but I didn't think I should when you were sleeping."

"You want to kiss me?" She swiped at a tear rolling past the corner of her lips.

"Well, I *did*, but now you're upset, and it doesn't feel right." She unbuttoned the collar of her coat and started unbuckling it.

"What are you doing?"

"Not traipsing through my parents' house as Song, that's for sure. Could I borrow one of your night dresses?"

Amelia didn't say anything for a moment as her tears subsided, and she sniffled. "Will you stay with me for a while? Just until I fall back asleep."

"Oh…sure."

Amelia scooted over in the bed to make room for her. Song removed her boots and coat, then settled in beside the woman. They sat in silence for a minute before Amelia leaned her head onto Song's shoulder.

"Why are you dressed like a pirate?"

"Because if Tsingsei Gould visited a seedy tavern in the red-light district, just to have a drink and play cards, it'd be the end of the world."

"Why did you go to a seedy tavern?"

"Because I'm bored. I have no idea how I survived my whole life trapped in this gilded prison, but I abhor it now."

Amelia giggled. "I rather like this gilded prison."

"You can have it," Song said.

"I'd rather have it with you here as well."

"Lucky you, I'm trapped."

The two talked for a little while longer, Song's desire to kiss Amelia never returning. Anytime she thought about it, the woman's terror at seeing a pirate over her entered Song's mind. It hurt a bit more than it should have—though she understood why Amelia had reacted that way. Perhaps it hurt because deep down, it's who Song would always be. The two could've been great together once. Maybe. But now one of them was terrified of what the other was. She resolved herself to still give it an honest try. Perhaps Amelia needed time to get used to her, and know that despite what she was, Song wouldn't hurt her.

She woke to Amelia shaking her. She hadn't realized she'd fallen asleep until that moment.

"It's morning!" Amelia hissed.

She grumbled and stared out the window at the fluffy pink and orange clouds in the grey sky. "So it is." She scrambled to wrap her coat, boots, and belt into a spare blanket, then yanked a nightdress over her clothes. "Right. I'll see you later."

She left in a hurry, rushing to her own room before anyone took a long look at her—at the trousers poking out at the bottom of the somewhat short nightdress, and the collar of her shirt jammed into the top and doing a terrible job staying tucked in all the way. Aside from a couple of maids in the hallway, who gave the black gloves on her hands a curious stare but said nothing, Song made it to her room unbothered. She hid her pirate clothing in the trunk, replaced the blanket over it, and headed for a bath to scrub away the smell of the tavern before starting her day.

THE HOUSE MANAGER FOUND SONG IN THE LIBRARY. HE STOOD over her and waited patiently as she finished reading a paragraph in the translation journal Sunshine had been working on for her.

She hadn't learned too much—few *aibhridh* pushed their limits, and the ones who had, had died from over-exertion. They tried to do big things too early in their Gifthood and it claimed their lives. The larger the action, the faster and more severe the cost became. It broke them and they died within minutes, hours, or days—always in agony.

One had fallen down dead while carving the temple into the side of the extinct volcano in Thìse. The temple's completion had taken more than a dozen Touched, each doing a small bit of work at a time, so no more of them died. Another had tried to rebuild her severed finger out of *kijæm*. She died after two days trying to maintain the digit as a workable, corporeal manifestation.

One of the more powerful women, whom they denounced as a heretic, had tried to raise the dead. She'd animated the body of her child who'd fallen into a river and drowned. The tome called him an unholy abomination puppeteered by his mother's power, with no real thoughts of his own and a body that continued to rot. After a day, the priestess died. Her *kijæm* evacuated the boy's body in a rush as though it didn't want to be there, and took the opportunity to flee the second she couldn't command them to remain. That at least set Song at ease that she herself had not died that day on the Dauntless and been raised by the *kijæm*.

Thus far, Song fancied herself to be the most powerful of the bunch, and it was still a mystery why she hadn't died. Perhaps she'd eased her body into the power, like submerging a little at a time into cold water to get used to it and not shock her system. Though, even her more powerful moments—like holding the Stars' Bounty together while pulling men out of the ocean and shoving another skyship off course all at once—far exceeded some which had claimed even advanced users. Never mind her also jolting men back to life afterward. It was no question—Song should have died that day. And even she didn't know why she hadn't.

What makes me so different from them? The drawing Bruce had made of her lying on the deck of the Dauntless flashed into her mind. *That can't be it. If anything, that should've made me weaker…shouldn't it?*

The house manager cleared his throat when she'd stared off at nothing in thought for several minutes. Her gaze snapped to him, and she gave an apologetic smile.

"Sorry, Leonard—" She studied the small crease which formed between his greying brows. "I seem to have either forgotten your name, or never paid attention to it in the first place. Which is it?"

"The latter," he said.

"You never corrected me."

"It's not my place to—"

"It's *absolutely* your place to correct someone who is disrespecting you in such a manner. You're a person, not furniture." She marked her place, set the book aside, and stood to hold her hand out to him. "Let's start again. Hello, my name is Tsingsei Gould."

A little smile toyed with his lips as he set his palm to hers to shake her hand. "A pleasure, Miss Gould. I am Leopold Kent."

"That's a Jashedarian surname, is it not?"

"It is, indeed. I'm a third generation Andalisian."

"Fascinating, truly. All right, Leopold, why have you come to fetch me? Is my mother demanding my attention on frivolous things again?"

He chuckled. "Sort of. She says there is a surprise for you in the parlor."

She let out an exasperated sigh and followed him from the room. When they reached the parlor, she stopped in her tracks. There, sitting on one couch, was Isabelle, a man she'd never seen before, and on the woman's lap was a small infant with bright blond hair.

"Next time tell my mother that this is an unpleasant sort of surprise, and to leave me out of it," Song muttered.

Leopold gave her a long look. "Noted, Miss."

Song didn't even force a smile onto her lips as she strode in and sat herself on the couch beside her mother. "To what do I owe the…whatever this is?"

"We wanted to welcome you home!" Isabelle said.

Song couldn't help but note she was rounder in the face than the last time she saw her. "You could've waited until the ball."

"Tsingsei, mind your manners. I thought you'd be happy to see your friend," Annie said.

She almost laughed, but instead clenched her jaw. Her eyebrows lowered as she met Isabelle's gaze. The audacity of this woman to have shown up in the Gould home after being the reason Song fled was something to almost be admired—if it didn't vex her so.

"We were all so worried when you disappeared," Isabelle said.

"I'm sure you were," Song said. She poured herself a cup of tea and held it up to blow on it, rather than looking at the woman.

She had an entire tirade waiting on the tip of her tongue. A lecture about her lecherous actions behind closed doors with a pirate who refused to touch her. She could reveal to the room that it had been Isabelle who had driven Song away after threatening to tell all the mothers that she'd kissed her. Now she wondered if Isabelle had told them at all.

"Where have you been all this time?" Isabelle asked.

"You haven't introduced me to your companion," Song stated, her tone bland.

"Oh, this is my husband, Wilfred. And my son Milton."

The husband in question had dark brown eyes and dark brown hair. The infant in her lap had bright blond hair and shining blue eyes…and looked nothing like the man.

"Strange," Song said.

"What?" Isabelle asked.

"You said *my* son, not *ours*."

A look of shame crossed the woman's face, but only for a moment. She forced a tight smile and made to reply, but Wilfred set his hand over hers.

"He is my son, though not by blood. I love him all the same," he said.

Song snorted. "Oh, the scandal. Do you even know who the father is?" She bit her lips together. "Sorry, I didn't mean it that way."

"Why don't we talk about something else?" Mrs. Gould said.

"Oh, yes, let's talk about the *weather* lest our minds be challenged by anything other than menial, bland chatter." She sipped her sea. "I would like to order some special teas imported from Armalinia. They have one that I've grown quite fond of."

"We can ask later."

"Oh, yes, and won't that be quite *thrilling*?" Song said in a mock of the excited tone Mrs. Gould often used.

"Your mother didn't mention where you've been this whole time," Isabelle tried again, forcing a smile.

Song studied the woman, her teacup hovering in front of her lips. She had half a mind to invoke her pirate name and see how Isabelle responded. In her periphery, though, her mother's fist tightened the smallest bit. Of course, the Goulds would want to keep a lid on the accuracy of the ballad, which told the tale of Tsingsei flying around the world with the infamous pirate captain and having a slave lover. Perhaps that's what Isabelle was so desperate to know.

"Traveling," Song said. "Seeing the world." She sipped her tea and set it back on the table.

"Have you heard that ballad about you?" And there was the confirmation.

"I have."

"How…true is it?"

Perhaps this was where she might find the worry over her heartache. Though, to be frank, she didn't want it from Isabelle. She would rather this woman had stayed away and at best sent a nice card for Song to burn without reading.

"It's very embellished," she said after a while. "The bard took plenty of creative liberties when he wrote it."

For the rest of the visit, Song pointedly avoided talking about herself and her travels. It became uncomfortable after a while, as the couple couldn't seem to take the hint that she wasn't interested in their visit. After some time, Song released a long sigh.

"I am so sorry, but I fear I must go lie down. This is just too much excitement for me."

"Oh, I was not aware you were ill, as well!" Isabelle said, already gathering her things to leave.

"Oh, yes, quite ill. It was a pleasure seeing you again, I think." Song escorted the guests to the door.

She shifted the baby in her arms. "We'll stop by again sometime, when you're feeling more yourself."

"Oh, no, there's no need to go out of your way."

"We'll see you at the ball, then."

"Yes, at the ball." Song tried not to make a face, then did so as the two exited the house when Leopold opened the front door for them.

Mrs. Gould leaned close as the door closed. "We don't talk about it, but everyone knows. Isabelle was raped by Captain Song. And that is his child."

She froze as fury blossomed within her chest. "She was *not!* And that is *not* Song's child!"

"You're questioning the word of a lady?"

"I'm not questioning anything. I am straight out calling her a liar. Song can't *father* children. And I have it on good authority that she practically *begged* him to touch her, but he refused."

"Maybe the captain is the one lying, Tsingsei. He's a pirate. They're all dishonest and dishonorable."

"Wrong. But what use is it arguing with you? You'd blame *me* if I'd the ability. After all, I'm less of a lady than Isabelle. And only a lady can tell the truth."

Mrs. Gould reached out to strike her, but Song's right hand shot up and grabbed the woman's wrist. Song glared down at her mother, then used her left hand to slap her. She stormed away, refusing to hear another word or even associate with her right then, lest she do worse than that.

Boredom had led Song into the night in her pirate garb before; this time it was frustration. Anger tumbled like an avalanche within her as she trekked through the city, searching for a tavern. She thought back on how Isabelle had been so eager to volunteer, and so ready for Song to do whatever a man would to her. Had the woman known she was with child and was looking for someone to blame it on? She had to be. But why lie?

She reached a tavern and pushed through the door, then paused to get her bearings. A card game was in session at the back of the room, and another hooded man sat at the table.

You'd think they'd have gotten the message. Then again, it could just be coincidence.

Song leaned to the bar. "A chilled whiskey, please."

Once she'd gotten her drink, she sauntered over to the table and dropped into the empty seat a little way down from the man. She gave the name Caleb, as before, but otherwise stayed quiet.

"So, Song, I was wondering if the rumors about the Gould girl were true," a man down the table from her said.

She opened her mouth to reply, but the other hooded figure spoke first.

"Which rumors?"

She pursed her lips at the blond goatee around his mouth. "Song doesn't have facial hair, you know. Just a boy, and all that."

"Funny thing about boys is that they grow up to be men." He didn't even look at her, keeping his eyes on his cards. "Now, what rumors?"

"Some people claim she's your lover."

Song bit her lips together to keep from announcing to the table how true it was, but only on lonelier nights when she had no other woman around to ease her desires.

"I wouldn't say *lover*, but…that is a dish I have tasted on many occasions," the imposter said.

She sneered at the very idea of it. Her left hand made a fist as her right didn't move, holding the cards steady as though nothing were amiss. At least the *kijæm* could keep its cool for her.

"What about the slave?" another man asked. "I heard there was a slave in there somewhere."

"He wasn't a slave," Song snapped.

"What do you know of it?" another man asked.

"You wouldn't believe me if I told you."

Now the imposter looked at her. A funny sort of trepidatious smile flickered over his lips a few times. "Do we have a copycat on our hands? If so, you're not a very good one, are you?"

"And you think simply raising a hood over your head makes you a good one?" she challenged.

"Are you aware of what happened to that other copycat?" he asked, his tone a threat which didn't even make her blink.

"I'm well aware." She dropped her cards face up and sighed at her losing hand she'd held onto for far too long.

"Song wins again," the dealer said, interrupting the tension.

The other men at the table grumbled and leaned back in their chairs.

The imposter sorted the new chips into the stacks in front of him. "Did you expect anything less of me?"

"Funny, because Captain Song is notoriously shite at cards," she said, as a new round flitted across the table to the players.

The imposter laughed. "You're one to talk! You haven't won a single hand!"

She stared at yet another abysmal lineup in her fingers. "Imagine that."

She listened to him brag for a while as she lost and folded hands, and he won more. The one thing she had to hand these impersonating fools was that they could weave a decent tall tale. If only they could redirect their energies to something more productive, they wouldn't have targets painted on their tongues.

After another hour of Song biting her own tongue and growing more furious by the minute, the imposter finished his drink, stretched, and cashed out. While the dealer's assistant counted up his winnings and disappeared into a room behind the bar, the imposter stood to go to the lavatory—the first one Song had ever seen *inside* a tavern, rather than forcing patrons into outhouses or using the alley outside. Truly, the country was advancing at a rate she hadn't been part of while trawling the skies for treasures. New conveniences meant little to a pirate, though she still found them intriguing.

She finished her drink and followed him. Song leaned on the closed door when she realized there was no lock on it. She waited, staring at his back as he used the long trough to relieve himself. If she'd a curious mind, she would look at the workings and investigate the lavatory, perhaps see if the two enclosures on one side were set up for women. As it was, though, she didn't care. She only cared about the man, now packing himself back into his trousers.

"What is it about Captain Song that makes liars like you claim the name?" she asked.

The imposter spun around to stare at her. "What makes you think I'm a liar?"

"I don't *think*. I *know*. And I would love to hear your sad excuse for claiming my name."

"Now who's the liar?"

She took a few steps forward. "Do you know your letters?"

"Aye," he said, slow and curious.

Song moved the flap of her coat and tucked it behind her revolver. She raised the weapon to display the initials on the butt of the handle. He didn't move, but his breath caught and resumed with a frightened waver, though his face betrayed nothing.

"Don't worry, I'm not going to shoot you." A slow grin spread across her lips as she holstered the weapon. "You know what happened to the last copycat." She withdrew her eilfass tusk dagger and gripped it in a fist.

They stared each other down for a minute before he withdrew his own dagger. He made the first move, striding forward to stab at her. She ducked and punched him in the gut. They swung at each other, neither able to meet their steel with flesh.

He pinned her arm against the wall, and she fell to her knees at the last second to avoid taking his blade to her shoulder. She dropped her dagger, and it tumbled behind him. Now unarmed, her right arm reached out to grab the blade of his weapon and twist at the wrist to yank it from his grasp. She switched hands, but the man knocked the weapon from her left.

They exchanged blows with their fists until he ducked, wrapped his arms around her waist, and rammed his shoulder into her gut as he slammed her against the door so hard it caused her back to ache, and the door to splinter, break off its hinges, and fall into the room with the two crashing down atop it.

Patrons skittered away from the fighting pair. Song rolled over the top of him. She raised her right arm and hit him hard enough to knock him unconscious with the single blow.

She released an exasperated breath and reached back to find his dagger in the doorway. Song leaned forward to pry open his mouth and start slicing through his tongue. He woke halfway through, and cried out, flailing beneath her.

"Stop squirming or I'll bollocks it up!" she shouted.

He, of course, did not stop. She gave up while a sliver of flesh still attached his tongue to his jaw. Song reached into his mouth with her right hand, gripped the muscle, and ripped it out the rest of the way. She threw it onto the door beside them and stabbed his dagger through it.

Song ignored his moaning and crying as she stood and rinsed her gloved hands in the basin in the lavatory, retrieved her tusk dagger, and strode around him. All eyes followed her in a terrified silence as she walked to the dealer's assistant at the bar.

"Give me my winnings."

"Y-your…?" he said.

She motioned at the sack clutched in his fists. "Those are Song's winnings, if I'm not mistaken. So, hand them over."

Rather than argue, he shoved the quoine into her hands. She opened the sack and took out a handful to set on the bar top.

"For the door and the mess. Next time, I'll try not to destroy anything."

"Y-you plan on returning?" the barkeep said.

She set three quoine before the barmaid and gave her a charming smile. "I rather like it here."

The woman blushed as her face twisted in discomfort. On one hand, as a woman, she understood the barmaid's discomfort. But on another, she knew that discomfort was also because the world had tarnished her name. Lies from women like Isabelle had put the name Song in the same line as a rapist. Nothing made her more furious and sick to her stomach than that vile accusation sticking to her as it had.

As she strode from the tavern, an idea formed in her mind. It was insane, perhaps. Maybe a bit reprehensible. But if she was being honest, she didn't care. She would get the record set straight about her dealings with ladies, no matter what questionable actions it took.

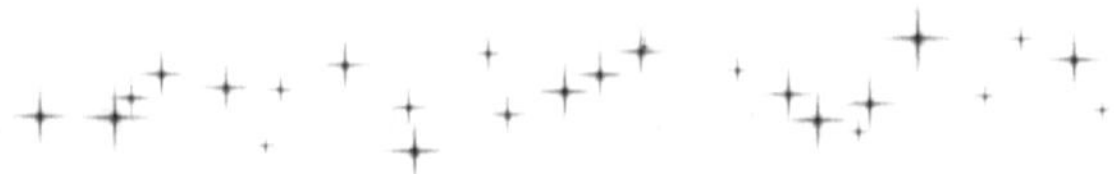

A WEEK AND ONE MORE TORTURED COPYCAT LATER, SONG STOOD outside a posh two-story. She'd hoped the imposter would distract her from the terrible idea she'd had. It had fluttered in and out of her mind as she questioned the morality of her plan, and whether erasing the accusations was worth it. She'd hoped she could brush off the lie. But nothing had worked, and so here she was with a vicious plan sprouted from the seed of ire.

Isabelle's home wasn't far from her own. Three blocks, to be exact, and about one-sixth the size. A reasonable home for a young couple coasting through life on their parents' quoine. Unfortunately for them, they didn't have a gate or a high wall like the Gould estate. Doubly unfortunate was the trellis of crawling vines against the side of the house, growing upward from the garden. It would be a stretch to reach the nearby window, but Song supposed she could do it.

She glanced around to ensure no one was looking, and—keeping to the shadow cast over the white two-story house by its taller neighbor—rushed to the trellis and scrambled up. The room behind the window was dark now, but she'd seen Isabelle enter earlier, carrying her little bundle of joy.

Song leaned over, gripping the sill to peek inside. There was his crib. Isabelle had left the door open a crack, so Song would have to be quiet. She removed her right glove, flicked out the sharp fingertips, and used them to pry the window open.

"Always lock your windows, silly girl," she muttered as it slid upward. "Even on the second floor. Wouldn't want a pirate to drop out of the sky and let herself in, now, would you?"

She climbed up a little farther, stretched out her leg to set her boot on the windowsill, and gripped the upper sill with her right hand. Song lowered herself in, listening for creaking floorboards. Once inside the room, she looked around.

She has to have one of those cloth things all mothers stick their little babies in to keep them close, Song thought.

And there it was, hanging on the wall like a large scarf with no ends. Song crossed the room one slow, cautious step at a time, removing her weight from a board when it creaked even the slightest bit. She tested floorboards ahead, choosing her steps with care. She walked on the balls of her feet, not letting her heels touch the hard floor. Song grabbed the sling and wrapped it over her shoulders, then made her way back to the sleeping infant.

Luck was on her side—the boy didn't wake as she settled him into the sling. She pulled the folded letter from her hip pouch and set it inside the crib, North Star stamped into the sealing wax facing up. She made her way back across the room just as slow and careful as before.

Getting out the window with the child on her chest was not as easy as she'd expected. She stretched and wriggled, before finally getting a grip on the trellis and moving over. She used the sharp fingertips to close the window again, then climbed down.

Song kept to the shadows, checking the streets before crossing them to make her way down alleyways. She reached her home and stared at it from across the street—she hadn't thought this far ahead. Normally she climbed into her bedroom window, but such a jump with a bundle that could wake up at the jostling was impossible.

With a huff of annoyance aimed at herself, she crossed the street and circled the house to the kitchen entrance. Just her luck that it was unlocked. She would have to make sure it was never that way in the future. Even gated walls couldn't protect them from pirates who dropped out of the sky. Though, to be fair, she was the only pirate bold enough to pull such antics.

She made it to her room undiscovered, thankful that she'd waited until such a late hour. She set the boy on her bed and changed into a nightdress and robe with her white gloves on. Afterward, she took Milton and traveled through the house to the servants' quarters. She found the room she knew to belong to Mabel and her husband, Jordan. The door opened after one knock, and Mabel stood in the doorway with her newborn at her breast.

"Miss Gould! What brings you here so late? Whose child is that?"

Song smiled. "I'm sorry to disturb you, but a dear friend fell ill and asked if I could watch her baby for a while. I don't know the first thing about caring for children, so I was wondering if you'd be willing to act as a wet nurse for him? Of course, I'll increase your pay for the month."

Mabel directed a motherly smile down at the blond boy. "Of course I would. Come in. Harriet isn't in the crib just yet, so he can stay there."

"What's going on?" her husband asked from the bed, still half asleep.

"We're watching another baby, dear. Go back to sleep."

"Very good, darling."

"Don't tell my parents of this," Song said. "You know how my mother can be."

Mabel nodded. "Of course."

She set the baby in the crib and gave Mabel a kiss on the cheek. "Thank you so much for this. Truly."

"I couldn't live with myself if a baby had to starve when I could help. Bless you for taking him in."

She smiled. "What kind of friend would I be if I didn't?"

Twenty-Four

D READFUL!" Mrs. Gould said, scanning over the news-paper again. "We should invite Isabelle and her husband over to comfort her."

Song sipped her tea, then pursed her lips. "I'm sure she'd rather stay home and take care of that ransom note." She looked over the headline, which had taken the first line of the letter she'd left behind.

A Boy Needs His Father

Of course, they wouldn't print the whole letter. What she'd written was:

'A boy needs his father in his life. I'll take good care of my son. Unless there is a secret you're not sharing with everyone. Perhaps it's time to tell the truth. Until then, he's mine.'

Song took the paper when her mother set it down. She scanned over it, reading the interview with a frantic Isabelle Clarksen, in which she begged for the return of her son. The woman had the perfect opportunity to tell the truth right there; she had the city's attention. And yet she'd chosen to keep it to herself. She would rather the world believed she was the mother to Captain Song's bastard child than admit that it was the bastard of someone else. What could possibly be worse than being raped by a pirate?

"What was that you said about the child not being Caleb Song's? Such a vile man."

"Well, if it is Song's child, then I don't see why everyone is so bothered. Milton is with his father. Isn't it admirable that he'd take such an interest in his son?" Song asked. "Other fathers would rather walk out and pretend they'd never even spread seed."

"It's not admirable!" Annie gasped. "How has such a villain caught you in his dastardly web?"

"Song isn't a villain, Mother. Just a pirate with a broken heart and a disdain for liars."

"You traveled with him, did you not? Could you go to him and reason with him?"

"He's being a good father! Why would I reason with him?"

"Kidnapping a child from his mother is not being a good father," her mother said.

Song took a patient sip of her tea and sighed. "And I think lying about a child's parentage to sully the name of another—no matter the quality of that person's character—isn't being a good mother."

"Tsingsei, how dare you pass judgment—"

"How would you feel if you were Milton? Growing up being told you're a product of rape and your father is the most infamous pirate in the world? Do you really think that her lie to spare her own secret will help that child later in life?

Do you think he'll be happy to have grown up as Captain Song's bastard? No! People are cruel and will judge him for it, as though it was his choice. Nothing could be worse for that child than a life with that terrible of an origin. And since I know for a fact it's not true, I choose to side with the child, and Captain Song, who is the only person in all of this interested in the truth for the sake of the child."

Mrs. Gould straightened. "And how would you know what he's thinking? You said he left port after you arrived."

"I said Song's *ship* left." When her mother said nothing for several minutes, she said, "Do we have anything exciting on the agenda today? Or can I go entertain myself with more interesting subjects?" She waited another minute before standing. "All right, then. I'll see you at lunch or dinner."

"How can you be so cruel to your friend?" she asked as Song reached the door.

"Isabelle was never my friend. In fact, she's been my enemy since we met. But you never cared about what I thought before, so why would you care that she's the reason I ran away in the first place? Well, that and your little suitor ultimatum. I would rather be friends with a pirate, no matter how infamous, than aristocratic wretches." Song swept from the room, a scowl on her face.

She didn't want to wait until nightfall to visit the tavern and drink away her frustrations or take care of an imposter, but she had to. Song paced the halls, too impatient and irritated to sit and read. She would enter her room, lift one of her many books she'd been studying, open it, and immediately close the book to resume stomping through the hallways.

Part of her nagged to return the child now, but a stronger part insisted she remain patient and stick to her plan. It had only been a few hours. The child was safe, and all Isabelle had to do was tell the truth. No mother would wait longer than a day to do what was demanded of her in order to get her child back, Song was sure of it. If it had been her, she'd have spilled her secrets at the top of her lungs out of the sheer stupid hope the kidnapper was near enough to hear.

"You've passed my room about ten times," Amelia said from her doorway.

"Sorry. I'm a bit restless."

Amelia glanced at Ryk'r, who stood at his usual meter behind Song. He gave her a gentle smile, but didn't move.

"Could I walk a bit with you? I'm quite bored."

Song glanced at the afternoon sun and released a weary sigh. "Sure." She held out her arm so the woman could lean on it.

They walked in silence, Amelia taking in sights she hadn't yet seen of the house. Down the hallway leading to her father's office, they stopped as Amelia stared at an old painting of three people—a woman and two men. One man had dark brown hair, and the woman's was black. Those two sat side-by-side on a small bench. The third man with light blond hair stood between the two, hands on their shoulders. The woman's skin was a deep golden tan. Her eyes were narrow and black, while the man's beside her were bright blue, and the one standing had brown eyes.

The woman had a strong jaw, and features one might consider more masculine—features Song recognized in herself and had always thought made her ugly. But this woman was beautiful. Her hair had been twisted into intricate braids with little gem-encrusted metal tubes encircling them. Her gown was white with a thick fur edge encircling her shoulders.

"Who is that?" Amelia asked.

"My great-great-grandparents, and…I'm not sure." She stared up at the blond man she'd never asked about, half recognizing his features, but unable to place them.

"She kind of looks like you. In the face shape…and the mouth."

She nodded and smiled. "She's my great-great-grand-mother. I was named after her."

Song had passed this painting thousands of times in her life. She'd known one was Tsingsei, and the man on the bench was her husband Benson. Everyone in the world knew who Benson was, of course. The brat she'd been had never bothered to ask who the second man was, though.

"Ladies," her father said, stopping to acknowledge the two before he passed.

"Welcome home, Daddy." Song set a kiss on his cheek.

"Senator Gould," Amelia said.

Elroy smiled up at the painting the two had been looking at. "Ah, are you acquainting Miss Sterling with our ancestors?"

"Somewhat," Song said. "I can't seem to recall ever learning who the third man is."

He met Amelia's gaze to ensure she knew he was talking to her. "World renown cartographer Benson Harold Gould the Second, his co-explorer Carlisle Weston, and…" His eyes settled on his daughter, a little smile crinkled at the corner. "Tsingsei Luⁿyâk-Gould. The three of them were…"

he glanced at Amelia and paused, as though thinking up a new word for her benefit, "…inseparable."

She stared at her namesake. Despite Song looking so much like her father, his eyes had always been a touch narrower than hers, and his skin a shade darker. She'd always thought herself and some of her cousins so oddly tan compared to everyone else. She'd always known it was because of her great-great-grandmother, but had no idea of the woman's home country. The features she possessed were unlike any she had encountered in her travels.

"Where was she from?" Song asked, when her own mind didn't even recognize the odd sound of the woman's second name enough to place it into a country she knew of.

"She called it Hrănchu—Home. It's somewhere to the north of Andalise."

"The northern lands," she said with a sigh. "I was going to explore there."

Elroy stared at her. "With Captain Song?"

She nodded. "Yes. We thought there was nothing there."

"As Benson and Carlisle intended. They burned their maps and told the world it was a wasteland. All because she asked them to, and Benson loved her enough to do it."

"Our navigator was going to map it out, and we were going to name it after him. I thought it was absolutely frigid up there."

He chuckled. "It is."

"But people live there?"

"They do."

"How do you know?"

"Because she wrote everything down in Common so she might pass the stories through our family. Unfortunately, she did not also pass down her native language, just a few words here and there."

"Andalise isn't interested in acquiring other languages, they'd rather have Common be the world language."

Elroy held up a finger. "That was Jashedar, my dear. Andalise was just the first to adopt it fully…with a few pronunciation differences, of course. Really, did your tutors sleep on the job?"

"You act like I was even listening." Song gave him a wry smile. "Can I read her book?"

He smiled as though he'd never been so proud. "Of course. Let me fetch it for you." He disappeared into his office and returned with an old tome, the spine worn so the cloth frayed at the edge of the hinges. "Please be careful. It's irreplaceable."

"Of course!" She kissed his cheek and held the journal close to her chest. "Thank you so much. I'll see you at dinner?"

"Should be soon. I must take care of a few things before then. Excuse me, ladies."

"Thank you, Senator Gould!" Amelia said, as he walked away. She released a long breath. "I think I'd like to sit down again."

"I'll walk you back." She tucked the book in one arm and held the other out for the woman.

Once Amelia settled back into the bed, Song took her leave and wandered to her room as slowly as she could, as though taking longer to do everything might make time pass that much faster. She sat in her room, looking over the journal of her great-great-grandmother. The book began with the story of how she, Benson, and Carlisle met while he and a team were exploring the northern land. Her great-great-grandmother and a few others from Hrănchu—Song couldn't be sure if it was the name of the village, or the name of the continent—had worked with the men, teaching them about the culture. Tsingsei Lǔnyâk-Gould used those moments to write it down, as though also teaching the reader the same lesson.

When dinnertime came, annoyance caused her brow to furrow into a scowl over the disruption in her reading, but she made her way there, anyway. It was still light out, which peeved her twice over. She escorted Amelia to and from dinner, as well.

After dinner, to while away even more time, she visited the servants' quarters on the far side of the house and knocked on the door with a crying baby on the other side. Mabel opened it, looking frazzled and tired.

"Is everything all right?" Song asked.

"He's upset about being around strangers. It's normal for infants. Here." She handed the boy to Song as she shut her inside the room.

Milton stared at her, his index finger jammed into his mouth as he cried over it, sending drool across his chubby hand. Song gritted her teeth and leaned away, but he leaned forward, setting his head to her shoulder. His cries died down to a whimpering pout.

"Oh, thank everything holy. You're not a stranger to him."

"I met him *once*," she said.

"Then perhaps you have a motherly touch?" She set about changing the cloth diaper on her daughter.

"You take that back right now."

Mabel laughed. "Still don't like children?"

"Never will."

"When you have one of your own, it's different. You don't mind the drool when it's *your* baby's drool."

Song sneered. "I will never have one of my own. You just solidified that fact by insisting I won't mind someone *drooling* on me." She retrieved a burping cloth from the dresser top and placed it on her shoulder to catch said spit. "Will he be all right here a bit longer?"

"He'll be upset, but yes. Hopefully, your friend isn't ill for too long."

Song smiled and nodded. "One can only hope."

She stayed with Mabel for a little longer, only because the woman asked her to keep the boy calm while she did some tidying. When Song escaped, it was dark out, and now was her opportunity to leave the mansion in search of some sort of entertainment.

Twenty-Five

T HE NIGHT WAS YOUNG, AND PEOPLE STILL MOVED ABOUT, completing their business for the day. City employees strode down the streets holding long poles with a hooded flame at one end. They stopped at each gas streetlamp to ignite it before moving to the next. Song passed one as the lamp overhead came to life with a sudden *whoosh* and a flicker.

She returned to the tavern where the beautiful barmaid worked, making her way through alleys and slipping inside without incident. Song didn't go unnoticed, but no one bothered her. There were no imposters, to her dismay. She could use the distraction. Perhaps her messages were finally getting across, or maybe they'd heard about the stolen baby and didn't want the blame to fall on their heads.

The barmaid approached her table. "What'll you have, sir?"

Song smiled. "What's your favorite?"

"I'm a fan of peppermint gin."

"Oh, that sounds lovely. Could I buy you one when you get off work?"

"I have a suitor, sir."

Song chuckled. She wasn't sure if it was true, since hiding behind a man—real or fake—was usually the only sure way to stop men from making overtures. Either way, she could take the hint. "I was only wanting to buy you a drink, not asking for a kiss. Does this man have any idea how lucky he is?"

She blushed, but remained calm. "One peppermint gin, then?"

"All business. Yes, please."

Once she had her drink, after letting the barmaid go about her business without the idle chatter, Song sat back and studied the room. The card game was going, and on a short stage at one end of the tavern, someone played a piano. She wished to play with Ponce and Sunshine again, with Qiicho setting up the music box for them. What she wouldn't give to go back to that simpler time. After a while, the liquor urged her to her feet and to the piano. She set two quoine on top and waited for the man to look up at her.

"Mind if I have a go?" she asked.

He took the quoine and stood. "One song."

"All I wanted."

Once she'd settled and positioned the bench where it was most comfortable for her, she realized the room had gone silent. No one said a word, no coughs or boot scuffs. Even the cards and chips were still and the liquors weren't being poured. She'd never performed this for anyone but her crew. Without Ponce and Sunshine and the music box, it might not have the same effect. She second guessed playing it at all. But she was already there, and everyone was waiting with bated breath for what Captain Song would play.

She started high with the music box tune, then did her best to play both the violin part and the low notes. She reached the part she knew best. Her fingers flew across the keys in a fury as anger pulsed inside her over having even made this song. Blame and guilt roiled through her and burned her heart.

Qiicho, Leslie, Pinch, Dashaelan, Altain, Alton, Doctor, Bones, Lucy, Blades, Leftie, Powder, McKay, Knuckles, Paddy, Bishop, Oliver, and Gerti.

They were all dead because of her. If she'd just done what was expected of her, instead of running away, all of them would be alive now. It was all her fault. And she pounded that fact into the keys one frantic note at a time until she reached the end.

No one clapped. All eyes stared at her, captivated. It was as though they were holding their breath in anticipation. She stood and moved aside for the pianist.

"What song is that?" he asked.

"I call it Song's Storm."

"It's breathtaking. You're truly a wonder on the piano, sir."

"As are you." She set two more quoine on the piano for him. "Play something a bit more lively."

In the back of the room by the bar, one person sprang to life, clapping. The barmaid, smiling wide as she stared at Song. A few others joined the applause as Song returned to her seat. She'd just gotten there when glass crashed to the floor.

She whipped around to find the barmaid beside a table, a man's hand out near her rear, though it was clear she'd dropped her tray and jumped away. The man grabbed her skirt to keep her from escaping. Song sneered at an action even she had regrettably done while drunk. It was rude at best. As Song strode over, he dragged the woman onto his lap.

Song gripped him by the hair and yanked his head backward. "Let her go. Now."

The man's arms opened so the barmaid could escape.

"Now apologize."

"Piss off."

Song threw him forward out of the chair and shoved his cheek into the broken glass. "*Apologize!*"

"I'm sorry, *I'm sorry!*"

"Miss, do you accept his apology?" she asked.

The barmaid nodded after taking a moment to calm down. "Yes."

Song released him and rolled him over, then tore his purse from his belt. She handed the whole thing to the barmaid. She strode away from the scene, leaving the woman standing there dumbfounded, and the man holding a quivering hand over his cheek, but not touching it due to the glass stuck into his flesh.

Song sat and returned to her drink, sipping it as she studied the scene. The card game resumed along with the music, as though they'd waited for her to finish her outburst. It didn't take long for the man's comrades to haul him out to find a doctor. The barmaid had disappeared into another room. The barkeep swept up the glass and mopped the blood and alcohol away.

Something didn't sit right with her, though—a nagging feeling in her mind that the man or his friends weren't finished with either Song or the woman. She waited for hours, savoring her drink to avoid getting drunk. Sometimes her mind would insist she was being paranoid. But on the off chance she wasn't, she remained there, watching the door and the barmaid.

Another part of her wondered why no one had gone to the authorities to report her mere presence, let alone what she'd done to the man. Were they afraid? Or did they have bounties of their own?

When the barmaid's shift ended, Song paid her tab and followed. She stayed a ways behind the woman, not wanting to frighten her—though, if Song was in her position and noticed the tail, it wouldn't matter how far behind the person was from her, she would have panicked.

Song wondered if maybe she should have offered to walk the woman home. That thought led to her utter annoyance that she hadn't once asked her name. She looked like a Moreen, if Song had to guess.

As she contemplated jogging up to probably-not-Moreen and talking to her like a normal person, a figure entered her line of sight, following the woman much closer. Then another. The third had a bandage on his face.

Bloody predictable idiots.

Song picked up her pace, taking long strides to catch up to the men. The barmaid turned to travel down an alleyway, the men followed, and Song entered right after. The woman glanced behind, then spun back around and walked faster.

"No need to be scared," one man said. "We won't hurt you."

Song reached into her collar to unbutton her long glove and shove it into a pouch. Her fingertips popped open, flicked out the sharp cones, then clattered shut again, like cards shuffling. One man turned at the sound.

"Looks like the wench brought the pirate with her."

The barmaid spun around, eyes wide and frightened.

"She's ours. Piss off," another man said.

"Men like you are so busy stalking women, you never realize when you're the one being stalked," Song said. "Leave now and you may live."

"And what are you goin' to do if we don't? There's three of us and one of you."

Song stared down at her metal hand as though inspecting her fingertips. "Are you with me?" she whispered to the dormant *kijæm*. Her vision shifted to that strange, colorful world; three heartbeats echoed in her mind. She had her answer. "You're right," she grinned and looked up at the men, who shifted in uncertainty at the glowing red eyes staring at them from beneath the black hood, "you're completely outnumbered."

She surged forward, sights on the one in the center. This time she would save the bandaged man for last, so he could watch her tear his friends to shreds. They'd had time to step back a pace or two before she was upon them. She rammed her hand—fingers forward like five tiny spears and joints glowing red—into the man's face.

He screamed high and shrill in agony. One of his eyes popped beneath her ring finger as his nose shattered against her palm. She curled her fingers. The tips scraped against bone, and tore backward, ripping skin and muscle from tendons. The sharp fingertips shredded his cheek open. Once her hand was free, she shook the flesh from her fingers, extended the little blade from her palm, and rammed it into his temple. He fell to the ground, silent.

Her sights set on the man to the left as the two darted away. She launched forward, sprinting after them. For a moment she wanted her *kijæm* back, so she could send it after them to do the work for her. However, she couldn't ignore the rush of excitement that made her heart flutter over the hunt.

Song launched up a stack of crates and brought her fist down on the man's head. He fell to the ground under her. Her arm lit red, propelling it forward. His skull gave way, and her fist met cobblestones.

She shoved to her feet to catch the last one. A shoe soared past Song's shoulder and hit the man in the back, causing him to stumble. Song dove on him and turned him over. She straddled him and lifted him by the collar.

"Mercy!" he shouted.

"I'm growing quite tired of that word."

"Please! I have children!"

She chuckled low in her throat. "Correction: you've got orphans."

She punched across his temple. His skull caved the slightest bit as his neck snapped and sent his empty gaze to the cobblestones behind him.

She released a long breath as her vision returned to normal. Part of her was sad it had been so easy. She wanted someone who would fight back. A worthy opponent. But none of these copycats or back alley filth were trained in anything but cowardice.

Song stood and withdrew her handkerchief to clean her hand—popping out the blade to get as much as she could, though she knew it would have to be opened up for a deep cleaning by Ponce. She stopped over the shoe in a dirty puddle, then looked at the woman cowering in a doorway.

"Nice shot."

"Please don't hurt me."

Song chuckled. "Is that why you helped me? Because you thought I wouldn't hurt you out of gratitude?" She held the bloody cloth in her right fist and lifted the shoe in her left. She stood over the woman, who cowered further into herself. "I know it seems suspicious, but I was following you home as an escort, not as a predator."

"Why didn't you just escort me like a gentleman?" she demanded, voice shaking, though she seemed to have relaxed a little.

"Would you have allowed me to?"

"No."

"There, see? Saved us an unnecessary conversation, because I would've followed you, anyway."

She accepted the shoe back and yanked it on. "But why?"

"You're too pretty to be a tavern wench. I had a bad feeling. And to be honest, I've been quite bored lately. This was… acceptable, as far as excitement goes." She held out her hand, and the woman paused to think before accepting it.

"You're supposed to be a reprobate."

Song scoffed and positioned herself to block the woman's view of the corpse as they passed it. "I'm not a reprobate."

"You can't think you're virtuous."

"Not at all. I'm just like everyone else: capable of doing good deeds and bad ones. Is what I did just now a good deed or a bad one?"

"I'd say it's a good one."

"Ah, but is killing someone good?"

"Well, no. But saving me was."

"What do you suppose that makes me, then?"

The woman accepted her extended elbow. "You do the right thing in the wrong ways, I suppose."

"Or I do the wrong thing for the right reasons. Being honest, I didn't need the excuse of protecting you. I just wanted a decent fight. It's their fault they took it so far, really."

She stared at the side of Song's hood, but said nothing.

"Let's get you home to your family and your beloved," Song said.

"I lied," she blurted. "I'm not spoken for. I just…you're Captain Song!"

"You were afraid I'd continue to flirt with you?" Song chuckled as the woman nodded. "I know how to take no as an answer. All you had to do was ask. I don't blame you, though, not in this city. Truth be told, it was all empty flirting, anyway. It's rare that I find a woman interested in someone like me."

"You mean a pirate who regularly assaults women?"

"I do not! I have never once taken more than a kiss without asking first."

"Are you going to kiss me, then?"

"Only if you want me to. I don't steal kisses anymore."

The woman gave her a teasing smile, and turned to continue walking.

"What's your name, by the way?" Song asked.

"Olivia."

"I like that."

Olivia blushed in the flickering light of a gas streetlamp.

"You can stop acting meek, you know."

She stared at the sidewalk. "I've no idea what you mean."

"You clapped when no one else dared so much as shuffle a card. You threw your shoe at a man after I slaughtered two in front of you. And you took my hand after seeing the literal blood on them. Your blush is a lie for the sake of a prudish world, because it's what's expected of women."

"And what would you know of what's expected of women?" Olivia asked.

"More than you dare to dream."

She guided Song up a short flight of stairs to a narrow brownstone. Song hadn't expected this, as it would imply some amount of wealth, and yet the woman worked in a tavern in the red-light district. It wasn't any of her business, though, so she didn't ask. Olivia fiddled with her key after pulling it from her handbag.

"Thank you for walking me home."

"You're welcome. Should I hang around the tavern to walk you home every night?" Song asked.

"If I said yes?"

"Then I'll be there. Goodnight, Olivia." She left her on the steps, wishing it could be that easy for her to woo a woman. But more times than not, once her hood came down, none of these charmed ladies would be interested.

Her thoughts drifted back to Lyella, and how her shallow desire to have a princess of her own had brought them together. If only she could visit her now, if for nothing more than to cure some frustrations and imprint the smell of the sultania's hair into her memories.

Twenty-Six

FOR THE NEXT FEW DAYS, SONG RETURNED TO THE TAVERN. She would play her song, have a drink and maybe join a few rounds of cards. Afterward, she walked Olivia home. Every time she did, the woman would hesitate before going inside, and Song guessed she wanted a kiss from the pirate captain. But Olivia didn't want a kiss from a woman, and so Song would turn and leave.

One night, though, she found an imposter at her table. She stopped at the bar and Olivia leaned to her.

"He insisted on sitting there," she said.

"Has he given a name?"

"No. But I can imagine which he'll give."

Song sat across the room from the man, though he knew she was there. She sipped a watered-down rum to keep her head clear. He stayed another half an hour before paying his tab and leaving.

Song paid hers and set a hand on Olivia's wrist. "I'll be back to walk you home."

She smiled. "I won't wait up, but I look forward to it."

Song followed the man at a slight distance to a large inn four blocks from the tavern. He disappeared inside, and she rushed to catch up. She spotted his coat tails retreating up the stairs and gave chase. She shoved the toe of her boot into the door as he shut it, then forced it back open.

"Predictable," he said, then launched at her.

"I could say the same thing." She wrestled against him, then hit him with her metal hand, knocking him unconscious.

She tied him to the chair and started cutting out his tongue. He woke with a scream as she cut away the last bit. Song sneered at the man. This time, his tongue wasn't enough; the message didn't seem to be getting across with something so simple. She bent over him and used one of her sharp fingertips to carve LIAR into his forehead. She wiped the metal cone clean on his shirt, then it flicked back into the fingertip.

"Maybe you will finally serve as a warning to all the others stupid enough to claim to be me," she said.

Song untied him and let him fall forward to cup his face in his hands and moan in agony. She took his dagger and shoved it through his tongue like a gruesome decoration on the inn room door. Something clattered from his pocket onto the floor. She stepped back inside and stooped to lift a metal thing and hold it up to the light. Her eyes rounded. A police badge. She stared down at the man.

What was an officer doing dressed as me?

After wiping her hands, she left. She'd only gone a few steps out the door of the inn when the shout stopped her.

"Caleb Song! Stop right there and raise your hands in the air!"

She blinked ahead of her on the street, where citizens stood at a distance, eyeing her with abject terror on their faces. Song turned toward the voice to find five policemen with firearms trained on her—two rifles and three revolvers. Behind them was a horse drawn wagon with solid walls, and a sturdy roof; metal bars covered the empty windows.

That's what an officer was doing dressed as me.

"Officers!" she called, a charming smile spread across her lips. "This is all just a misunderstanding! The man you want is upstairs."

"Raise your hands!" another shouted.

She lifted her hands over her head. "How did you know I'd be here?"

"Because you can't resist a copycat," a man in a long tan coat with his collar raised to the chill of the night said as he walked around the front of the horses. "That's the thing about your kind: you're predictable."

"And who are you?"

"Detective Inspector Zion Foggerty."

Song snorted, then barked a laugh.

"Something funny?"

"I am amazed you said that name with a straight face. Your parents must have *hated* you. Why else would they name you *Zion*?"

"Where is the Clarksen infant?" he asked, unamused.

"I haven't the *foggertiest* idea."

His brow lowered as she witnessed him lose the last of what little patience he had. "Arrest him already. We'll get the answers through other means."

He patted the shoulder of an officer, who shuffled forward, revolver trained on her and sweat dripping down his face. He hesitated every other step, and the closer he got, the slower he walked.

"What's your name?" she asked.

"Daven."

"Oh, I like that name." She tilted her head to the side and let out an impatient sigh. "Oh, come on, man. At this rate, you won't have me in cuffs until after breakfast."

His pace quickened the slightest bit.

"Are you afraid I'm going to hurt you?"

He didn't say anything, but pressed his lips together.

"Smart man," she hissed as he drew close enough for her to bat at his gun hand.

He pulled the trigger, and the bullet zipped past her shoulder. Her metal hand gripped his wrist tighter, causing him to cry out and drop the weapon to the cobblestones. She grabbed him by the throat and spun him to shove her chest against his back to use him as a shield against his comrades.

Song grinned over his shoulder at the other officers. "Next time, send a man with stones."

Foggerty raised his own revolver. "Release him, now!"

"Or what?"

"Or we open fire."

She laughed outright. "Go ahead! I dare you!"

"Come quietly, and—"

"Are you absolutely mental, Foggerty?" she scoffed. Song removed the glove from her right hand and flicked the sharp spikes out. She pressed them to Daven's neck where his pulse flickered, betraying his panic. "Learn to read a situation better. I've got the hostage. The upper hand is mine."

"Tims, give the captain a warning."

A man with a rifle took a shot. Song ducked her head behind Daven's as the bullet whizzed past her ear. She unholstered her revolver, peeked past the officer's head with one eye, then reached around and shot. The man formerly named Tims dropped his rifle as a hole burrowed into his forehead and exploded out the back. He fell forward to the ground and the other officers shifted in uncertainty.

"Who's next?" she bellowed.

Foggerty's wide eyes snapped to her from the corpse on the ground. "He had a family!" he thundered, his calm veneer cracking for a moment.

"Everyone has had a family at one point or another. I fail to see how that makes him so special," she said. Maybe with enough prodding she could make the detective inspector's shell crumble to expose the sort of man he was underneath. If she'd had more time, it could have been fun.

"Of course, a heartless bastard like you wouldn't care."

"I am *not* a bastard. My parents love me very much, thank you."

"You don't see people, do you?" he continued. "You see targets to take down with a single shot." He was trying to unsettle her by analyzing the sort of person he thought her to be. It wasn't working, and he was incorrect, anyway.

"I do have astonishingly perfect aim, don't I? Thank you for noticing."

"That wasn't a compliment."

"I beg to differ," she said with a haughty air. "And by the by, I do see people. I see an entire group of people in front of me, just one stupid twitch of an itchy trigger finger away from tasting one of my bullets. Would you like to wager who of you will hit me before I send you to meet Tims, the family man?"

"Remain steady," Foggerty said to the antsy men beside him. He stared down at the body, then looked at her again. "He wasn't going to hit you."

"Of course not. That's why he aimed for my head, right?"

"We want you alive, Caleb."

Behind.

The thought entered her mind. Not so much as a word, but an urge. She twisted her head to find three more officers, one with a rifle taking aim at her back. She didn't wait for him to fire. Song turned, dragging her hostage with her, then shot the aiming officer in the head.

"Your comrades are trying to get you killed," she hissed in the man's ear as she dragged him backward toward an alley.

"Please. I have children," Daven said.

"Everyone has children. Pick another cliché." She glanced over her shoulder to ensure the alley was clear of officers.

Vagrants picked themselves up from the ground and took off for the other end.

The officers collected at the mouth of the alley, following one step at a time as she continued to back down the narrow passage.

Rooftops.

Her gaze darted overhead. "How the bloody hell do I get on the roof?" she growled to herself.

"The flat at the end of this alley has one of those new emergency ladders for fires," the man in her grasp said.

She froze. A grin spread across her lips. "Daven! You're helping me? How delightful." She looked over her shoulder, and sure enough, there was a wooden ladder that led to a series of balconies connected by wooden stairs.

"Between us, I'm a fan of your work. I heard *The Princess and the Slave* a while back. What you did for the Gould girl was…honorable."

"Oh, you'll make me blush."

Foggerty took a few steps ahead of the other officers. "Caleb, we can—"

"I don't actually like being called Caleb," she said.

"Song, then. We can lay down our weapons and talk about this like civilized men."

She chuckled low in her throat. "No, we really can't."

"Release him and come quietly—"

"Are you daft, man? Really? I already said no! Besides, I kind of like Daven. I might keep him." She glanced behind. *Almost there.*

Once close enough, she raised her gun and shot over the men's heads. They flinched, a few ducking low. While they were distracted, she holstered her firearm, shoved Daven forward, spun on the ball of one foot, and sprinted for the ladder. She clambered up, her strength and metal arm making the action effortless and swift.

The first shot from the officers embedded into the wall beside her, sending brick dust and fragments flying at her. She didn't stop or falter as she raced to the top. She ducked behind the stairs as bullets lodged into the wood. Then came time for the reload.

Song ran around the stairs and bolted up them two at a time. By the time she made it across the balcony and to the next set of stairs, the gunfire resumed. Without a clear line of sight to their target, the bullets slammed into the stairs or zipped between steps, right past her foot.

Foggerty and two others ran forward and clambered after her. The gunfire stopped as she reached a second ladder which led to the roof. She scrambled up and took off running across the long, flat rooftop.

As she reached the end, she had the inexplicable urge to run up a set of tiered chimneys; her gaze settled on the exact bricks to place her feet on to boost her into the air. She ignored it like an intrusive thought. Song skidded to a halt at the edge of the roof and cast her gaze down into the gap of an alleyway.

"Bollocks." She glanced at the three-tiered chimney beside her and let out a breath. "Oh. I see, now."

She backed up as the officers shouted and ran at her. She took off at a run, but knew her momentum was too slow this time to make it up the structure. Instead, she threw herself over the edge with a slight jump upward, hoping it was enough. Her chest crashed against the wall of the neighboring building, but her hands found purchase on the ledge. She dragged herself up and rolled onto the roof, hand pressed to her aching sternum.

"Bollocks again," she groaned.

On the previous building, the officers didn't slow as they reached the edge. Song shoved to her feet and took off running. The next building had a dormer roof—the spine higher than the one she was on, but the gutters lower. Again, her sight glanced across a path where her mind urged her to place her feet to run up the edge and sprint along the narrow peak of the dormer roof. She slowed and tensed in anticipation, setting her foot in the first position, then the second. Her body tried to move to the next position, but she over-thought it and faltered.

Her momentum dropped, her foot set on an awkward joint between the roofs, and she slipped onto her side. She slid down the dormer roof toward the gutter and the cobblestones below.

"Bollocks!" she shouted at herself.

Her right hand's fingertips clattered open and closed, then dug the sharp cones into the metal roof to slow her fall with a piercing shriek that made her teeth ache. She came to a stop dangling from the gutter, where her hand gripped tighter. Her arm jerked in the cuff, threatening to fall out as the straps pulled tighter than was comfortable. She gasped and flailed in panic.

"Captain Song!" a man shouted from the street below.

She glanced over her shoulder at the policemen training their firearms at her. "I'm a little busy!"

"There's nowhere for you to go," Foggerty said from the ledge overhead, the three focusing their revolvers on her.

"I said bugger off!" She didn't have time to think, and she needed to.

No...I don't need to think at all.

"Right. Your turn. Get us out of this," she muttered.

Her body moved in what felt like her doing, and yet she knew was not. It was more like a memory in her muscles; an urge she had to follow, but not consciously so. Her left arm gripped the gutter and her legs swung from side to side. Song's body launched sideways toward the corner of the connected building. Her left hand gripped a round drainpipe as the fingertips of her right hand jammed into the bricks and slowed her descent to the ground. Her fingers left a trail of scratches and billowing brick dust in their wake.

The constables stared at her in dumbfounded shock. Her body turned and took off running before she could deliver a witty remark she so desperately wanted to say. It happened so fast she was still disoriented, but her body knew where it was going without her having to comprehend where she even was. It was terrifying. And yet it was exhilarating.

Song's left foot planted on a stack of crates, and she launched up to grip the cloth awning over a storefront. Her legs swung forward, and back, then again to build enough momentum before her feet planted on the bar on either side of her hands. Her grip released and her legs straightened to launch her upward, where she grabbed a windowsill on the second floor. She clambered onto the roof using windows and uneven brickwork to aid her ascent, and paused to assess the scene.

The officers and citizens on the street below were stuck in a sort of mute shock. On the dormer roof, Foggerty and the two constables ran along the spine of the roof. She spun and took off as the detective leapt into the air.

"Song, stop!" he bellowed, breathless after landing.

"No, thanks!" she shouted back, laughing.

One foot in front of the other, she let her body surge forward, doing her best to not think about anything, lest she get in her own way again. Her foot planted on the red bricks surrounding a chimney, then her other on a thick divider between two connected buildings as she cleared it with no effort at all.

She couldn't see the next roof, but she knew she'd reached a part of the city where two and one-story houses were more common than three floor buildings. Her legs didn't slow as she reached the edge of the roof. Her feet planted—one on a chimney and the other on the ledge.

Panic gripped her when the other building came into view, one story lower and quite a distance farther away than the small alleys had been. Her legs tucked under her, pointing her knees toward the next building. Her arms circled in the air at her sides to keep her upright.

To her surprise, she made it to the other roof. Her legs extended to catch her. Her body doubled over itself, curling to roll and dampen the fall. She came out of it back on her feet, able to resume her sprint.

"Captain Song!" Foggerty shouted from far behind when she reached the next roof.

She stopped and stared back at where he stood, hands planted on the ledge of the three-story she'd leapt from. He looked winded and defeated.

"Goodnight, Detective Inspector!" She saluted him, then resumed her run along the roofs.

Song ran until she knew she was safe, then she slowed and dropped back down to the street in an alleyway. She recognized this neighborhood—Olivia's home was a few blocks away. She looked down at her arm and smirked as she laughed through her nose.

"We make a good team."

And all you have to do is say the words, she thought. Her teeth clenched. *No. I don't need it. It'll only kill me.*

But she had to wonder if it would. She'd been using *kijæm* passively since it had gone away. It was still part of her, strengthening her and making her faster; giving her more stamina and endurance. And now, it seemed, being the eyes at the back of her head, and teaching her to run across rooftops in a manner she'd never heard of being done before.

Song stuck to the alleyways behind the houses, skulking through shadows and hiding from any questionable noise. Going by the location from behind, Song guessed which house was the right one. She jumped the back fence and strode up to knock on the door. A minute later, a woman with dark skin and upturned eyes opened it.

"Oh, bollocks," she said, her accent a faint Zardiian.

"I'm sorry, wrong house—"

"You're here for Olivia?"

"Oh. Yes. Who are you?"

The woman waved her inside. "Roommate." She walked to the stairs and shouted up, "Olivia, your pirate is here!"

A man leaned on the doorway to the parlor and stared at Song. He had blond hair and dark eyes. "Igriid only let you in because Olivia likes you. You're not bringing trouble with, are you?"

Song licked her lips. "No. I'm just…stopping in to make sure she got home all right."

"That's Captain Song?" a young boy asked. "I thought he'd be older. With a beard. And a pirate hat."

Song chuckled. "Not many pirates actually wear those hats."

"I thought he'd be taller," a little girl said, popping out from the same room and rushing over to look up at Song.

"How many people can you fit into that parlor?" Song asked with a laugh.

"About ten," Olivia said from the stairs, wrapped in what had to be her nicest dress robe.

"And how many people live here?" she asked.

"About ten," she said again. "You can come up, Song."

Igriid and the man gave each other wicked smiles.

"She likes to cuddle afterward," Igriid said to Song.

"After what?" the little girl asked.

"Nothing. Get your teeth brushed. It's time for bed."

A chorus of children groaning followed Song up the stairs to where Olivia stood, blushing.

"That's…not why I invited you up."

Song smiled. "That's not why I came up." She followed the woman into a room with a single small bed and meager furnishings. "I wanted to make sure you were all right. Sorry I took so long."

Olivia closed the door and lingered close to her. "How gentlemanly of you."

"Tell me about your roommates." She crossed the room to investigate the humble vanity. "Why do you have them? And whose children are those?"

Olivia sat on the bed and smiled. "Igriid, Conrad and I have been friends for a long time. We share this house, because otherwise we couldn't afford to live anywhere alone. The children are orphans each of us have brought home a time or seven. Strays that needed somewhere to stay so they wouldn't freeze or starve."

Song's lips spread into a genuine grin. "You three are wonderful for doing that."

"Don't say that. We have to send half of them away, I think. Our landlord just raised our rent, and now we can't afford to feed so many mouths on top of it." She released a long, exhausted sigh. "It gets harder every day."

"I'm going to come clean about something," Song said, suddenly conscious about her reason for being there. "I'm here because I'm hiding from the police. Laying low before I move on. Giving them time to give up the chase."

Olivia didn't move, as though processing the information.

"If you want me to leave, I will. I didn't know you had a bunch of kids here. I'd hate for something to happen because of me."

The woman released a long sigh. "You can stay for an hour. I'm sure you won't put any of us in danger."

She smiled. "Thank you."

For the next hour, Song sat with the woman and talked. She let her unload all the financial fears she had. If the landlord raised their rent again—which she suspected he would—then they'd have to get rid of the children, or all end up on the street. As the woman talked, Song formed a plan in the back of her mind. She would enact it the very next day.

When the hour was over, Olivia walked her to the back door. Song kissed the top of her hand, and disappeared into the shadows of the night.

Twenty-Seven

Aﬅer the encounter with the police, Song decided it was time to stay in the mansion for a while. She sent Ponce on her behalf to buy the property Olivia rented, and she ordered him not to take no for an answer. She even had him pay extra to expedite the whole process—she would have called it a bribe, but in wealthier circles they called it incentive. Once he had the deed in his hands with her name on it, Song had him hire inspectors, who would check the structure's stability and state of repair.

He also hand-delivered a letter to the tenants, stating that the property had been bought, and their rent had been reduced to one quarter of what they were paying—just enough to cover property upkeep, and Song wouldn't even turn a profit. It wasn't about profit for her. It was about keeping the tenants and children off the street, and having a place in the city to hide if she needed.

Over the next few days, she would look out the window and see a lot more officers about. Her father was busier, as well. One of the days he came home for any amount of time, he told her to stay put—that the city wasn't safe.

"What's happening?" she asked.

"Your dear captain friend has been wreaking havoc across the city. The police set up a trap of an imposter. Song's pride is predictable. It worked, but he escaped custody."

She forced a gasp. "How dreadful!"

"The police are combing the city for him. Searching every establishment, inn, and home. Someone is hiding Song, but we'll find him," Elroy said.

"Should I make myself presentable for when the constables come?"

"Are you hiding a pirate in the servants' quarters or the stables?" he asked, as though unsure if he knew whether she would or wouldn't do something so bold.

"Absolutely not, Father. I can promise you there are no pirates with the servants or horses."

"You're not hiding Captain Song anywhere?"

She maintained her innocent smile. "I'm not hiding Song anywhere."

"Do you know where he is hiding?"

She stared at him, her smile gone. "If I knew, do you really think I would tell you?"

Elroy let out a long, impatient breath. "Tsingsei, I'd rather not have scandal brought down on this family."

"Are you warning me to keep my mouth shut about my relationship with the captain, even to the authorities?"

He lowered his voice. "I'm asking you to think of our family and the livelihood of those in our employ before you do anything rash, be it aid Captain Song in hiding, or telling the wrong people just how close you are to him."

"And how close do you think I am?" she whispered.

"No one burns down half a city for a mere friend," he whispered.

"You're right, they don't. I won't talk to a single soul about Song. You have nothing to worry about."

He nodded in uncertainty.

"I'll go make sure my room is in order, so they can search easier," she said.

"There's no need. They will not be searching our home."

She blinked in shock. "Whose homes *are* being searched?"

"The east side, where people have spotted him on more than one occasion. He frequents a tavern on that side of the city."

Song squared her jaw. "I see. Good luck, Father." She strode away, relieved that her items were safe from discovery, but also furious that the authorities were targeting the area around her secret new safe house.

The next morning, Song woke with a warning tangle in her stomach, but had no idea why. She hadn't gone far into her day when she realized she hadn't seen Ponce at breakfast; nor had he been in the library when she checked. Her father wasn't home, and her mother was pointedly avoiding being in the same room as her daughter for longer than breakfast.

Song followed the sound of the piano accompanied by a violin to find Sunshine and Johanna playing together. Johanna had a sweet smile on her face as her eyes flicked to the man every few seconds. Song smiled and let them finish before entering.

"Thersiàl, have you seen Henry this morning?"

Sunshine's brow furrowed. "Now that you mention it, no. I haven't."

Her handmaid busied herself collecting up the sheet music, her facial features forced into a look of disinterest. But Song almost recognized the expression behind the mask.

"Johanna?"

"Yes?" the woman directed a flicker of a smile to her before looking away again.

"What do you know?" she demanded.

"I don't know any—"

"Don't you *dare* lie to me. What do you know?" Song snapped.

Johanna straightened and let out a long sigh. "I heard a commotion in the night and followed the sound. Your father had Mister Barton taken away by constables."

"What? Why?" she shouted.

"I don't know."

Song returned to her room and made herself presentable. She had a carriage prepared, seething the whole time as she watched the stable hands secure the horses to the vehicle. Johanna, Sunshine, and Ryk'r accompanied her to the police station. No one said anything on the ride there. If they had, Song would have yelled at them. Perhaps that's why they remained so quiet.

Once the carriage stopped, she shoved out into the winter chill that bit her cheeks and promised snow soon. She stomped into the precinct, straight to the reception desk.

"Where is my father?" she snapped.

"Who is your—"

"Don't give me that bollocks. You know damn well who I am, and I'd put quoine on you knowing where he is right now."

The woman held up a finger, signaling for Song to wait, and shuffled away from the desk.

"How do you even know he's here?" Sunshine asked at her shoulder.

"Because he would never stay out of it. Even if he stands in the corner and doesn't say anything. I know my father is here interrogating Ponce," Song said.

The woman returned a minute later. "Senator Gould is busy—"

Song strode around the desk to make her own way through the rows of desks toward the back hallway, even though she didn't know where she was going. The receptionist chased after her, and Ryk'r followed.

"Miss Gould!"

"I have been told my entire life that my father is too busy to see me. Forgive me if I'm tired of waiting."

A woman looked up at her from the other side of a desk where an officer stood. The name plate on the desk read 'DI Z. Foggerty'. Song recognized the man as Daven—he seemed older in the well-lit precinct, his eyes a soft green with a shock of brown splitting the left iris in half. Foggerty was nowhere to be seen.

Her eyes settled on the woman, then. Olivia. She had a stack of photographs in her hands. She was there to identify the man under the hood. Again, that thrilled shiver ran through Song as the woman stared her in the face and gave no hint or expression of recognition.

She strode past them, avoiding the clerk who continued trying to grab her by the arm. Once in the hallway, she started opening doors. By the third door, she had several people after her, trying to hold her back from opening more or continuing down the hall. Ryk'r put himself in the way of some to prevent them from grabbing Song. She lurched away and opened the fourth door to find Ponce handcuffed to a table, Detective Inspector Foggerty on the opposite side, and her father in the corner with his arms folded. She spun and slapped a man across the cheek as he wrapped his firm grip around her biceps.

"Don't you dare touch me!" She backed into the room and slammed the door as Ryk'r loomed over the crowd, barring their entry. She turned to glare at her father. "What is the meaning of this?"

Ponce sat up straighter, his forlorn expression softening to one of hope as he stared at her.

Elroy set his palm across his eyes and massaged his thumb and middle finger against his temples. "You shouldn't be here."

"*Henry* shouldn't be here! I don't care where I should or shouldn't be. You've taken an innocent man into custody. For what?"

Foggerty stood, his back straight as though not only showing her the respect her family demanded, but also making himself seem more authoritative. He'd styled his brown hair in a manner similar to her father's, parted on one side with delicate waves to it. It wasn't oiled under control, and so had drifted forward to tickle his forehead. He settled his patient hazel eyes on her. He was younger than she'd thought when meeting him the other night—somewhere in his mid-twenties, if she had to guess. A detective inspector his age had either obtained the position without merit—

perhaps nepotism, or even bribery—or he was a force to be reckoned with. For her own sake, she hoped it was nepotism.

"Miss Gould," Foggerty said, "it is highly inappropriate for you to barge in here. However, as you are close with this man, I will at least give you this: we know he is Captain Song. It's only a matter of proving it."

She released a single *ha!*

"I'm telling you, there is no proof," Ponce said. "I'm not Captain Song."

"Sooner or later your lie will slip," Elroy said.

"It's not a lie!" Song shouted.

"You lot give me far too much credit," Ponce said. "I'm not great enough a man to be Song. And I'm not stupid enough to claim the name for a moment of unearned glory. Even if I didn't see the gallows, Song would take my head."

His loyalty made her want to smile, but she bit her cheek until it stung, rather than letting herself show any sort of approval at his words.

"So he leads by fear?" Foggerty asked, falling back into the interrogation as though he'd already forgotten she stood there.

"No. Song earned our loyalty. Treats us kindly. Protects us. Lesser men buy loyalty with quoine or demand it through fear. Song gave us purpose. After Dash died, some talked of leaving the crew. But the mere fact that he'd made Song captain on his dying breath swayed us. Anyone trained by our former captain is worth standing by and protecting, the same way Song protects us."

Her heart swelled over what he said, and she resisted reacting. Ponce didn't look at her. A detective and a senator could read body language like that, Song knew. However, his brow nearest her raised the slightest bit as though he was resisting the glance.

Her own father was usually a master at picking up on subtle clues—a risked glance, a shifting foot, a twisted sentence. But the day before, he'd revealed his blind spot: his own daughter. She'd twisted her words to give him the truth he'd asked for while obscuring the facts behind fancy phrasing. And he'd looked right at her and accepted it at face value. Or had he?

No, he'd seen through what she said, but had come to the wrong conclusion.

"This is because of me," Song said, her eyes glued to her father. "I told you I wasn't hiding Captain Song anywhere!"

He released a long breath through his nose. "Yes, and Henry wasn't hiding, was he? In fact, he was out buying property where a known associate of Song's lives."

Foggerty hissed a warning at her father to keep quiet.

"You misunderstood me!" she said.

"Then speak more plainly," Elroy replied on a sigh, as though too exhausted to deal with her right then.

"How can I speak plainly when you hunt those I care most about?"

Foggerty turned on her. "You care about scoundrels, thieves, and murderers, Miss Gould. And if I find that you had aught to do with the actions of pirates, I will try you alongside them."

"Zion!" her father barked.

"My apologies, Elroy, but no one is above the law. Not even your daughter."

Song took a few calculated steps toward the detective inspector. She settled her gaze on his, capturing it and holding on like a threat. "I would focus more on the criminals stalking and raping women in your streets, rather than accusing me of something unseemly. I would also suggest rethinking if going after Song is even worth it, knowing the sort of man he is."

"And what sort of man is he?" Foggerty didn't budge. He held his ground like a saint.

"Song has influence in many places around the world. Places who wouldn't take kindly to his execution."

She was, of course, talking about her betrothed in Armalinia. Though she had to imagine it was common knowledge now that the sultania was betrothed to a woman. Whether people knew that woman was Tsingsei Gould was a mystery, so she couldn't attach that fact to the man they knew as Song. She also meant the three pirate havens, though getting the people out of them to avenge her was unlikely, and other pirates might dance on her grave. The third was Aibhànocht, where she had an open invitation to join the church—if they hadn't deduced that it was she who stole the words from their sacred text. Not to mention her possibly being the chosen of their God. And of course, there was always Telbhaniich-Zardi, where her loyal whore and her honorable fence resided. Both would hide her at a moment's notice, though only one knew her face beneath the hood.

Now that she thought about it, Lyella was likely the only person who would miss her or seek revenge. This realization hit her like a punch, though she remained impassive.

"Pishing wants him alive," Elroy intoned, though she heard it.

"And you intend to deliver him to them?" she snapped. "Since when does Andalise extradite its own citizens to that barbaric country?"

"There are matters I and the senate attend to, which you and the public need not know about."

"Your adoration is plain, Miss Gould," Foggerty said, before she could demand more information from her father. "You love him, don't you?"

"Am I being interrogated now?" she asked.

"You *are* in an interrogation room, after all."

Ponce shifted in his seat, a smile drifting over his lips. "Anyone who knows Song, loves him. He would die to protect one of us. It would be an honor to do the same for him." He leaned back in the seat, relaxing as though that was the last he would say on the matter.

"Work with us and we can grant you immunity in whatever crimes you've committed," Foggerty said to both of them.

Neither spoke.

"Tsingsei, take the deal," her father said.

She squared her jaw. "I would love nothing more…than to watch you fumble around being outsmarted by Captain Song at every turn. You'll never catch him. And if you do, you'll never keep him."

"I'm with her. Song is the most powerful Touched to ever exist. What are you besides some angry sod with a badge?" Ponce said. "You'll never get anything more than that out of me."

"Then you'll hang," Foggerty said.

"I have faith that Song will save me. Do your worst."

Elroy cradled his temples again. He sent a glare to his daughter. "Tsingsei, go home now, and we will talk later."

She nodded once, then captured Ponce's gaze with her own. "Stay strong, Henry. Song will fix this." She stared at Foggerty. "Have a good day, Detective Inspector Zion Foggerty." She spun on her heel and strode from the room, waiting until the door closed to allow herself a small snort of amusement over his name.

In the lobby, her father caught up with her, anger painted across his face. "Tsingsei, do you have any idea what you've just done?" he demanded.

"Argued with a detective and my father."

"We almost had him!"

Her lips twisted into a humorous half smile. "No, you didn't. He was just being less openly defiant before. Henry was never going to give you what you wanted."

"He was about to admit to being Song!" Elroy growled.

Sunshine coughed a laugh beside them. "Henry? He ain't Song."

"Then who *is?*" he snapped. "You all deny it's Henry, and yet refuse to give a name!"

"Because Captain Song is Captain Song. And expecting any of his crew to turn on him is as laughable as you yourself being Song."

She smiled at her father. "I'll see you at home, Daddy." She kissed his cheek, despite how furious he still was.

When he said nothing more, she turned and strode from the precinct. Johanna, Sunshine, and Ryk'r followed.

Twenty-Eight

NIGHT HAD FALLEN, AND SONG HADN'T BEEN ABLE TO FOCUS on anything. Her mind was too preoccupied with the issue of Ponce. At first, she'd feared he would say something or reveal her to be Captain Song. But now that he'd reaffirmed his loyalty, she had to deal with the matter of getting him out of the position her father had put him in—give her up or hang in her name. She couldn't allow it.

She *wouldn't* allow it.

"Amelia is asking about you," Johanna said in the doorway. "I know it's not my place, but…you've been neglecting her."

"Am I meant to spend every waking moment by her side?" Song asked.

Johanna released a long, weary sigh. "It might not seem it to you, but she is unwell in her mind."

"Like she should be committed?"

"No. Like she shouldn't be left alone or treated like her pain is inconvenient to you."

Song furrowed her brow. "I do not—"

"Yes, you do. You avoid her, though maybe it's not intentional. I understand. It's easy to leave the victims behind to pick up the pieces alone."

She clenched her jaw and looked the woman in the eyes. "Do you speak from experience?"

Johanna stared at her, unwavering.

"Who helped you pick up your pieces?"

Her gaze remained locked on Song's, though she didn't say anything for a long minute. "She doesn't need to be coddled or forced to get better. She just needs to know she's not alone. Amelia shouldn't be shut away like an inconvenient reminder that the world is cruel to women." She took a long breath, as though it was a relief to get it off her chest. "She cares deeply for you, and it breaks her heart to not be able to move about so easily as she recovers. Go walk with her or something. Get her out of that bed. Show her you care about her, too."

She raised an eyebrow and meandered to the door, studying the woman. "You imply we are more than just friends?"

The woman chuckled. "Tsingsei, I helped raise you. You have never once looked at a man half as adoringly as you looked at the girl who cared for you before me."

"So, I did have another nanny!" Song gasped. "What was her name?"

"I don't remember. I only met her the one time. You absolutely loved her. She was young—a teenager. Old enough to be married, so anywhere from fifteen to nineteen."

"With honey-colored hair? From Pishing?"

Johanna thought, her brow furrowed. "Yes, I believe so. Your memory is sharp."

A sad smile flickered over her expression. "Her name was Fiyora."

"I heard she traveled to Jashedar after. Your father bought her passage. Begged her to stay, but she seemed to be running from something. I wonder how she's fared since then."

"She died," Song said with a bitter frown. "I'll go visit Amelia, now." She lifted the oil lamp with a chimney from the side table by the door and strode past the woman.

My drunken mind had dredged up memories, not made them up.

The memories had plagued her after resurfacing. She'd thought a lot about them. And contemplated even more after learning that the name of Leslie's childhood sweetheart was Fiyora. The odds were good that it was the same girl. The missing pieces of the puzzle bothered her, though. Who was Fiyora running from? How had she died? What was she doing in Garda? Song determined she would never know the answers to these questions, and so tucked them away in the back of her mind, so she could focus on more pressing concerns.

She stood in the doorway to Amelia's room. After a moment, the woman looked up and gave her a shy smile. Song returned it.

"I'm sorry I've been so preoccupied. I have trouble sitting in one place all day," she said.

"I don't need you to sit with me all day, Tsingsei. Just a few minutes here and there would be nice."

Song nodded and thought. She didn't want to sit in the stuffy room, not for five minutes, and especially not for longer. Johanna had suggested a walk, and Song determined it was the better choice. "Would you like to see my favorite part of this house?"

Amelia grinned. "I would!"

They walked through the halls, arms hooked together, Amelia carrying two throw blankets. Song led her up a flight of stairs, and another. At the end of a lonely hallway on the third floor, Song opened a door which hid another set of stairs. She let Amelia enter first, then followed, closing the door behind them. They ascended the creaking, dusty stairs one after the other.

The attic reeked of undisturbed dust and mildew from the wooden beams clinging to whatever moisture they could. Song took Amelia's hand and guided her across the protesting floorboards to a long window. She unlocked the panes and pushed them open, then climbed over the sill to stand on the wide peak of the roof that ran between the attic and the ballroom. She helped Amelia out through the window and walked a few steps to stand in the middle.

The two sat wrapped in blankets and stared over the city, taking in the glimmering lights, and the steam from a train and a few nearby cars. Skyships docked and departed at the harbor. Song released a long sigh and set her chin on her knees, wishing she was on one of those skyships.

"I feel like any second I could fall," Amelia said.

"You're fine, so long as you don't scoot too close to the edge."

"Are you not scared?"

Song shook her head. "I've never been afraid of heights. I've always liked coming up here, or climbing trees. The world looks so different from above. I love it. Father is terrified of heights—mostly balconies, though. It's how my grandfather died."

"Falling would be an awful way to die."

She closed her eyes and relived the thrill of leaping from the Stars' Bounty and the Stars' Reprisal to land on sailers—though she'd used a rope with the latter. "Falling is such a rush, though. There's nothing like it. Jumping from the skywalk in Telbhaniich-Zardi was exhilarating. They're higher than the tallest buildings, there."

"How did you stop yourself, though?"

"My *kijæm*. It would catch me and set me safely on my feet."

Amelia shivered, but not from the chill of the night. "You're incredibly brave."

"Not all the time. Not right now."

They stayed silent as Amelia stared at Song's profile, the light from the oil lamp flickering on the other side of her.

"My father took Henry into custody last night. He thinks Henry is Song. And I don't know how to prove he isn't without proving I am." She clenched her jaw, feeling like maybe she should cry, but her heart didn't care to. She was overwhelmed, and instead of breaking down, her emotions had shut down and left her cold. "So, do I let my friend hang as a scapegoat in my stead? Or do I take my rightful place at the noose?"

"Your father wouldn't let his own daughter hang, would he?"

Song shrugged and shook her head. "I don't know. Even if he wouldn't, could he override the laws he himself put into place? His reputation would be destroyed."

"Do the other senators need to know?"

Song stared out over the yellow-lit city which flickered with the streetlamp flames that reflected from windows and illuminated brick walls. "Maybe they don't…"

Amelia reached a slow hand over to wrap in Song's. "Maybe find a way to tell him."

"If I tell him in private, he'll be sure to pin the blame on someone else. But if I show the world that the man accused is not the real Song, then he'd have no choice but to release Ponce. After that, I don't know. I'm sure he can come up with some sort of excuse to get me off the hook as well."

"Show the world your hood, but not your face. All to save your captain's assistant. Your friends really are the luckiest people in the world to have such a devoted woman fighting for them."

The words left a bitter taste in the air, and Song clenched her jaw. "Not Altain. Not Leslie. I failed them."

"But you *tried*, didn't you?"

"Aye."

"In the end, that's what counts."

"Years in the sky have made me think otherwise. When lives are at stake, the world only deals in absolutes. You succeed or you fail. You live or you die. Trying is just what you do in between. And it doesn't matter how hard or little you tried, the end result is the only thing people remember. The outcome is all that history will record. You commend me for trying, but I will be remembered for failing."

Amelia frowned out at the city. "The years have been unkind to you. The Song I found on the beach would say trying is what counts. Do your best, and anything more than that is beyond your control."

"The Song you met was an idiot with a death wish. The worst kind of naïve, as well. She was a fool. It's no wonder all her friends have wound up dead."

"I'm not dead."

Song bit back the witty reply she might have given to her crew, but would hurt the woman's feelings. *You're not my friend*. It was cruel, and she wasn't sure if it was entirely true. Instead she said, "Yet."

The two remained silent for several minutes, lost in their own thoughts as they stared out over the city. Regrets plagued Song's mind. If she could go back and change just a few things here and there, she'd be in the skies, Dashaelan and Leslie beside her on the Stars' Bounty, reunited as father and son. As much as she'd enjoyed being captain over the past two years, she would give it up in a heartbeat to resurrect the dead.

Amelia scooted the few inches between them to press closer to Song's side. After a while, she leaned her temple on Song's shoulder. They remained like this for several minutes.

Amelia tilted her head to look at Song. "You're the only girl I've ever kissed."

She blinked out at the city, then shifted her gaze down to the woman. "Really? That's a shame. I was terrible at it."

"I didn't think you were!"

"I was rubbish."

Amelia giggled. "Have you learned more since then?"

"I have."

"Show me."

Song smirked at her. "If you wanted a kiss, you could just ask."

"But then it wouldn't have felt genuine."

"It doesn't feel genuine like this."

Amelia sighed. "What would make it feel more natural, then?"

She thought, her eyes narrowed. "Perhaps wooing."

"And how would you woo me?"

Song turned her torso to face the woman as she rested on her arm and studied her features. She wasn't near as beautiful as Lyella, but she was pretty in an unusual way. "I would tell you that the stars aren't half as spectacular as the sparkle in your eyes. That faces like yours are ones men go to war for."

"You're lying."

"You asked me to woo you. It's half flattery, you know." She gave the woman a mischievous grin. "You're like a rare jewel. Someone could hold you in their arms and have no idea what sort of treasure they'd discovered. You're the sort of woman others mourn the loss of."

When she paused to think up more, Amelia surged forward to press her lips against hers. Song leaned into the kiss. Regardless of the strange limbo where her feelings on Amelia seemed to be content residing, she couldn't deny her hunger for a woman's company. She slid her hand into the blanket to wrap it around Amelia's waist. The woman squirmed, then jerked away, tearing the intruding hand from her body.

"I'm sorry," Amelia said, as she buried her face in her hands. "I can't do it."

Song released a long sigh. "No need to apologize. It's my fault. Should've been satisfied with a kiss." She tucked a lock of Amelia's hair behind the woman's ear.

"I was such an idiot."

"Don't say that."

"But it's true. I was so afraid of losing myself and becoming a servant—a decoration—that I completely ignored all the warning signs."

Song shook her head, though Amelia wasn't looking at her. "You can't blame yourself for the actions of others. If you do, you'll go mad."

She released a humorless laugh. "Am I not already mad?"

She let out a heavy sigh and leaned back on her palms to stare out at the city. "We're all a bit mad, though, aren't we? Everyone out there, going about their night, is a little crazy. We have to be, don't we?"

"Why do you say that?"

"Because in order to live in a cruel and dangerous world, you have to be equally cruel, brave, or insane. Most people are cowards, so I'd wager they're mad."

Amelia smiled at Song. "You're incredibly brave."

"Are you kidding? Me? I lost the plot long before I ever found it." She laughed as Amelia giggled. "What was so important to you that marrying some shite weevil was the worse option over pirates?"

"Freedom," Amelia said. "Existing as a woman, as myself, in a world that would rather keep me caged up and silent."

Song sucked in a long breath and released it just as slowly. "I see we have more in common than I suspected."

"I don't think we're as alone in the idea as society would have us believe. We're expected to smile and be pretty, anything but that and we're too demanding."

"Sit down, be quiet, and let the menfolk make all the decisions."

"And anyone who complains is a problem. They weaponize us against each other to keep other women in line against our own interests." Amelia shook her head. "I hate it."

"I hate it, too."

Amelia leaned against Song in a manner she assumed was weariness.

"Would you like to go back to your room?"

Amelia took a deep, contemplative breath. "I would, please. But only because it's getting cold."

Song stood and helped Amelia to her feet. They gathered the blankets and the oil lamp and shuffled back across the roof, hand in hand to steady one another. They made their way through the house in an almost comfortable silence.

Song thought over everything that had just happened — mostly about their momentary intimacy. Half of her was upset — she'd been trying to connect with Amelia, and the woman seemed to still like her, but Song was having trouble scraping up the same feelings. The other half of her mind, however, was furious that Amelia had even had the adverse reaction to a simple touch. If Song could kill the pirates who'd abused her again, she would. She would take her time, though. Savor their suffering. And she would let Amelia join in the torture, if she'd the stomach for it. Unfortunately, she couldn't kill them over and over, and there was nothing she could do to undo what they had done to Amelia.

As she helped the woman back into the bed, she had to wonder if she actually liked her, and could love her. Being honest with herself, she had no interest in an actual relationship. She wanted a woman she could spoil with pilfered trinkets and enjoy while docked, but otherwise wouldn't demand her exclusive affections, or deny her the freedom she missed with every fiber of her being since arriving in Garda.

She didn't think Amelia was the type of woman to fit those requirements. She was a homebody. Perhaps that's what kept Song at an emotional distance from her. And though she tried not to, as she sat beside Amelia and read the smiling woman poetry, she found herself missing Zeriida-Khiin and Lyella. And she couldn't even count the days until she could see either again, because she wasn't sure if she ever would.

Twenty-Nine

ESPITE SONG'S RESERVATIONS ABOUT GETTING TOO CLOSE to Amelia, she stayed by her side the next day. Together, they devised a plan to not only free Ponce, but prove him innocent.

Song penned a letter to her father as Caleb Song, demanding an invitation to the upcoming ball. He would then have Captain Song in exchange for Henry Barton. She added a list of stipulations to protect her own identity during the event, and instructed him to send the invitation with 'your daughter's friend, Thersiàl'. That way, Sunshine could leave, have a drink somewhere, and hand her the invitation when he returned. She folded up the paper and sealed it with her stamp. Afterward, with a sigh that told her just how beneath him the task was, Ryk'r slipped the letter in with the post, which her father would look over after the evening meal.

Song spent the day with her stomach in knots, though Amelia tried to comfort her. She worried he would pass up the opportunity, or see it as a ruse. If so, she wasn't sure what else she could do to clear Ponce's name. At dinner, she sat in agonized silence, unable to eat as every possible outcome raced through her head. Afterward, she hovered outside her father's office—Ryk'r forced to stay out of sight halfway down the hall—waiting for a sign.

It came when he strode out with two sealed envelopes in his hands. Song followed him at a distance, then watched from around a corner as he handed both to Johanna. She curtsied and headed the other direction, toward the servants' quarters and the stables. As her father came back down the hall, Song rounded the corner, an innocuous expression on her face.

"Oh!" she feigned a gasp upon seeing him. "You scared me. What are you doing out of your office so early?" She looked over his shoulder as Johanna disappeared around the far corner. "Where's Johanna going?"

His lips tightened with his all-too-familiar annoyed expression. "It's nothing to worry about, my dear. If you'll excuse me, I have some important letters to return to."

Song smiled. "Of course." She kissed his cheek. "Goodnight, Daddy."

"Goodnight, Tsingsei." He kissed her cheek and strode to his office.

She pursed her lips and rushed after her handmaid. However, Sunshine met her halfway, worry furrowing his brow.

"What's the matter?" she asked.

"Your dear old *daddy* sent Johanna to deliver a letter to the police and to the address you provided."

"He was supposed to give it to *you!*" Song growled.

"Get to that location before anyone finds her," Sunshine demanded. "You couldn't have picked a seedier place if you tried."

She gave him an unamused expression. "It was supposed to be you, not her. And no one was supposed to be going there!" she hissed, eyes scanning for any prying ears. "Don't blame me for the change in plans!"

"Just go make sure nothing bad happens because of it," he snapped.

Song's eyes widened in shock before she smiled. "You fancy Johanna?"

He scowled in response.

She giggled. "I'll go save your damsel in distress, lover-boy."

"Call me that again and your arm will end up in a horse stall."

She made a rude face at him, then strode away. To her delight, Ryk'r didn't object or stand defiant as she dismissed him for the evening. He saw her to her bedroom, and continued to his own. As Song changed into her pirate clothing, scrubbed her face, and tied her hair into a tight ponytail at the nape of her neck, she fumed over her father's disobedience to the demands. If she hadn't been his daughter, she would have retaliated in some way. Once her belt was on and her coat buckled, she leapt out the window, lifting her hood on her way to the ground. She raced across the city, using the rooftops to shorten the time. Johanna would likely arrive long before she did.

When Song reached the address, she dropped to the sidewalk and stopped to catch her breath. The carriage sat stationary a block down. As she made her way to it, though, voices emanated from within the nearby alley. Curiosity led her feet to follow the sounds—and a fortunate thing, too, as Johanna seemed to have gotten lost. But she wasn't alone. There was a man in a long coat, his hood over his head and a thin sword at his waist. He'd pressed Johanna into a doorway, and whatever he was saying had painted an expression of terror across her face.

"A respectable lady like yourself shouldn't be out alone at such an hour," he said.

"I have a message."

"For who?"

"C-Caleb Song."

The man laughed. "Let's hear it, then."

Song's feet stopped their silent approach. Was he really impersonating her? Had he not seen the reports of what had happened to the others? Did he really not know there was an outright manhunt of police combing the city, looking for the man in the hood?

"How can I be sure you're Captain Song?" Johanna demanded.

"I shouldn't have to prove nothing to you, wench."

Song tutted low. "Ah, sir, it seems to me a man who can't prove his identity is using a false name." She spoke lower than was comfortable, hoping to fool Johanna.

He spun to face her. "And who are you, boy? Just some brat, eh? Go run along home to mummy."

Song advanced one slow step at a time. "Madam, what do you know of Caleb Song?"

"I know plenty," she said with pride.

"What are you," the man demanded, "a fanatic?"

Johanna's cheeks grew pink. The way she'd spoken of the captain had always been strange to Song, almost like a masked admiration. She read about pirates in the way one might read up on their favorite hobby. It was a fascination barbed by fear, Song suspected. The woman had fallen into the trap of romanticizing something dangerous, like many women had. But, like any upstanding citizen, she would never admit to her fascination out loud.

Song smirked. "Madam, what sort of weapon does the captain carry?"

Johanna straightened. "He carries many. First it was an Armalinian flatblade."

"Right," Song clapped. "Next?"

"A Garda saber he nicked from Captain Hugh."

"What's this got to do with anything?" the copycat demanded.

"Patience." Song held up her palm to him. "Continue, madam."

"Most recently, he wielded the sword of his right-hand man."

"What sort of blade is it?" Song coaxed.

"Pishing sorrowstone."

"Good. Thank you. Your knowledge is rather impressive. I'm flattered." She turned her attention back to the man. "Tell me, sir, what sword do you wield?"

He withdrew his and pointed it at her with an implied threat, preparing for a fight.

Song released a dramatic scoff. "A rapier? Really? If you're going to impersonate someone, at least do it right. I mean, do you even *have* a gun?"

"You shut your mouth, brat!" He launched at her.

She withdrew her eilfaas tusk dagger and ran the blade parallel to her forearm to block his halfhearted swing.

"Lesson one." She batted another swing of his rapier away, then lurched forward to slash at his belly. "Impersonating someone is only a compliment when you do it accurately."

He stabbed at her, and she shifted sideways.

"Lesson two, do your research."

"You're not Caleb Song," he insisted. "You're just a brat."

"A brat with a monogrammed revolver," she said, tossing her dagger into her right hand to withdraw her sidearm. She pulled back on the hammer and pointed it at him.

He dropped his sword to the ground and raised his hands up by his head. "Please, I wasn't meaning nothing by it."

She strode at him; he backed up at each of her steps. "Lesson three, Captain Song never harms a lady and rarely gives second chances to those who do."

"Spare me," he begged.

"Why?"

He shook his head, sputtering for an answer.

"Captain," Johanna called over Song's shoulder. "Just let him be."

"You're one lucky bugger." She smirked and holstered her revolver. "If I ever hear of you claiming my name again, I'll kill you. Now get out of my face before I change my mind."

He ran as fast as he could and left the two alone in the alley. Song sheathed her dagger and kicked his sword into her hand to look at the blade. The rapier was poorly made and had never seen combat outside of the short spat with her.

Johanna cleared her throat. "Rather blunt warning."

Song chuckled. "There is no point dancing around the subject. At least this way he knows exactly what I meant." She threw the sword into a corner and turned on Johanna, doing her best to cast as much of her face below the mask in shadow as possible. "Now, madam, what brings you to a dark alley in such a delightful part of the city?"

She released a nervous laugh. "Looking for you, sir."

"Me?" she asked, feigning shock. "How fascinating, because I was waiting for a Mr. Saigh. Unless you're hiding something under those skirts of yours, I doubt you're him."

"The senator sent me in his stead."

Song scoffed. "Typical of a Gould. Can't follow simple bloody instructions. Now, to this business you've come for." She held out her hand.

Johanna reached into a pocket of her coat and produced the invitation. Song tucked it into one of her pouches.

"You're not going to read it?"

"I know what it is, darling. No need to check that it's accurate." Though she would double check later, just to make sure. "Might I accompany you back to your carriage, madam?" She extended her elbow.

Johanna scrutinized the figure before her, trying to figure out just what sort of game they were playing. She relented and wrapped a hand through Song's elbow. "I don't understand…"

"How can a ruffian pirate be so courteous?"

"There was never a question of your charms." She released a soft, nervous laugh. "What they say about you, though…"

"I have never once harmed a lady."

"You're not suggesting those ladies all lied?" Johanna gasped, stopping to stare at the side of the hood.

"I'm not *suggesting* anything. I'm saying plain as day those ladies are liars."

They resumed walking, Johanna keeping her lips closed against another objection.

"It's hard to trust the word of a pirate over several ladies claiming the same story. But I promise you, their claims are utterly erroneous."

Johanna stopped beside the carriage and spun to face Song, her face set in an indignant scowl. "A woman would never lie about being raped."

Song stood close, hoping the smell of her unwashed coat covered the perfume she hadn't had time to rinse from herself. "Madam, I don't have the means, nor the desire, to rape a woman."

"What's that supposed to mean?" she demanded.

Song bowed, planting a soft kiss on Johanna's hand. "The night is deepening. It's best you head home." With that, she spun on her heel and sauntered away.

Once out of sight of the carriage, Song broke into a sprint. At an intersection, she stopped, eyeing the constable on the corner. She used crates and a ladder to get up to the rooftops and run along them instead.

She stayed above the city, letting her *kijæm* instinct guide her feet to the best places to boost off, or land and roll to prevent injury without stopping her momentum. She could run like this for hours, just for the rush. But as she reached her home, she had to drop to the ground and wait for the street to clear before sprinting across in a dark patch between two streetlamps, whose light couldn't quite reach each other.

She slipped into the gate and skirted the wall. The carriage was already in the stables, and the stable hands were unhooking the horse. For a split second, her mind let her reflect on how she didn't even know the stable hands' names, or the name of the horse, for that matter. Once out of sight of it, though, she shoved the thought from her mind in order to focus on ascending to her balcony and slipping in through the doors. She shut and locked them, then drew the curtains closed.

A faint light illuminated the room, and behind her, a woman screamed.

Thirty

SONG DROPPED HER HOOD AND RIPPED HER MASK OFF, EYES wide on Johanna in her doorway. The woman shoved her palm over her mouth to shut herself up when she saw Song's face.

"Johanna!" someone called.

Footsteps thundered down the hallway toward them.

Song dove under the bed, tucking her feet into the bed skirt as someone arrived at her doorway.

"Johanna, are you all right?"

"I, um…" The woman made a few uncertain noises.

Song held her breath, ready to start bribing or killing the house staff.

"I thought I saw something." Johanna gave a reserved, nervous chuckle. "Just…just a shadow, I think. Oh, that was…something." She forced another laugh.

"Turn up the lamp when entering a room, right?" the man said, then chuckled.

"Good idea. Goodnight."

The door closed and locked. Song didn't move. Johanna's heels clicked across the tile floor and stopped beside the bed. She knelt down and lifted the bed skirt to meet Song's wide eyes with her own.

"Please tell me this is just a costume," Johanna hissed.

She blinked at her. "Why would it be a costume?"

"Well, there are copycats…?" She held out her hand to help drag Song out from under the bed.

"Copycats who keep ending up maimed."

Once standing before her, Johanna lifted the hood and deflated at the familiar stranger beneath it. "Oh…bugger."

Song chuckled and dropped her hood, then began unclasping her coat. "I told you I have neither the means nor the desire to rape women."

"Have you always been Song?" she hissed.

"Yes. It's a nickname an old friend gave me just after I left home."

The woman pursed her lips as thoughts whirred behind her eyes. "This changes so much of the stories told about you."

"I know." Song smirked as she started shoving her things into her trunk. "My father was supposed to give this damned letter to Thersiàl. He was going to waste some time at a tavern, then come back and give it to me."

"Why did he send me?"

A knock sounded on her door, and both women froze.

"Miss Gould?" Sunshine said through the door.

Song let him in, then locked the door behind him.

"Miss Burke," he said, almost shocked to see her there. His gaze bounced between the two women, then he released a sigh. "Well, that *rebhidh* is out of the bag."

"Why did you come in here, anyway?" Song asked Johanna.

"I came in here to tell you of your father's questionable delivery. What is it?"

She paused in her undressing to retrieve the letter from her pouch and open it. "I presume you already spoke to my father, assuring him you delivered it into my hands?" She held up an invitation for the ball with the name 'Caleb Song' written on it. "The world needs to see that Henry Barton isn't Captain Song."

"Why?"

She recounted her thoughts to Johanna over the whole debacle with Ponce. Johanna sat on the side of the bed, listening, her brow furrowed. After a long silence as Song put away her clothes and fished out a nightgown, Johanna took a deep breath.

"It's a good thing you told me. There's no possible way you could get yourself ready for the ball after already being late." Her eyes settled on Song's harness system.

"That's your biggest concern?" she asked.

"Well, you're right about your father covering it up unless you make a public spectacle. I may not agree with your alter ego and all your activities, but your parents didn't hire me to have an opinion about that. I'm paid to get you ready for the day and see to your education."

"You're only saying that because I've bribed you my whole life."

"I'm not disagreeing." Her eyes looked over the corset and belts again. "What is that?"

Song draped her nightgown over the end of the bed and unbuttoned the glove from the shoulder pad. She held out the metal arm and let the woman investigate it. "My bones were shattered. Sunshine—Thersiàl—gave the order to have it removed before it killed me."

"She was a right pain in the arse for months about it," he said. "Still hate me for it?"

Song gave him a wry smile. "I stopped hating you ages ago. I would've died. Plus, now I have this unexpectedly useful tool."

Her fingertip cones popped out, then back in. She curled her fingers and the palm blade shot out. Johanna jumped in shock both times.

After Song dressed, she sat on her bed and made a plan for the night of the ball. She would show up as Song first. Then, if her father let her go, she would rush to her room and Johanna would help her change so she could make her appearance as the returned Tsingsei Gould.

Johanna sat in an uncomfortable silence when they'd finished. Song started to ask what was wrong, but the woman spoke as she opened her mouth.

"Did you really kidnap that baby?"

Song nodded.

"Where is he?"

"Safe. He's being well cared for. I may not like children, but I wouldn't hurt one."

"Why did you take him?" she asked.

Song sneered. "Because Isabelle has been telling people I raped her, and that her child is mine! And everyone takes her word at face value because she's a lady. The truth is, she presented herself to me, and I didn't touch her. She'll have her child back when she admits the truth for all to hear. Call me whatever you like, but I *will not* have my name sullied by the word rape."

Johanna released a long breath. "I suppose that makes sense. But there had to be another way besides kidnapping an infant."

"Maybe, but I didn't think of any. So, here we are. Honestly, I expected to return him the next day. You'd think a mother would admit the truth without a second thought for the return of her child."

"Do you think your mother would have?"

Song narrowed her eyes. "No, actually. In fact, I doubt she noticed I was missing."

Johanna frowned and tilted her head as she shook it. "Tsingsei…your mother was the first to notice. She was up for hours searching every inch of the house for you. She looked in all the little cupboards and hideaways you've tucked yourself into before—your favorite spot up on the roof, and even little nooks you haven't fit into since you were a child."

Song stared at the woman, dumbfounded and unable to think of something to say.

"Your mother is cold and distant. She has expectations for you and this household. But she knows you better than you think. And she loves you dearly."

"Then why does she always force me to do things I don't want to do?"

"In the hopes you might like something she does. Common ground for you to bond over."

Song scoffed. "Why didn't she try something I like?"

"Because you get your stubbornness from your mother," Johanna said with a laugh.

Sunshine yawned from his position against the wall beside the door. "Sorry, ladies, but I'm afraid it's past my bedtime."

Johanna stood, a small smile on her lips. "I have to agree. We can talk more tomorrow," she said to Song.

"Walk you to your room, Miss Burke?" He extended his elbow.

Song snorted a laugh as Johanna wrapped her palm around his arm. The woman shot Song a quick warning scowl.

"Oh, yes," Song said, "maybe you could tuck her in, too!"

As they left the room, Sunshine made a rude gesture which Johanna didn't see. Song broke down into giggles as the door closed.

WHEN SONG ENTERED THE DINING ROOM IN THE MORNING, HER mother sat alone at the table, staring at her eggs. Song was late to breakfast, but normally others would already be there. Instead, Mrs. Gould had herself as company.

Song thought over what Johanna had said that night. With a heavy breath, she entered and sat in the seat nearest her mother — which was not a place she ever chose. Since she'd been old enough to choose her own place at the table, Song had always sat far away from Annie, closer to her father.

"Good morning, Mother." Song served herself from the dishes set at the center of the table. Once she'd filled her plate, she stared at her mother, who stared at her with tired curiosity. Instead of asking the question she knew the answer to, she refreshed her mother's tea from the pot kept warm over a candle, dropped in one cube of sugar, and a splash of cream.

"How are you feeling?" her mother asked, a skeptical note in her tone.

"Quite good, actually. I had an interesting talk with Johanna last night." She loaded a piece of toast with beans and scrambled eggs, then took a bite too large.

"Oh?" Mrs. Gould started eating the food she'd been pushing around, as though the thought of conversation had returned her appetite.

"Yes," Song said, then held up her hand for her mother to wait as she chewed and swallowed. "She told me I'm a terrible daughter, and you're a stubborn mother. And I stayed up thinking…why can't we meet in the middle? I don't like the things you like, and you undoubtedly hate the things I like. So why don't we both try something new?"

Annie paused her chewing to stare at her daughter during this speech. The wheels turned behind her eyes, and when she swallowed, she said, "I…think that could be fun. Did you have anything in mind?"

"Not entirely. I've never seen you ride horseback. We could try that."

Her face paled. "I could never…"

Song smirked. "It's all right to say you're afraid, Mother. It's braver to admit it than to hold your tongue."

Annie stared at her plate, a look of shame on her face. "I…have been terrified of horses since I was a child."

"See? That wasn't so hard."

Her mother scrutinized her for a silent minute, which, in the past, would have unnerved Song. Now, though, she stared right back as she ate her eggs on beans on toast, wolfing it down as she'd grown used to on the skyship. Her aristocratic shame had been all but erased—not that she had tried to get it back. Perhaps at a dinner party she might break out her manners like fine porcelain dishes. But this was breakfast with her mother, and she would be lying if she didn't admit that it was partly to get on the woman's nerves and see just how mannerless she would allow her daughter to be before chastising her.

"You've changed so much," Annie said. "I never would have thought you could unlearn everything I taught you, but you managed it."

"Everything Johanna taught me," Song corrected. "I haven't forgotten it. I just don't feel like it's me."

"And who are you, then?"

Song leaned back with her teacup. She took a thoughtful sip. *I'm not only a ruddy pirate, I'm the most infamous captain in history. Are you proud of me now, Mother?* "I am a woman who has learned to wear masks to appease others… Just like you. Just like Daddy. Our life in this house is a farce. A masquerade. It always has been. You don't like Captain Song, but at least Song won't smile at people he hates. That sort of honesty is refreshing."

"A man like that would stab his best friend for a bounty."

She shook her head. "You heard the song. *The Princess and the Slave.*"

Annie nodded.

"The slave in that story was Song's best friend. Why do you think Carliolace burned that night? It wasn't for some heartbroken aristocrat." She released a long breath. "You speak of things you don't understand, Mother. Maybe if you understood, you wouldn't be so quick to judge."

"He's a pirate."

"A pirate who will look you in the eyes as he kills you, instead of stabbing you in the back like a coward. Existing with that kind of honesty is freeing. You should try it sometime."

"Perhaps we can start with an activity we'll both enjoy."

Song smiled, happy that it, at least, was something. "I'm sorry I was such a brat."

"I'm sorry I didn't ask what you wanted enough. I should've listened when you said you didn't want a welcome home ball. And now it's too late to cancel."

"Oh, no. That's all right. The timing is fortuitous. I'm looking forward to the whole thing."

"You never got fitted for a gown."

The corner of her lips rose. "I have one that'll be sure to leave people talking."

She was, of course, referring to the special one Stitch had made based on the dress Miriad had given her in Pishing. It was a scarlet version with copper-colored accents, and she'd been eager for an opportunity to wear it. Her eyes stood out in it so intensely that when she'd tried it on, Stitch had been struck dumb. She was most excited for the scandal it would cause when her bare knees were on display for all to see. Song may have murdered the girl's stepfather, but at least Miriad's dream of her own fashion spreading to Andalise could come true.

Footsteps entered behind Song.

"Oh, that smells good," Ponce said.

She lurched to her feet to grip him in a relieved hug. "They let you go!" She leaned close to whisper in his ear, "Did you tell them anything?"

"Of course I didn't," he said.

"Sit. Have breakfast," she said louder. "I'm sure the jail's food is atrocious."

She sat with the two and had more toast as they all spoke. Her spirits rose. After breakfast, she would have to pull Ponce aside and fill him in on the plan, but for now, it was enough to sit and talk.

Thirty-One

THE NERVOUS KNOTS TIGHTENED SO HARD IN SONG'S STOMACH, she thought she might vomit. What she was doing was insanity at best. But it was the only way her father would clear all charges against Ponce. He had to see the real Song, in the flesh. Sure, she could do it in a less public way, but he could deny it and keep the secret. He could make Ponce a scapegoat to protect his own daughter. Song was many things, but a coward was not one of them, and she would not let one of her dearest friends suffer the punishment that should have been hers.

She didn't want the punishment, of course. And that's why she was banking on her father not wanting the public shame. She could blackmail him without a word. Revealing her as Captain Song would ruin him and their legacy. He would be jobless and their family ostracized. Elroy Gould would keep her secret, either out of love for his daughter, or fear for his own reputation.

She and those in the mansion who knew her secret had planned and planned again. She'd timed walking through various areas of the house, counting each step. And now it was show time. Everyone was in place and would play their part, including Captain Song.

The guests had all arrived, and now Leopold stood at the top of the stairs alone, in case there were latecomers. The music echoed up from the ballroom through the cracked door of the linen closet she'd been hiding in for hours. When the music stopped and the crowd grew quiet, Amelia's voice reached her as the woman began the 'special treat' they'd planned.

"Welcome, everyone," she said, her voice carrying through the conic megaphone they'd set up for her. "Before we present our guest of honor, Miss Tsingsei Gould," she had to pause as the guests clapped, "we have a special performance. This is a piece written by Captain Song himself! And they say that if you play it, and leave a bench open at a piano, the captain will be unable to resist sitting down to play."

Murmurs rippled through the crowd.

"What do you say? Should we see if the captain appears? Or are we too scared to test this tall tale?"

After a moment, the applause started. Song chuckled. The woman was surprisingly good at showmanship.

"To play the song tonight, I present Henry Xavier Barton the Third of Anarchaia."

Applause filled the room, then died down.

"And Thersiàl Saigh of Aibhànocht."

The crowd clapped for Sunshine before dying down again.

"And now, ladies and gentlemen, I present to you: *Song's Storm.*"

The music box tune started, amplified by the brass cone. As Sunshine joined with his sorrowful, sweeping violin, Song sneaked out of the closet after making sure no one was looking. She approached the stairs as though having come from the front door, her invitation clutched in one hand. She stopped beside Leopold, who gaped at her. Song held up a shushing finger, then handed him the invitation. He took it and motioned for her to head down the stairs.

Once Amelia's head tilted to grin up at the hooded figure, the rest of the audience turned one at a time to see what she was smiling at. Off to the side stood Foggerty, Daven, and her father with Ryk'r shadowing him at her order. It didn't surprise her that Elroy would have called the detective inspector. What surprised her, though, was the woman beside him: Olivia. She wore what had to be her nicest dress, though it was still a rag compared to the expensive silks of the other guests.

The crowd parted for Song as she reached the bottom of the stairs, none daring to get too close. She felt like she'd been walking forever, like time had slowed to a desperate crawl and the closer she got to the stage, the farther away it drew. Her gaze landed on Ponce and she took a deep breath, forcing herself to remain calm for his sake. But there was still that fear that someone would rip her hood down and ruin the entire plan.

She reached the stage unhindered after what seemed like an eternity, though it had only been a minute. She sat on the piano bench and started her part at the right time. For a moment, the entire world melted around her. She was alone in a room with her piano. Nothing else mattered as she poured her heart onto those keys, the tune pattering out like sorrowful rain, as though made from every drop of blood she'd shed, and every tear she'd cried. Her heart swelled and clenched and thrummed with the music, tightening with the crescendo and settling in her throat as a tight mass of excitement and sorrow and nervous chaos.

The song ended. She folded her hands in her lap and stared down at the keys, begging her eyes not to spill the tears they desperately wanted to release. The music box continued until it slowed to a mournful stop. The silence afterward was louder than any applause the stunned crowd could have given.

Song took a deep breath and slid from the bench. She descended the stairs of the stage and stood before her father.

"Miss Paige?" Foggerty stared down at the woman, who gave Song a giddy smile.

"Hello, Olivia," Song said, and took her hand to kiss the top. "Are you working with the police now?" She spoke with the uncomfortably low pitch in the presence of her father.

"She's just—" he began.

"She can speak for herself."

Olivia took a breath, a grateful smile on her lips. "Only to confirm the face under the hood. And since this is as much of your face as I've ever seen, I can assure you, Detective Inspector, that this is Captain Song." She settled her gaze on Foggerty. "Now draw up those citizenship papers for Igriid."

"You betrayed me to keep your friend in the country?" Song asked.

A look of hurt and shame contorted Olivia's features.

"I would've done the same, if the roles were reversed." She smiled and Olivia returned the expression.

"I almost didn't trust you would actually show up," Elroy said, interrupting any more conversation she and Olivia could have.

Song turned her smile onto her father. "But I did. Do you intend to uphold your end of the bargain?"

"A meeting in private in exchange for Mr. Barton's freedom. We can talk in my office."

She looked at the detective inspector. "You may handcuff me for the short journey, if it makes Senator Gould more comfortable. I only ask that my hood remain up."

"Acceptable," Elroy said.

"Turn around," Foggerty said.

She did so and waited as he locked the metal around her wrists. He took an extra second with her right arm, but she couldn't see what he was doing with it. Perhaps he'd figured out it was too cold and too hard. She could worry later about him figuring it out or not. For now, she smirked at the crowd as they looked right at the person they'd come to welcome home, though none of them had any idea.

As the officers each took an arm to lead her behind her father, Ryk'r a few paces behind, she wondered if it would ever get old. Would she ever tire of people looking right at her, unable to recognize the person they were looking for? She almost wondered if it was wrong to have that twisted glee ripple through her at remaining unrecognized. But she enjoyed it far too much to ever wish it would stop.

Isabelle surged forward, held back by her husband. "Where is my baby?"

Song stopped to grin at her. "Where is my apology?" She shook her head when the woman said nothing. "What is more important to you? Your child or your lie?"

"You sick bastard!"

Foggerty released Song to block Isabelle from getting to her.

"Where is my baby?"

Song resumed walking. "Let's go, Senator. Unless you want to break our deal?"

Elroy held out a hand to soothe Isabelle. "We'll get your son back. All in good time."

The woman stepped back into the crowd, allowing her husband to comfort her. Foggerty gripped Song's arm, and they resumed walking.

"Thank you, Detective Inspector. I'd hate for our agreement to be voided over a hysterical brat."

"Shut your mouth, Song," Foggerty said.

She gasped as though wounded. "After all we've been through? That hurts."

They started up the stairs, and the music resumed in their wake. Song walked in silence after that, half sure one of them would yank down her hood before they reached her father's office. If they saw her braid, it would be over. The only way out of it then would be killing the officers before they could tell anyone else.

They reached Elroy's office on the first floor.

"You have five minutes of my time," he said.

"In your office," she reminded him. "Alone and preferably without handcuffs."

He pursed his lips, eyes darting between her and the officers.

"I promise not to harm you. I'm a pirate of my word."

He glanced between them again, and nodded. The two removed the handcuffs and stepped aside. Daven's eyes flitted to a spot to her right, but she ignored him. She couldn't afford to let him distract her in such a juvenile way. The officers eyed Ryk'r as the three found places to stand in the hallway. She entered the office and waited as her father shut the door and turned the lock.

"Lock it."

He stared at her. "I did."

"No, you didn't. You twisted the dummy lock meant to trick people into thinking you did, so you can't be held hostage in your own office." She reached out and pushed the button hidden behind the knob, which would release the bar to truly lock the door.

"How did you know about that?"

"Don't shout," she warned on a whisper, then gripped the edge of her hood. "All right?"

Elroy nodded, and she took down her hood and raised her mask. His eyes rounded. "*Tsing*—" He glanced at the door and they moved away from it as she shushed him. "Tsingsei," he hissed. "What are you doing in that getup? Take it off, now. This isn't a joke."

"You're right, Father, it's not a joke. I am Captain Song, and always have been."

"You're lying to spare Henry."

"No, I'm not. Well, not the lying part. Exposing my secret to you in order to spare him from the accusations and the thieves' necklace, yes. I won't let any friend of mine be a scapegoat."

"The threatening letter with the Garda's Pride?"

She chuckled. "I didn't think it was that threatening. Then again, if I had signed my given name, neither would you."

Elroy sat in one of the two chairs in front of his desk and set his head in his hands. "You lied to me about not hiding Song."

"No, I didn't. I wasn't in the stables, or the servants' quarters. I wasn't hiding at all. Thank you for steering the search away from *our* home. One look in my chest and the jig would be up." She strolled to his tray of liquors and poured brandy into two glasses.

"Do you have any idea what this will do to my reputation? I would—"

"Lose your job, your memberships to clubs, your friends, your livelihood, and the whole family would be ostracized. Mother would divorce you and latch onto some other rich man who might repair her public image so she can continue living a lavish life as a spoiled brat. Yes, I had thought about it. Though, I'm not actually sure, now, that Mother *would* do that." She handed him a glass, and sat in the chair beside him, raising her feet up onto his desk and crossing them at the ankles. "I'd meet the gallows and probably win against it. I'm quite hard to kill, you know."

"What am I supposed to do with you, Tsingsei?"

Song took a long drink and stared at the painting of her as a fifteen-year-old hanging on the wall. "Turn me in and be the hero, collect the quoine on my head. Or reveal who I am to the wrong people and lose everything. Or…keep my secret to protect your job, your lifestyle, and your little girl."

"I…need more proof." He turned to scrutinize her as though the proof was written across her face.

Song dropped her feet and leaned forward to set her drink down. "Common knowledge that Song is Touched, right?"

"Yes."

"Well, not anymore. I…shut it off, like closing a faucet, I suppose. However, I do still have something." She unbuckled her coat and pulled it off.

Something hard hit the floor at her feet. She stared, then picked up the green glass bead cradling a dark metal. Song set it on her metal arm and cursed when it stuck. A magnet. Foggerty must have placed it there, and now he knew about the prosthetic—or at least that something metal was up her sleeve. She set the magnet on her father's desk and draped her coat over the chair. Song unbuttoned the long glove covering her right arm and dragged it off. She held her arm out and moved it, showing him how the joints glowed blue with each movement.

"What is that?" he asked, taking it in his hands.

"The price I paid for saving my crew." She unbuckled the strap around her biceps and pulled off the prosthetic.

Elroy gasped and stared at the end of her natural arm. "How…?"

"The bone shattered. My men held me down and cut it off at Sunshine's order. I was furious with him for months, but now I know he saved my life. The arm was dead, and would have taken me with it."

"Who is Sunshine?"

"Thersiàl. Because of his sunny disposition, of course."

"Of course he's a pirate. And Henry?"

"Captain's Assistant. I had to make up a title for him because the men think my cabin boys are cursed. They keep dying, and only one was my fault. Two asked for it, one was a hothead who got herself killed, and one…well, we all miss that little bugger. Adored him." As she spoke, she counted out the cabin boys on her right hand.

Elroy stared in confusion and transfixion at the limb moving on its own while she still held it in her left hand. "That is…an interesting ability."

She stared at the arm. It went limp as though playing dead, causing her to almost drop it. "When it behaves, it's fantastic. I could kill a man from another room. Other times it likes to do…things. Sometimes it helps me, sometimes it makes these weird gestures. It's the *kijæm*. Got a mind of its own, you know."

A fist pounded on the door. "Five minutes is up, Song," Foggerty shouted on the other side.

She let out all her breath and sat in the chair to pinch the arm between her thighs to secure it back on. After a moment of her fiddling with the buckle on the straps, her father crouched in front of her to help secure them.

"Thank you. That's normally Ponce's job. Henry, I mean. Call him Ponce because of his aristocratic upbringing."

"How did you manage these past few days without him?"

"Just had to figure it out. Sunshine helped."

Foggerty pounded on the door again. "Senator Gould?"

"I'm fine," Elroy shouted.

She looked over her shoulder at the door, then at her father. "So, what are you going to do?"

After a minute in which Elroy looked tortured over the decision, and she wasn't sure what he would choose, he stood, grabbed her coat and glove, and shoved them into her arms. He took her by the arm and led her to the other side of the room. He set his hand on the corner where the two walls met. It creaked open, revealing a way into the neighboring library, covered by the world map tapestry she'd looked at her entire life, but had never moved.

"Get in here," he whispered, "and wait. I'll bring them into my office. Once the hallway is clear, get to your room and put on your gown. The guests will only wait so long before growing suspicious."

Song threw her arms around him in a tight hug. "Thank you, Daddy." She kissed his cheek and entered the library, then closed the wall passage.

Instead of leaving, though, she put her ear to the false wall to listen.

"Sorry about that. Come in," Elroy said.

"Where is Song?" Foggerty demanded.

"Come inside and we can discuss that. You, too."

The door closed.

"What are you playing at, Senator?" Foggerty demanded.

"Trust me when I tell you we should not apprehend Song. We need to find some way to explain away tonight. But Captain Song had some intriguing propositions, which I am very interested to hear more about."

"And where is he?" Foggerty demanded again.

"I let him out the window, after he promised to return later."

"And you trusted him?" he thundered.

"I do," Elroy said. "He may be a pirate, but even they have honor codes. Song will keep his word."

Song smirked and raised her hood, then slipped out of the library to rush for her room. It was time for Tsingsei Gould to make her grand debut.

THERE WAS ONE THING THEY'D FAILED TO ACCOUNT FOR IN THEIR planning of the night: Annie Gould. Song knew how meddlesome her mother could be, and how controlling she would get to ensure an event went off without a hitch. And so it shouldn't have surprised her to find her mother standing in her bedroom, her face red from irritation, with an uncomfortable Johanna doing her best to stave her off.

"Of all the stunts to pull," she said the moment the door closed. "And tonight of all nights. Get out of that and put on your dress." She didn't stop to let Song undress herself—she hadn't even lowered her hood, yet. Mrs. Gould strode over and started working the coat buckles for her. "The guests have been asking after you this *whole time*, and I've had to assure them you would appear once everyone was here, since it is *your* night, and you wanted to make a grand entrance."

"Mother—"

"I have been lying through my teeth for you!"

"How long have you known it was me?" she demanded, slapping her mother's hands away so she could undress herself.

"It's the way you defended Song from every criticism and had none of your own to contribute. You defended the name like someone defends themselves. Add to that what you told your father. He thought you meant Henry, of course, but I didn't say anything of my suspicions. You just confirmed it when you played that song."

"It's just a song! Anyone could have played it!"

"Yes, but not everyone dances when they play. You move your elbows more than most, and when you finish playing, you've always folded your hands in your lap in a particular way."

She stared in shock at her, then shot an expression to Johanna as though to ask, 'Can you believe this woman?'

"I told you, your mother is more observant than you give her credit for," Johanna said.

"Why did you do this tonight?" Annie asked.

"Because I had to show myself publicly, otherwise Father would have pinned my name on Henry, and made him pay for being someone he isn't."

She released a long sigh through her nose. "All right, get ready. I'll stall a little longer. But tomorrow, you, your father, and I are going to have a long talk about this." Her mother slipped out the door and shut it behind herself.

Song met Johanna's gaze, her eyes wide. "She figured it out?"

"Your mother is quite observant. She just keeps her mouth shut. It's not her place to be smart, so she doesn't let on how intelligent she is."

Song put her clothes away, retrieving a small trinket before locking her chest, and pulled her dress on while Johanna worked to apply her makeup as best she could in a hurry with a moving subject. Next, Song sat still while the woman worked her braid free and styled her hair. She shoved her feet into a pair of high-heeled ankle boots, and the two left the room together, Song locking it behind them. Johanna rushed ahead to slip into the crowd as Song approached the stairs for the second time that night.

This time, the nerves in her stomach tangled tighter because she didn't have the protection of her coat and mask.

She may as well have been naked. Leopold announced her to the room, and they all clapped as though her mere presence were a performance unto itself. So she gave everyone her brightest smile and bowed her head graciously. Tonight she would earn that standing ovation.

Well-wishers and acquaintances stopped her every chance to express their relief at her return. Bachelors tried their hand at charming her. She danced with each and played the affluent damsel part to perfection, a mask of gold and jewels hiding her discomfort and desire to run away again and never return. Her mother gave her a secretive yet approving smile—a momentary slip of her own mask which Song now knew existed. Her father kept his eyes glued to her as though if he looked away for even a moment, she would turn back into the captain.

Once left alone to breathe, she wandered out to the sprawling brick patio. Ryk'r had returned to shadowing her, and planted himself in the doorway to keep watch. Isabelle leaned on the stone banister, staring out at the hedge maze in the garden. Song set her hands on the railing beside the woman. It was cool beneath her left palm, as the cold spring night bit at their bare skin.

"It seems so very long ago, doesn't it?" Song asked.

Isabelle's gaze dropped as a frown tugged at her lips. "It does." They stayed in silence for a minute before the woman asked, "Did you run because of me?"

"Yes," she said. "It was one of two reasons."

"I'm sorry. Truly. I never told anyone. I couldn't admit a girl had kissed me, even if it meant getting you in trouble."

"As apologies go, that one was shite, and I don't accept it."

"Then what apology would you accept?"

Song slipped her fingers into the little pocket at her waist. "There is only one thing I want from you," she said in her lower tone.

Isabelle jolted and spun toward Song, scrutinizing her face. "What did you say?"

"You spread your legs for a pirate who wouldn't touch you, and claim your bastard is the result." She pulled the locket out and let it dangle in the air between them. "There is only one apology I will accept from you. Or is your lie more important than the man in this locket and that child you've done nothing to get back?"

Tears sprouted in the woman's eyes. "Y-you're…?"

"Say it," she hissed.

"You're Song?"

"Aye. Tell anyone and you'll never find your son—no, I won't kill him. I'm not a monster. But I want the world to know you lied and sullied my good name. I never touched you. I never touched any woman who did not consent. And I especially didn't father any child."

Isabelle closed her eyes, her makeup-tinted tears rolling colored streaks down her face. "My son is his."

"Whose?"

"The man in the picture. My parents threatened to disown me if I didn't break contact with him."

"Your orphan boy."

"Yes."

Song opened the locket to stare at the man in the picture. "You sacrificed the love of your life for superficial comforts."

"I still see him in secret," she admitted on a whisper.

"So, your child was conceived in love, and you're letting everyone believe he was conceived in violence and hate. And people say *I'm* a reprobate?"

"I would lose everything, if…" Tears trickled down her cheeks as she closed her eyes in shame.

"Sounds messy, and I'm not interested in other people's messes." She dropped the locket into Isabelle's hand. "It doesn't matter what you say beyond the truth about me. I want you to tell the world you lied. Song never touched you. After that, I don't care. But you'll get your baby back when the rest of the world knows I have no claim to him."

"The police told me to keep my mouth shut. They've been setting up a trap for Song—for you. It's been killing me. Please—"

"He's safe and fed. He will remain so until you admit the truth. As for the trap…I've already escaped enough of their traps. But thank you for the heads-up." Song stared in at the dancing crowd. "If you love your son, you'll be honest. And you'll keep my secret. Enjoy the rest of the ball, if you can." With that, she walked away, leaving the woman there to cry in the cold, alone, clutching a secret locket to her chest.

Thirty-Two

In the morning, Song snatched the paper up to skim through it before her father could. "Oh, good, my knees made the front page. It's nice to know they have their priorities straight. Lovely picture of me, though." The picture in question had her posed at the top of the stairs, so the entire dress was on display.

"Where did you even find such a dress?" Annie scoffed.

"It's an upcoming style from a girl in Pishing. I happen to like it." She returned to skimming the paper.

Smaller than the headline about the Gould ball, but still on the front page, was an article detailing a late-night visit to the editorial office from Isabelle Clarksen.

"'Song was nothing but a gentleman to me. I took advantage of his unusual kindness and told what I thought was a victimless lie. I regret the decision, and I hope Caleb Song will accept this apology and clearing of his name. He is not the father of my child. I miss my son dearly.' Well, would you look at that? She does have some sense in her."

"Will Captain Song be returning the child, then?" Elroy asked, his sights settled meaningfully on her as he accepted the newspaper.

"He will. All he wanted was his name cleared, and she's finally done that."

He diverted his gaze to the paper. "I hope we'll also see an end to the mutilation of copycats."

"Song never did like liars," Ponce said. "Especially not ones who'll steal a name."

Elroy's gaze flicked to the man for a minute before returning to the paper. "I'm sorry for the accusations, Henry. It's good that your name has been cleared."

Song smirked at the odd round-about way they spoke of her with others present. "As long as weak men stop taking a name that isn't their own, then the mutilations should stop."

"Hate to be the bearer of bad news," Sunshine said behind his own newspaper. "But there's been someone flying around Pishing as Song."

"You mean weeks ago, right?"

"No. They stopped a noble vessel just two days ago."

"What?" she snapped. "It had better not be the Reprisal," she hissed across the table at him.

"No… Do you remember that big, black ship we saw?"

"Darkness. Of course I remember it."

"That's this new Song's ship."

Song clenched her jaw. They'd been within interception range of an imposter and hadn't even known it. "Can we alert the post that any person claiming Song's name who doesn't fly on the Stars' Reprisal is an imposter?"

"I'll see what I can do. We've been keeping a close eye on the situation," her father said.

"I know someone who would *love* to keep an even closer eye on it. And perhaps put a stop to it."

"Song is not going after anyone," Elroy intoned, half distracted by an article. "It's not worth the risk."

She folded her arms as she rolled her eyes. "It's not a risk. The imposter doesn't stand a chance."

But her father wasn't listening anymore, as whatever he was reading took his full attention away. She scoffed and shoved too much scone into her mouth, then struggled to chew it through her aggravation.

THAT EVENING, AFTER SONG HAD SENT JOHANNA OUT TO DELIVER the infant to the police precinct, claiming the captain had left him on their step, Senator Gould called his daughter into his office. Song sat across from her father, hands folded in her lap as they waited for her mother. When Annie entered the room, Leopold closed the door behind her and the three were left alone in the silence.

Elroy finished sorting through documents, then threaded his fingers together and set them over a stack of papers. "As you both know, my colleagues and I have been going through negotiations to stave off the impending war over Captain Song's antics surrounding Pishing."

"The *impost—*"

"No, Tsingsei. This goes back far longer than that person has been causing problems. This is *your* fault."

"I didn't do anything!"

"You, an Andalisian, were cutting off trade to and from another country, with whom we have had a tenuous relationship for decades. It doesn't matter why, or if you were acting on behalf of someone in the Andalisian government, they are choosing to view it as an act of war."

Song sat back, her jaw clenched tight. "So, what's happened to the negotiations, then?"

"King Bartlett gave a single term that would mend fences, as it were. It's a common practice there, and the rest of the senate agreed it was a reasonable…solution." He released an exasperated breath.

"And it involves us?" Annie asked.

"It involves Tsingsei."

A thought entered her mind, and she prayed she was wrong. She didn't want to voice it, or even ask what, in case doing so would manifest her worst nightmare into existence.

"They would like for you to marry a royal. Probably one of the princes."

And there it was. Her wildest, most terrible idea had been right. She slid down to slouch in her seat and scowl at the wall. "No."

"There has to be another compromise that can be met," Mrs. Gould said.

"There isn't. We've tried. They suggested this shortly after you returned home, but I put it off, hoping something else would appease them. They see it as a unifying of our nations. A royal of Pishing, and the most famous Andalisian woman."

"The princess of Andalise, the king of the skies," Song growled.

"What?" Mrs. Gould asked.

"Nothing. Something someone called me once." Song sat up with determination. "How do I get out of this?"

"You don't," Elroy said. "As I said, this was the final measure. And I agreed to it today, *after* you revealed to me *you* are Captain Song. This is your mess, and you will help clean it up by any means necessary."

"You're all right with selling your own daughter?"

"No!" he shouted. "No, I am not. But it's this or war. Would you really put your own selfish wants over the good of two countries?"

"Yes, I would!"

"That's too bad. You should have thought of that before you started a fight with one of said countries."

"I didn't start a fight! I was upset and angry."

"With an entire country?" he demanded.

"No, with Roman Duchamp…and the country that allowed him to exist as a high lord." She folded her arms and huffed.

"Tsingsei, need I remind you that you killed him and his son, massacred almost his entire royal guard, and burned down half the city? You had your revenge and then some. Everything after that was you throwing a temper tantrum over a slave."

Song lurched to her feet and slammed her metal fist onto the top of his desk—it creaked and a hairline fracture ran along the edge. "*He was not a slave!*" she thundered. "He was a free man. And he was worth more than all the lives I've taken in his name combined. I would burn this entire world to ash for him." She fought to catch her breath. "And no one even knows his name. He was the most important person in the world to me, and it's like I'm the only one who gives a damn that it was murder that Roman carried out, not justice or the law."

He released a long breath. "And if you had left it at that, then we wouldn't be having this conversation. But you dragged two *countries* into your quarrel *after* you'd already gotten your vengeance. You hurt thousands upon thousands of innocent people. Either you pay at their gallows as Captain Song, or you pay at their altar as Tsingsei Gould. Either way, my dear daughter, this is the price, and even I cannot escape it."

Song straightened and clenched her jaw until it hurt.

"And I would prefer you choose the second option." Elroy stood and circled the desk to set his hands on her shoulders. "Even though I say all these things, know this is not what I want. I would erase the bounties for your head if I could—I'm actually working with a few colleagues to… rewrite a few things. To protect you from the price you've brought on your life. But I was also out-voted. The other senators agreed to the terms. The details, however, are on us to set in order."

Furious tears clouded her vision. "They already agreed to it?"

"Yes. And signed. And…if you disappear again, they will see that as breaching the treaty. It was my idea to at least let you choose the man you will marry."

She let him press her down into the chair. "I don't want to marry anyone, especially not a man, and especially not some stuffy lord I don't know, who is probably twice my age."

"We'll choose a handsome one," Annie said.

"I don't care about looks, Mother! I'm attracted to *women*. I enjoy sleeping with *women*. No amount of handsome in a man is going to change his utter lack of honeypot!"

"*Tsingsei!* Watch your language," her mother snapped.

"I will bloody well not. What good is making love to someone if you can't then fall asleep on breasts? It's the second best part!"

"Oh! My heavens," Mrs. Gould gasped, covering her mouth in the sort of shock only a high society prude could muster.

"Don't 'oh my heavens' me, Mother. I know how babies are made now. And I know what's in those naughty brown-paper books you hide from everyone. As awful as it is to even think about, you're not some innocent, untouched woman. And I bet Daddy has slept on your breasts plenty of times." She gave her a half smirk, half sneer, convinced that she'd won an argument—though she was the only one having it.

At that moment, she realized what she'd been saying. She was so used to the people around her knowing she preferred women over men that she'd forgotten she had still kept it from them. She hadn't anticipated blurting her secret out to her parents, but her anger had gotten the better of her. To her shock, though, neither looked taken aback or even a little bit surprised.

Elroy released a long, patient sigh, his eyes closed to the vulgarity and argument. "Why not just choose the prince, then?"

"Because it's what they want, so I don't want to do it," she said, folding her arms over her chest again.

"What if I chose for you?"

"No, I don't want *no* say."

"What about a ball?" her mother offered, having recovered from the earlier fluster.

Song sat up. "A ball in which the eligible bachelors all wear masks. Like the one I wear, so it covers their hair, too. Then I won't even know the ages of some. Or if they're bald. But I'll dance with them. They have one dance to convince me to choose them."

"Why only one dance?" Annie asked.

"Because it's like a good duel. You can really tell a lot about a person by how they dance or fight. If he lets me lead, he might be a more agreeable sort. Someone who won't domineer me or try to own me."

"What if they just go on about how pretty you are?" Elroy asked.

"Well, I'm not, so that won't be a problem."

"My dear daughter, you are beautiful when you're not scowling."

She scowled deeper. "Make it a masquerade, then. Just like my bloody life at this point. One big farce of people hiding their true selves. I'll wear a gold mask, guests wear black, and bachelors wear silver. One dance. Then I make my choice at the end of the night." She sat upright, her chin raised. "Is that agreeable?"

"As long as it is to you, then I will agree to it," he said.

"It's not, but I don't have any better ideas that don't involve running away again…or killing a bunch of people."

He breathed out, closing his eyes for patience. "Please do not kill the king."

"Who said I was going to kill the king?"

"Or the princes."

"Who said I would kill the princes?"

"Or the senators…" He directed his weary gaze at her, willing her to stop being difficult.

"What if I marry an old man and he has a mysterious cardiac episode on our wedding night? Is that within the realm of things that will get me in trouble, or would they accept it as an act of their gods and let me rule in his stead?" She gave her father a mischievous grin.

"Tsingsei…"

"I hate that disappointed tone so much."

"That's why I use it," he said.

"I'm just covering all possible unforeseen situations which could cause complications."

He said nothing, just stared at her with strained disappointment.

"All right, then…when am I to be sold?"

"You're not being s—"

"I most certainly am! It may not be for quoine, but you are selling me to those barbarians, and the price is peace. Would I still be the sacrifice if I were a man?"

Elroy thought, then nodded. "If everything was otherwise the same, yes, perhaps. Though you'd marry the princess, instead."

Song sat upright. "*Can* I marry her?"

A long silence settled over the room as her parents stared at her.

"Why are you acting like I commented on the weather when I just admitted my darkest secret to you?"

Annie scoffed. "Everyone in this house has known or suspected something like that about you since you grew old enough to be attracted to someone. I had hoped it was a phase, or maybe that you might like both… But I see that's not something you grew out of."

"And like it or not," Elroy interjected, "we live in a society which finds these things uncomfortable. Pishing is no better. And so, my dear, beautiful daughter, you must marry a lord or prince, rather than the princess."

She squared her jaw. "You're not mad at me? I thought you'd be mad. It's…it's why I ran away!"

Her mother shifted in her seat. "I…was upset. Losing you sort of made it irrelevant. I'm happy to have you back, as you are. And now you don't have to keep pretending Amelia isn't your sweetheart!"

"You are far too enthusiastic about that, Mother. Also, she's not my sweetheart. I have a…betrothed, though."

Elroy blinked in shock at her. "A what? You what? Since when? Whom?"

Song picked at the fingertips of her right glove, her lips pursed together. She withdrew the necklace tucked beneath her bodice. "The sultania of Armalinia. She wanted the Andalisian princess, same as Pishing. This is why Ryk'r follows me everywhere I go."

"Can we negotiate with her?"

"No. I tried. But she'll only claim me if I return to her country, so I'm mostly in the clear, so long as she doesn't find out about this whole debacle. No one needs to know, right?"

He released a long, thoughtful breath. "Right. At least for now."

"Can I make demands?" she asked after a long pause.

"What kind?"

"Things like…separate bedrooms. A personal stylist, like Johanna, so no one sees my arm."

"Your arm?" Mrs. Gould asked.

"Long story, but my right arm is fake." Song rapped a knuckle against the forearm to produce a hollow ringing. "Also, I'd like it made clear that both parties may have a mistress or mister—whichever they prefer."

Her father nodded. "I'll send the masquerade proposal to Pishing. Work on your terms while we wait."

"How long will it take?" she asked.

"As long as it needs to."

"Find something to occupy your time, dear," her mother said. "*Not* tavern crawling and mutilating men claiming to be Captain Song."

She made a face. "What if I'm not tavern *crawling*, and just happen across a copycat on the street?"

"Tsingsei," her father warned. "No more mutilations."

"Fine, fine. I'll just go read that book Pishing will execute me for owning." She smiled, stood, and left the room without elaborating as they gaped after her.

Elroy reached up to press his thumb and fingertips to his temples.

Thirty-Three

Over the next week, Song did what her parents had asked, and stayed within the estate. When she wasn't spending time with Amelia, she would read the books she wasn't allowed to own, along with her great-great-grandmother's journal.

She received at least one bit of good news. In light of the proof that they were dealing with an imposter circling Pishing, her father had managed to convince the other senators to draft up a privateer contract for Song and her crew. Once everything had calmed down, she would take to the skies to apprehend whoever it was. Unfortunately, they wanted the man alive, so they could question him, and clear Andalise of the accusations that they'd hired Song as a privateer in order to disrupt trade. She didn't care who was responsible or why; she wanted that man's head mounted to her wall.

The days drifted into the next week, which again found her lounging and reading the book on Jinjran. She'd learned a great deal, but didn't know what she could ever hope to do with such information.

Song sat upright, eyes wide on the tome. What she recognized as *The Song of Freedom* in its original form sat on the page, and beside it was the translation. What caught her eye, though, was the name. *Stevnaa Baalmoru - Baalmoru's Call.* She marked her place and dug through her trunk for the holy book of Aibhànocht and the translation. She retrieved her family journal from her nightstand, and rushed to the estate's library.

She scoured the shelves for the book of children's stories she knew to be there. Once she had that, she added it to the pile. Song scanned over spines in the world section which she'd avoided her whole life due to lack of interest, praying there was something there on Armalinia. After a while, she found a book on their culture. She searched the glossary at the back and found the word she wanted, then added that to the stack. Next was a book on folklore and legends of Jashedar.

With a growl, she rushed from the room to find Leopold. He was in the kitchens organizing the dinner courses for the evening. She waited until he finished—which earned her a curious look from the staff—then pulled him into the hallway.

"Who has the most knowledge of what books we have in the library?"

"That would be me, Miss," he said.

"Oh, splendid. I'm looking for anything on Kerriwen or Telbhaniich-Zardi. Specifically local legends, folklore, or religion."

"Why?"

She flipped her hand in the air as though brushing off his concern. "Just trying to educate myself on the world. Do you know if we have any?"

"Telbhaniich-Zardi doesn't really have its own culture or folklore. It's all bits and pieces from everywhere else. We do not own any texts on Kerriwen—I'm not sure many even exist. I can order some, if you like."

"Please do, thank you. How long would those take?"

"Anywhere from a week to a few months—longer if we have to import."

Song made a face. "All right, order them. Thank you."

She returned to the library and opened each text to relevant pages based on the glossary and read through the information. After that, she reread the legend she'd grown up with—as most children in Andalise had. *Balamora's Legendary Treasure.*

Ponce poked his head into the library. "What's going on in here?"

"Get Sunshine and meet me in the schoolroom," she said, tucking papers into the tomes as bookmarks. "It's the next door down." She pointed left.

"Oh. All right."

Song lifted the books, only for Ryk'r to ease them out of her arms. He carried the heavy stack to the schoolroom she'd spent her days in as a child and adolescent. She organized the books on the tutor's desk and moved the clean blackboard behind it as her guard found a spot nearby to plant himself. Ponce returned and slid into the single student's desk. Song moved the tutor's chair for Sunshine.

"All right, go on," Ponce said.

"Right." She lifted the children's book and wrote the word *Balamora* on the board. "Andalise has a story about a lost treasure belonging to a man named Balamora. Just a children's tale, right?"

"Right," Ponce said.

Sunshine shrugged. "I think I heard it once or twice."

"We grow up on it," she said. "Everyone knows the legend. From the wealthy elites to boys who beg on the street. Now, a name *you* might know, Sunshine…" She wrote *Bhalemorai* beneath the first word. "The name of the Aibhànocht god. Have you heard it before?"

"Of course I have." His brow furrowed on the two words. "They're spelled so similar."

"But sound nothing alike." Song nodded. "It gets stranger." She wrote the next words under the first two, and stood back to stare at her list as though just writing it out confirmed something in her mind.

Balamora - Andalise

Bhalemorai - Aibhànocht

Balemari - Armalinia

Baalmoru - Jinjran

Balmor - Jashedar

Bălĕmir - Hrănchu

"I don't know about Kerriwen, yet, and Telbhaniich-Zardi doesn't really have one of their own. So these are what we have to go with."

The men leaned forward, brows furrowed at the list.

"What are Hrănchu and Jinjran?" Ponce asked.

"The Northern Lands and Pishing. I don't know that there is a Pishing-specific legend with that word, but seeing as it was Jashedar who invaded Jinjran, then it doesn't matter, as each country already had their own legend about it." She pointed at the Jinjur word. "I just discovered this word in a book that Pishing authorities have burned every copy they find. It's a song called *Stevnaa Baalmoru* which translates to: *Baalmoru's Call*. I recognized the lyrics as a sort of base form of *The Song of Freedom*. And here is where it gets stranger. In Aibhànocht, a priestess or whatever she was—Myrmhin— hummed *The Song of Freedom* as something other Touched have heard when they envision this place they call *Au Caesaries*. Leslie…" She froze in anticipation of the tears or a knot in her throat. To her shock, neither happened, so she continued. "He told me that some have said the song is a guide. What if it's not a spiritual guide, but a physical one?"

"To where?" Sunshine asked.

"I don't know. Balamora's Treasure? *Au Caesaries?*"

"What if *Au Caesaries* is Balamora? And the treasure is a place," Ponce said.

She shook her head and lifted the Armalinia book. "I don't think it is. Every mention implies the legend is about a person. For simplicity, let's call him Balamora."

"Him?" Ponce asked.

"The priestesses in Thìse have a statue of a man, whom they claim is their god."

Sunshine's brow furrowed. "Do they?"

"Yes. So, let's assume he is the person in question. Which also means someone has seen him before, otherwise how would they carve a statue of him? Now, to Aibhànocht, he's

God. To Armalinia, he's a noble spirit—they even have a symbol for him." She drew the North Star on the blackboard, and both men's jaws slacked. "They refer to Touched with his name as well, only capitalizing when talking about the spirit, rather than a Touched person."

"Nochties consider *kijæm* a gift from God," Sunshine said, deep in thought.

"That's two countries with *kijæm* being tied to Balamora," she said.

"But who is he?" Ponce asked.

"I don't know. Every tale is different. God in Aibhànocht. Noble spirit in Armalinia. To Andalise, he's an inventor who sailed into the sunset to never be heard from again—"

"Ingenuity propaganda," Ponce said with a scoff.

"True. Because that's what Andalise has always valued most. Armalinia values individuality of people's spirits."

"Aibhànocht values their religion," Sunshine said.

"Who is he in Jashedar?" Ponce asked.

"An explorer who—" she lifted the book to read the passage, "—'discovered lands beyond his own', so I imagine places other than Jashedar? He sailed off into the Great Ocean to never be seen again—same as Andalise. Some endings have him swallowed by a sea monster," she said. "Jashedar valued exploration and conquest in previous centuries, like when they invaded Jinjran."

"Still do, in a way," Sunshine muttered.

"In Hrănchu, he was a great chieftain who was supposed to lead the unaltered people to—" She lifted the journal to find the page, "'a haven in the stars.'"

"What does it mean by unaltered?" Sunshine asked.

"I have no idea."

"So what's Pishing's legend on Balamora?" Ponce asked, leaning forward to hang on every word. "Er, whatever it used to be called."

Song shook her head. "Jinjran. In the original version of the *Song of Freedom*, it's a call for help from a man trying to get home. The opposite of the other tales. But if read with the world in mind…I think the lyrics are directions—points on the map."

"Directions where?"

"His treasure maybe? If we believe that version of the tale. If we believe Aibhànocht, maybe it leads to *Au Caesaries*."

"All right, let's say it is," Sunshine said, "where does it say to go?"

"I haven't gotten that far."

"Are you sure it's even connected?"

"Myrmhin told me that other Touched who've melded as far as me have had visions. They saw smoke and heard the tune for the Song of Freedom."

They fell into a thoughtful silence. Song jolted, remembering the scroll Myrmhin had given her. She rushed from the room to search through her trunk of belongings. When she returned to the schoolroom, she pulled the ribbon free. Ryk'r had moved from his spot by the wall to study the words written on the blackboard.

"You *really* think it's all connected?" Sunshine asked.

"Think about it. Every legend has a reason for you to go find him," she said.

"What's that?" He stared at the scroll.

"Myrmhin gave it to me and I completely forgot until

now." She unrolled the page and stared at the drawing. "There are those funny symbols again," she intoned.

At the bottom of the page, Myrmhin had written a single word in the odd lettering Bruce had used before. But this time, she couldn't read them. Above the symbols was a bust of a woman. She had a rectangular medallion on her jacket lapel, like the statue of the man had. The woman was average in features, with big doe-eyes, though they didn't make her look oblivious, but rather observant. She had a thin nose and thin lips, making her seem small but stern. Her hair was pulled back into a high ponytail, bangs framing her face, and an odd rectangular item, like a plain barrette half-hidden within the hair on the right side of her head.

She set the page down to show the other two and pressed her lips together. "The statue of your god had a lapel pin like this. I think she's got something to do with Balamora."

"Maybe even gods have wives," Ponce said.

Sunshine chewed on the inside of his cheek, lost in thought. They waited for him to say something.

He took a breath and scrutinized the open books and the drawing. "We need to get this song to Maps. He'll know how to read it better than any of us."

THE NEXT DAY, SONG WROTE AN ORDER FOR HER CREW TO RETURN to Garda. With any luck, they'd all gone to Talegrove. Of course, with that letter she included a package for Shadow along with a note apologizing for not visiting. Hopefully, the Andalisian accordion shutter camera would appease him. It was an expensive gift, as newspapers could only afford one, and most citizens could only hope to see one at a photography studio. She could rent a little dinghy of a skyship for what the device cost. She only regretted that she wouldn't see the man's face when he opened it.

Much to Ryk'r's chagrin, she ordered him to accompany Sunshine. He complied after more silent, uncooperative placement of himself nearer to her than to Sunshine. She needed Ponce with her, and she didn't want Sunshine going alone. It wasn't until she promised not to go anywhere outside the manor until he returned, that he released a long breath and strode across the room to take up root beside Sunshine. She, of course, had no intention of keeping that promise.

The men packed, and Sunshine spent his last night in the city with Johanna. He said he was getting a tour in before he left, but Mrs. Gould later admitted she'd made a reservation at the most exclusive and romantic restaurant, where the Goulds had an open tab. Song almost laughed outright, but it was rather touching to see him so embarrassingly smitten.

She and Johanna saw them off the next day, waving from the docks, not knowing when they would return or with whom. Ideally, she would get her entire crew back. Realistically, she imagined she'd have to replace most. That was nothing new, of course, but Song hoped certain faces returned.

Waiting was the hardest part. In that time, she found moments to sneak out in her pirate garb to walk Olivia home or get into a ravern brawl. The copycats had all but disappeared, save for the one still in the skies around Pishing. She also continued to read the books, trying to piece together a shared truth within all the legends from each country. Perhaps with enough mixing, she could create a story akin to the truth. The trouble would be knowing if it was the truth at all.

Her Balamora research was selfish, of course. Song wanted answers about the *kijæm* that even now was a part of her. Though she couldn't wield it—refused to wield it—she imagined she still qualified as Touched.

They received the reply from the King of Pishing, who had taken the liberty of arranging Song's masquerade ball. He would make all the preparations, and they would hold it in his castle. Invitations were being sent to every eligible royal in the entire country. All she had to do was show up and dance. It was conveniently easy, but perhaps that was the only easy part.

When Sunshine returned, it was with the Stars' Reprisal and most of the crew, save for one face she never expected to be missing. Ryk'r had wordlessly informed Sunshine of his departure, refusing to be negotiated with. Obviously, Sunshine had no idea where he'd gone.

Regardless of the missing man, she had Sunshine collect signatures of all those willing to rebrand—in writing only— from pirates to privateers. Of course, it was everyone, since she didn't plan on changing how things ran. Government-sanctioned piracy was a convenient cover. Elroy had only managed it by assuring that the actual Captain Song was determined to catch the imposter terrorizing Pishing. The senators were desperate to resolve the tensions between the two countries. There was only so much the forced marriage could accomplish if the Andalisian pirate continued to cause trouble.

Song prepared for the ball, having a dress made that was similar to the scarlet one from her welcome home ball. This time she asked for black with golden embellishments to match her custom-made golden mask. She loved the outfit. It was unfortunate that it was being wasted on a betrothal she didn't want.

Thirty-Four

WHEN THE DAY OF DEPARTURE CAME, THE GOULD FAMILY skyship—loaded with supplies and house staff—left port at midmorning. At noon, the Stars' Reprisal departed from Garda, Captain Song at the helm and two irate lawmen watching from the docks. She stared at Foggerty, letting him know with that unseen eye contact she knew how furious he was over the deal she'd struck with the senate.

Once out of sight of the city, Song descended to the cargo hold, where they'd constructed a makeshift passengers' quarters using folding wall dividers and heavy curtains. She entered the first one and stared at her mother and father, whom she'd smuggled aboard in the night, alongside Johanna and Amelia.

"How are the accommodations treating you, Senator?" Song asked with a playful smirk.

Her mother scoffed and spoke before Elroy could. "I still don't understand why we're traveling in squalor."

Her father set his hand over hers and directed a pinched smile to the curtain opposite their quarters. "She is the most infamous pirate in history, dear. I think she may know a thing or two about safe passage."

"Thank you, Father." Song beamed. "We're on a pirate ship because pirates are less likely to stop us. They want the easy target. The Gould ship is an easy target with high-value occupants and items. So, when it comes down to it, you can either travel comfortably or safely. You can't have both."

"We could have hired a better crew—" Annie started.

"There is no better crew," Song snapped. "You seem to think you can trust any ordinary man to protect you. Out here in the skies, they have no reason to. Dead men can't spend quoine. No matter how much you pay them, hired swords will not die for you. In fact, they're more likely to hand you over to anyone who pays more. Double the profit and half the work. The men on this crew know who I am and are loyal to me. Not to a Gould or a faceless man under a hood. To *me*. Because I am loyal to them. As unseemly as you find it, Mother, there is no safer place for you."

"You expect me to stay down here for two days—"

"No. We brought some nice chairs on board just for you, so you may sit out on deck and complain up there instead of down here. Father even stocked the galley with expensive foods for Thumbs to turn into amazing dinners for your *refined* palate. We're doing our very best to accommodate you, and I really wish you'd be a little more grateful. I could've just taken Johanna and Amelia and left you two to the whims of any pirates you crossed paths with."

"Annie, just try to enjoy an unpleasant situation in any way you can," Elroy said. "And trust that our daughter, who has been living in these skies for four years, might know how to survive in them."

"Also," Ponce said from the doorway, "Thumbs is by far the best cook on any vessel—land, sea, or skies."

Song salivated as she thought of a bowl of Thumbs's stew. It may not have been expensive or high society, but damn if it wasn't a sinfully delicious concoction. "You're making me hungry." She smiled at her parents. "Make yourselves at home as best you can. Please. Now excuse me while I go steal some of those fresh mushrooms you paid for."

"There are radishes, too," Ponce said, moving aside for her.

"*Radishes!*" With that, she jogged up the stairs to raid the galley, leaving her parents to decide what they would do.

A few hours later, her family wandered up from below while she perched on the bowsprit, taking in the wind and sun, and greeting the sky like an old friend she hadn't seen in far too long. She stared over her shoulder at them. They seemed lost and so out of sorts that they might flee, if only there were anywhere to run.

Amelia, though, had caved in upon herself. She gripped her shawl tight to her chest, her shoulders hunched, and stared around at the crew on deck. Jerome approached with a chair, a smile on his face. Despite his grin, she shied away, pressing herself into Johanna so hard that the woman almost toppled.

Song hopped over the railing and strode to Amelia. "Would you like to sit in my cabin?"

Amelia shifted to press closer into Song, instead. "Please."

The other three followed her as her crew finished setting up the deck chairs. None of the men gave Amelia funny looks—even Jerome wasn't offended. They'd been there.

They'd seen her. The crew knew, without asking, that it wasn't personal.

Her parents took in her cabin with critical eyes as Johanna urged Amelia to the bay bench. Their eyes settled on the wanted posters and Bruce's drawings over the piano.

"What happened to Captain Krell?" Elroy asked.

"He died," Song said. "Another pirate crew attacked us. He took a bullet to save him." She motioned at the poster for Leslie. "We didn't even know at the time that Leslie was Dash's son. Well, Dash did. But there hadn't been time to tell us."

"Any father worthy of the title would sacrifice himself for his child." He gave Song a loving smile. He wandered around the cabin to take in her trinkets on shelves and hanging from nails on the wall. "You seem more at ease and…natural here than I've ever seen you at home."

"You wanted me to be so much more. I know. But this is just…who I am. I seem more at ease, because I *am*. I have never belonged anywhere more than I belong in the skies."

"If you didn't, then I doubt you would've become quite so infamous," Johanna said.

The woman seemed thrilled beyond belief to be aboard the pirate ship, her eyes taking everything in as though memorizing it to cherish forever. Now that Song knew of her odd fascination with criminals, she understood the excitement. She didn't share the sentiment. Perhaps it wasn't so easy to find fascination with the darker side of society when she belonged to it.

Song ate meals with her crew, allowing her family to use her cabin's table. A few faces were missing from when Song had left, but they were men she hadn't known well. The crew told her of the small adventures they'd gone on. They'd stopped a few passenger ships, offloaded in Telbhaniich-Zardi with her fence, then gone to Talegrove for a vacation after the merchant country. It hadn't felt right to keep going without her leading them. Toothy had done a fine job, but it wasn't the same. Her heart melted, and she leaned to either side to hug Toothy and Thumbs—the crew had all scrambled to be the ones to sit closest to her, but those two had won, Thumbs using his position as cook to threaten his way into the spot.

At noon on the second day, they stopped over the mountain mass at the northern tip of Pishing, which cradled Argwin, the capital, and protected it from all sides. When they didn't see the Gould ship, they circled, all hands with spyglasses to their eyes. An uneasy feeling churned in Song's stomach. The family ship had left hours before, and should have already been there, waiting. The plan had been to meet up and transfer their secret passengers and herself to the other ship to make the last leg of the trip in the more stately craft. That way they could arrive without raising alarm or suspicion, like the Stars' Reprisal was sure to cause.

When the ship appeared on the horizon, they turned to intercept. Song swung across alone and met with the captain in his cabin. Captain Davies was a somewhat overweight man, with kind eyes and a friendly smile—at least for Tsingsei Gould. For Captain Song, he had a scowl and pursed lips.

"You're late," she said.

"Yes, well, your echo stopped us."

She froze while staring at his fancy compass set up on a map on his desk. "My echo?"

"Aye. The one who flies Darkness," Davies said.

"Another cheap copycat?"

"No. If I didn't know you had a deal with the senator and his family, I would have thought this man was you, Captain Song. He wears a near replica of your coat. He's built like you and walks the same—that same careful swagger like you own whatever floor your boots are on."

She paused in her pacing and stared at her feet. "I wasn't aware I walk like that."

"He talks like you, too. Your accent, your inflections, the confidence in your tone. Straight down to the exact way you breathe. This man is your double. The only difference is vocal pitch, and a little height."

"Someone studied me to duplicate me with the most convincing replica they could find. I'd say I'm flattered, but honestly, I'm furious. Was anyone hurt?"

"No one fought back, as Senator Gould instructed, so no, there were no casualties or injuries."

"Did he take anything of note?"

Captain Davies shook his head. "He searched for jewels, like any pirate would. But that didn't seem to be what he actually wanted."

"And what did the false Song want?"

"Based on questions, and his rage after discovering the lack of Goulds aboard, I would bet my life that he was aiming to kidnap Miss Tsingsei."

Song had changed into her dress and let Johanna style her hair and make up her face, but she'd done it all in a daze. The imposter had stopped her family ship to kidnap her. But why?

"He wants to stop the betrothal," Song murmured.

Her father stared at her from where he double checked that nothing precious would be left behind — he would ride with the pirates, but Song knew he wouldn't trust them to return lost items. She could have set his mind at ease, but to be honest, she was too preoccupied. And besides, it was amusing watching him crawl on the floor to perchance find a cufflink he may have lost under the cot.

"Who? What?" Elroy asked.

Song frowned and told her father everything the other captain had said. "The imposter must know about the betrothal and is trying to stop it. It's a private affair, I thought?"

"Yes, we're keeping it as quiet as possible until the wedding."

"He wants war." She stared up at him as they frowned at each other. "I did what I did out of anger and hurt. This man's aims are political, and have been since he took to the skies. I don't know what is going on, but I will not abide by it. Captain Song was never political. I *loathe* politics because of you."

His eyebrows pushed together. "I suppose that's understandable."

"So, Senator, use your political prowess to determine what plot could be afoot."

Elroy paced a moment, finger tapping his lips. "Either

this imposter is someone close to the king, or someone close is pulling the strings of a puppet."

"How do you explain how well this echo takes my place?"

"One of your crew may have turned on you. Can you think of any man who might have been swayed against you?"

Song released a long sigh. "Hardtack. He was with us for a while. I don't know that it was long enough for him to know me so well, but I did often find him staring. Studying me, perhaps."

"What happened to him?"

"He was on an enemy ship and got left behind. I later attacked that ship and gave no quarter. If he hadn't already been killed, he might have thought I'd turned on him. It was nothing personal against him. It was about Darian and his damned deadly ship."

"Let's get going," Ponce said from the doorway. He'd put on a nice grey suit, and it complimented his eyes, making the brown seem clearer.

"Ponce, who would you put money on being able to copy me so perfectly they *could* be me? Accent and all."

He gave her a long look, his lips pursed like they wanted to say something, but had to force it back. "Hardtack, if he's alive. Only former crewman I can think of who'd care enough. The others are dead, apathetic, or really not someone I'd wager smart enough to pull it off."

"After this ball, we have about a year to catch him for the senate," she said. "Then I have to submit myself to the torment that is marriage. Gods have mercy on my soul. Or don't. I'm sure no punishment is crueler."

They crossed to the Gould skyship, and the captain once again was that kind man with the smiles for her family. He pulled her father into his cabin as the rest descended to the passenger section to wait for their arrival in Argwin.

Thirty-Five

T HE GOULD SKYSHIP SLID INTO THE DOCKS, THE PASSENGERS standing on deck like a presentation. In the center of them all was Song, an elegant maroon mask over her face to match her travel dress. The king stood waiting, flanked by guards, his wife, and one short girl with bright blonde hair. The princes wouldn't be there, since they were in the pool of bachelors. No bachelor was to be wandering the halls. If they had to, they couldn't speak to her, and were required to wear the masks until the entire affair concluded.

"King Chiron Phillip Anton Bartlett the First," a man in a black suit said as he gestured at the king, who wore a fine royal blue suit and a crown upon his head.

Song curtsied before the king. "A pleasure to meet you, Your Grace," she said as he took her hand and kissed the top.

"And you, Miss Gould," he said.

"My parents, Elroy and Annie Gould."

King Bartlett shook her father's hand and kissed her mother's.

"And Henry Xavier Barton the Third."

Amelia pouted beside Song, but said nothing, knowing she was not the sort one introduces to a king.

Song, however, caught the expression and decided her mother's idea of proper decorum could drown, for all she cared. "And of course, my dear friends Amelia, Johanna, and Thersiàl."

He regarded each with a patient smile. "This is my wife, Edina, and my daughter, Fiyora."

Song stared at the latter. "Such a beautiful name." She had to stop herself from giving a flirtatious 'It suits you, my dear.' Instead, she said, "I've heard it a few times. That's quite a common name, isn't it?"

The princess gave her a tight-lipped smile. "It is. Like Poppy in Jashedar."

"The endless cleverness of parents naming their daughters after flowers. At least they didn't name you Vyaantr?"

Fiyora giggled. "Oh, that would be the worst! Luckily, fiyoras are a beautiful flower."

"How fitting," Song said. She forced her smile to remain sweet instead of turning flirtatious.

The woman gave a silly giggle. "You're too kind."

The king cleared his throat. "Come, I will show you to your rooms."

"Surely your house staff could—" Mrs. Gould bit her mouth closed.

It must have occurred to her they wouldn't have paid staff, but slaves or indentured servants. Song had made it clear she would not tolerate being waited on by any during her visit.

As though the king understood her sudden silence, he gave them an uneasy smile. "It's no trouble."

"Papa, you're being silly. Come on." The princess steered him away and gave Song a wry smile.

"Are you absolutely *certain* I can't marry the princess?" Song hissed once the royals were out of earshot.

Elroy shot her a look and followed behind the king.

Song stayed put a moment longer, though, as she stared at the guards with light blue clothing and breastplates adorned with stag horns. The royal banners were light blue cloth with stag horns on a halo at the pommel of a longsword pointing down. She met the gaze of the nearest guard, as though he might have been the man who'd let her into the parlor office of Duchamp Hall so she could murder Roman. He likely wasn't, but she had no way to tell past his helmet. And so she followed the others, a sinking feeling in her gut.

Once they were situated in their respective rooms, Song wandered back into the halls to see if she could happen upon the princess. She had tried to get Amelia to go with her, but the woman was sulking in her own room, and Song didn't feel like trying to comfort her again.

It had been a struggle to not yell at Amelia every time someone reminded her of the betrothal. She knew Amelia was hurting, but she treated Song as though she'd chosen to betray her. There was only so long they could huff about it and give silent treatments before it all came to a head, and Song started yelling—which would be unbecoming of her to do in the Argwin Palace.

She found Princess Fiyora in a courtyard garden, reading poetry aloud beside a planter filled with the strange flowers Song remembered from the monument in Talegrove. She approached without a word, gave a quick smile when Fiyora glanced up, and bent to smell the flowers. Song closed her eyes and made a noise of approval.

"Aren't you supposed to be staying in your room, like the suitors are?" the princess asked.

Song smirked. "Supposed to be, yes. But I didn't want to."

"Are you looking for anything in particular?"

She contemplated saying nothing, but boldness got the better of her. "You."

"And why are you looking for me?"

"I wanted to talk. Bonus for getting to smell your flower."

Fiyora cleared her throat, though gave Song a shy smile. "You should be careful with your tone and phrasing, Miss Gould."

"Why?"

"Because if you weren't a lady, I'd think you were being lewd."

Song feigned shock, even though she knew precisely what she'd been doing. She had hoped to get a laugh out of the princess—some indication of a rebellious side, and perhaps even a curiosity Song could help her explore. But now it was plain that crude humor of that sort was something the upper echelon of both countries could never appreciate. On top of that, it meant Fiyora was less likely to entertain the idea of breaking a few gender norms and expectations. And there went Song's hope for a royal mistress.

"I am so sorry. I didn't even think before I spoke! Forgive me."

Fiyora laughed. "I forgive you."

"It would be such a shame to remain locked in my room

for the entire visit, never seeing the castle, or its spectacular views," she said on an airy sigh.

She narrowed her eyes. "Don't be coy. Just tell me you want a tour of the grounds."

Song grinned. "I like you. You don't pussyfoot around or play games."

"It's better to just say what you bloody mean," she said, her voice low as she leaned forward to avoid others hearing. "So, how about a personal tour from me before we join my parents for supper?"

"That sounds like a perfect tour, and I wouldn't dream of anyone else being my guide."

The princess snapped her book closed, stood, and took her place beside Song. "First, we have my *private* garden, which you weren't supposed to enter without my permission."

She grimaced. "Oh, bugger. I'm sorry. Should I leave, then?"

Fiyora hooked her arm through Song's. "Absolutely not. Next, we have the Hall of Reflection."

The princess led Song out another direction into a hallway with mirrors running along the walls. Some were stained glass, some reflected distorted images of the two, and some were put together in beautiful shapes and patterns.

"The Hall of Reflection," Song said. "What an alarmingly unimaginative name."

Fiyora giggled. She guided Song all over the castle, showing her sights she'd never imagined.

Artifacts hung on the wall in a room Song wasn't supposed to be shown, and she recognized some as deities and cultural designs of the Jinjur people. Now they were here as trophies, their history long expunged from the world. And this wide-eyed princess had no idea that any of these were once sacred to someone, that they were proof of the attempted—and near-successful—erasure of an entire culture, an entire people whose descendants were now subjugated and made to be slaves at worst and peasants at best.

At the end of the tour, as though she'd planned out the route to end there, the princess guided Song to the private royal banquet room, where dinner was about to be served. Song sat with her parents, taking note that no one else had been invited. This was just for her, her parents, and the royal family, minus the princes. It was her chance to make a good first impression—or rather a bad one, considering it was Song, after all. She knew herself well enough that she didn't expect this to go well unless she kept her mouth too full of food to speak, which was unladylike and might prove worse than any wit that might tumble out at the royals.

As they ate, a lone musician stood in one corner with an instrument that looked like a guitar, but was played by cranking a knob at the end and pressing keys at the neck. She had never seen one of those before, but she loved the sound. It must have been an instrument native to this continent. She wanted to ask about it and maybe acquire one of her own, but that was for another time, if she remembered.

For the most part, the conversation remained light-hearted. The princess settled her wide brown eyes on Song.

"I heard Captain Song stopped your skyship! That must have been terrifying!" Fiyora said.

"Oh, goodness, was it? I missed the whole thing." Right

after it left her lips, she realized it was quite possibly the stupidest response she could have given.

The royals stared at her in astonishment as Annie blinked, trying to think up her own lie, and Elroy gave her a disappointed glance. She would no doubt hear about weaving convincing lies later.

"That is to say, an old friend asked me to fly with them for most of the trip so we could catch up. We parted ways just before arriving, as they were headed for Jashedar. I had no idea my family's skyship was stopped!"

"We felt it prudent not to worry you," her father said.

"Well, let's hope that imposter is on the other side of the continent by the time we leave."

Queen Edina furrowed her brow. "Imposter?"

"Yes. You can't believe that's the actual Captain Song."

Elroy set his hand on hers. "Tsingsei, now is not the time."

The king leaned forward in his seat. "No, no, please explain yourself."

Song chewed at the inside of her lip as her gaze bounced between her father and King Bartlett. She was supposed to keep her mouth shut about her rumored relationship with the captain, and not even hint at the ballad, since they had banned it in Pishing—though there was no way the king hadn't heard it before banning it. "Well, you see… It's um…" The most obvious answer occurred to her after an embarrassing amount of time. "It's the wrong ship."

His brow furrowed. He lifted his goblet to sip his wine. The king's unwavering gaze settled on her. "Go on…"

"What do we know of Captain Song's ships? The Stars' Bounty and the Stars' Reprisal, right? Both have a star on the front. This new one is called Darkness, and the figurehead is a *vyaarblisu draaku* skull painted black." She paused, her breath hitched in her throat as she wondered if knowing about the mythical fire breathing sky serpents from Jinjur legends gave away that she had access to forbidden knowledge.

One of his eyebrows arched higher as he studied her. "You know a lot about the ships."

Song gave a dismissive laugh, relaxing as his focus fell to the ships rather than the creature. "Oh, just a fascination. I'm sure we all have dark interests we delight in from time to time. Mine happens to be pirates." She gave Elroy a sweet smile. "The more I know about them, the better I can follow in my father's footsteps. Perhaps I could make him proud."

"Ladies can't be senators," the princess said, as though she knew the laws of Andalise—though she wasn't wrong.

Song made a show of deflating. "Oh, right… Oh! But I could do it as a High Lady or Princess of Pishing! Help get that pest of an imposter out of your hair, using what I've learned from my father."

"That is especially not becoming of a member of the royal families," the queen said. "We'll have to get you into some etiquette training before the wedding."

Song took a long drink of wine, her gaze never wavering from the queen's, then set the empty goblet down. A servant stepped forward to refill it.

She set her hand over the top. "Are you *paid* to refill my glass?"

The woman stared at her like she'd slapped her with the metal hand. Her eyes shot to the king, asking his permission to respond.

"I made it quite clear, your highness, that I refuse to be attended by slaves."

When no one said anything, or even attempted to move, Song grabbed the carafe from the woman.

"Leave the room before I pay you for your service," Song snapped. She had almost paid the woman anyway, but feared it would cause retaliation aimed at the slave. With a glare on the king, she filled her own glass and swallowed the contents as fast as she could. She refilled the goblet and released a heavy sigh as the door closed, and the woman was gone.

"Is our wine to your liking?" the princess asked, as though trying to lighten the mood.

Said wine was already getting to her head and warming her cheeks. "I'd rather have a whiskey, but it'll do."

"Did you develop a taste for whiskey in your travels?"

Without giving herself enough time to rethink blurting something stupid, she gave the princess a flirtatious smirk. "Yes. Among other things."

Under the table, her mother kicked her ankle, and Song sat more upright. The princess took a long drink and looked away from Song, her face red.

"Oh, goodness me, that came out wrong," Song said. "I just mean that ladies taste quite nice—"

Her mother kicked her ankle again.

The queen sputtered at her plate. "Miss Gould, I'm not sure what—"

"*Cannibals!*" Song blurted.

Everyone froze. Her eyes widened, as the outburst had shocked even herself. She grabbed her goblet and started gulping it back so fast she hoped she drowned.

"Tsingsei, slow down on that wine!" her mother demanded.

"Which ones?" the king asked, causing the muttering queen and princess to go quiet.

Song stared at him, still trying to catch her breath.

"I can't imagine the Quodinlau welcomed you for a meal. Was it in Aibhànocht?"

Her mind stopped reeling and settled on one question. "There are cannibals in Aibhànocht?"

"Yes! Interesting bunch. It's an excommunicated branch of their religion. What is it called?" He directed the question at no one.

"The um, *Thiurin Bhalemorai*," Song said.

"Yes, that's the one. The priestesses in this sect not only kill men who have *kijæm*, but they eat him as well, to absorb his Gift into themselves. They also eat priestesses once they reach a certain age, in order for the dying to pass their Gift onto their sisters. It's fascinating, really."

Song leaned forward. "Oh, that's an interesting thought. Do you think the *kijæm* really transfers that way, or does it pass through their bodies unabsorbed?"

"I would imagine it would be absorbed."

"Oh, but I've heard *kijæm* is like another life-form entirely. So don't you think it would choose to leave the corpse before the priestesses could consume it?"

"I have never heard that theory before! Do you believe a parasite to be smart enough to exit the host to avoid being eaten?"

Song released a thoughtful noise. "I'm not sure it's a parasite, to be honest. One could make the argument that Touched people are the parasites, with how they use the *kijæm*.

Though I imagine it to be more of a symbiotic relationship."

The king nodded, something like a sparkle of excitement glittering in one eye. "Right. Good point. It leaves you to wonder why the priestesses believe so strongly that they are absorbing the Gift from the dead. I wonder what the Quodinlau believe that urges them to partake in cannibalism. Is that who you dined with?"

"No. It was um…" She blinked at him, thinking fast. "A village in the Blind Woods. Apparently, that's why people never make it out of there alive."

"Except you."

"Well, they found me charming and let me go. That and I made them laugh with what I chose."

"Dare I ask what you tasted?"

"*Lady Lips*," Song said, giving him a wry smile that twisted with just enough fake embarrassment to be believable. "When I tell you how shocked I was to learn they were not, in fact, the lips you talk with, well…" She sipped her wine as the table fell deathly silent around her—even the musician had stopped playing to stare in shock. "They were quite delicious," Song murmured against the rim of her goblet, as though it made any of what she said less revolting.

The queen looked ill; the princess had nudged her plate away; her mother was holding a napkin to her mouth—though Song suspected it was not to hide queasiness—and her father had set his brow into his palm to massage his temples with his thumb and fingertips.

After an entire accursed minute of aghast silence, the king bellowed a laugh. He raised his glass toward Song. "I quite like you, Miss Gould."

As though that was the cue she was waiting for, the musician resumed playing in the corner, eyes still wide and face set in horror.

Song flushed and presented the king with a smile more confident than she felt as she raised her glass. "I quite like you, too."

They drank together as the rest of the table still sat frozen in a moral disgust they couldn't quite come to terms with.

"What is your pedigree, if I might ask?" the king asked.

It was more a gentle question than something she felt obligated to answer. As his eyes swept over her features and then her father's, she suspected he saw the bit of Tsingsei Lurnyâk-Gould in them.

"Mostly Andalisian, and just a touch of something a *bit* more exotic," she said.

He gave a thoughtful nod, then turned his attention to her father. "Senator, I know we agreed to a fair game, but I would enjoy having your daughter around for more lively discussions such as this. What would one of my sons need to do to win her heart?" He gave Song a charming smile, and she returned it.

"We can discuss it after dinner, if Tsingsei is all right with two of the bachelors having an advantage." He looked to her, so she could answer for herself.

Song gazed around the room, her eyes settling on Princess Fiyora for a long second, before flitting back to the king. With her filter having all but been washed away by the wine, she said, "I think I would rather enjoy being a princess. Imagine the things I could get away with!"

Thirty-Six

Song woke on the day of the ball with a sick feeling in her stomach that she could only identify as terror. She ate little of her breakfast, and stayed in her room reading or staring off into the ether, imagining all the ways she could escape. But she'd given her word that she wouldn't, and so she didn't.

The time came for her to dress. She let Johanna and Ponce help her into her arm and dress. Johanna styled her hair in a series of curls and braids that looked almost like flowers and vines at the nape of her neck. Her makeup wasn't as important, but Johanna made her look breathtaking, anyway.

They secured the mask over her face—it stretched lower on one side, reaching the corner of her mouth as though it had melted into a point. On the other side, dangling from the edge of the nosepiece to the corner at her temple, just beneath the eyepiece that covered her cheekbone, was a chain with a little brightsteel North Star.

Her parents had refused her request to wear her hairpin at all during the trip, and so she'd chosen that charm in minor protest. Hopefully, no one read more into it. Though, if they did, she didn't care. The amount of things they could assume was quite long, and she'd already prepared a lie about Armalinia's revered spirit.

The dress didn't faze her mother this time. She grumbled about her daughter's exposed knees under lace pantyhose, but otherwise didn't make a scene. A servant—or slave whom they'd dressed in nice clothes to hide their status during the visit—came to escort them to the ballroom. Song entered as a man introduced her. She stopped to curtsy and play the expected part, grinning and waving.

The sheer amount of silver masks caught her off guard. Half the guests wore them. This would take hours if she didn't take any breaks in between. The truth swelled to the front of her mind that they were here for a possession, not an equal. She would be the trophy on their arm, not the woman they would trust as a partner.

They served a quick dinner at tables positioned around the outer edges of the room. King Bartlett, Song's father, and a few other men dined at a long table at the front of the room. Two seats beside the king had been left empty; she suspected the princes would usually sit there. Not far from that table was one for the women, where the queen and princess sat with other ladies. Song sat with her mother, Amelia, Johanna, Ponce, and Sunshine, at a table nearby. Leopold was not there as a guest, and so had taken up a position against the wall, waiting for the dancing to start. Leopold held Song's dance card in his hands like a precious jewel. It was four pages long, and she couldn't look at it.

Song watched the suitors eat, studying them and noting any recognizable features she could place on the ones who ate like animals. She kept her meal light, so she wouldn't vomit on someone after spinning around the room on a full stomach—though it likely would have proven to be a highlight to the evening.

Far sooner than she was prepared for, the ball commenced. The suitors were to go to Leopold and tell him whatever identifier was written on the list. After that, they would dance with her. For the first hour, it was one after another in painful repetition. They danced to the same slow tempo, and all blithered about their riches and estates. They wooed her and tried to charm her, having no idea she was immune.

After she insisted on resting her feet for a few minutes, the line resumed. The first interesting man to approach was tall and narrow, with a charming smile and softer jawline, which Song at least approved of. If nothing else, she wouldn't hate looking at him, so long as the rest of his face was pleasant. He was tall enough that he didn't look silly beside her in her heels, and his build was—as best she could tell under his suit—sturdy, but not stout. He could be wiry under those clothes, or he could be fit. The tightening of the fabric at his biceps told her it was the latter.

"Let's hope this one can dance," she hissed to her mother.

"Oh, you like this one?" Annie asked.

"He looks delicate."

Her mother laughed. "Are you looking for a man you can break in half?"

Song smirked. "If that's what it comes to, I suppose." She smiled as the man approached.

He took her offered hand and bent, kissing the top as all had done. He leaned closer. "You look bored, Miss Gould."

"Is it that obvious?"

He chuckled and escorted her to the dance floor. The music stopped and something a little more lively began. He led her in a faster waltz across the floor. He was less commanding of being led than others had been, letting her prove she knew what she was doing. By the end, she was smiling. He led her back to her seat, and she curtsied as he bowed. As the man walked away, Leopold approached and leaned to hear her verdict.

"I like that one," she said.

Her mother smiled. "Good. If you only like one, it's enough."

"They're only forcing me to marry *one*, anyway. Unless I'm mistaken." Song let out a long breath and sipped her wine. "Can we stop there, then?"

"Unfortunately, no. This is what you agreed to."

"Spend the night making each bachelor feel special?"

Annie nodded. "Precisely. Stroke their egos a bit. Make them all feel like they have a chance, even if they've already lost."

Song set her wine on the table behind her. "Mother, how did you feel when this was you?"

"As you did. Resentful of having to entertain middle-aged men."

"And then father swept you off your feet."

Her mother laughed, nodding as they both looked over at the king's table, where Elroy Gould sat to his left, looking like he was at a meeting, not a party. The next man approached Leopold. She cringed at the greying of the hair long enough to show from beneath the mask, and growing girth at his midsection. Mrs. Gould jammed an elbow into her daughter's waist.

"I can say no to any of them!" Song hissed.

"The agreement was you *dance* with them," her mother replied.

"One thousand quoine says he cannot dance worth spit."

Annie giggled into her glove. "Tsingsei, that's not very lady-like." Her lips formed into a reserved smile as she scrutinized the man. "One thousand five hundred says you're right."

Song laughed outright. Amelia smiled beside her, but said nothing otherwise.

The man approached and bowed before the ladies. Song offered her hand as expected, and he set a soft kiss on the back of her glove. She clenched her jaw through the dance, trying to maintain a kind smile rather than laughing, since standing near him revealed she was far taller than him in her heels, and would still be so without them. When the dance ended, she curtsied and returned to her seat.

Leopold approached and leaned down as he did after every dance, but this time he did not wait for her to speak. "I took the liberty of crossing him off the list, miss."

"Was it that obvious?" she asked, laughing.

"Painfully," Amelia said beside her. She seemed on edge, though trying to have as good a time as possible.

Song danced with more, thankful for the breaks in between to rest her feet. Still, none had been as delightful as the man who'd chosen the faster song. Leopold approached after a long break to whisper in her ear.

"That seems to be the last of them, Miss Gould."

She sank and sighed. "Thank the stars."

She rested for a long time, letting her feet relax. A man entered, dressed in black like the others, but with silver accents on his jacket and tall boots. His mask was silver on black cloth to cover his hair, like the others, but his collar was upturned. The ensemble was made complete by an elegant tricorn hat—also black with soft silver accents. The ladies all watched as he strode straight for the king's table, bowed, and sat to his right in the chairs she'd suspected to be for the princes.

"Who do you suppose that is?" Mrs. Gould asked.

"Doesn't matter, he's late. I'm done dancing," Song said. "I've made my choice."

"If I ask to dance?" a woman said behind her, her Armalinian accent thick, but words more sure than Song remembered.

She spun around, eyes wide, and shot to her feet. Flustered, she curtsied low, casting her gaze to the sandals on the dark copper toned feet. "Sultania, what brings you…" She swallowed as she looked up.

Lyella was in a curve-accentuating knee-length black dress that tied behind her neck and had a back that dipped low to her hips, plenty of cleavage on display. Her face was unveiled, but hidden behind a lace mask over the upper half, with long tassels as a sort of makeshift veil covering to her jaw.

"…here?" It had been two years since she'd laid eyes on the beautiful woman, and she wasn't prepared for how it took her breath away to look into those gorgeous smiling eyes.

"You have dance for *ghidja*." She laughed.

"Where is your *cadarrik*?"

"Only two know. I sneak." Lyella pointed over at Ryk'r just steps away, and her personal bard, who spoke with the orchestra.

Song leaned around the sultania to shoot the guard a glare, hoping he could see it despite her mask. He returned a self-satisfied grin.

Annie cleared her throat as she stood at Song's elbow. "Who…is this?" She didn't even hide the scrutiny of the sultania's outfit.

"*Mother!* This is—"

"Sultania Ky'r," Lyella interrupted, "of Armalinia."

"Is that the sort of dresses you're wearing over there?" Annie asked, a hand on her stomach as though it made her ill.

"Yes, mother," Song hissed through her teeth. "I have one of them."

Lyella's smile never dimmed, her amber eyes remaining locked on Song. "So. Dance, *yr ghija?*"

She swallowed. "I don't think that would be…appropriate."

"Why?"

"Ladies don't dance with ladies in this culture."

Her smile remained. "They do in mine."

"But—"

Lyella grabbed her hand. "I tell you."

"Command. You're commanding me." Song let out a long sigh. "As you wish, your highness." She curtsied again.

"Tsingsei," her mother hissed.

She leaned in close. "This is the princess," she hissed in her ear. "You want me to refuse the *future ruler* of Armalinia? *And* the woman who tricked me into an engagement?"

"*That* is your…?"

"My *other* betrothed. Yes."

Wide-eyed, her mother dropped into her seat as Lyella returned from speaking to her bard. He'd brought the strange upright stringed instrument with him, and the others were looking over a page of music. The sultania had come prepared.

"You know the dance," Lyella said.

Song almost asked which, but the sparkle in the sultania's eyes told her exactly which dance they would be performing. She nodded once, keeping to herself that it was especially inappropriate for ladies in this culture. Lyella held up her palm and Song set hers to it. The music began. It was the dance she'd practiced many times: the wedding dance.

It started simple—right palms pressed together. They turned and set their left hands together. The music sped up as the two twisted and turned around each other, bending and spinning. Because of her height, Song had learned the more dominant role of the choreography. Her job was to support Lyella in spins and dips—a metaphor, Leslie had said, for a partner's devotion to the other.

The music grew faster and faster until Lyella was spinning so fast her skirt flared out, exposing far more of her thighs than any of the aristocrats and royals were comfortable seeing. But the two didn't stop. They spun and twisted, their arms and legs seeming to tangle together, though they slipped effortlessly apart. The song came to an abrupt end. Song's left hand clasped Lyella's right in the air over their heads, their other arms wrapped behind each other's backs as they pressed their chests together. Lyella grinned, and it infected Song.

The sultania took her hands and held them between the two. "That pleased me."

"That pleased me, too. I'm actually happy to see you." Song laughed, then curtsied low.

"I am glad to see you."

It wasn't until a single person's slow clap echoed from the vaulted ceiling that Song realized the room had gone silent when the music stopped. The source of the sound was the latecomer sitting beside the king, smiling as though he hadn't been quite so entertained in some time. Song ignored him and walked with Lyella back to her seat, where Mrs. Gould looked flustered and Amelia was observing her hands in her lap.

"Go enjoy the rest of your night," Song said.

Lyella bowed her head. "I will."

Once sitting again, Song took a deep breath and straightened as though unbothered by some of the rude looks she received. Instead, she cast her gaze over to her father, preparing to feel the shame from his expression. However, he was not looking at her. The latecomer had moved seats to speak with him without the king between them. Soon enough, though, a few men approached one at a time to say something to her father. He smiled and nodded to each, though it was a tight smile and she could see in his eyes just how unimpressed he was. His expression fell to one of annoyance when they walked away. The man beside him remained impassive through whatever was vexing her father.

Elroy motioned to Leopold so he could look over her dance card. He found what he was looking for and pointed it out to him. They spoke for a minute before Leopold returned to Song and leaned to her ear.

"You've one last suitor, miss."

She growled. "No."

"Your father insists."

"Tell him I'm done. I've made my choice. Is that not enough?"

"It also was not a request, miss." He smirked and chuckled.

"Bloody hells."

Mrs. Gould pushed Song's shoulders back up as they sagged in annoyance. "Just one more. Then you can announce your choice and we can leave so you can go…be *you* in private."

Song knew her mother meant 'be anything but dignified,' but it wasn't something which should be said aloud. "If it's that man who just arrived, he can sod off. He was late. He can accept the rejection without his chance to waste my time."

Leopold cleared his throat. "He also asked me to tell you to trust him."

She looked over at her father, who was smiling at her in a way he hadn't done in so long she almost wondered if it was a hallucination. "*Fine*. I'll humor him. Won't change my mind."

A minute later, the man dropped his hat into his seat, spoke with the musicians, then approached. He bent a little at the waist and she set her fingertips in the palm of his black-gloved hand. He did not kiss the top, though, which she found curious. When he said nothing as he led her to the dance floor, her eyebrow rose behind her mask.

"The others were already trying to win me over with their riches by this point. You're losing," she said as he remained silent.

His eyes—a pale green in the room's amber lighting—settled on the star charm tickling her cheek. Whatever he made of it, he did not voice, nor did his lower face's expression betray a single thought. It was unnerving more than anything, if she was being honest. All the others didn't hesitate to talk themselves up, but this one was quite content keeping his silence. The song started and, like all the ones she'd rejected, was slow.

"The others loved to listen to themselves talk. Do you even speak?"

He didn't respond.

"How am I supposed to like you if you don't tell me anything about you?"

He smirked in response.

Something about this man was unsettling to her. It wasn't the silence—that was actually somewhat refreshing, despite being so strange. Whatever it was, it crept up her spine and settled at the back of her mind, refusing to come forward. Was she afraid of him? Or was it some other emotion dying to break free, and yet too timid to do so? The feeling made her desperate to rip his mask from his face to see what sort of monster hid beneath. He must have been a monster, she decided, for not much else set her instincts on edge the way he did. If she could get a good look at him while standing still, perhaps she could figure out what her subconscious was whispering in the darkness behind her mentally counting out dance steps to avoid standing on his toes. As it was, though, she couldn't. And so she shoved the entire thing from her mind.

Now that she knew he had no intention of speaking to her, she decided to keep her own comments to herself. Just as she started to test him by trying to lead, the music adjusted and quickened. It sped to an exciting pace, and he led her into a quick-stepped dance, spinning her around the room. Her eyes widened and before her mind reminded her that this sort of dance was unladylike, she smiled and gave a small laugh of excitement.

When she was sure of the pace, she tried to lead, expecting him to resist. Not only did he not fight her for control, he smirked and allowed her to take charge of the dance. He took it back for a few turns, only for her to get it back. It felt more similar to a sparring match than an actual dance. His light eyes sparkled with the same amusement she knew was in hers.

When the dance finished, he dipped her low, and held her there a moment, jaw clenched and an odd intensity in his gaze he'd locked onto her. He pulled her back up, took both her hands, and slowly bowed, this time avoiding looking up at her, as though in those seconds he'd changed from a lord to a servant. Again, he didn't kiss her hand. He escorted her back to her seat, nodded to her mother and Amelia—which none had bothered to do before—and returned to the seat beside her father.

Leopold bent to her ear. "Should I cross that one off?"

"Don't you dare."

He chuckled. "That's two, miss."

"Now you've a choice to make," her mother said. She leaned closer. "I think that was a prince!"

"Why?" Song hissed.

"Extravagant clothes, sitting beside the king. And why else would your father go out of his way to have you dance with him?" She looked from that man to the one Song had liked before. "Yes. I think the two you need to choose between are the princes. Either one and you'll be Princess Tsingsei Bartlett. Oh! I envy you."

Song looked over at the king's table, but the man was paying attention to her father speaking, rather than staring the way many other men continued to do, even now. Her gaze swept around the room at the faces masked with silver. The one benefit to not seeing their faces was it made the choice feel less personal.

She could tell a lot about the men just by the brief conversation and the way they'd danced with her. With only a few minutes to convince her they were the right choice, many spoke of their riches and what they occupied their time with. None of them asked her questions or tried getting to know *her*. All of them, save the two she hadn't crossed off, had been domineering in the dance, treating her as a subordinate.

If any of them knew who she was and what she'd done—knew the Jewel of Castildi was not only in her possession, but around her neck and tucked beneath the half-jacket to remain hidden—they would either run, have her arrested, or try to claim her even more so.

"All these Lords," she said to her mother and Amelia, "and I have to smile and pretend I don't outrank some of them."

"Outrank them how?" Mrs. Gould asked.

"Captain," she said with a grin.

Her mother made a few flustered noises and looked around for anyone too close. She pursed her lips at Song. "I'm sure that doesn't count. Besides, that all has to stop."

Song glared straight ahead. "No. I will make sure the man I marry knows exactly who is in charge of me—not bloody anybody but me."

She and her mother locked stern gazes at one another for a minute before the king interrupted them. He stood and held out his hands for silence.

"The night is winding down, and I think it is time for our guest of honor to announce her choice among all these suitors." He smiled and nodded over to her.

Song let out a long breath and stood. But as she did, so did Amelia, who then took off running for the door. Song didn't pause or think before she broke out running after her. She chased Amelia down the hallway, calling to her.

"Miss Gould!" Leopold shouted behind her. "Your choice!"

But Song didn't stop as she raced after the woman.

Thirty-Seven

W HEN SONG ENTERED THE ROOM ACROSS THE HALL FROM hers, Amelia was already sitting on the bed, crying into her hands. She'd flung her mask across the room, and now it lay crumpled in a corner. Just before she closed the door, Lyella slipped in to stare between the two.

"Amelia…" Song said with a sigh. "What's wrong?"

"All of this," she said. "You having the time of your life with those men—"

"You really think I'd rather be out dancing with *them* rather than dancing with *you?*"

"Tsingsei can have fun," Lyella said, lowering herself with effortless grace into a chair and crossing her ankles.

"Who are you?" Amelia asked, jealousy spiking her tone.

She smiled. "Sultania Ky'r, Tsingsei's *ghija.*"

"If I return to Armalinia," Song reminded her of the caveat.

"Yes."

Amelia sniffed. "Your what?"

Song let out a long breath and closed her eyes. "I accidentally accepted a marriage proposal from her. Well…she tricked me into it. She is the princess."

"The…princess…of…" Amelia said.

"Armalinia. All of it."

The woman smiled. "My father is a good sultan."

"You…you're already *engaged?*" Amelia demanded.

"Technically…"

"It is all right," Lyella said, still smiling. "She may have her own *ghija* or *ghida*, and this *ghidja*, too. And you! She may have you."

The woman on the bed shook her head. "I don't understand."

Song sat beside her. "In Armalinia, the upper classes, should they choose, may take many wives and husbands."

"I wanted a princess," Lyella said. "Andalise princess." She laughed, pointing at Song.

"I'm not a princess," she muttered.

"Close enough," Amelia said, her demeanor overcome with morose realization. "And then you'll marry the prince of Pishing. If you marry the sultania, then you're also the princess of Armalinia, aren't you?"

"Yes," Lyella said.

Amelia tried to resist, but lost the battle with the wry smile that overtook her lips. "You'd be the most powerful woman in the world with so many countries looking to you."

Song laughed. "I'm already the most powerful woman in the world."

Amelia laughed, too, though her sadness polluted the sound. "Right."

Lyella released a wistful sigh as she stared at Song. "My king of skies. You anger Pishing."

"That wasn't me."

Lyella gave her a disbelieving smile.

"Mostly."

On the bed, Amelia's tears had slowed so she could echo Lyella's expression at Song.

"All right, I started it. But the one causing all the trouble these past months is not me. Bastard is tarnishing my good name."

Amelia blinked. "Your *good* name? The name linked to hundreds of murders, thousands in riches stolen, at *least* two skyship explosions, *regicide*…not to mention that child you kidnapped! *That* good name?"

Song stuck her nose into the air, indignation settling over her expression. "Yes. Not once was it political, like this imposter. He's the reason I have to marry some mute prince—oh, gods of Jinjran, I really do hope he's mute. A man who can't talk back or boss me around would be a gods-send."

"You did not choose," Lyella said.

"Oh, bollox." Song deflated.

"Who were you going to choose?" Amelia asked on a near whisper, as though she didn't want to know.

"I want to say that last one. The latecomer. But something in my gut doesn't trust him. At the same time, there's something compelling me to choose him just so I can see the man under the mask."

"What's so scary about him?"

"I don't know. I don't even know if it's fear I feel for him, or something else. Just…some sort of vague urgency in my mind. That's the part that scares me—having that nagging, but no idea what it's trying to tell me. He could be a lovely prince, or he could be a monster, for all I know. And yet…"

The woman on the bed shivered. "Maybe you should choose the other one."

"Yes. He'd be the safer bet. Safe is good." She twisted her lips into a wicked smirk. "Then again, there's something thrilling about monsters."

"You, of all people, have no reason to fear one." She released a small laugh that turned into a whimper. "But what will happen to me?"

Lyella moved to sit on the bed and dab at Amelia's tears with a handkerchief. "Tsingsei will keep you."

"You make me sound like a pet."

"Oh, but Pet is such a cute nickname," Song said as she crossed the room. "How are you, Pet? You look lovely, Pet." She sat on the bed. "Give us a kiss, my Pet."

After a nervous giggle and a glance at Lyella, Amelia inched forward to set a small peck on Song's lips.

"There, see? Nothing to worry about." Song took her hand and kissed the top, then did the same with Lyella's hand. "It's a miserable situation, but we can still make the best of it."

The sultania wrapped Song's hand in both of hers. "One tell of you."

"Demand."

"One demand."

"What is that?"

Lyella smiled. "You marry me before prince. You were mine first. I get you first."

Song thought, then gave a single nod. "All right, it's a deal. But how will I marry a Pishing prince if I'm trapped with you?"

"I do not trap you," Lyella said, her voice sharp with indignation. "I would never trap you."

"But that's why I ran! I didn't want to be forced to stay in Armalinia forever!"

She scowled. "You should ask! You are free spirit, Tsingsei… Song. I could never cage you." She leaned forward to plant a firm kiss on Song's lips, as though punctuating her statement.

"Well," Song said when she released her, "don't I feel silly." She took Amelia's hand in her free one again. "There, see? I've room enough for you, even if I'm a princess twice over. Besides, I've been working on a list of demands, including that both parties may have mistresses, should they choose."

"What if I don't want to be a *mistress?*" Amelia said.

Song stood and stalked across the room. "You think I want it that way? This is the only solution I've got, Amelia!"

"Run away again!" she shouted.

"I promised I wouldn't!"

"They can choose some other senator's daughter!"

"They don't *want* another senator's daughter! My father tried! I told you that, but you've been sulking and shutting me out."

Lyella frowned. "They want princess of Andalise." She dabbed at Amelia's tears.

"They want the famous missing girl," Song said. "Amelia, please, I am *trying.*"

Amelia sniffled. "Can I be alone for a while? To think."

She nodded. "Of course." She strode over to lean down and kiss her cheek, then left the room with Lyella in tow.

They crossed the hall into Song's room and stood together in the silence on the other side of the door. After a minute of staring at each other in uncertainty, Lyella tore her mask from her face and dove at Song lips-first. They got lost in each other's mouths for several minutes, hands wandering over each other. A knock sounded through the door, jolting into Song's back. She checked her lip color in the mirror as Lyella tugged her mask back on. When Song opened the door, Leopold stood on the other side.

"Sorry for the disturbance, miss. Your father would like to speak with you in his chamber. He asks that you bring your demands."

"Oh. All right." She gave Lyella an apologetic look, and the sultania smiled back.

Song grabbed the page of terms she'd been working on, and followed the man a short way down the hall to where her mother stood outside the door to the room they had put her parents in.

"He wants a word in *private*. *Tch!*" Annie said.

"I'm sure he's telling me the hottest gossip and you're missing out," Song teased.

"That's not funny."

Song laughed anyway as she entered. Elroy sat at a drawing table, looking over some papers.

"Working on holiday?" she asked with a wry smile.

"You consider this a holiday?"

She made a face. "I wouldn't have been dancing with men all night if it were."

"And one woman." Her father turned in his seat to give

her his full attention. "I've not asked about your…travels, but I would like to know who that woman was."

"Swear you won't say a word?"

"On my honor."

"The sultania. She is not supposed to be here, especially not without her entourage, *and* without her veil." She smiled. "Quite the little rebel."

"How did she find out about this event?"

"Ryk'r, of course. Sneaky bastard. I always suspected he can talk, he just refuses to. This gives weight to that theory."

"Why did she come?"

"To dance with me as a reminder…and to inform me that Pishing can't have me until I wed her. I was hers first, after all. Don't worry, no one needs to know, and she won't force me to stay in Armalinia." She sank back against the wall. "Everywhere I go, people want to get their hands on me for one reason or another. Pishing wants a peace offering; Armalinia wants a princess; Andalise wants their famous senator's daughter; Aibhànocht thinks I'm chosen by their God. And everywhere wants me to hang as a pirate—except Pishing, suddenly. They want me alive, and I've no idea why. Do you?"

"I don't, unfortunately."

She released an exasperated sigh. "It's all so tiring. I just want to fly around and have an adventure."

"What you were doing was mayhem, not adventures."

"They absolutely were adventures. And I don't plan on stopping."

Elroy let out a long breath. "You'll have to reduce your

activity dramatically, if not stop altogether once you're married."

"Speaking of which, your write-in bothered less than the others. Wouldn't even say a word to me."

Elroy smiled. "So, you like him?"

She picked at an invisible string on her sleeve, avoiding her father's gaze. "He's not terrible."

"Aren't you glad you trusted me?"

"I suppose. Hopefully, he's always that silent. Less back-talking. The dance was almost as inappropriate as the one with the sultania, so maybe he won't be so overbearing and I can get away with a few of my less dignified hobbies."

"Tsingsei, you don't have dignified hobbies."

"*Exactly!* What did he say to you that you added him to the list?" she asked.

"He was already on the list, but they'd crossed him off early. Apparently he wasn't interested in even attending the event, but showed up last minute. He was here as a regular guest, but only had the one mask. Your dance with the sultania caught his interest. Asked a lot of questions about you, and I tried to make you sound more lady-like without outright lying. The other suitors also spoke to me after, but to express that if chosen, they planned on getting you 'under control.' And, well, we're trying to make peace, not push tensions into an all-out war with you running him through on your wedding night." He laced his fingers together.

"Who's to say I won't do that, anyway?"

"Because you liked that one."

"I haven't chosen, yet."

Elroy smiled. "Your mother and I discussed the two you liked. I made the final decision to select that man. Something about him is…trustworthy."

"Something about him unsettles *me*," she said, just above a whisper.

"Nothing *you*, of all people, can't handle. I'm sure of it. You don't get a reputation like yours by being a damsel in distress." His brow furrowed. "Did I make the wrong call?"

She forced a smile. "No. I can take care of myself. He's a prince, either way, right?"

"Given that only two men knew just how to get your attention, and I gave the king those insights for them, I'm inclined to say yes. But otherwise, I am as clueless as you."

"They didn't have names on the dance cards?"

"No. They gave each suitor a number on their invitation."

"As thankful as I am for the advantage given to those two, I…"

"What?"

"Nothing." She let out a long breath. "None of them asked me questions about me. Just talked about themselves the whole time. They don't care about *me*. It would've been nice to have just one care about the person they were trying to win. They want some pretty face they can sit down, keep quiet, and forget about." She thought back to what Amelia had said on the rooftop. "They want a coat rack."

"And you're very young."

"Probably think I'm naïve. I should've just told them all I'm not chaste and *they* would've crossed me off *their* list."

Elroy's eyes widened on her and she pressed her lips closed. "Years with no filter on that mouth, it's a wonder you can trick people in public at all. I'm sure it won't matter. No one has to know what you've done with women behind closed doors."

"And one man."

"Oh." Elroy shrugged, as though nothing his daughter could ever say would shock him anymore. "How are your terms coming along? You'll be meeting your betrothed tomorrow, so if we get it to him tonight, it gives him time to craft one of his own."

"Yes, I have a few things on it." She unfolded the paper to look over the list she'd started. "Full autonomy. I included having a mistress, and he may have one, too—or a mister, whatever he likes. Freedom to come and go as I please, including going…"

"With your crew."

Song nodded. "And…no slaves will ever serve me, clothe me, or do *anything* for me. Everyone will be paid."

"Tsingsei, their culture—"

"I told you about Leslie," she hissed, then let out an angry breath, her nostrils flaring. "He meant the world to me. And being a former slave is what got him murdered. So, no, I will not bow down and accept their backward customs. I will not live in a house where slaves are kept. And if this man tries, then, well, they'll all mysteriously go missing one night and you'll have some new citizens in Garda. Am I understood?"

He stood and pulled his suit jacket down. "Sit down."

She clenched her jaw, but did so. He read over her terms, which were mostly ideas in an unorganized list. He took out his folder and fountain pen, handing her the latter, and set a clean sheet of paper on the drawing table.

"In short, clear, and diplomatic sentences, list your terms. I will take it to him, and tomorrow the two of you can discuss after you officially meet."

"Thank you."

"I know I haven't always been the best father, but at least I can try before taking care of you is some other man's job."

"I can take care of myself."

"You always could. It's just a sentimental phrase."

She gave him a soft smile, then set to rewriting her list in clear statements as an actual contract.

- *Both parties may have a mistress or mister, if so desired.*
- *Neither party will exercise control over the other.*
- *Miss Gould will not tolerate the ownership of slaves.*
- *Miss Gould requires the freedom to travel at her leisure with minimal oversight.*

Elroy took the finished contract and looked it over. "What are these at the bottom? A personal tailor? Your own horse without a side-saddle? Separate bedrooms?"

"When I was ten, you were writing out a list of items for a bill. You put a few silly things on the list and told me—"

"It's good to add in a few items specifically for removing during negotiations."

She smiled. "I don't have any of those things now, so why should I care when he asks me to trim it down a bit?"

"You are frighteningly clever sometimes." He set it down and drew two lines.

"Dash said it made me a terrifying pirate." She signed where he pointed.

"He wasn't wrong." He rolled up the paper, and she tied a ribbon around it. "Wait here."

Mrs. Gould came in and sat on the bed after he left, directing an expectant stare toward Song. "Well?"

"Father is taking him my demands."

"Of course. But he told you which one we chose?"

Song nodded, ignoring the knot in her stomach. "Thank you. He's the one I would've chosen."

The two spent the next several minutes talking about the suitors and the ball, waiting for her father. He returned and breathed out a sigh, as though expelling all the excitement of the night from his fraying nerves.

"Well?" Song asked.

"Since he wasn't originally part of this whole thing, he had other engagements to get to. I caught him as he was leaving," Elroy said.

"So, I won't be meeting him tomorrow?"

"No. We'll have to arrange another time."

"And the demands?"

Elroy gave a small half smile. "He read them."

"And?"

"Laughed."

Song blinked, taken aback. "He laughed? Like it was funny to him?"

"More…amused, really. He took it with him, so I assume he'll want to make counter terms."

She nodded and released a breath, much like her father had. "Excuse me. I'd like to take off my dress and relax now."

"Goodnight, my dear daughter," Elroy said, then kissed her forehead.

"Sleep well, my darling." Annie stood to hug her. "I'm so proud of how you handled tonight."

"Thank you Mother, Father. Goodnight."

She returned to her room, giving Ryk'r a perturbed smile. He grinned from his position beside her door, then fell into his usual straight-faced, alert state.

Lyella had stretched out on the bed, admiring a painting she'd taken off the wall to study. "This art is different from Armalinia." She stared at something beautiful, and yet she looked so sad.

"What's wrong?" Song sat beside her.

Without asking, Lyella sat up to help Song out of her clothes. "There is much I do not know. You are worldly. I am…"

Song set her palm to the woman's cheek, realizing for the first time that she, too, might be a caged bird just like herself. "You know more about your country and its citizens than I could ever hope to. You don't need to be worldly, so long as you know how to rule your people when it's your turn. Knowing about art in Pishing or tattoo meanings in Kerriwen will not help you govern Armalinia."

Lyella gave her a small smile as she met her gaze through her eyelashes.

"Besides, I think Armalinia is better than all the other countries in the world. If you did force me to stay put, I would've been happy it was there, instead of someplace like Pishing."

Lyella leaned forward to capture Song with a passionate kiss. She tore at her clothing more desperately, as Song undressed her as well. They crawled beneath the covers and Song extinguished the lamp on the table. Song slid lower, kissing a trail down the woman's stomach.

"You're going to have to be quiet," she whispered.

Lyella grinned. "I will try."

As Song ducked her head, the sultania grabbed a pillow and shoved it over her own face.

SHE WOULD NEVER GROW TIRED OF THE OCEAN WINDS ON HER skin. Of the sun flickering on the waves, and the promise of adventure on the horizon. Song stood out on the bowsprit, feet planted in place, hair loose, her coat and prosthetic left behind in her cabin. She raised her arm up over her head and smiled as the breeze tangled through her fingers like ribbons made from ghosts.

Her cabin door opened, disturbing the silent deck in the sunrise-painted morning. Hands reached around her waist, and Lyella set her chin on her shoulder. She had her actual veil on, now, and she moved with a comfort Song understood. It was the same comfort she felt wrapped inside her pirate coat.

"Good morning, my desert flower," Song said. She made a face. "And that's the last time I say that out loud. What an awful phrase."

"I like it. It is romantic."

Her nose wrinkled. "Sorry, but I can't bring myself to say it again without laughing or wanting to die." She lifted the veil to plant a kiss on the woman's lips.

She had skipped out on the breakfast with the king, since her new betrothed wouldn't be there, anyway. She used that morning alone to make up for lost time with the sultania—it wasn't as fun when the woman couldn't scream openly, but that didn't stop her enjoyment. Song had convinced her parents to let her escort Lyella and her bard home, and invited them along. Her father had to get back to the senate with an update on the situation. Her mother didn't want to go without him. Amelia had refused to get back on the pirate ship, even though she knew it would be safe. They'd left Argwin together and had transferred ships once over the mountains.

Amelia's fears, while understandable, bothered Song—which made her feel terrible and selfish. She wanted the woman to be better, and not terrified of pirates. But there was no way to magically cure her, and in fact Song had no idea how to even help someone who'd been through what Amelia had. Were there medicines or concoctions she could take to ease her mind? Herbs she could ingest to calm her down? Song didn't have the answers, but she had vowed to herself that once she returned home, she would find someone who did. She would get the help Amelia needed, since so far doing nothing had—quite predictably—done nothing.

Song knew the refusal to join her on her ship wasn't personal, either. And yet she couldn't help but feel like it was. Amelia couldn't stand to be around pirates, so how long would it be before she realized that Song, at her heart, was a pirate, too?

Johanna had joined, though, making the excuse that it was to remain by Song's side. However, the fact that in a full day, she'd stayed below to socialize with the men while sitting with Sunshine revealed just how thorough a lie she'd told. Not that it bothered Song. She was quite content to be spending this time with Lyella. She didn't want romance. Song didn't think she loved her. But she'd be lying if she said she didn't adore the sultania, and enjoy getting to know her better, now that Lyella spoke Common so well.

It turned out they had a great deal in common—at least in Song's former life, trapped in Garda. Lyella had a beautiful spirit, as well. She'd never thought it was something one could see, but now she understood it. It was a sparkle in someone's eye, or the smile they gave without thinking. If Lyella's spirit was a light, she would have been blinding. The woman loved to love and did so without caveat. And Song thought—feared—that maybe Lyella had somehow, somewhere, fallen in love with her. She hoped she hadn't, though, since she still had not found it in herself to love her back. Not in the way she deserved. And she couldn't help but think of how Leslie had loved her, and it might have broken him. She didn't want to break Lyella, too.

They spent the days talking, and listening to crew members play instruments. Jerome used a bucket as a hand drum to play the Ebrinar Jig with Sunshine. It was lively, and Lyella loved dancing to it. But what the man said afterward dragged Song's mood down just a little.

"We used to play that with our friends. We played the drum. Peyton played a fiddle, and Tark a guitar. When Leslie could visit, he played his recorder." He stared at the bucket and smiled. "We miss them."

"Where did the others go?" she asked from the steps.

"Don't know. Well, Peyton, yes. He went and got himself a spot on the royal guard. A respectable position for an orphan."

Song frowned. "Was he a Duchamp guard?"

Jerome furrowed his brow. "I sure hope not. Otherwise you killed him."

"I didn't kill *all* the guards. There was one…" Now that she had the chance to think more about the king's family crest and the guard uniform, she thought back to the man outside the parlor office in Duchamp Hall.

"What?" Sunshine asked.

"A member of the king's guard unlocked the door for Roman's office after I told him straight out I planned to kill Roman."

"Probably knew you'd kill him if he resisted."

She furrowed her brow in thought. "Maybe. But why be so…suspicious."

"What are you thinking, Song?"

She took a deep breath and released it. "Nothing. Whatever it was, that was two years ago, and it's still none of my business. Politics is my father's thing, and I'm happy to stay out of whatever Pishing has going on."

"Except for the whole you becoming their princess thing," Ponce said.

She made a rude face. "Unfortunately, yes."

Just over a week later, they delivered Lyella and her bard to Pajisr in the night, when no one would spot the star at the figurehead. The sultania hesitated for several minutes, kissing Song over and over. She would turn for the door to join Ryk'r on deck, but spin back around for more kisses. The guard had to pry her away, and hold the face covering of the shemagh up so she couldn't tear it down and leap back into Song's arms.

Sunshine joined Song in the doorway to watch the three disappear into the city. "I don't know why, but that woman absolutely adores you."

"I don't know why, either. I'm a right bastard for running out on her before, and we've hardly seen each other in two years."

"Absence makes the heart grow fonder…"

"I think it's more than adoration," Johanna said. "I think she loves you."

Song scoffed. "What codswallop."

"It's the way she looks at you. Like you're the sun in her sky, or the moon of her night."

"She only wanted me because I'm Tsingsei Gould."

"It's more than that now, dear." Johanna released a loud sigh. "Some people would give anything to be loved so deeply."

"And it's wasted on Song," Toothy said.

Song gave him a rude gesture.

They waited for Ryk'r to return, then left port. Song watched the city disappear into the darkness from her bay windows. For just a moment, she regretted not staying. She could have been happy in this sandy cage with the woman who adored and possibly loved her. She could have even found contentment in at least being free to exist as she was without shame. But a small part of her screamed that she'd made a promise to her father, and now she had a second royal waiting for her. Unfortunately, that small part was quite loud, and so she glared out at the night and seethed, rather than having Sunshine turn them around so she could escape a prince and run to a sultania.

WHEN THEY RETURNED TO GARDA, SONG FIRST STOPPED IN TO check on Amelia. She seemed to be doing better, but there was a shadow in her eyes. And so, Song left her there to find Leopold so he might hire someone more suited to helping the woman than anyone within the estate could.

After her long bath, she met her father in his study.

"How was your breakfast with the king?" Song asked.

"It was fine. The princes were there, as well."

She jolted. "Both? But you said the one had to leave."

"As it turns out…you only liked one of the princes. The other took his chances and ignored what Chiron told him."

"Oh, no, you're on a first name basis with the king of Pishing." She made a face and giggled as he waved away her comment.

"I rather like him as a man. He's not at all what I expected."

"So…who am I betrothed to?"

"I didn't get a name, but I did get an unfiltered opinion on him from one of the princes."

She adjusted in her seat. "Oh? And?"

"It's…not good."

A stone formed in the pit of her stomach. "How so?"

Elroy sighed. "They call him the Bastard Lord. Say he's illegitimate. Apparently, most were glad to hear he wouldn't be attending. It was their absolute worst nightmare for you to have chosen him. So…cheers to that, I suppose."

"Oh, bollocks." Song wilted in her seat. "I knew I had a bad feeling about him. What does that mean for the treaty?"

"Well, the king seems to like him, so anyone else's opinions are moot." He observed her for a minute in silence. "Would you have chosen the prince if you hadn't chased Amelia out of the room?"

She leaned back, massaging her eyes through the lids in a delicate manner to avoid smudging her makeup. "I don't know. Maybe. Probably not. I hadn't quite made up my mind. I still haven't." Song frowned at her father. "It's too late to change my betrothed, isn't it? Or would they make an exception since you're the one who chose? And because it's the Bastard Lord."

"Doubtful. But I can write to the king and ask."

"Please do. I don't need to be more of a social pariah there than I already will be." She sank in the chair to rest the back of her head on the seatback. "I almost feel bad for him, though."

"Hmm?"

"The Bastard Lord. He didn't ask to be born an illegitimate child of some Lord who couldn't keep it in his trousers."

Her father nodded. "Sins of the father become the sins of the son."

"Maybe I *should* marry that one and help boost his status. Get rid of that ridiculous nickname."

"How noble of you."

"I'm doing it."

He raised his eyebrows at her.

"Is it not fitting? The most backward woman they could have chosen, choosing to marry the one person they don't want me to?" She laughed and clapped once. "I like it. Even if it's for the simple fact that I'll be infuriating every royal by doing it."

Elroy chuckled. "That's my girl. Now, if you'll excuse me, I have work to do."

"Goodnight, Daddy." She stood and leaned over his desk to kiss his cheek.

"Goodnight, Tsingsei."

She left his study and wandered the halls, wondering what to do next. What could she do? She had to wait for the wedding date, and would have to stay available for the planning and preparations. Or…she could let her mother handle all of it, and trust she would make it something Song wouldn't hate. Which was asking a lot, as she already hated the very idea of the marriage, never mind the wedding itself.

She would also need to find out a date from Lyella for that ceremony. It would have to be a secret, so word didn't reach Pishing that she'd wedded the sultania of Armalinia. A private event sat more comfortably in her stomach.

Until all of those happened, she could spend her time in her favorite tavern, doing some empty flirting with her favorite barmaid. Then, once her father gave his approval, she could head into the skies to capture the imposter. Or 'accidentally' blow him out of the air. At least that way, there was no chance of him escaping. Then again, she wouldn't be able to look at the man under the stolen hood and spit in his eye.

She turned in early that night, opting to lie with Amelia as some sort of comfort for the woman. She received a sad smile, though Amelia cuddled up to her all the same. If Song didn't love Lyella, then she wondered if maybe she could love Amelia. She just needed the right woman. That was another thing she could do in the meantime. She could try harder with this woman, and hopefully help her start to heal. Perhaps she could soothe the nightmares that woke Amelia—though she hadn't found a way to cure her own, so she doubted her ability to help anyone else with theirs.

Song closed her eyes, breathed in the scent of Amelia's clean hair, and resolved that she would do her best to enjoy herself until her wedding day. Then she would marry a pariah and either boost his status or ruin her own. Or kill him. That option would always be on the table. Yes, she decided, it was going to be a good year, whether or not it wanted to be.

Thirty-Nine

Two weeks had passed since Song returned from the skies. She'd fallen into a routine of spending time with Amelia and even her mother. She included them in things such as her research into other cultures' legends of Balamora, and even looking into cannibals around the world out of morbid curiosity, as well as more conversation to have with the king at a later date. Her mother was happy to take over preparations for the wedding and started making plans before the king had even hired the Pishing planner.

Twice a week, Amelia had to go to a doctor's office. This wasn't a medical doctor, but a mental doctor. It fascinated Song, but she was not allowed in the room during the sessions. She almost thought of hiring one for herself, as the thought of waking up and stabbing her future husband in the neck sat on her mind as an intrusive thought. Not that she opposed such a happenstance, but it wouldn't bode well for her or the treaty, unfortunately.

She wondered if a mind doctor could make her arm stop hurting, too. The arm wasn't there; it was all in her head. And yet every so often it would ache like she'd fallen asleep on it and it was waking up with all the pins in the world. There was nothing she could do about it, either. The missing limb had been a ghostly curse on her body for two years, now. If there was any hope of stopping the pain, she would try it.

At night, she would dress in her pirate garb and go to the tavern near the docks. She would stay until Olivia's shift ended, and then walked the woman home. She'd asked where Song had gone, and received the half truth of providing protection to the Gould family on a trip. The woman accepted the reason.

This night, Olivia fidgeted on the doorstep. She stared up into the hood. "Can I ask you a question?"

"Of course."

"Why don't you ever try to kiss me?"

Song gave her a rueful smile and tucked a lock of hair behind the woman's ear. "Because you deserve more than a kiss from a ruddy pirate whom you've never seen the face of. You deserve a kiss from someone who isn't lying straight to your face without saying a word."

"What if I invited you inside so you could take your hood down?"

"I would rather not break the illusion you have of me. If it please you, I give you permission to kiss me in your dreams, and imagine the face beneath this mask. But for now, I can't bring myself to ruin it for you."

"May I ask for a kiss on the hand?" Olivia asked, lifting her right hand into view.

"You may." Song took the offering and set a soft kiss to the coarse, under-moisturized skin of a working woman. "Sweet dreams, Olivia."

"And you, Song."

She smiled as the woman disappeared inside the brownstone. After a moment to get her bearings and convince herself she'd made the right call, she jogged down the steps and headed home. When she reached the mouth of the alley that opened across from the Gould estate, she froze. Her mind sobered as she stared at a black zeppelin with spiked collars ballooning up behind her home. There was no doubt what ship that was, as no other like it existed.

Darkness.

The imposter had grown bold enough to leave the skies over Pishing. He had failed to capture her before the betrothal, and now she knew he was there for her.

Song flagged down a carriage. "You! Call the constables!"

"What?" the driver demanded as the woman in the carriage stared out the window.

"The Goulds are under attack! Hurry!"

He spun in his seat to look at the manor. By the time he turned back, Song was circling the carriage to race through the gate. As the carriage clattered away at a faster pace than before, she ran to her window, jumping to boost up the wall and grab the floor of her balcony. She hauled herself up and checked inside. Her door was still closed. She let herself in, then reached into her trunk for the sorrowstone blade. She secured it to her belt and moved to the door. Song walked on the balls of her feet, creeping through the hall, listening.

Each door she passed, she opened—if the knob would turn. In a linen closet, she found several servants huddled in the darkness. Song put a finger to her lips as a young woman opened her mouth to scream and a man covered her lips with a palm.

"Where are they?" Song asked on a whisper.

Perplexed, the man blinked. "You'll never find the Goulds."

"They made it to the safe room? Thank the gods of every nation."

"Are you the real Song?" another man hissed. "The one Senator Gould trusts?"

"Aye. I'm here to help. Where is Amelia?"

"I saw men heading to that part of the house," the girl said after moving the first man's hand.

"Henry Barton?"

"I saw him go toward the servant quarters with a sword," the man said.

Song nodded. "Right. Stay here. You'll be safe." She took her master key from her pouch, closed the door, and locked it.

Down one hall and around a corner, she found pirates looting her father's office. She used her eilfass tusk dagger to slit the first man's throat from behind. When she turned for the other, he drew his sword. She blocked his swing with the sorrowstone blade, and after a short duel disarmed and dispatched him. As she sheathed the sword, a woman's scream echoed down the hallway.

"Amelia!" she hissed, then took off running through the halls.

Near the stairs for the next floor up, she found Sunshine wielding a sword, defending Johanna and Amelia. While one pirate distracted him, another grabbed Amelia's hand and yanked her away. Johanna took her other hand and held fast as Amelia screamed in terror.

Song charged forward and leapt onto the man's back, burying her dagger into his collar over and over until he collapsed to the floor. She made a quick decision to throw the dagger at a pirate rushing toward Sunshine. The handle made contact with his throat. He wrapped his hand over his neck and stared at her in dumbfounded shock and abject confusion.

"Should've practiced that more!" Sunshine said, chuckling despite being in the midst of combat. He killed the man and readied for more.

"Button it, old man." She strode past Sunshine.

In one swift movement she hadn't thought to do, her right arm snatched the dagger from Sunshine's belt, flipped it into the air, caught it at the tip, and launched it so the blade buried deep into the invading pirate's throat.

She stared at the hand and scoffed. "Show off."

It made a fist and raised the thumb up.

Her face contorted into annoyed curiosity. "What does this mean?"

"It's your arm, you tell me," Sunshine said.

"I told you, it has a mind of its own! Right pain in the arse sometimes."

A woman screamed on the second floor.

"Worry about your hand being peevish later," Johanna said, clinging to Amelia, who was shaking so hard she could barely stand. "The closet under the stairs!"

Song ran to said closet and opened it. "My parents?"

"Upstairs."

She shoved Sunshine in after them. "No hero business."

"Let me help," Sunshine said.

"No. You protect these two." Before he could protest, she closed the little closet.

As she made her way up the stairs, she found bodies in the hallways—servants and a few pirates. A thumping reached her from inside her parents' room. The door stood ajar. Men had crowded into the room, some launching a small battering ram against the section of wall which hid their panic room door, others going through her mother's jewelry. She was not foolish enough to think she could take all of them, so she stood to the side, revolver and sword ready, her back pressed to the wall as she formed a plan.

"We just want the girl!" one said.

A man let out a loud sigh. "This was supposed to be a simple grab." The tone of his voice sent Song on edge. "You bloody fools have made a mess of everything."

Song blinked in shock as the man spoke so much like her it was eerie. His accent, tone, and inflections mirrored her own, though his voice contained a rough growl. It was as if this man *was* her.

As the pounding quickened and the wall crunched under the strain, Song closed her eyes and took a deep breath. She spun to put herself in the doorway.

"Oi, milksops! Tsingsei's not in there!" she shouted.

The imposter spun, his upper face covered by a black mask. His icy eyes swept over the sword in her grasp. "Where did you get that?"

"Come find out," she taunted, then took off running.

"After him!" the man shouted.

Footsteps thundered behind her. Song rounded a corner and spun herself into a hidden cubby in the wall. The frightened breathing of two individuals sounded behind her. She turned and stared into the darkness, blind. She hissed a soft *shh*.

The footsteps rounded the corner and continued past, a few stragglers taking the time to search rooms in that hallway. Door after door opened and closed. A woman screamed in terror before it cut short with an agonized gagging.

Song would be lying if she had told anyone she felt confident right then. Face to face with her echo for the first time had jolted something inside her. He'd taken everything that made her Song—copied her down to her accent, her coat, her mannerisms. The bastard even had blue eyes. It occurred to her, though, that there was one aspect that no one could copy. No one could replicate the nature of her *kijæm*.

In all her recent studies, there was one truth that no one could take—she was the most powerful Touched in written history, whether the rest of the world knew it or not. Without her *kijæm* she could be anybody, but with it she was the true Song. She needed it, just as it needed her. And so she closed her eyes and took a few deep breaths.

"Please, please," she whispered, "I will do anything. Anything you want. Just return to me."

Three words formed in her mind—ones she'd known all along and had heard in her nightmares. Now she knew that this was the *kijæm* all along, whispering the phrase for her to reclaim her power. And so this time, she whispered it with them.

"*Zechnif… Dlro'w oleh-h.*"

Warmth crawled through her veins as an image entered her mind. Tall black cliffs made with volcanic rock, a cone-shaped mountain spewing smoke to cast a shadow over a small island. Not another piece of land was in sight. Then, as though carried on a breeze which wasn't in the cupboard with her, words spoken by a man whispered into her ears.

Help me. Find me. I need to get home. Ahrek…it worked. Oh, God, I'm such a fool. It worked.

The vision faded, and when she opened her eyes, she could see everything in the little space, as though through a blue glass in dim light. The two figures looked into her eyes and shied away. Her mind collected itself as she realized what she'd just seen—*Au Caesaries*. It was real…and she'd seen it before. Years ago, when she was just some brat on a stolen skyship.

As though it had never left her, just hid itself, her *kijæm* returned the entire language to her mind.

"Should've said anything but bloody *that*," she grumbled as she pressed her ear to the wall.

When no sound came from the other side for a minute, Song opened the wall and slipped out, closing it behind her. Not a soul remained in the hallway. When she reached her parents' room, two men had remained behind to break through the wall. She walked in and unholstered her sidearm, shooting each in the back of the head before they could turn around. Mrs. Gould screamed frominside the panic room.

"Who are you?"

The hairs on the back of her neck stood on end. She turned to face the replica of herself. He was, indeed, a near perfect echo.

"The real Song," she said.

"False. You are a pathetic copycat. Flattering, but annoying, nonetheless."

"Funny, I was about to say the same about you."

"Where is the Gould girl?" he asked, withdrawing a white handled sidearm.

"Escaped through the tunnels in the basement already. What do you want with her?"

The corner of his lips rose in a sadistic smirk. "Wouldn't you like to know?" He raised his gun and shot as Song dove sideways.

She grunted as the bullet grazed across her left biceps. When she landed on the floor, she lifted her own revolver and emptied the remaining four bullets toward the door, where he no longer stood.

She shoved to her feet and ran into the hall as she emptied the cylinder and loaded new bullets into it. Silence surrounded her as she sneaked through the hallways, trying to find the echo. She hissed a command, and her vision shifted to that odd colored world. The people throughout the mansion came into view as red and orange blobs, even through walls.

A commotion drew her down the stairs. To her left, a pirate stomped toward the ballroom, carrying a set of gilded candelabra. She shot him in the back of the head and strode the direction he'd been running.

"Song!"

She spun to stare at Detective Inspector Foggerty, gun drawn, but aimed at the floor. A pirate rounded the corner over his shoulder and raised his sword. Song lifted her revolver and shot.

Foggerty raised his weapon, flinched, and looked over his shoulder as the man fell down dead. By the time he turned back to her, Song had already spun on the ball of her foot to continue to the ballroom. There she discovered the point of entry—a large broken glass wall panel, which men poured out of and clambered up ladders hanging from the side of Darkness.

"*Mih-h kairb,*" she hissed at the last remaining man.

The mist shot from around her, shifting from blue to red. It slammed straight into his back and threw him to the ground. His screams echoed from the vaulted glass ceiling and the massive windows as his body contorted in unnatural ways. Each of his bones broke within him one at a time. A single man at the bottom of a ladder stared wide-eyed at the figure with glowing red eyes under a dark hood. He turned to clamber up and shout for the ship to leave.

As though clouds parted, the moonlight flowed into the window just in front of her. Darkness turned and flew away from the manor, toward the ocean. Once clear of the buildings, two massive canvas wings spread from its body to catch the updrafts.

Her vision returned to normal. The man on the floor stopped screaming and stopped breathing. She sneered down at him, then spat in his wide-open eye.

"*Pish ehth oot em kait.*"

She held out her arms as the *kijæm* swirled around her and lifted her feet off the floor. The bright mist carried her through the broken window and lifted her higher and higher. It pressed against her back and rushed her forward. Her *kijæm* took her around the side of the ship and set her on the deck.

"Captain!" someone shouted.

There he stood at the helm. He stared down at her, but she couldn't make out his expression in the darkness under his own hood. He released the wheel and jogged down the stairs, unsheathing a shining silver saber as he went. They locked blades, battling for the upper hand.

"You'd think someone impersonating me would be better with my sword of choice," she said.

"You'd think someone impersonating *me* would fight with the proper hand," he said.

Again, his voice caused the hairs to raise on the back of her neck, but she couldn't quite place why. The distraction was enough to open her up to a strike. She caught his blade in her right hand, twisted it from his grip, and tossed it over the side of the ship.

"It seems I underestimated you," he said. He spoke strong and sure—loud, so everyone on deck heard their captain exchanging words with an accused imposter.

But he was the imposter. And a good one at that. It was as though he'd studied the way she stood, the way she moved. Her exact accent flowed through his lips with the same lilt and cadence as hers. This man, whoever he was, was her exact copy in every way she could tell. It gnawed at her gut, but she ignored it and focused. She knew what she had to do. She had to take his head and then unmask him. Damn what the senate wanted.

"You did. Now you get to die." She lunged to stab him in the gut, but he spun away.

The echo brought his foot up and kicked her hand, causing her to release the sword. It tumbled through the air and clattered against the railing. Song dove for it, but the sorrowstone blade plummeted over the side toward the ocean below. Fury rose inside her, though at the back of her mind she knew she could get it back.

"Fair fight. Me and you," he said. "May the best Song win."

For a moment, she thought about popping out her sharp fingertips and ramming them through his neck. But he'd made her curious with the suggestion.

"You and me," she said, turning around to glare at him even though he couldn't see into her hood.

He came at her, fists raised. They punched and kicked each other in near equal skill and practice. She did her best to not hit him too hard with her metal arm, her ego wanting the fair fight. He was impressive, she couldn't deny. But could he keep up with her?

"I can go for hours," she said after a while.

"As can I."

His entire crew stood gaping at the spectacle. Minutes passed as the two battled in a stalemate.

But then he did something she hadn't expected. It's not that she wouldn't have been prepared for the maneuver, it was that his graceful form sent her back years to a hot day when an untrained brat caught a forearm across her chest, tripped over a leg hooked behind her own, and crashed to the deck. Leslie's smug, self-satisfied smirk entered her vision, and she sucked in a sharp breath.

Song blinked, and the full moon replaced the sun. Where Leslie had stood was a black figure silhouetted against the bright orb. The echo straddled her and placed his gloved hands to her throat.

She scrabbled against him, trying to grab his hair to yank. Instead, her hand came away with his black mask. She struggled for breath, but his weight on her was too much to knock away. The fingers of her right hand curled, the palm kicked back, and with a sharp *shwing*, the blade ripped through her leather glove. The echo noticed the white dagger and threw himself sideways to avoid it.

Song rolled onto her knees, coughing. He stood, his hood having fallen back. In the dim lighting of the moon behind him, her air-starved mind saw the most familiar face staring back at her under his short, dark hair. The bright, kind eyes. The slender nose. Those lips that had given her countless smiles and had kissed her so desperately.

Leslie.

She squeezed her eyes closed, as though erasing the image from her sight. *Why his face?* She opened her eyes to get another look, but he'd lifted his hood back up.

"You cheated," he said. "He's all yours, boys!"

His crew converged on her, and she knew she'd lost. She would have to slaughter them all.

Her mind was reeling. She wanted to drag that hood back down and see the man who was really under there. She wanted to assure herself that she was hallucinating.

Even if it could have been Leslie, that man acted too much like her to have been him. Leslie had been too honorable and good to be this male version of her watching as these men advanced. And he especially would never have stolen her identity and gone parading around as though it belonged to him.

No. She had to take his hood down. She had to see his real face.

Song ignored the tears burning her eyes and fought the men, stabbing through them with her palm blade. But the blade was short, and soon they had her swarmed.

This isn't over.

She backed to the railing and threw herself over the side toward the moonlit ocean below.

Song's feet set on the hardwood floor just inside the broken window of the ballroom. The shards of glass crunched beneath her boots, disturbing the otherwise hollow silence. Foggerty stared at her, his revolver raised to point toward the ceiling. He didn't say anything, and neither did she. The sorrowstone blade, illuminated by a blue glow, flew in through the window behind her and slapped its handle into her palm. She sheathed it, then stepped around the detective.

"You saved me," Foggerty said.

"No. I killed a man who didn't belong here. Your presence changed nothing." She jogged up the stairs and opened the cupboard where Sunshine and the two women hid. She handed Sunshine the master key. "I locked several servants inside a linen closet near Tsingsei's room."

He nodded and took the two with him down the hall.

Foggerty stood at her side. "You have a key to the mansion?"

"Senator Gould and I have an arrangement."

He made a thoughtful noise, then strode to meet with officers who trickled in around the corner. He lifted his hands as a few raised their firearms. "Song is here at the request of the senator. Holster your weapons." He craned his neck as she headed up the stairs. "Where are you going?"

"To get the senator and his wife."

He followed her up, saying nothing. She could almost hear the questions scrawling out as a list in his mind. He stopped to check bodies for anyone still alive, but she continued on, knowing they were already gone or close enough.

She reached the panic room door and knocked like she'd learned as a child. Her father had made two special knocks, one for if she was in trouble, and one for if she was safe. She tapped three times, once, then twice—the signal for safe. The same sequence knocked back. The wheel turned to retract the metal bolts from the frame. It clicked open and swung wide.

Without a pause to check the surroundings, Annie Gould launched herself at Song, wrapping her arms as tight as she could around her daughter as she cried in relief. Ryk'r stood in the doorway of the panic room, his blood-covered kris in hand. His gaze landed on Song, and she nodded her thanks to him. He nodded back and found a cloth to clean his dagger.

"Mrs. Gould," Song said. "Senator."

Elroy looked over her shoulder at the detective in the doorway. "Ah, Zion. When did you get here?"

"Not long ago. Someone came to the station claiming Captain Song demanded we rush over. It was either a trap or a legitimate report." He released a sigh. "I'm glad I'm not afraid of traps."

"Detective!" An officer entered the room with a man beside him. "This man has information for you. He saw everything."

Foggerty withdrew a notebook and pen. "Do you know who attacked tonight?"

He eyed Song. "It was Captain Song…one of them, at least."

"The imposter," she said. She frowned as the face of a ghost in the moonlight flashed through her mind.

"What did he want?" Foggerty pressed.

"Came here for Miss Gould," the man said.

"Why?"

He shrugged.

"Where is Miss Gould?"

"Safe. She escaped through the tunnels before—" He stumbled back as Song advanced on him, dagger drawn. "Help, *help!*"

"Song!" Foggerty barked, his hand settling on his revolver as a threat.

"He's part of the imposter's crew." She sneered and pinned the man against the wall, blade to his throat.

"How do you know?" her father asked behind her.

"Because the only people who know Tsingsei is in the tunnels are me and the imposter."

"Tunnels?" Annie asked, perplexed.

"Why would they think she's in tunnels?" Elroy asked.

"Because that's what I told him," Song said.

"I don't follow," Foggerty said.

"There are no tunnels under the Gould Estate," Elroy said.

"I lied as a distraction." Song locked her sight on the man in her grasp.

He sneered as realization hit him. "You can't keep her from him."

"Why does that imposter want Tsingsei Gould?"

"He's not the imposter. You are."

"Why does he want her?"

"Why does any man want a woman?"

"Liar," she spat. "I don't like being lied to."

She kneed him in the stomach and threw him to the floor. Before anyone could stop her, she straddled the man and cut his left ear clean off in one quick swipe. He screamed and cupped the side of his head.

"*Song!*" Foggerty bellowed a warning. He drew his revolver and trained it on her.

"Tell the truth!" She hit him in the face with his own ear.

"Get him off me!" he shouted to the officers.

"*Ere'rab.*" Blue exploded from her and surrounded the two in a sphere of light that would keep the police at bay. "The more annoyed I get, the more body parts you lose."

"I can't let you torture a man in front of me," Foggerty said.

"I'm not *torturing* him! I'm *punishing* him! Now turn around, so I'm not in front of you when I take his nose."

"All right, I'll tell!" the man shouted as her dagger touched his nostril.

"See? It worked. No one likes me when I'm irritated."

"Not you," he said. "I'll tell the detective, but not you."

"Rude." She stood, dropped the barrier of light, and took a few steps back.

Foggerty eyed her, then knelt over the man to look at the damage to his ear. "All right, tell me—"

"Not until he's gone."

Song released an indignant scoff. "I have never been so insulted in my life! We were having a good chat, and—"

"Captain," her father said. "Would you mind retrieving my daughter from her panic room?"

She made a face. "*Fine*. The most powerful Touched in the world will play fetch, *Senator*." She turned on her heel and strode away.

Song reached her room and found Johanna, Amelia, and Sunshine sitting inside. She locked the door behind her.

"Father sent me to fetch Miss Gould," she said. She crossed the room and closed the curtains, then stripped.

"What do we know?" Sunshine asked.

"It was the imposter. He was here for me."

"Why?"

"I don't know. One of his men stayed behind—under the echo's orders, I assume. He tried to claim he was house staff. He's with the police now."

Johanna helped bandage the wound on her arm after her *kijæm* burned it closed, then aided her dressing in a gown dark enough to hide if it started bleeding again. After she'd dressed, cleaned, and been made up, she crouched in front of Amelia. The woman looked through her in a daze.

"Are you all right?" Song whispered.

Amelia didn't move or respond.

"Go, Song. We'll stay with her," Sunshine said.

She hesitated, then nodded. The invading pirates may well have just undone all the work the woman had started with the head doctor.

She made her way through the house. When she neared officers, she shifted, as though slipping on her Tsingsei mask, and put on a show for them. She squeaked in shock as she passed the bodies, and bit her cheek until it forced tears into her eyes from the pain, which she could pass off as distress. Officer Daven found her at the bottom of the stairs and held out a friendly hand.

"Miss Gould, it's best not to look at the bodies," he said.

"But there are so many of them!"

"I know. You don't want to give yourself nightmares, though."

"You're probably right." If only he knew it was too late to prevent her nightmares, and these dead bodies were the least of her worries.

He guided her upstairs to where they had the man tied to a chair, his head bandaged.

"Mummy! Daddy!" Song called and raced into their loving embrace. "I was so scared!"

"As were we. I'm so glad you're safe," her father said.

"Who is this?" she asked, staring down at the man in the chair.

"A member of the pirate crew that attacked your home," Detective Foggerty said.

"What happened to his head?"

"Song did."

"He said the imposter came for me. Why me? What does he want?"

"That's the detective's job to find out," her father said.

She fixed an expectant stare on Foggerty.

He stared back. "Let's get him some medical treatment and into the interrogation room at the precinct."

"What about all these bodies?" Mrs. Gould asked.

"I already sent for a coroner."

Song followed behind Foggerty and her father as her mother stayed behind to detail her account of the night to another detective. Ryk'r stood at Mrs. Gould's shoulder, letting her grip his arm as some form of emotional support. Daven offered Song his elbow to escort her through the halls and distract her from the gruesome display on the floor.

"I don't know if I can sleep at all tonight," she said.

"I should be off duty and in bed now, too," Daven said with a chuckle.

"I'm sure you can't wait to get home to your wife and children."

He gave her an odd look. "I don't have children, Miss."

You bloody liar. She forced her expression into one of shock. "Oh! I'm sorry. I just assumed that someone as handsome as you would have already been domesticated by now."

"No need to apologize. Honest mistake, right?"

"Officer Carson," Foggerty said as they reached the parlor; Daven snapped his attention to him. "Please escort this man to the wagon."

"Excuse me, I must check my office safe for valuables," her father said. "Goodnight Zion. I'll stop by the precinct in the morning."

"Be sure to get with Joniss and give him your statement before you turn in, Elroy."

Her father made a noise and disappeared around the corner.

Song smiled at the detective as they were left alone in the entry hall. "Goodbye, Detective Inspector," she said, eager to escape to check on Ponce. "Thank you for all you've done."

"I hope you can get some rest, Miss Gould," he said.

She spun away to head to the servants' quarters.

"Oh, one more thing."

"Yes?"

As she turned, something flew through the air at her face. Her right arm rose to catch it as she flinched. It smacked the metal with a muffled *clang* through her glove. She looked at her palm—at the big bead of green glass sitting in the center. Her eyes flicked up to stare at the detective.

Foggerty strode forward and plucked the magnet from her hand. He then set it right where he had the night she'd appeared at the ball to turn herself in. It stuck there and his brown eyes settled on hers.

"Clever detective," she whispered, then ripped it off her arm and glanced around for anyone looking, though they were alone. "How?"

"Did I guess?" he asked.

She nodded.

"The first clue was when you called me by my full title and name at the precinct…even though we've never actually been introduced to one another. I thought maybe someone had told you. But when you said my name, the corner of your lips rose like you wanted to laugh. You managed to supress it, though, and I almost missed it."

"Bollocks," she hissed, cursing herself with more colorful language in her head. "What are you going to do?"

He leaned closer to whisper. "I'm going to wait and watch. And when you're no longer under your father's protection, you'll receive the punishment you've earned."

"And what about Pishing?"

"I don't care that they want you alive—"

"Not that," she said.

He tilted his head in curiosity.

"I'm marrying one of their royals to stop a war. Didn't you know?" She gave him a wicked smile.

Of course, he didn't know. They wouldn't be announcing it until she'd met her betrothed, and they set a date.

Realization settled in his eyes.

"I wonder how they would feel about you not only hanging the captain they want alive but also their little token of peace. Probably as cross as the sultania of Armalinia if she found out you harmed her soon-to-be-wife." She nodded, her lips in a sad, grave pout.

Frustration flickered across his expression.

"I would keep my mouth shut if I were you, Detective Inspector Zion Foggerty." She giggled at his name, which made his glower deepen. "Unless, of course, you wish to be the man responsible for starting a war with two countries. That's assuming I even *can* be killed. You've seen but a fraction of my power. *Nothing* can stop me." She straightened his tie and presented him with a cordial smile. "Watch me like a hawk, detective. Because that's all you *can* do."

"Your confidence will kill you, one day…Song."

A cord in her neck tightened at his use of her pirate name while she wore her aristocratic face. It felt like blurring a line she didn't want blurred—though it was too late for that, where the detective was concerned.

"It's kept me alive this far, *Zion*. Go home. Lie in your bed, and dream of the day you catch me, because that's the only place where it will happen the way you want it to."

"All villains pay eventually."

"Good thing I'm not a villain, then."

"You think you're a hero?"

She laughed. "Absolutely not. But neither are you. This isn't some epic tale, Detective. It isn't even a spirited game of cat and mouse. This is you failing. Get used to the feeling if you choose to keep pursuing me."

"Justice comes for everyone, eventually. Even kings can fall."

"Not this king." She shoved his magnet into his hand, turned on her heel, and strode away. "I'm sure you know your way to the door."

Her heart thundered as she rounded the corner. *What a rush!* It was more exhilarating than people looking right at her and not seeing the pirate they sought. Having someone know her secret and be powerless to stop her was a new sort of satisfaction she hadn't expected. She was untouchable.

Dawn was breaking, and the coroner had finished clearing away the last of the bodies. They had blocked half the mansion off, so no one wandered the blood-soaked hallways and rooms. Ponce had come up with bandaged injuries. Mabel proclaimed him a hero. He'd staved off five men and protected a handful of estate workers in a room. Weariness claimed him, and he'd gone to sleep some hours ago. Johanna turned in earlier than that, with Sunshine following to set up a chair and sit to keep watch outside her door.

The coroners and doctors were leaving, but officers would remain a while longer. Song retreated to Amelia's room, where the woman had gone and demanded to be left alone. She was still awake when Song let herself in, using her *kijæm* to unlock the door. Amelia stared up at her from the center of the bed, where she sat wrapped in a blanket, gripping her knees.

"Are you all right?" Song asked.

She shook her head as tears rolled from her eyes.

"We're going to get him back for this. I promise. I'm going to kill every last one of those bastards for even daring to step foot in our home."

Amelia frowned and brushed a tear from her chin. "Song, I…"

"What?"

"I can't do it. I can't keep living in fear of pirates."

Song furrowed her brow. "Once I kill him, you won't have to."

She shook her head. "No. You have to choose."

"What?"

"It's me or piracy."

Song crossed the room and gazed out at the pink sunrise. It would have been beautiful, if not for the terrible night they'd just had. She said nothing for a long time as Amelia sniffled behind her. It wasn't a difficult decision. In fact, she'd made it long before the woman had voiced the demand. What was difficult was what Song had to do next.

"An ultimatum is something you make when you're confident the other person will choose you," she said. "How confident are you?"

"Fairly. Because you love me."

Song closed her eyes and let out a disappointed breath. "Oh, Amelia… No. I don't. And if I did, I still would not pick the person demanding I choose between who I am and who they want me to be." She turned to witness the twisted expression of shock on her face. "You will not force me into a decision based on how valuable you think you are to me. That's the thing about pirates, dear. You ask us to choose between us and someone else? We're selfish bastards who choose ourselves every bloody time."

"Why would you say such hurtful things?"

Song approached, one slow step at a time. "The truth is often hurtful." She took in a deep breath and let it out just as slow. "I'll arrange for my mother to keep you as the daughter she wanted, which I'll never be. She likes you, anyway." She strode past Amelia.

"Wait!" she gasped. "Where are you going? Shouldn't we talk—"

"We won't change each other's minds. No point wasting breath. Where am I going? To talk to my father about getting me into the sky to catch an echo. After that I might get me a drink. Maybe a woman. Or I might just lie down and sleep like the dead. I haven't quite decided yet." She turned on her heel. "Get some rest." With that, she left.

Song clenched her jaw against the pain it caused her to have been so cruel to Amelia, especially after the night they'd just been through, but it was high time she stopped lying to both of them. She would never love Amelia, so this was the kinder option. What they'd had so long ago was nothing more than two girls over-eager to have found a kindred. It wasn't love. It would never have been love. Ultimately, the two were vastly different people; one too stubborn to change for someone else, and one too traumatized by the very thing the other was.

Forty-One

SONG STARED OUT THROUGH THE BROKEN WINDOW IN THE ballroom, tears streaming down her cheeks as she sobbed in silence. Her fists clung to the canvas she'd ripped from the nails holding it in place over the opening. It had been two days, and she'd been replaying that night in her mind, trying to see the actual face behind the hallucination of Leslie's. But no matter how she tried to reimagine it, it was still Leslie. It was still his face.

Ponce found her there and stood in silence, listening to her gasp and sputter. "We'll restore your reputation. We'll make sure everyone knows that man isn't Song."

"I saw…Leslie," she whispered.

"What do you mean?"

"I think I was hallucinating. The echo throttled me." She lowered her collar to show him the brown bruises from the man's hands. "I couldn't breathe, and my vision was blurry, but…"

"You think you're going crazy."

She nodded.

Ponce wrapped an arm around her shoulders and squeezed her close. "You know, even now, I'll see someone who looks just enough like Nebhàr that I question everything. I used to call out to them… It gets easier, Song. I promise."

"I've never seen his face on another person, though. Not once. Even when I was drunk. Why do I feel like I'm losing my mind? It's been two years!"

"Nebhàr's mother told me we all heal in our own time. You're healing in your time. Some of us just take longer."

"Damn it, Ponce, I *was* healing. I could say his name without crying. And now… I don't want to take longer. I want to be all right. And I want someone to look at that imposter and tell me I'm wrong, so I can finish healing."

"Perhaps he just looked similar enough that—"

"I can't rest until I take his hood down and see for myself." Her breathing stuttered in her chest as her sobs turned into desperate gasps. "W-what if it is him? What…what do we do? And why? Why would he—"

He pulled her into his embrace and let her sob into his shoulder. "There, there. We'll catch that bastard and prove to you it was just your mind playing tricks. That's all."

"How can you be so sure?"

"Because Leslie would never do this to you. Claim your name? Try to kill you? Go after your family and you as Tsingsei? No. He didn't have an ounce of this sort of cruelty in him."

"It's something I would do, though."

"We all know Leslie was the only thing keeping you in check. He would never stoop to the same levels as you. It's not him. You're still grieving."

"Promise?" she asked, struggling to regain her composure.

Ponce stared out the window at the harbor and the ocean beyond, but said nothing.

With the help of the senators, Elroy Gould drafted another contract for Song and her crew to sign. This time, it was more specific as to their purpose—catching the imposter. It wouldn't give them immunity from the law, but it would grant them certain liberties and leeway when it came to apprehending the fake Song.

A few of her crew didn't want any part in this new mission, on the grounds that they weren't bounty hunters and it was not a risk worth taking. So Toothy had set about hiring new members. Now that it was an open secret that Song's crew was working with the senate, her men could visit the Gould manor as they prepared to take flight. They brought her manifests and supply lists, and even profiles of men wanting to join. One such person was a teen looking to be a cabin boy. She clenched her jaw and ordered Toothy not to even entertain any more prospective cabin boys.

As the days counted down for departure, Song spent more time in her cabin on the ship, and would visit her father at his office in broad daylight, hood raised and pedestrians giving her a wide berth. A few senators interacted with her, though most kept their distance.

At home, she did her best to avoid Amelia. The woman had since tried to reason with Song about staying with her and renouncing piracy. Song didn't want to hear it, and wouldn't change her mind. Annie Gould was all too eager to take Amelia in as a daughter when Song suggested it. She'd already been taking etiquette lessons, and so Mrs. Gould reassigned Johanna to see to Amelia's formal education as well. Song's mother even floated the idea of adopting Amelia, and changing her surname to Gould.

They were one night from departure, and Song was organizing her cabin as her crew checked every nook and cranny, every nail, and every board to make sure all was secure and everything was in working order. Normally they weren't so thorough, but the ship hadn't been in a battle in months, since they had stayed in Talegrove while Song was trapped in Garda. On top of that, they planned to stay in the skies for a long time. They loaded their cargo holds with supplies instead of keeping the larger one empty for pillaged goods. There was only one treasure they were after.

Someone knocked on a window of her open doors.

"Come."

The footsteps entered behind her, one slow step at a time. Ryk'r stiffened and set his hand inside his wide belt where his kris hid.

She glanced over her shoulder and almost dropped the liquor bottles in her arms that she'd been arranging in the cupboard after dusting inside. She shoved them onto the table as she passed. Song settled her hand on her revolver as she studied the man with short black hair, his brown eyes taking in the new ship.

"Hardtack," she said.

He raised his eyebrows and looked at the hand on her sidearm. "Hello, Captain. I like the new ship." He glanced at Ryk'r, who circled as though to block the exit on Song's command.

"You're alive."

He blinked at her. "Is that why you fired on the Harpy's Claw without stopping for parley? You thought I was dead?"

"Yes. And I was angry. We lost eleven men the day we lost you…and Leslie soon after…and then my arm."

"Which one?"

She raised her right arm. "This one. I got a new one, though."

Alton's brow furrowed. "Blimey." His eyes landed on her left hand resting on her gun, again. "You don't trust me?"

"Where have you been?" she asked.

"My loyalties never shifted, Song. I signed your contract, and haven't signed another since. But I've been crewing with Darian."

"For two years?"

"Aye. I was getting you answers about your friend."

"For *two years?*" she repeated, her voice growling out between her teeth.

"Darian is a hard man to escape from. I'm lucky to be able to talk to you now. He's been careful not to berth if we see a ship with a North Star at the bow. He's terrified of you."

She glanced out through her doors at the figurehead covered by canvas. "He doesn't know I'm here. How did you know?"

"Saw too many of your crew for it to be a coincidence. Bells told me what your new ship looks like."

"Why is Darian here?"

"Came back to get the Dauntless out of permanent dock. He wants to fly a smaller crew." Alton chuckled. "He *needs* to fly a smaller crew. It's been hard filling the ranks since you tore the Claw to pieces. No one wants to risk their lives. And besides, a lot joined that new Song. Idiots think it's you, and therefore think they're safe."

"How convenient. We're leaving port tomorrow to apprehend that imposter. The cowards get to die by my hand, anyway." She released her revolver and folded her arms. "Will you be departing with the Dauntless? Or will you be departing with the Reprisal?"

"Is there room on your crew for a couple of loyal men?"

She raised an eyebrow. "A couple?"

"Aye." He met her eye for a minute.

She sighed at him, realizing he had no intention of elaborating. She fished the crew list out of her drawing table to see the headcount. "We've three openings. Lucky you. Bring your friend here at dawn, and you may return. But remember, if you are playing me—"

"Only a fool would play you, Captain Song."

She stepped forward to hug the man. "I'm glad to see you, even though I didn't quite like you."

"We didn't exactly get off on the right foot," he said on a laugh.

"Toothy is below, if you want to say hello."

He grinned as he stepped back. "Ponce and Pinch, too? I've missed those three bastards."

Her lips twisted into a frown. "Ponce is at my house. Pinch…was one of the men we lost in Darian's attack."

His mood shifted. "Oh. I'll have to give my condolences. Goodnight, Captain."

"Goodnight, Alton."

He left, giving Ryk'r a wide berth, and descended into the ship. Song stared out at the empty deck for a long time, wrestling with the urge to go onto the Dauntless and sabotage it somehow. The part of her mind that urged her to ignore it, because she was leaving in the morning for a more important target, eventually lost.

Song ordered Ryk'r to stay put as she exited her cabin and strode with purpose down the dock. He didn't follow, but watched from the edge of the ship. Her gaze scanned over the skyships for the little one she almost couldn't remember. She'd gone halfway to the end of the walk when she spotted the small ship, only sure it was the right one because of the name painted at the bow.

There wasn't a soul to be seen on deck. She carried herself across on her *kijæm* and stood at the center, spinning around in a slow circle to look at the ship from her memories. It seemed so much smaller than she remembered. Echoes of a bratty teen raced across the deck, or sat on the edge to dangle her feet and stare down at the ocean. Her memories felt like they belonged to another girl from another time. And yet, as she realized it had been a mere four years ago, that timeline felt like a lie.

A latch clicked behind her and she turned to stare at the captain's cabin door. She spun on her heel and crossed to it. It was locked.

"*Kawl-nu.*"

The door unlocked and she let herself inside. It was dark, curtains drawn over the bay windows, but just enough moonlight to show silhouettes of items. She resisted having her *kijæm* aid her in seeing in the dark, since it would cause her eyes to glow. She took a few steps in, pausing to listen as she thought she'd heard something. A board creaked. She took another step.

The door slammed, and arms wrapped around her from behind. She lurched backward to ram them into the door. A man's deep voice grunted in her ear. The two wrestled until she was free of his grasp. She punched at him, holding back so she didn't kill him, just incapacitated him to interrogate. They shuffled around the room, landing blows and missing some.

He ducked as she swung at him. He straightened behind her. A strong arm wrapped around her neck as the other gripped the back of her head. He squeezed softly at first, then harder, as the initial pressure only angered her. She thrashed in his grip. His added pressure on her throat kicked in, depriving her head of the blood flow it needed. Her right arm continued to fight as her vision spotted and her strength failed. As her legs collapsed beneath her, and her eyes fluttered closed, he gripped her close and whispered into her ear.

"It's all right, love. I've got you."

Enjoyed the book?
Please consider leaving a review!

Glossary of Terms

Miscellaneous	Pronunciation	Translation
Qet-Qet	keh-t keh-t	A city on the northern coast of Kerriwen
sor	soh-r	Zardiian gender neutral term used in place of sir or madam
Balmor	ba-l-moh-r	A name from Jashedar
Bălêmir	ba-lay-meer	A name from Hrănchu
Hrănchu	hr-ann-chew	Secret home of a people in the northern land

Armalinian	Pronunciation	Translation
akh'tilak	ah-kh-tih-lah-k	warrior
ank	ah-nk	you
baelimra	bay-lihm-rah	kijæm/Touched
byrrnd	bye-r(roll the r)-n-d	love
caddarik	cah-dah-rih-k	The protective detail of decoys that surrounds a future sultana.

Armalinian (cont.)	**Pronunciation**	**Translation**
Castildi	cass-till-dee	Ancient Armalinian queen.
Djori Cove	Joh-ree Cove	A pirate haven in the north of Armalinia.
drr	(roll the r)	from
ghida	gh-ih-da	nonbinary fiancé/betrothed
ghidja	gh-ih-ja	male fiancé/betrothed
ghija	gh-ih-zha	female fiancé/betrothed
jrra	zh-r(roll)-ah	ma'am
kharak	kh-ah-rah-k	sky
Ky'r	k-eye-r	The royal family's surname.
ly	lie	I
Pajisr	pa-jih-s-r	Capitol of Armalinia
Srkar	s-r-car	Pirate haven in Djorri Cove
sultania	suhl-tan-ee-ah	princess
yr	eye-r	my
yrshi	eye-r-shee	west

<u>Jin</u>	<u>Pronunciation</u>	<u>Translation</u>
Baalmoru	bal-moh-ruh	a name
Gemestha	g-eh-mess-thah	Named for the Jinjur goddess
Gemesthie	g-eh-mess-thee	Jinjur/Pishing goddess of the sun and light.
Jin	jihn	The language of the Jinjur people.
Jinjran	jihn-j-ran	The name of Pishing before it was colonized by Jashedar settlers.
Jinjur	jihn-jer	The native people of what is now called Pishing. They're known for their red hair.
Myooru	mee-yoo-ruh	A Jinjur name.
Stevnaa	steh-v-na	A call/cry
vyaarblisu draaku	vee-yahr-blih-ss-uh drahk-uh	A mythical fire-breathing flying serpent similar to a dragon.

<u>Nochtie</u>	<u>Pronunciation</u>	<u>Translation</u>
aibhridh	eye-vree	priestess
Au Caesaries	ow kay-sar-eez	The land of the Aibhanocht God.
Bhàlemorai	vaal-eh-moh-ray	The God of Aibhanocht
rebhìdh	reh-vee	A fatty rodent with sweet, gamey meat.
thiùrin	hyoo-rihn	church

Acknowledgements

Thank you to my alpha readers. L. Lindberg for making the first half of the book seem less meandering. Your tips and advice never cease to not only amaze me, but also improve my writing. To Grace, for assuring me that certain characters and story threads were fine as-is. Also a huge thank you for encouraging me to lean into Song's heritage I'd been terrified to include even in the first edition of book one. Her story is all the richer because of you

Thank you to my beta readers. Laura, who refused to let my careless writing turn Amelia into a non-character; whose comments throughout the manuscript shifted from 'I love this' to 'god damn it, Song, you idiot. I love you but stop'. I'm glad you love Song enough to know she'll always make the wrong choice, no matter how much you yell at her. Malaena, for yelling at me for making you cry and laugh in the same scene, and for being my 'uhm akshually' for more than a few sciency facts.

And thank you to you, dear reader, for sticking around this far into the series. Just one book left! I know you won't be disappointed. ;)

About the Author

Shalaena Medford is an American author, editor, researcher, desktop publisher, artist, and definitely not a lizard person. She has attended university for creative writing, with focuses in fiction and screenwriting. She has always had a passion for books and the written word.

Visit her website at:
www.shalaenamedford.com

www.ingramcontent.com/pod-product-compliance
Lightning Source LLC
Chambersburg PA
CBHW022013300726
48970CB00003B/871